Praise for the
Lady Arianna Regency Mysteries

The Cocoa Conspiracy

"This Regency mystery is well plotted and fast-paced. The story is full of intrigue and adventure. . . . The growing romance between Sandro and Arianna is delightful. This is an excellent view into the society, personalities, and governments of the Regency period."　　　　　　　　　　　—MyShelf.com

"[A] compulsively good read . . . with heart-pounding suspense and sword-clashing action played against a plot rife with international intrigue in the Napoleonic era."
　　　　　　　　　　　　　　　—Reader to Reader Reviews

"[A] fascinating story. . . . Readers will be held spellbound by the events portrayed in *The Cocoa Conspiracy*. The verbal sparring between Sandro, Baz, and Arianna is a delightful backdrop to the danger they find themselves in."　　　　—Fresh Fiction

"The author writes great characters and plots in this Regency mystery and creates a mystery that is rich with the pomp and circumstance of the European royals in that era. . . . The newlyweds are extremely charming and very much in love, and the story is fascinating reading. Andrea Penrose is an expert in combining conspiracy and chocolate."　　　—Once Upon a Romance

"[A] terrific tale. . . . The story line is fast-paced from the moment Arianna beats up a foreign thief . . . and never slows down as she works the case of the Cocoa Conspiracy."
　　　　　　　　　　　　　　　—Genre Go Round Reviews

continued . . .

Sweet Revenge

"Andrea Penrose bursts into the world of historical mysteries with a book that will delight readers. *Sweet Revenge* is replete with swashbuckling action, taut suspense, and a heroine feisty enough to give the most rakish Regency cad a run for his money. I can't wait to get my hands on the next installment!"
—Tasha Alexander, author of the Lady Emily series

"A mouthwatering combination of suspense and chocolate!"
—Lauren Willig, national bestselling author of
The Garden Intrigue

"A mysterious lady, bent on revenge, and a mystery-solving lord will take you on a thrilling ride through Regency England in this smashing debut novel."
—Victoria Thompson, national bestselling author of
Murder on Fifth Avenue

"Penrose deftly combines a cleverly concocted mystery with a generous dash of romance in this historical mystery."
—*Chicago Tribune*

"An absolute delight for lovers of mysteries, Regency romances, and chocolate." —*The Historical Novels Review*

"Andrea Penrose whips up a scrumptious chocolaty treat for her debut historical mystery. . . . Ms. Penrose layers politics, murder, history, suspense, romance, and recipes to concoct an intoxicating mystery. . . . *Sweet Revenge* spoons out a potent cocktail laced heavily with sordid intrigue and unconventional characters that will have you savoring every last drop." —Fresh Fiction

"A satisfying surprise inside the perfected shell from the Regency world." —Goodreads

"Intriguing story lines, intelligent characters, and interesting dialogue." —Blue Moon Mystery Saloon

Other Books in the
Lady Arianna Regency Mystery Series

Sweet Revenge
The Cocoa Conspiracy

RECIPE FOR TREASON

A LADY ARIANNA REGENCY MYSTERY

ANDREA PENROSE

AN OBSIDIAN MYSTERY

OBSIDIAN
Published by New American Library, a division of
Penguin Group (USA) Inc., 375 Hudson Street,
New York, New York 10014, USA
Penguin Group (Canada), 90 Eglinton Avenue East, Suite 700, Toronto,
Ontario M4P 2Y3, Canada (a division of Pearson Penguin Canada Inc.)
Penguin Books Ltd., 80 Strand, London WC2R 0RL, England
Penguin Ireland, 25 St. Stephen's Green, Dublin 2,
Ireland (a division of Penguin Books Ltd.)
Penguin Group (Australia), 250 Camberwell Road, Camberwell, Victoria 3124,
Australia (a division of Pearson Australia Group Pty. Ltd.)
Penguin Books India Pvt. Ltd., 11 Community Centre, Panchsheel Park,
New Delhi - 110 017, India
Penguin Group (NZ), 67 Apollo Drive, Rosedale, Auckland 0632,
New Zealand (a division of Pearson New Zealand Ltd.)
Penguin Books (South Africa) (Pty.) Ltd., 24 Sturdee Avenue,
Rosebank, Johannesburg 2196, South Africa

Penguin Books Ltd., Registered Offices:
80 Strand, London WC2R 0RL, England

First published by Obsidian, an imprint of New American Library,
a division of Penguin Group (USA) Inc.

First Printing, December 2012
10 9 8 7 6 5 4 3 2 1

*For the British Art Center at Yale University,
whose exhibits and study rooms are a source of constant
wonder and inspiration*

Adversity is the first path to truth.

—George Gordon Byron

1

From Lady Arianna's Chocolate Notebooks

Whole Wheat Oatmeal–Chocolate Chip Cookies

2¾ cups rolled old-fashioned oats
1 cup whole wheat flour
⅔ cup (1½ ounces) wheat bran (or germ)
1 teaspoon baking soda
1½ teaspoons baking powder
1 teaspoon fine-grain sea salt
1 cup unsalted butter
1 cup natural cane sugar or light brown sugar
1 cup firmly packed Muscovado or dark brown sugar
2 large eggs
2 teaspoons vanilla extract
10 ounces semisweet chocolate, chopped and shaved
into chunks and splinters

1. Preheat the oven to 350°F, placing racks in the middle. Line two baking sheets with unbleached parchment paper and set aside.
2. In a medium bowl combine the oats, flour, wheat bran, baking soda, baking powder, and salt. Set aside.
3. Either by hand or using an electric mixer, cream the butter until light and fluffy. Beat in the sugars for 3 or more minutes, scraping down the sides of the bowl a few times along the way. Incorporate the eggs one at a time, then the vanilla, scraping the sides of the bowl another time or two.
4. Add in the dry mixture, and stir until the ingredients barely come together. Then stir in the chocolate, mixing until it is evenly distributed throughout the dough.
5. Using a small ice cream scoop, spoon, or ¼ cup measuring cup, make uniform dough balls. Arrange the cookies at least 3 inches apart on the prepared baking sheet. For extracrisp cookies, bake until deeply, deeply golden on the bottom, about 15 minutes. Rotate the pans once about two-thirds of the way through baking—back to front, top to bottom. If you like your cookies a little chewier, bake for less time.
6. Cool on a rack.

A jolt of the coach bounced the open book in her lap, rousing Arianna, Lady Saybrook, from a fitful half sleep. Wincing, she shifted against the leather squabs and flexed her aching shoulders.

"Hell," she muttered as the wheels hit another frozen rut. *This was truly the Devil's own journey.*

Though instead of rolling through fire and sulfurous brimstone, they seemed to be entering a bleak realm of ice and frigid vapors. With each passing mile, the landscape looked more and more leached of all color.

Touching her numb fingertips to the page, Arianna couldn't help but wish that the handwritten recipe for hot Spanish chocolate might transform from ink and paper into a pot of steaming, spice-scented liquid. Despite the fur throw wrapped around her, she was chilled to the bone by the damp cold seeping in through the creaking woodwork.

And the weather looked to be turning worse.

December was not an auspicious time to be traveling from London to Scotland. *Not that there had been any choice,* Arianna reminded herself with an unhappy sigh.

Peering out the windowpane, she saw that large flakes of snow had begun to fall, smudges of dull white against the grim grayness of the windswept moors. A shiver skated down her spine. There was something about the dark, desolate surroundings that stirred a prickling of unease.

Her two companions, however, appeared untouched by worry. Alessandro Henry George De Quincy, the fifth Earl of Saybrook—and her husband of little more than a year—was slumbering quietly on the facing seat, his long legs wedged against her bench to steady himself against the bumps. Basil Henning, his good friend and former military comrade, was not quite so peaceful in repose. His raspy snores were growing louder by the minute.

But then, Henning was always a little rough around the edges—stubbled chin, wrinkled clothing, irascible temper . . .

A clench of guilt squeezed at her chest. He wouldn't be forced to make this miserable trek if it hadn't been for his loyalty to her and Saybrook in previous adventures.

"Damn Grentham," swore Arianna under her breath, tucking the wrap tighter around her middle. The government's Minister of State Security was renowned as a ruthless, manipulative master of intrigue. Most people feared him and didn't dare to challenge his authority.

But not me.

"He is not a good man to have as an enemy," she acknowledged in a wry whisper. A fact that hadn't stopped her from jabbing a needle into his puffed-up vanity on several occasions.

She had won those skirmishes. But as for the war . . .

Another lurching bump. And then all went very still.

"Why are we stopping?" she asked in a louder voice.

Saybrook came instantly awake. Leaning close to the opposite window, he brushed a hand to the fogged pane and squinted into the swirling shadows. "Perhaps a tree has fallen across the road."

Henning was slower in opening his eyes. "Auch, or perhaps a bloody rein has snapped, or a spoke has cracked," he grumbled, rubbing at his unshaven chin. "There are a hundred—nay, a thousand—things that can go wrong on these miserable rutted roads of Yorkshire."

"Thank you for the cheery note of optimism, Baz," quipped Saybrook.

"If you want sweetness and light, you should have headed south and caught a ship to the balmy shores of Catalonia," retorted his friend. The earl was, in fact, half-Spanish, a fact that only added to his reputation for eccentricity among the Polite Society of London. "Heaven knows, we would all be far more comfortable there than in this godforsaken wilderness."

"I'll step outside and see what the problem is. If there is an obstacle blocking the way, José may need a hand." Saybrook buttoned his overcoat and, after a hint of hesitation, eased the carriage pistol from its holster by the door before reaching for the latch.

Arianna frowned. "You expect trouble?"

"It is always wise to be prepared—"

CRACK!

One of the windowpanes suddenly exploded in a shattering of silvery shards.

"Get down!" ordered the earl calmly as he ducked low and shoved the door open with his shoulder. "Arm yourselves. The dueling pistols are in their case under the chess set, and the cavalry weapons are in my valise," he added. "Baz, you guard the left while I reconnoiter on the right." And with that, he rolled out into the gloom.

Henning's sleepy scowl vanished. Like Saybrook, he was a battle-toughened veteran of the Peninsular War. The bullet did not spark panic, merely a short, sarcastic laugh.

"Ah well, we did ask for things to get a bit warmer." His lips pursed as he pulled out the rosewood box and checked the priming of the sleek pistols. "Here, you had best keep one of these fancy barking irons, Lady S. You've already proved you know how to use it." The matched pair had been a gift from the Russian Tsar, who had professed his undying admiration for her marksmanship during their recent stay in Vienna. Her shot had saved . . .

Be damned with old enemies—there were new ones to face.

Arianna took the pistol and then slipped a sheathed knife from her reticule and pushed it into her pocket. The long, slim blade was deceptively dainty looking. Its steel was lethally sharp.

"There is something to be said for possessing an unladylike expertise with deadly weapons," she replied.

Henning's chuckle died away in the sound of splintering wood as another bullet smashed through the casement. "Stay here and keep low." He crawled over her tangled skirts and unlatched the far door. "I'll go cover Sandro. Whoever is out there is in for a rude surprise."

"Rude, indeed," she echoed before following on his heels.

Cold spiked through her as she hit the ground and slithered into the shelter of the spoked wheel. The light, gray and grainy as gunpowder, was fast fading behind the weathered clefts of granite, leaving the narrow road through the ravine shrouded in shadows.

Squinting, she tried to bring the hazy shapes into focus. Sounds were just as muffled—all she could hear above her pounding heart was the nervous snorts of the horses and the rush of a nearby mountain stream tumbling down through the rocks.

Damn. Arianna drew in a deep breath and held herself very still. No sign of movement up ahead, no stirring of . . .

A scuff—and then a step, coming from the rear of the carriage.

Easing back the weapon's hammer to full cock, she moved forward for a better angle of view.

Swoosh, swoosh. The faint whisper of wool brushing against leather. A moment later, the dark flutter of a greatcoat, skirling around a pair of well-worn boots.

Not those of her husband or his friend.

Arianna tightened her grip on the butt. Her hands were so cold that she could barely feel any sensation in her fingers.

"Ha." With a low hiss, the stranger dropped to a crouch by the wheel and raised a rifle. "I see you now, behind that rock," he muttered under his breath. "One . . . two . . ."

"Drop your weapon before I count to three," said Arianna, moving the pistol to within a hairsbreadth of his temple. "Or you are a dead man."

His jaw twitched in shock.

"And in case you are wondering, I'm an excellent shot," she went on. "Not that any aim is required at this distance to blow your skull to Kingdom Come."

Snarling a low, savage oath, he tried to swing around, but the rifle barrel knocked against the iron rim and went off with a deafening bang.

At the same instant a sharper shot rang out, and a gurgle of blood spurted from the man's jugular as the earl's shot tore open his throat. He pitched forward and fell facedown on the hard-scrabble ground, a viscous black pool quickly spreading over the snow-dusted stones.

Wrenching her gaze up from his lifeless form, Arianna spotted Saybrook moving along a ridge of rock.

"Sandro—behind you!" she cried in warning as a second silhouette rose from the murky shadows, too close for her to dare a shot.

The earl whirled and lashed out a kick that caught his assailant's knee, knocking him to the ground. The man rolled out of reach and sprang to his feet, flinging a rock at Saybrook's head. It missed by a hair, the echoing ricochet sounding like gunfire in the swirling wind.

"Bloody hell, Jem—what are you waiting for! Shoot the bastard," cried the assailant to some unseen cohort as he whipped a hand up from his boot and cut a slash at Saybrook's chest.

"He's got a knife, Sandro," called Arianna.

"Yes, yes, don't worry," he responded, parrying a thrust with a quick flick of his forearm. "Stay where you are."

Ignoring the order, she edged along the side of the carriage, alert for any other sign of movement. *Where was Henning?* she wondered. *And what of their coachman?* A low groan from the driver's perch seemed to indicate that José had survived the first attack.

Questions, questions—but they would have to wait.

A flurry of wild thrusts had forced Saybrook back several steps, giving her a clearer shot at his assailant.

"Tírate al suelo," she called to him in Spanish, ordering him to duck down.

"Aim for his knee and not his heart," called her husband. "I want him alive for questioning."

"Jem!" cried the assailant, his voice turning shrill.

A shot rang out from somewhere on the other side of the coach, followed by a scream. One of the horses whinnied in fright, spooked by the flash of fire.

"Ye'll be getting no help from Jem." Henning's voice rose above a wispy plume of gun smoke.

"I suggest you throw down your blade," said Saybrook to his attacker. "The lady is a crack shot."

"As if any bloody female could hit the broad side of a barn," jeered the assailant, but he sounded a little shaky.

"Oh, I assure you, my wife is no ordinary female."

Arianna angled the pistol's barrel a fraction. "I'll aim a touch high. If I miss, it will hit his cods rather than his knee. Either way, he won't be walking very steadily for quite a while."

Her *sangfroid* seemed to spook the man. Cutting a last half-hearted jab at Saybrook, he suddenly turned and bolted for the tangled wildness of the looming moor.

"Dio Madre!" She was about to pull the trigger and drop him with a shot to the leg when her husband took off after him. Cursing her flapping skirts, she scrabbled up to the top of the ledge and followed as fast as she dared.

2

From Lady Arianna's Chocolate Notebooks

Toasted Pecan–Chocolate Toffee

1 cup (2 sticks) butter, cut into chunks
1½ cups sugar
3 tablespoons corn syrup
3 tablespoons water
2 cups well-chopped pecans, toasted
*8 ounces chocolate, cut into chunks, your choice of milk,
semi- or bittersweet*

1. Cover a baking sheet with parchment paper and set aside.
2. In a medium, thick-bottomed saucepan over medium to medium-low heat, add the butter. Wait a minute or two until the butter really starts to soften and melt. Stir in the sugar, corn syrup, and water. Cook, stirring regularly, until the mixture is bubbling (lava-style) and a candy thermometer registers 300°F.
3. Remove from the heat and stir in 1 cup of the pecans.
4. Pour the hot toffee out onto the prepared baking sheet. Depending on how thick you like your toffee, spread it out

into a round 10 to 12 inches in diameter. Set it aside to cool.

5. While the toffee is cooling, melt half the chocolate in a microwave or double boiler. Be sure the toffee has set up a bit before you spread the melted chocolate over the top. Immediately sprinkle with ½ cup of the remaining pecans.

6. Wait 20 minutes, or until the chocolate has firmed up. Carefully flip the toffee over. Melt the remaining chocolate and spread it on the second side. Sprinkle with the remaining ½ cup pecans. Let cool.

Henning quickly caught up with her. "Steady, Lady S," he wheezed as she slipped on some loose scree. "No need for you to risk your lovely ankles. I'll handle it from here."

Arianna snapped a rude oath and forged ahead. Henning was no aficionado of physical exertion, and his breath was already coming in ragged gasps. "Stubble the manly bravado. My ankles—and my wind—are likely a good deal stronger than yours."

"Auch, much as it pains me to admit it, you are probably right." He climbed up a twist in the footpath and paused to catch his breath. "But it appears that Sandro has no need of us."

Up ahead, she saw that her husband's long, loping stride had narrowed the distance between him and his quarry. As the path narrowed to cut through a cleft in the rocks, Saybrook suddenly picked up his pace and angled through a patch of scrubby heather to cut off the man's escape.

Sensing the danger, the assailant veered sharply and began climbing over a tumble of boulders. The earl was right on his heels.

Pushing past Henning, Arianna started to run.

Saybrook lunged, catching hold of the man's coat.

Kicking, cursing, the assailant struggled desperately to break free, but the earl held tight. Spinning, swirling, their shadows blurred in the wind-whipped snow. They both crested the stones at the same time and fell together in a pelter of whirling jabs and punches.

"Damn." Arianna skidded to a halt just as the assailant landed a vicious kick and broke free. His boots scraping over the rough rock, he lurched to his feet and made a wild, running leap across a narrow ravine.

"Damn!" Saybrook's oath echoed her own.

The jump fell a few inches short. Arms flailing, the man fought to catch his balance on the lip of the ledge, but the slippery snow and gusting wind were against him. With a strangled scream, he fell backward and disappeared into the chasm.

It took a moment or two for Arianna to climb to her husband's side.

"Damn, damn, damn," he repeated in frustration. "Damn the fellow for breaking his bloody neck."

"They might have been naught but thieves, hoping to prey on prosperous travelers heading north for the holidays." Even to her own ears, the suggestion sounded hollow.

"We deliberately chose a route that avoided the main roads," he replied tersely. Despite the cold, he stripped off his coat. Tiny tendrils of steam licked up as the flakes swirled, white against white, and melted on his sweat-dampened shirt.

"Sandro," she began, eyeing the treacherous fall of jagged rocks leading down to the body. Already a thin scrim of ice was glazing the surfaces. "It's not worth the risk of a broken leg." *Or worse.*

"On the contrary, we can't afford to overlook any clue." Finding a handhold in the fissured stones, Saybrook started to descend. "Having a medical man as a traveling companion does have its benefits," he quipped over the chuffing of the wind. Henning was a skilled surgeon whose ministrations had saved the earl's leg from amputation during the war. "God knows, his ill-tempered mood has so far provided precious little comfort. But at least he can tend to any bodily injuries."

His friend, who had finally managed to scramble up the slippery stones, huffed a harried gasp as he bent over and braced his hands on his knees. "I have bloody good reason to be in a foul humor," he retorted, once he had caught his breath. "Being friends with you has a habit of leading into some very nasty situations, laddie. We haven't even crossed the border and already some unknown enemy is trying to kill us."

"Let us not jump to conclusions," said Arianna. She winced on seeing a sliver of granite break off beneath Saybrook's boot. "As I said, this may be a case of simple robbery."

Henning answered with a low snort. "Nothing concerning you two is *ever* simple."

True. Unfortunately, the surgeon's words were not mere hyperbole.

"Oh, Basil, I'm sorry you've been dragged into yet another viper's coil," she said softly. "I shouldn't have taunted—"

He cut off the apology with a brusque wave. "Auch, in truth, it's me who's to blame for this present predicament, and I damn well know it." A puff of pale vapor swirled as he exhaled another short, sharp breath. Turning abruptly, he crouched down and peered over the ledge.

"Find anything?" he called to the earl.

"Nothing in his pockets, save for this," answered Saybrook. A leather purse arced out of the gloom and landed at the surgeon's feet with a muffled thud.

Henning undid the drawstrings and peeked inside. "How gratifying to see that our hides were worth gold instead of silver."

"Any clues offered by the man's clothing?" asked Arianna, shivering as the melting snow started to trickle beneath the upturned collar of her coat.

"No." A muffled oath. "There seems to be something inside his leather waistcoat, but the thongs are too knotted to work free."

"Here." She tossed down her knife.

"How lucky for me that my wife carries a dagger, rather than a dainty little bottle of vinaigrette."

She absently rubbed at a spot of blood on her cuff. "It's a

wonder I don't fall into a permanent swoon, considering the things I see when I'm with you two."

The earl spent another few moments examining the body before turning the dead man facedown and climbing up from the ravine. Shaking the strands of wet hair from his brow, he pulled a small object from inside his glove and handed it to Henning. "Does this mean anything to you?"

The surgeon subjected it to a long scrutiny. "Yes." He returned it without further comment.

"Put this back on, before you catch your death of cold," said Arianna, draping his overcoat over Saybrook's shoulders. "And let's get moving. Further discussion can wait until later. We need to return to the carriage and tend to José, not to speak of getting you into some dry clothing."

"What about *him*?" asked Henning, gesturing at the corpse. He shifted his gaze to the earl. "Do you intend to report this to the local magistrate?"

"No, I think not," replied Saybrook after a slight hesitation. "There is nothing to gain from involving the authorities, except unwanted questions." His mouth thinned to a hard line. "Let us leave him and his fellow varlets for the wolves and the carrion crows."

"Or a skulking *renard*," muttered Henning grimly.

Renard. The French word for "fox" seemed to rumble through the rocks, low and menacing like a predator's growl.

Arianna carefully uncocked the fancy dueling pistol. They were heading to Scotland in order to hunt for a cunning traitor known only as Renard. A clever operative who reveled in deception and death as he moved within the highest circles of London Society, betraying government secrets to a foreign enemy.

But the question of who was hunting whom had just taken a dangerous twist.

"The nearest town looks to be no more than five miles away." Saybrook looked up from the map and glanced out the far window. Although the temperature had dropped several degrees, the squall had blown over, and in the silvery twilight, the snow-dusted landscape had an eerie tranquility. "Barring any further mishap, we should be there within the hour."

Henning's response was a sardonic grunt—in French, which added an extra *soupçon* of sarcasm. *"Grâce a Dieu."*

God willing, repeated Arianna to herself. Though she feared that it would take special effort on the part of any higher deity to counteract the Devil's influence on the upcoming mission.

Uncorking a silver flask of strong Scottish malt, Henning took a long swallow, then offered the rest to Saybrook. "There's a wee dram left, though most of it went down José's gullet." The coachman had been knocked unconscious by a rock during the initial attack. But with his head bandaged by the surgeon and his belly warmed by the whisky, he had insisted he was fit to drive.

Arianna finished tucking a makeshift drapery over the shattered window and turned to her husband. "Drink," she ordered, before the earl could demur. He still looked half-frozen, despite having changed out of his wet shirt and breeches. Adding a low oath, she spread a blanket across his lap.

Saybrook took a small sip and handed it back. "We can fill ourselves with warming spirits once we reach an inn. Right now—"

"Ah yes, right now, we had better have one of our jolly little councils of war," interrupted Henning. "And here I thought that resigning from the military would mean an end to mortal danger from flying bullets and blades."

There was an extra edge to his voice that Arianna found disturbing. He was always irascible—which was, she admitted, something she found rather endearing. But this new razor-sharp note was like steel scraping against flint.

It was only a matter of time before such friction set off dangerous sparks.

"Yes, we had better talk now," replied Saybrook, seemingly oblivious to the tension in the air. "For no matter what José says, I intend to relieve him of the reins shortly."

She frowned but remained silent, knowing it was useless to argue.

"Once we reach the inn, there are things that can't be discussed," he went on. "We must assume that the walls have ears."

The creaking of the paneling seemed to grow louder as the earl's oblique warning hung heavy in the chill air.

It was Henning who broke the silence with a brusque cough. "Well, to begin with, we need not fear being taken up by the authorities for murder," he muttered. "It's highly unlikely that anyone will stumble over the bodies, even come spring." He and Saybrook had hidden the other two dead men deep in a crevasse far from the road. "But as for other threats . . ."

He rubbed a hand along his bristled jaw. "I cannot believe this was a chance attack. Someone knew we were heading to Scotland and must have had men watching the routes north." The rasp of whiskers was audible against his callused palm as he settled his gaze on the earl. "Yet only a very small circle of high government officials were privy to our mission. What does that say to you, laddie?"

"It simply repeats a fact that we've known for some time, Baz," pointed out Saybrook. "The French traitor Renard has access to privileged information. That's why he—"

"Or *she*," murmured Arianna. "Let's not forget that a woman can be just as dangerous as a man when it comes to duplicity and deception." She paused. "I ought to know."

The earl's mouth quirked up at the corners at the reminder of how they had met. She had been masquerading as a male chef in an aristocratic household, hoping to smoke out her father's murderers and bring them to justice. But when the Prince Regent was poisoned by one of her decadent desserts, the earl had been called in to investigate because of his expertise in chocolate . . .

A soft laugh recalled her to the present.

"Point taken, my dear." The earl's amusement then died away just as quickly. "Whether a he or a she, Renard has an uncanny ability to uncover government secrets and use them to foment chaos, as well as to destroy lives. That is why we must trap the Fox and put an end to the trail of bloodshed."

"A pretty speech, Sandro," said Henning. "What you've left out is the ugly fact that Renard is almost certainly a highborn English aristocrat. And an even more sordid truth is that the ambush may have been ordered by the double-dealing spawn of Satan, Lord Grentham."

"*Dio Madre*, you are like a terrier who refuses to drop a bone, even though the meat has been chewed off," growled the earl. This wasn't the first time Henning had suggested that the Minister of State Security might be in league with the French. "I don't like Grentham any more than you do. However, in this case I think him innocent of any intrigue. Much as he loathes us, we're the only ones he trusts to unmask the traitor, regardless of Renard's power or prestige. So for the moment, we're worth more to him alive than dead."

"Perhaps he's pulled the wool over your eyes, laddie," responded Henning. "As far as I'm concerned, what happened in Vienna is no proof of his innocence. Indeed, the fact that the culprit there turned out to be the son of a prominent peer of the realm makes me even more suspicious."

"You really think it's possible that Grentham is Renard?" asked Arianna. "I have perhaps the most reason to hate the bastard, but . . ."

The surgeon was quick with a reply. "He's a man who has devoted much of his life to deception and manipulation. Whether it's by the stroke of a pen or the squeeze of a trigger, murder is a weapon he uses with impunity if it suits his purposes." A scowl pinched his face. "In truth, the whole bloody circle of officials privy to this mission are a bunch of arrogant aristocrats who think themselves gods among mortal men."

"I trust you do not include Charles on your list of suspects," said Saybrook softly. His uncle, Charles Mellon, was a senior diplomat in the Foreign Office, and it was because of him that the earl had first become involved in investigating murder and treachery within the inner sanctum of Whitehall.

"I don't know who to trust anymore," muttered Henning.

Oh, hell, thought Arianna.

Friends, family, country . . . Loyalties were going to be tangled and tested in unimaginable ways by this mission. The special bond between the surgeon and her husband had been forged in the fire of the brutal Peninsular War. But were the ties of blood and Scottish heritage tugging at their camaraderie?

"I know this endeavor is fraught with emotion for you, Baz," said Saybrook. "But don't let your heart overpower your head. We must use cold logic in order to vanquish all our enemies— and like you, I'm aware that there may be more than one lurking out there."

For an instant, Henning's expression turned even darker. But then his bony face relaxed into a throaty laugh. "We Scots don't have hearts, merely chips o' Highland flint, liberally watered with whisky. However, you are right—we're a clannish people, and I've let my blood rise to boil on account of the threat to my sister's son. I shall try to temper my personal feelings."

"I know that this stirs political as well as personal conflicts for you," replied the earl. "If there were a way to avoid your involvement—"

"Well, there isn't. Not with Grentham using my nephew as a pawn in his dirty games," snapped Henning. "Without my help, you haven't a snowball's chance in Hell of getting any information out of the locals in St. Andrews. They aren't, to put it mildly, very chatty with strangers."

He drew a deep breath and let it out in a long hiss. "Sorry. I don't mean to be biting your head off, but my nerves are stretched tight as a bowstring right now. My sister is sick with worry over Angus, what with the lad being incarcerated at Inverness prison. The Sassenach jailers there are notorious for their mistreatment of Scottish prisoners."

Sassenach. Henning had unconsciously used the Gaelic term for "English," noted Arianna. It was not a flattering moniker.

"We understand," she said.

Saybrook shifted against the leather squabs. "I was not going to say anything until we arrived in Edinburgh, but I had one last meeting with Grentham before we left London, and I managed to wrest a concession from him regarding your nephew. As you know, the original agreement was that he is to go free only after Renard is apprehended. However, the minister agreed that your nephew will be released as soon as we reach St. Andrews." The earl's lips curled in a faintly mocking smile. "Grentham called it a good-faith gesture that we will not renege on our promise to capture the traitor."

Henning spit on the floorboards. "The bastard is all heart, isn't he?"

"Grentham doesn't need such an organ to pump blood through his veins," quipped Arianna, trying to lighten the mood. "A hunk of coal is all that he requires to blow smoke and brimstone through his body."

As she had hoped, Henning chuckled. "Aye, no wonder the air around him always stinks of sulfur."

"Enough jabs at Grentham," counseled Saybrook. "Let us save all our punches for whatever enemies lie ahead. This attack was likely just the first exchange of blows. I'm sure our strength will be sorely tested in the coming days."

"True enough." The glint of amusement died in Henning's eyes. "Don't think I'm ungrateful, laddie. I know the high-and-mighty minister does not give his favors for free."

Instead of answering, Saybrook reached into his valise and withdrew a slim leather portfolio. "I've made some notes of what we know—and what we don't. A review of the facts may help spark an idea of how to go about picking up Renard's trail."

"Given what happened in Vienna, the trail has probably gone cold. He's likely become even more careful," pointed out the surgeon.

"Or more desperate," pointed out Arianna. "If Napoleon really has ambitions to escape from Elba and re-seize his crown, he must act sooner rather than later—which may force him and his operatives to take risks. The peace conference is making headway with drawing new borders and forging new alliances. Once Europe is rebuilt from the rubble of war, the Powers That Be will be loath to let anyone plunge the Continent back into chaos."

"Perhaps," conceded Henning.

Paper rustled as Saybrook arranged his notes in his lap. "The former Emperor is not easy to defeat. Yes, we managed to spike his guns, so to speak, during our trip to Austria. But he's a genius of battlefield tactics. He will regroup and attack from a different angle."

"And his operative Renard is just as canny. The last time, he sought to twist the Scottish fervor for freedom to his own nefarious purposes," added Arianna. "God knows what he'll try next."

Hunching his shoulders, Henning stared meditatively at his scraped hands. "Judging by what we found inside that brass eagle, you have every reason to fear the worst."

"I trust you are still willing to make an introduction to the chemistry professor at the university in St. Andrews." Saybrook's words were half statement, half question.

Grentham had not sent them rattling off to Scotland merely out of spite. In recounting to the minister what had happened during their Vienna mission, Saybrook had been required to explain in great detail about the chilling chemical discovery that he and Henning had made. The surgeon had recognized the diabolical design for an explosive device from an article he had read in a scientific journal from the university at St. Andrews. Further tests on the liquid had confirmed his surmise—the compound was a lethally dangerous concoction, far more powerful than traditional gunpowder.

Arianna slanted a sidelong look at Henning and her husband.

That the substance was linked with Renard had sent a rumbling of alarm through the halls of the British government. And so Grentham had wasted no time in manipulating the three of them into undertaking this journey to Scotland in order to hunt down the traitor.

Whatever his other faults, the minister was just as cunning as Renard in wielding the weapons in his arsenal.

Heaving an inward sigh, she noted the surgeon's slight hesitation in responding to her husband's query.

"Aye, Connery and I have known each other since we were wee lads. He'll talk to me . . . and to you, with my vouching. But we have to approach him slowly and very carefully. Despite our friendship, he won't be overly eager to expose a fellow Scottish professor to the wrath of the English government, so we must be subtle in our inquiries."

"You know I've no interest in doing Grentham's dirty work for him regarding the Dragons of St. Andrews or any other secret society dedicated to democratic ideals and independence from the Crown," assured the earl. "I'm only after Renard and his cohorts. The identities of any other people I meet will be safe with me."

"I don't doubt *you*, Sandro."

"But you are uncertain of whether that is good enough protection for your Scottish friends?" pressed Arianna.

Henning gave a cryptic shrug.

"Grentham has given me the name of the government's contact in St. Andrews, who will help arrange the release of your nephew and provide any other local assistance that we may need. I shall be discreet in my dealings with him."

"You have to be discreet about a lot of things, laddie," said Henning flatly. "First and foremost, if it becomes known that you and Lady S are fancy English aristocrats, I could beg until I am blue in the face and the Scots won't talk to ye. Never forget, they hate the Sassenach."

"You have been very diligent in reminding us of that," said Arianna softly.

The surgeon blew out his cheeks. "Lady S, ye grew up in the New World, so I daresay it's hard for you to comprehend the bitter hate and distrust ingrained in the Scots, the Welsh and the Irish by centuries of subjugation by the English. In many ways, the mighty British Empire is a seething powder keg, ready to explode."

"You've always said that violence is not the right way to effect change," said Saybrook. "If your beliefs have changed, tell us now, Baz. I respect your feelings and will not ask you to go against your conscience. But on the other hand, I must know whether I can count on you as an ally."

The silence seemed to grow louder with every passing heartbeat.

"Aye," Henning finally answered. "You can count on my loyalty. I am a radical when it comes to abstract notions of freedom and equality, but I'm not a revolutionary. France has shown us the horrors of writing change in blood rather than ink."

"Thank you." Saybrook was quick to move on. Taking a small object from his pocket, he handed it to Henning. "Earlier, you said you recognized this."

"Yes," replied the surgeon, fingering the silver fob. "It's the badge of the Dragons of St. Andrews."

Arianna craned her neck for a closer look. She knew that the Dragons were a secret society dedicated to creating an independent Scotland, governed by democratic rule and the principles of individual freedom. Its members were mostly idealistic university students, but during their last mission, they had learned that the group had come under the control of Renard, who had used the young men for his own objectives. "Your nephew was arrested by the English for being a cell leader."

The surgeon nodded. "Sandro and I found a similar one in David Kydd's rooms before you two left for Vienna."

She closed her eyes for an instant, trying not to picture the blinding flash, the grisly explosion of blood and bone. The young diplomat, a brilliant protégé of Saybrook's uncle, had been a friend. He had also been an unwitting pawn in Renard's sinister games.

"You think that the French still control the group?"

"It seems a logical place to start," answered Saybrook. "Especially given what Baz remembered reading in the technical journal from the university at St. Andrews."

Henning nodded his assent, though he didn't look overly happy about it. "Speaking of starting places, once we cross the border into Scotland, I think it best for you two to assume the new identities we've agreed on. As I said, my friends won't be keen to confide in an English earl or countess, no matter how much I assure them that you are trustworthy. Presenting you as an old Spanish comrade from the war will raise far fewer hackles, Sandro . . . though as I said, the Scots tend to be wary of all strangers."

"That should present no problem," said Saybrook. "I would hope that an air of lordly arrogance and entitlement has not yet attached itself to my person."

Arianna smiled. Her husband was perhaps even more radical than most revolutionaries when it came to his views on inherited wealth and privilege. "Nor mine either," she added. "But then, I've had far less practice."

Though the daughter of an earl, Arianna had lived most of her life in poverty, her aristocratic birth of no consequence in the day-to-day struggle to survive. "My Spanish is excellent, as is my American accent . . ." She switched to a flat drawl. "The role merely requires me to slide into one of my old skins." There were three—maybe four—to choose from.

"The skills acquired during your stint with the theatrical troupe in Barbados have certainly proved useful," said Saybrook.

"Most husbands would not find the fact that their wife is a master of disguise and deception a mark in her favor," replied Arianna, her gaze locking briefly with his.

The smoky flicker of the carriage lamp caught a momentary ripple of amusement in his chocolate-dark eyes. It was gone in an instant, for despite his Spanish blood, which proclaimed itself in his raven-dark hair, olive skin and lean features, it was his more reserved English nature that dominated the expression of his emotions. She had never met anyone quite so in command of his feelings as the earl.

"One man's poison is another man's pleasure," he quipped.

"I never tried to poison you," she protested. "I just tried to prick you with a knife so you couldn't chase after me."

"Just," murmured her husband.

The scuff of Henning's boots on the floorboards interrupted their teasing exchange.

"Dio Madre, Baz, you are jumpy as a cat on a hot griddle," said Saybrook. "We've been perilously close to the fire before and danced over the coals without being burned. I've every intention of coming through this adventure unsinged as well."

Folding his arms across his chest, the surgeon only grunted.

That Henning refused to take part in his usual hard-edged banter with the earl was not a good omen, thought Arianna.

"If something is bothering you, I wish you would tell us what it is," she said. Like her husband, his friend hid his feelings very well. At times, both of them reminded her of hedgehogs, rolled tightly into little balls with prickly bristles pointing outward to fend off any touch.

"Are you worried about something specific?" she went on.

"Aye," he said glumly, "I'm worried about when the next body is going to appear. And whose it will be."

3

From Lady Arianna's Chocolate Notebooks

Double Chocolate Scones

3 cups all-purpose flour
¼ cup sugar
4 teaspoons baking powder
¼ teaspoon salt
½ cup (1 stick) butter
3 large eggs
½ cup milk
¾ cup mini chocolate chips
1 tablespoon grated orange peel
¼ cup white chocolate chips

1. Preheat the oven to 450°F. Grease a large cookie sheet. Stir the flour, sugar, baking powder, and salt in a large bowl. Use a pastry blender or two knives to cut the butter into the dry ingredients until coarse crumbs form.
2. Beat the eggs and milk in a small bowl with a wire whisk or a fork. When thoroughly blended, stir this mixture,

along with ½ cup of the mini chocolate chips and the orange peel, into the flour mixture just until blended.

3. Shape the dough with lightly floured hands into an 8-inch round on the prepared cookie sheet; dust with flour. Score the top of the dough into 8 wedges with a sharp knife.

4. Bake for 20 to 25 minutes, until golden. Cool completely on a wire rack. Meanwhile, stir the remaining ¼ cup mini chocolate chips and the white chocolate chips in separate small, heavy saucepans over very low heat until melted and smooth. Drizzle each chocolate from the tip of a spoon in random lines over the tops of the scones. Let stand for 15 minutes to set the chocolate. Cut the scones into wedges along the score lines.

Gray on gray, the distant church spire was silhouetted against the sky, a dark needle piercing the gloomy mists. Below it, the ancient rooftops of the town floated in and out of view, hide-and-seek spectres. Dark, slightly menacing.

The university town of St. Andrews did not appear very welcoming. *Perhaps it senses that we are intruders,* mused Arianna. *Hostile forces, come to make war.*

Heaving an inward sigh, she watched as their coach rolled closer and closer.

To the left, beyond the dark swaths of rain-swept grass and gorse, the pewter gray ocean was rising and falling in sullen swells, with occasional whitecaps foaming like flashes of teeth. The wash of the waves hit upon the rocky strand with a rough, rasping sound, so unlike the tropical lilt of the Caribbean waters.

Oh, at times how she missed those faraway islands—the spicy warmth, the vibrant colors, the humid breezes, humming with music.

Much of her childhood in the West Indies had been grim. Her father, forced into exile for his less-than-honorable business gambles, had been murdered when she was fourteen, leaving her alone in the world and forced to fend for herself. *Jamaica, Barbados, Martinique* . . . She had floated around more rum-drenched hellholes than she cared to count before returning to England.

And a chance for revenge.

But strangely enough, she had come to care more for justice than for retribution.

A glance at Saybrook's profile, his aquiline nose and slanted cheekbones sharp in the muted light, provoked a tiny smile as she recalled that from the very first, she had been struck by his unyielding sense of honor. They had clashed—and still did—she the cynic, he the idealist, though he would likely bristle at the notion.

Her eyes moved to Henning, who sat slouched on the far side of the seat staring moodily out the window, and her smile faded. *Grim. Gray.*

Another sigh, this one audible. The last two days, which had been spent visiting his sister in Edinburgh, had not been a comfortable interlude. The surgeon's relatives were not un-friendly, just . . . dour. Chiseled faces, burred voices, granite dwellings, hardscrabble landscape—everything in Scotland seemed hewn out of rain-lashed stone.

"What are those men doing?" asked Saybrook, pressing closer to the window to get a better look at the pair poking at a gorse bush with long wooden sticks. "Hunting rabbits?"

A gruff chuckle sounded from Henning. "Hunting featheries—that is, a stitched leather ball filled with feathers. They are playing golf."

"Golf?" repeated Arianna.

"Aye. It's a game. One whacks a ball around a course filled with hazards, like sand bunkers, streams and bushes. The object is to knock it into a small hole in the ground with as few strokes as possible."

Wind whipped against the coach, the pelter of rain rattling

like a hail of bullets against the window glass. "And that is considered amusement?" she asked, raising a skeptical brow.

"It's quite popular here in the north. Indeed, it's considered a national sport of sorts."

The Scots seemed even more incomprehensible, she thought.

"St. Andrews is considered the birthplace of the game." He made a face. "So fer God's sake, don't ridicule it in public."

Had Henning taken offense at her teasing? It was so unlike him to have such a thin skin.

"On the contrary, I have a great respect for your game of golf," said Saybrook, quick to smooth any ruffled feathers. "I have heard that it requires careful strategy and precise execution, for so many variables affect the outcome of each shot. One must plan ahead, exercise patience, and be ready to improvise." A pause. "Rather like the game we are playing."

Henning leaned down to fasten the buckles of his valise. "In golf, the loser forfeits a pint of ale, while we will pay for defeat in blood." Metal chinked against metal. "Make yourself ready to begin the chase in earnest. We're almost at our appointed lodgings."

Arianna drew in a lungful of the damp, salt-roughened air. *Time to start sniffing out the scent of a very clever—and very dangerous—fox.* One who meant to wreak death and destruction at the heart of the British Empire, not merely within a country henhouse.

Arianna watched her husband break the wax seal on the note that had just been slid under their door. He quickly skimmed over the contents and then dropped it into the fire.

"Let us hope Grentham's operative is as well-informed about other things here in St. Andrews as he is about our arrival," he murmured as the paper turned to ash.

"If he was, Grentham would have had no need to blackmail us into his services," she replied darkly. "Will you be going out?"

"Yes." Taking a seat at the small dressing table, he donned a fresh shirt and began to knot a cravat around the upturned collar. Their lodging—at a small, spartan hotel catering to visiting scholars and lecturers—had been arranged by the minister. Arianna assumed the proprietor was part of Grentham's extensive network of spies and informers. Like some great, sinister spider, the minister had probably woven his web into every corner of the globe, she thought. And from there the strands likely dipped down into the deepest pits of Hell.

"The note invited me to come at the usual time to share a wee dram at the Rock," went on Saybrook. "As you know, Grentham set up a code name for the rendezvous point and time before we left London."

"I trust you will not go unarmed," she said softly.

His dark eyes met hers in the wavering reflection of the looking glass. "From here on, I shall always be carrying a turn-off pocket pistol somewhere on my person." The small Italian weapon was designed to fit into the palm of a hand. While useless at long range, it was highly effective in close quarters. "I suggest you do the same."

She nodded and continued unpacking her trunk. "My knife shall keep it company." The flutter of thick-woven wool stirred a sigh as she shook out the skirts of her gowns and hung them in the painted pine armoire. "Be on guard," she murmured after another moment. "I can't quite put my finger on it, but something feels wrong about all this. Even the shadows here in Scotland seem steeped in malice."

Saybrook tweaked the folds of starched linen into perfect alignment before answering. "That's because they have been colored by centuries of blood and betrayal, my dear. We'll find no easy answers in this country. As Baz has warned us, getting information will be as hard as chiseling at Scottish stone with a silver spoon."

"I'm not convinced we'll find *any* answers here in the north. We've no real evidence to go on, merely suspicions—which at the moment feel flimsier than the finest Chinese silk."

"It may be a wild-goose chase," agreed Saybrook. "But we can't afford to leave any stone unturned in the hunt for Renard."

Arianna chuffed a low, harried exhale in response.

"It's not like you to sound so uncertain," observed her husband. He turned and fixed her with a searching look. "We've faced other complex conundrums, each just as nebulous as this one."

"I know, I know." Her husband's reasonable words only exacerbated her unsettled mood.

"And yet . . . ," he pressed, giving voice to the doubts that she had left unsaid.

"And yet, I keep feeling that in this case we are letting emotion dictate our actions, rather than logic. That's dangerous."

His mouth tipped up at the corners. "Allow me to remind you that the reason we met was because you were hell-bent on seeking revenge for your father's murder."

She allowed a reluctant smile. "Put that way, I sound like a flighty female, who flits from one extreme to another."

"No one in his right mind would ever accuse you of being a featherhead. If you have concerns, I wish to hear them."

"I can't quite explain it . . ." Stirred by a draft of air, the double branch of candles flared, the two flames like malevolent eyes peering out from the devil-dark gloom. "But I simply have a bad feeling about being here."

His flicker of amusement disappeared. "My wartime experience has taught me to trust intuition. We must both be extra vigilant. If trouble means to strike, let us try to get in the first blow."

His voice, strong and steady despite the softness of its tone, helped calm her nerves. "It's likely just the unremitting cold and damp that has me on edge," she replied, chafing at her arms. "And the haggis."

The previous evening, Henning's sister had served them the national dish of boiled oatmeal and minced sheep organs, encased in a length of chewy intestine. It was not a meal she cared to repeat.

"Many things about Scotland are an acquired taste," he quipped, a brief smile flitting over his lips. "Look, should you wish to return home while I continue—"

Arianna silenced him with a rude oath. "What I wish to do is go over what we learned in Vienna, to make sure we aren't overlooking a vital clue." She paused to refold a paisley shawl and place it in the chest of drawers next to the armoire. "We started to do that with Basil but were distracted. Perhaps it's better that we continue on our own—it may allow for a more frank discussion of the situation."

"Is that a polite way of saying that you are worried about his loyalties?" asked her husband.

"I've no doubt that the bond between the two of you is incredibly strong. But there are a number of conflicting forces pulling at his conscience, and he is, after all, only human. Something may eventually snap."

"I shall do my best not to tug too hard on him." The earl made a careful check of his coat pockets. "Damn Grentham for maneuvering us into this situation. I'm aware that we must tread very carefully around our friend as well as our enemy."

"The devious bastard is determined to see that none of us escape from this mission unscathed," muttered Arianna. "He would be just as happy if we perish along with Renard. There is an old adage about killing two birds with one stone—well, in this case, he hopes to hit four."

"Even Grentham doesn't have such an accurate aim," replied her husband lightly. "If he hurls a missile at us, I'll make sure that the ricochet hits him in the arse."

"Ha, ha, ha." Her halfhearted attempt at mirth sounded awfully hollow. "In all seriousness, Sandro. If it were up to you, would we be here in Scotland? Or would we be concentrating our efforts on investigating the Duke of Lampson's wayward son? After what happened in Vienna, it seems to me that Lord Reginald's world is where we will find the key to unlocking this conundrum."

Looking pensive, her husband squared the set of silver brushes on the dressing table. "Like you, I have a feeling that the trail to Renard will lead us back to London. But we cannot overlook the terrible chemical threat we uncovered in Vienna."

A chance discovery. A stroke of luck. She shuddered to recall how close to disaster they had come.

"I trust Baz's scientific expertise, if not his emotional state at the moment," continued her husband. "And as he feels the work was likely done here at the university, we had no choice but to come see for ourselves."

"You're right, of course," said Arianna. Still, the sensation of a chill finger teasing against the back of her neck wouldn't go away.

After a quick look at his pocket watch, the earl swore under his breath. "Sorry, we'll have to finish discussing this when I get back. My contact will be waiting and I had better not be late."

"Are you taking Basil with you?"

The hesitation was so brief that she might only have imagined it. "Yes. Without him I would likely stumble around all night, trying to find my way through these dark, twisting streets. And as we have been saying, we can't afford even the smallest misstep."

A light touch eased the warehouse door open, its well-greased hinges yielding nary a sound. Saybrook quickly slipped inside, followed by Henning, who drew it shut. Darkness enveloped them, the dank air thick with the briny smell of fish and dried seaweed.

"You made good time from London." A voice rumbled within the shadows, followed by the metallic scrape of a lanthorn shutter being lifted. But rather than illuminate the speaker's features, the beam of light was deliberately directed at Saybrook's face. "Any trouble along the way?"

The earl blinked, blinded by the sudden glare. "None to speak of," he replied slowly.

Behind him, Henning quietly backed up a step and shifted out of the flickering light.

"I'm glad to hear it," went on the speaker. "The roads here in the north can be awfully rough, especially if one is unused to the hardships demanded by a clandestine mission."

Saybrook ignored the man's faintly mocking tone. "Lord Grentham appears to think me up to the challenge."

The mention of the minister's name silenced the other man's sneer.

"Lower that damn light and let us get down to business," the earl went on brusquely. "I daresay both of us will be happy to keep this rendezvous as short as possible."

"It would help if I knew why you and your companions were sent here," said the man. It was evident that he was not happy at having strangers trespassing on his turf.

The earl answered obliquely. "I am hoping you might have some useful information to share with us. We've been told that you have been in place here for several years as the proprietor of a bookstore near the university, and as such I would imagine that you hear whispers if there is any unusual intellectual activity taking place."

Grentham's operative took a step closer and lifted the light higher, revealing a long, thin face and pale gray eyes that accentuated the beady gleam of his dark pupils. "What sort of intellectual activity?" he asked, his nose twitching like that of a bird dog seeking to catch a scent in the air.

"Alas, I am not at liberty to tell you the specifics," answered Saybrook coolly. "Just tell me of all that you have noticed over the last several months, and leave me to decide if it helps narrow my search."

"Who the devil do you think you are, snapping orders like a bloody lord at me?"

"I imagine Grentham informed you of my identity. I'm Castellano, and during the Peninsular War, I was a liaison from the

Spanish army working with Wellington's staff. My work seems to have satisfied the duke, because he dispatched me from Paris to Lord Grentham for this mission," said the earl. "In case you haven't been informed, I am visiting the university because of my interest in Highland botany."

The man's lips pinched to a scowl. "I have been running intelligence operations for the ministry since my arrival here. I don't need a lecture from some snotty-nosed Spaniard telling me how to do my job."

"And yet, London felt compelled to send me here, Mr. Rollins," answered Saybrook softly.

"I've accomplished quite a lot," he said defensively. "Thanks to my surveillance, a number of dangerous revolutionaries have been arrested and are now languishing in Inverness prison, awaiting execution." A low laugh. "That is, assuming they live that long."

Henning drew in a sharp breath as if he meant to speak, but then let it seep out in a long exhale.

"Who's your companion?" asked Rollins, finally deigning to acknowledge the surgeon's presence.

"You haven't answered my question about scholarly activity," said Saybrook.

A shape shifted in the deep shadows, a ripple of black on black. "Indeed, Rollins, our visitor from London is right. It's our duty to cooperate with the minister's investigators." As a figure materialized from the gloom and came to stand next to Rollins, a wink of scarlet and gold flashed from beneath his dark cloak. "I've been informed that you have a third member of your party. A female, registered as your wife at the lodging house. An odd arrangement given your mission . . ." A fraction of a pause. "Mr. Castellano."

Saybrook regarded the newcomer for a long moment. "On the contrary, I think it reinforces the story that we are here on a purely scholarly trip."

"Perhaps."

The earl ignored the shrug. "I take it you are Lord Stoughton, colonel in command of this region?"

The military officer smoothed at the fancy frogging of his cloak, setting off a muffled jingling of metal beneath the thick wool. "At your service." His smile did not belie the sarcasm shading his reply.

"Excellent, Colonel." Saybrook parried with his own edge of steel. "You have a young man by the name of Angus MacPhearson incarcerated in Inverness prison. I want him released without delay."

Stoughton's eyes narrowed. "That would require an order from the highest authorities at Horse Guards."

"So it would." The earl took a packet from his coat pocket, its outer wrapping festooned with ornate wax seals, and held it out. "I trust you will find everything in order here."

The colonel reluctantly took it.

Saybrook returned his attention to Rollins. "You have yet to answer my question about the university."

Grentham's operative flicked a quick look at Stoughton, who gave a barely perceptible nod to proceed.

Clearing his throat, Rollins grudgingly complied. "It's been fairly quiet since we rounded up the rabble and locked them away. I've caught wind of some conversations that make me think a new print shop for seditious pamphlets is being set up somewhere by a new group of student radicals."

"Anything else?" prodded the earl.

Another sullen silence. "As I said, it would help if I knew what, specifically, you were looking for."

"And as *I* said, that is confidential information." The earl made to turn. "If you've nothing more to add, I suggest we call an end to this meeting. Neither of us will be of any use to the ministry if we are spotted in a clandestine meeting by the locals."

"But first we had better set a time for the next rendezvous—" began Rollins.

"There will be no set meetings," interrupted Saybrook. "If I have need of anything from you, I shall contrive to pass you a message in your bookstore without attracting undue attention. And if you have any urgent information to convey to me, send a book to my lodgings, along with a note inviting me to share a wee dram at a certain hour. We are, after all, going to pretend to form a scholarly friendship over your inventory of books."

He paused, drawing out the sliver of silence. "By the by, I've read several of the dispatches you have sent to London. You really ought to use a less primitive code than a simple Caesar shift."

Rollins spit on the earthen floor. "It's not as if the local Scots would have a clue as to how to puzzle out the meaning. They are naught but hairy savages . . ." He grunted some low, feral animal sounds. "A primitive people, little better than animals. It's a pity that the Duke of Cumberland didn't slaughter them all after the Battle of Culloden."

Stoughton laughed, leaving Saybrook and Henning standing in stony silence as he and Rollins traded a few more disparaging quips.

"Shutter your light. We are leaving," snapped the earl at Rollins, as soon as the last chortle died away. To Stoughton, he said, "I shall expect to have MacPhearson delivered to me without delay."

The colonel wordlessly tucked the packet from London into his cloak pocket.

Saybrook waited until darkness shrouded the warehouse before moving to the door, with Henning right on his heels.

A blade of light appeared for an instant and then disappeared, followed by a soft *snick* as the latch fell back into place.

Outside, fog swirled over the narrow walkway in silvery waves, muddling the scudding moonlight with the yawing shadows of the buildings. The sound of the sea breaking against the rocky shore drowned the sound of their steps on the cobblestones as Saybrook and Henning hurried across the deserted street. Hats pulled low, heads bent to the gusty wind, they passed through several winding alleys before pausing to survey the surroundings.

Satisfied that they hadn't been followed, they slipped out onto Pends Road, keeping close to the looming cathedral walls.

It was only after they turned yet another corner onto South Street that the surgeon expelled a low hiss through his clenched teeth. The vapor rose like steam from a kettle on hot coals.

"God rot their damnable Sassenach bones."

"I understand your outrage—"

"Nay, you don't," said Henning bitterly. "Not by half."

"Baz, I've been called a degenerate mongrel more times than I can count," replied Saybrook. "That the heir to one of the oldest earldoms is half-Spanish sends shudders of disgust through the mansions of Mayfair. Trust me, the high sticklers of Society think their blue blood is far too precious to be tainted by dark-skinned Mediterranean scum. So yes, I do understand your feelings concerning such pompous prejudices."

His friend blew out his cheeks. "My apologies, laddie."

"None are necessary."

"It's just that such insufferable arrogance makes my blood boil," growled the surgeon.

"Don't let them ignite your emotions, Baz," counseled the earl. "Keep a cool head and we shall beat them at their own game."

"Those two bastards put Angus in prison."

"And we are going to get him out."

His friend looked away into the night, masking his craggy face in the shadows.

"Rest assured that I intend to stay well away from Rollins and Stoughton from now on," added Saybrook. "I had no choice but to make contact with them on our arrival, but like you, I don't trust them."

The pungent scents of tobacco smoke and spilled ale drifted out from a tavern as two men bumped through the door and stumbled off into the night. The surgeon stopped abruptly. "Bloody hell, I need to wash the sour taste from my mouth."

Saybrook hesitated, his gaze shifting from his friend's grim profile to the iron-studded door. A light mizzle had begun to fall, and in the spill of lamplight from the windows, the fine mist looked like a shower of sparks. "As you wish," he said softly.

"Not here," said Henning, shaking the beads of water from his shoulders. "There's a place on High Street that caters more to the university lecturers. I may as well begin renewing my acquaintances with old friends. The sooner we can make contact with the chemistry professor I have in mind, the better." He turned up his collar. "Before this whole bloody trip blows up in our faces."

4

From Lady Arianna's Chocolate Notebooks

Chocolate Oatcakes

¼ cup hazelnuts, finely chopped
⅔ cup all-purpose flour
⅓ cup Dutch-process cocoa powder
¼ cup wheat germ
½ cup rolled old-fashioned oats
½ teaspoon freshly ground cardamom
¼ teaspoon ground cinnamon
⅛ teaspoon fine salt
½ cup (1 stick) unsalted butter, softened
¾ cup sugar
2 large egg yolks

1. Preheat the oven to 350°F. Line 2 mini muffin tins with mini muffin liners, or set out 20 mini muffin liners on a baking sheet. Lightly spray the liners with nonstick spray and sprinkle the hazelnuts into the bottom of each muffin liner.
2. Whisk the flour, cocoa, wheat germ, oats, spices and salt together in a medium bowl.

3. With an electric mixer on medium speed, beat the butter and sugar in another bowl until combined, about 2 minutes. Add the egg yolks and beat together. Add the dry ingredients and mix until just combined.

4. Scoop 1 tablespoon of dough (about ¾ ounce) into each mini muffin liner, on top of the nuts. (Alternatively, drop heaping tablespoons of the dough onto a parchment-lined baking sheet and top with chopped nuts.) Bake until the cookies are cooked through and the nuts are toasty, about 15 minutes (drop cookies will bake slightly faster). Transfer the cookies to a rack to cool.

Turning away from the sting of salt, Arianna pushed the flapping bonnet ribbons from her cheeks and continued walking along the pebbled path. A gust kicked up a spray of sand from the nearby strip of beach, tangling her skirts and tugging at the wicker basket looped over her arm.

Wind, water, weathered stone. Scotland had a bleak beauty, she admitted, watching a pewter gray skirl of fog dance around the ancient stones of St. Rule's Tower. However, the dull, heavy dampness felt oppressive. As if a lead weight had settled on her shoulders.

She tried to shrug off the feeling and lift her spirits. *Chin up—every little step is bringing us closer to our goal.* As Henning had warned, it was slow going, but after nearly a week in St. Andrews, they were beginning to make some progress. Her husband and his friend were meeting this morning with one of the visiting lecturers in chemistry, while she was making another foray to the market stalls off High Street.

A flock of gulls swooped overhead, their raucous calls interrupting her thoughts.

"You know on which side your bread is buttered," murmured Arianna, as they wheeled and dove for the scaly scraps tossed aside by the fishmongers. "As for me . . ."

She paused for a moment, surveying the jumble of carts and barrows clogging the street. Her interest in the local produce and baked goods had helped break the stony reserve of the local women. Food was a universal language among females, she thought wryly. As were recipes.

"Gud dae te ye, Mrs. Castellano," called an elderly crone with a face nearly as fissured as the harbor breakwater. "Did ye and yer husband enjoy my scones?"

"Delicious," she replied. "You must tell me your secret for plumping the sultanas."

"Uisge beatha," she said with a throaty cackle. "Ye soak them in gud Scottish malt—or whisky."

Arianna reached into her pocket and pulled out a piece of paper. "Here is the recipe I promised for my spiced chocolate cake." Her many unorthodox talents included finely honed cooking skills. In fact, she was an expert, as was the earl, in the uses of *Theobroma cacao*—or chocolate. While Saybrook was writing a scholarly treatise about its history and uses, she was compiling a cookbook based on his grandmother's journal and notes.

The crone's eyes winged up in skepticism. "I still canna quite believe that one may *eat* chocolate as well as drink it."

Wrapping her tartan shawl tighter around her shoulders, a woman from the neighboring stall edged closer. "Chocolate as an ingredient in pastries? I think ye be pulling me leg."

"I promise you that I am not. Please try it," replied Arianna. "I think you will be pleasantly surprised."

"Sounds too foreign fer my taste," chimed in one of her friends.

"Well, we strangers to Scotland find haggis a trifle odd," she said with a smile.

The comment elicited hoots of laughter.

"We invented it specially to poison the Sassenach invaders," piped up the fruit seller.

"I don't blame you. We in the New World have no love for the English either." She moved on a few steps and picked up a small sack of nutmegs, then a jar of candied orange peel. "I should very much like to learn how to make your Dundee cakes, Mrs. MacDonald."

"Auch, with pleasure. I'll scribble out the instructions. Stop back and see me afore ye leave the market."

"And I wud be happy te share my draught for a cough," added the woman tending a barrow full of herbs. "Yer potion for soothing aching joints worked wonders fer me Pater."

"Oh, well, I have another one that is good for gout . . ." After trading recipes, Arianna continued to meander through the crowded stalls, taking her time to sort through the offerings and make her purchases. Smoke from the warming peat fires drifted in the air, mingling with the scents of the foodstuffs and murmur of voices. The women were now comfortable with her presence, and all around her, the talk was not just haggling over prices, but also local gossip.

Gossip. In her experience, if one wanted to learn all the secrets of a place, one had only to find a spot where its females gathered. Cooks, maids, washerwomen—they knew the intimate details of a household's daily life. By keeping her eyes and ears open, mused Arianna, she just might learn more than Saybrook and Henning would within the male bastion of the university.

Men tended to be more tight-lipped unless well lubricated with brandy or other strong spirits.

Reaching the end of the lane, she turned and squeezed in between two covered stalls selling medicinal powders and potions. Half-hidden by a stack of barrels was a display of dried Highland herbs that looked interesting . . .

A rustling behind the sailcloth screen of the near stall interrupted her musings. Then a muffled voice, distinctly female, rose above the faint crackling of the canvas.

"By the bones of St. Andrew hisself, the bang frightened me near te death, Mavis."

Bang. Arianna went very still and cocked an ear. Had she heard right? The Scottish burr was hard to understand.

"Auch, he claimed it was but a wee bit o' liquid on the burner." The woman dropped her voice a notch. "But it blew the copper pot clear through the ceiling. There must have been flames as well—the woodwork was singed something awful."

"I wuddna want te work fer such an odd employer, Alice," said Mavis. "No matter that he pays a few pence more fer a maid."

"Aye, likely all that fancy study at the university has addled his head," replied Alice. "They say he be a very learned man, but he frightens me. Strange mumblings, locked doors, shadowy visitors late at night—I dunna like it at all. Mayhap he's a warlock, or a . . ."

A blustery breeze ruffled the canvas. Swearing silently, Arianna inched closer to the cloth, straining to catch the whispers.

"Bessie may know of another position," offered Mavis. "Let Professor Girton find someone else willing te put up with him and his quirks. I swear, it be the Devil's work if a man uses his own house fer brewing up mischief."

The Devil? Arianna pursed her lips and slipped back into the shelter of the barrels. Then perhaps they were on the right trail after all.

"I feel as if we're trying to trudge through a vat of boiled oats." Saybrook hung his coat and hat on the clothes pegs. "It just sits there, thick as glue, resisting every effort to make headway."

"I warned ye that the Scots are slow te warm up te strangers," said Henning. "My friend Connery is doing his best to sniff out what's going on in the laboratories. But he must be discreet in his questions. We don't want to spook our quarry." He moved to the sideboard and poured himself a glass of whisky. *"Sláinte."*

The earl let out a disgruntled sigh. "At this rate, it will be the next century before their reserve thaws."

"Try some oatcakes." Hearing the men return from their meeting, Arianna came into the sitting room from the bedchamber. A gesture indicated the platter on the tea table. "They are fresh from the market."

"I'd rather you feed me some useful information," grumbled the earl as he took a seat in one of the worn leather armchairs. "I'm starved for progress."

"I may have something that will sweeten your mood, but I thought I would let you eat first—you are always snappish when your bread box is empty."

"And we are all aware that you claim to think better on a full stomach, Lady S." The surgeon lifted his glass in salute. "Actually, it makes perfect medical sense. Just as a stove needs fuel to keep the fire burning, a body needs sustenance to perform at its best."

"Then my wife must be a veritable genius." The earl raked a hand through his damp hair. "Though how someone so slender can consume so much without becoming as fat as the Prince Regent is a scientific conundrum."

"I like food," said Arianna. "A fact for which both of you ought to be profoundly grateful."

The earl sat up a bit straighter.

"You see, I was able to melt some of that flinty Scottish suspicion of strangers with a few of my chocolate recipes."

"Chocolate is fast becoming England's secret weapon," quipped Saybrook. "Though it's really my Spanish ancestors who deserve the credit."

Henning downed his whisky in one quick swallow. "Much as I appreciate your expertise in chocolate, might you continue?"

"Of course." Her expression turned serious. "For the last few days, I've been spending time at the market, for you see, cooking provides a common ground for women."

"Trial by fire," murmured the earl.

Her mouth quirked up at the corners. "In a manner of speaking, I suppose. The point is, the locals here have come to accept me as a kindred soul, despite my strange accent. And as they don't view my presence among them as a threat, they feel comfortable talking among themselves."

Saybrook steepled his fingers and placed the point beneath his chin. "Go on."

"I've made a point of taking my time in wandering through the stalls. I look at the goods for sale, I buy . . . and I listen."

"I take it you have heard something interesting," said Henning.

"Very." Arianna moved to the door and took a quick peek into the corridor. "Perhaps we should take a walk on the strand. Seeing as Grentham arranged our quarters, there is a possibility that the walls have ears."

Her husband nodded. "A prudent suggestion. Baz?"

The surgeon poured himself another measure of whisky and drank it down. "Aye. I don't trust the minister or his lackeys farther than I can spit." He pursed his lips. "No word yet from that gold-braided donkey's arse about Angus?"

Arianna bit her lip. The malt had lit a dangerous glint in Henning's eye. For the present it was only a small spark, but it wouldn't take much to fan it into a flame.

"You know military bureaucracy," counseled Saybrook. "These things often move at a snail's pace, despite orders."

"We don't even know what Grentham wrote in those fancy sealed papers," retorted the surgeon.

"It is not in the minister's interest to make enemies of us," pointed out the earl.

"That," said Henning darkly, "depends on what his true interests really are."

"Instead of spinning round and round in circles on this, let us try to move forward." Arianna put on her coat and bonnet. "Put the arrogant Colonel Stoughton and his scarlet regimentals out of your mind. The only shade of red that ought to concern us is the cinnabar flash of a cunning fox."

Bundled up against the biting wind, the three of them cut across the golf course and took the footpath down to the rocky stretch of beach. The tide was ebbing, leaving pools of dark, foam-flecked water among the smooth stones. Storm clouds hovered on the horizon, ominous bands of charcoal smudging the steel gray sea.

As they picked their way along the high-water line, Saybrook linked arms with Arianna and signaled for his friend to do the same. "I think we're now safe enough from being overheard," he said dryly. "Feel free to be succinct. I feel a sudden craving for hot chocolate coming on, fortified with a generous splash of rum."

"I shall," she said through chattering teeth, and quickly recounted what she had overheard.

"Girton," mused Henning. "Just this morning Connery suggested that we add his name to our list of people who merited a closer look. Though I confess, I did not put it at the very top."

"I suggest you reconsider," said Arianna.

The surgeon looked pensive. "What—"

Saybrook swung around, turning them all back in the direction of town. "Let us get out of the cold, before Arianna turns into a block of ice," he counseled. "We can discuss strategy at a coffeehouse. But it seems to me that we ought act on this without delay. A late-night visit to his residence for a private audience might be in order."

"Aye." Henning's voice was muffled by the knitted scarf wound around his neck and the lower part of his face. "I'm sure that with the right encouragement we can convince him to be candid about his current activities."

Arianna quickened her pace. Her feet were going numb despite her sturdy half boots. "I agree. The sooner we move, the better."

"I am not sure your new lady friends in the market would approve." Saybrook arched a brow as he eyed her snug-fitting black breeches and coat. "Scots are rather rigid in their notions of traditional propriety."

"I'm sure that according to their rules, I'm guilty of a multitude of sins." She checked the sharpness of her blade before sliding it into her boot. "One more won't matter."

The earl opened a small traveling case, revealing several more small pocket pistols. He chose a pretty pearl-handed model and after checking the action of the hammer held it out on his palm. "Manton had this in his shop. It was made by a craftsman in Italy who specializes in discreet weapons for ladies and should fit perfectly in the hidden breast pocket of your coat."

"I prefer the Tsar's dueling pistols," replied Arianna. "As you pointed out, these tiny toys are only effective at very close range."

"Take it," he said softly. "You'll have the other weapons as well, but I prefer that you carry a spare. One can't be too careful, my dear."

"You are growing cautious in your old age," she replied, smiling slightly.

"Call it wiser." *Click, click.* The well-oiled steel moved with perfect precision as he examined the priming of his own pair of firearms. "Though many people would question my sanity for allowing my wife to be part of these little adventures."

"On the contrary. You are smart enough to know the futility of forbidding me to be involved in the action. I don't take orders well."

Click, click. "And yet the traditional vows of marriage include a promise to honor and obey."

"I lied," said Arianna without a hint of hesitation. "Which should come as no surprise to you, given my background." *Click, click.* She made her own quick examination of the tiny pocket pistol and tucked it away. "If you wanted a traditional wife, alas, you made the wrong choice."

Candlelight glinted off the polished metal, catching the spark of amusement that lit in his eyes. "Ah, well, there are benefits to being leg shackled to a lady who refuses to conform to convention. Life is rarely dull."

She put on her hat and tugged the wide brim down low. "It's time to go. Henning and his friend will be waiting."

The surgeon had suggested that he ask his friend Connery to accompany them to Girton's residence, explaining that the chemistry professor might be more forthcoming if a colleague were there to urge cooperation. Both she and the earl had agreed that it could do no harm, for Henning had sworn that his friend could be trusted to keep their secrets.

Easing the bedchamber window open, Saybrook angled a look up and down the alleyway. Signaling for her to follow, he slipped out to the ledge and slid along to the corner of the inn, where the corniced stone allowed enough of a foothold to climb up to the slated rooftop. Crouching low, he moved stealthily to the adjoining building, using the chimney shadows for cover.

The moon was naught but a thin crescent, noted Arianna as she slid her gloved hands over the rough tiles. Even if Grentham's lackeys were spying on them, they should have no trouble evading pursuit.

At the end of the block, the earl dropped down to a deserted storage pen, and from there they emerged onto a quiet side street.

"This way," he whispered, drawing her toward the harbor.

Henning and Connery were waiting in the lee of the cathedral's east wall. "It's colder than a witch's tit," grumbled the surgeon.

"Auch, London living has made ye soft, Baz," whispered his friend. "It's balmy fer this time of year."

"Let's hurry," advised the earl. He did not introduce Arianna to the professor.

Yes, some things were best left unsaid, she thought, falling in step behind her husband.

Connery led the way, threading a path through a series of narrow, twisting alleyways before pausing in front of the ivy-covered back gate of a walled garden. "It's locked," he whispered, "but Baz told me that won't be an obstacle."

"None whatsoever." Saybrook needed only a moment of probing with a thin metal pick before the mechanism released with a soft *snick*.

Moving quickly in single file, they followed the yew hedge up to the rear of a modest stone house. Save for a faint glimmer of light seeping through the shutters of the far ground-floor window, the place was as dark as a crypt.

"That's Girton's workroom," whispered Connery. "Shall we knock on the back door?"

Henning looked to the earl.

"No," replied Saybrook. "Let's enter first. You can alert him to our presence once we're inside."

Once again, a lock yielded easily to the earl's probing, allowing them to cross through the scullery and into an unlit corridor.

The house was silent . . .

Too silent, thought Arianna, aware of a prickling at the back of her neck. She eased off a glove and slipped her hand inside her coat, feeling for the butt of the pistol tucked into her waistband.

Connery inched around a corner and pointed up ahead at a paneled oak door, outlined by a thin bead of lamplight.

Saybrook signaled him to approach and knock. He, too, had his hand inside his coat.

"Girton? It's Connery. Forgive me for disturbing you at this hour, but I've something urgent to discuss with you."

Silence.

He cleared his throat and repeated the words.

Again, no response.

The earl stepped forward and pressed a palm to the door. It swung open with a low groan . . . which was quickly echoed by Saybrook's oath.

"Oh, bloody hell."

5

From Lady Arianna's Chocolate Notebooks

Chocolate Cherry Brownies

2 cups dried cherries
1 cup port wine
½ cup whole wheat pastry flour
⅓ cup unsweetened cocoa powder
½ teaspoon fine-grain sea salt
2 teaspoons baking powder
10½ ounces dark chocolate chips or chunks
5½ tablespoons unsalted butter
2 cups sifted Muscovado or dark brown sugar
4 large eggs
½ cup crème fraîche or sour cream
1 cup chocolate chips or chunks
Butter for greasing the pan

1. A day or two before you want to bake the brownies, place the cherries in a medium bowl and pour the port over them. Cover and set aside. Stir every twelve hours until ready to use.

2. Preheat the oven to 325°F and place a rack in the top third. Butter and line a 13 x 9 x 2–inch rectangular baking dish with parchment paper (an important step if you want to eventually get these brownies out of the pan).

3. Sift the flour, cocoa powder, salt, and baking powder into a bowl and set aside.

4. Make a double boiler by placing a stainless steel bowl over a small pan of gently simmering water—the bottom of the bowl should not touch the water. Place the dark chocolate chips into this bowl along with the butter and sugar. Stir just until the chocolate has melted and the ingredients come together into a mass. Transfer to the bowl of an electric mixer and allow to cool.

5. Mix on low speed and add the eggs, one at a time, incorporating each before adding the next. Scrape down the sides of the bowl with a spatula a couple of times along the way.

6. Add the flour mixture and stir by hand until combined. Add the crème fraîche, the remaining 1 cup chocolate chips, and the cherries with the port. Stir until just combined.

7. Spoon the mixture into the prepared pan and bake for about 1 hour, or until just set. The center of the brownie should be set and not at all wobbly.

8. Allow to cool completely in the pan. You can cover the pan tightly with plastic wrap at this point and the brownies will keep for a couple of days. Chill before slicing if you want small, precise squares.

Arianna pushed past a confused Connery to join her husband on the workroom's threshold.

"Damnation." She let loose her own oath after a quick glance around.

The massive pine desk had clearly been ransacked. An ink-well had been knocked to the carpet, leaving a splattering of black blotches over the scattered quills and penknives. The drawers hung open, and the contents had been strewn helter-pelter on the floor.

"Any sign of Girton?" Henning stepped gingerly around the jumbled pile of papers and peered under the worktable, as if expecting to find a corpse hidden in the shadows.

"I'll check the bedchamber," volunteered Arianna.

"No, I'll do it." Saybrook drew his weapon. "You stay here with Baz and see what clues you can find."

"I—I don't understand," stammered Connery. "What—"

A look from Henning speared him to silence.

"The worktable appears to have been swept clear of all implements," observed Arianna as she slowly rounded the desk and ran a hand over the waxed wood. Frowning, she stared up at the ceiling, where a jagged hole, its edges black with soot, marred the whitewashed plaster.

Henning crouched down and thumbed through several of the books that had been pulled from the shelves. "It would seem the intruder came for something specific."

He and Arianna locked eyes for a long moment before she looked away.

"Damn," she repeated under her breath, stepping to the hearth. A flicker of orange showed that the embers still had a bit of life. She was just about to take up the poker and stir up a flame when a curl of singed leather within the ashes caught her eyes.

Shoving aside the fireguard, she dropped to her knees and fished a small notebook out from the coals.

"What's that?" asked Henning, hurrying to her side.

Arianna swatted out the sparks, wincing as the heat burned her fingers. "I'm not sure yet." A cursory peek beneath the cover revealed pages filled with a scrawled script. "Time enough later to examine it more closely." She rose and carefully tucked it away in her pocket. "Come, let's see what else we can find."

They moved to the storage cabinets. "Why don't you check through these, while I see if I can find a letter case. If there are any suspicious chemicals, I wouldn't recognize them."

"Hand me one of the glass-globed lamps. An open flame would be too dangerous—"

The clatter of Saybrook's steps on the stairs cut off Henning's reply.

"Half the clothing in the armoire is gone, and a valise seems to be missing from its peg," announced the earl. "It looks as if our professor has made a hasty departure." He turned to Connery. "Does he own any sort of conveyance—a cart, a carriage?"

"I . . . I don't think so."

Saybrook thought for an instant. "The laboratory! Where does he do his experiments at the university?"

"St. Salvatore's College, in the wing closest to Butts Wynd."

"Don't just stand there, Connery. Lead the way!" He gave the professor a small shove. "And quickly!"

Shaking off his lingering shock, Henning's friend finally roused himself to action. Boots skittering on the waxed wood, he bolted off down the corridor, the earl right on his heels.

"Hurry," called Saybrook over his shoulder. "There may be a chance we can catch up with Girton."

Giving thanks for her breeches, rather than the cursed encumbrance of flapping skirts, Arianna raced after them. She heard Henning swear and slam the cabinet doors shut. Then his footsteps were echoing somewhere in the gloom behind her.

She didn't dare look back. The fog-swirled streets were as dark as Hades, and with precious few of the buildings showing even a flicker of light, she knew that falling behind would leave her hopelessly lost. Spurred on by the thought, she quickened her pace, even though the cold air was painfully sharp against her lungs and a stitch was stabbing at her side.

For a brief stretch Henning caught up, but she heard his breath turn wheezy and his steps begin to fade.

The surgeon knew the town, she reminded herself. He could find his own way, if need be.

After what felt like an eternity, Connery cut away from the slick cobblestones and darted through a gap in the buildings, where finally he slowed to a walk as he reached a swath of grass.

"There," he gasped, pointing to a looming building of square angles, crenellated towers and pointed spires silhouetted against the cloudy night sky. "St. Salvatore's—the laboratories are on the first floor. Girton's is at the very end, and in the back, overlooking the sea."

"Thank you." The earl looked around and spotted Henning limping down from shadows of North Street. "Go home now, Connery."

"What is going on here, Mr. Castellano? Who the devil are you?"

"It's best you don't know," answered the earl grimly.

The surgeon's friend hesitated, but only for an instant. The Scots, reflected Arianna, had a strong streak of pragmatism to go along with their flinty courage and stubborn pride.

With a brusque nod, Connery backed off and disappeared into the mists.

Still breathing hard, Henning hurried to rejoin them.

"Are you all right?" asked Saybrook.

"I'll live," replied his friend curtly. "What's the plan of attack?"

The earl didn't answer right away. He stood, silent and still, observing the building. Though she couldn't see his expression, she sensed the coiled tension of his muscles. If not for the rhythmic wash of the surf, she was sure that the thrum would have been audible.

"I don't like the situation—there are too many unknown variables. But we've no choice." He seemed to make up his mind. "Baz, I need you to wait here, both to watch our backs and to prevent Girton from escaping if he slips through my grasp. Arianna will come with me."

A scudding of moonlight caught Henning's grimace, but he didn't argue.

She, too, remained silent, despite wanting to point out that in a chase, she was more likely to succeed. Intuition told her this was not the moment to question his command.

"You're armed?" added Saybrook.

"Aye, laddie. I haven't forgotten all our training from the Peninsular War."

"Good. I suggest you take cover there . . ." The earl pointed to a thicket of gorse by the edge of the grass. "Three sharp whistles will be the signal for you to join us inside."

Henning nodded his assent. "Godspeed."

Saybrook turned to her. "Stay behind me, and do exactly as I tell you." Without waiting for an answer, he started forward.

The porter's entrance to the end tower was unlocked, allowing them access to a set of circular stone stairs. Narrow glass-paned windows, mimicking ancient archery slits, were the only source of illumination. With the clouds hazing the heavens, the gloom was thick enough to cut with a knife . . .

Arianna touched the top of her boot as she edged along the wall, loosening the slim blade in its sheath.

Saybrook thumbed back the hammer of his weapon to full cock, taking care that it made no noise.

She did the same.

"Stay close," he whispered, the heat of his breath against her ear amplified by the cold air. "And stay alert."

"I'm used to facing danger," she reminded him.

"I'm not," he said. His dark eyes seemed to spark for an instant, and then his chill lips brushed hers. Without another word, he started up the first turn, shoulder pressed to the center stones, his steps as light as those of a stalking cat.

At the first landing, he eased forward and darted a look through the half-open door. She waited for his signal to follow him into the corridor. The wall sconces were unlit—a glow of lamplight from the doorway up was the only man-made illumination.

The other rooms lining the way were shut tight, the blackened oak portals and forged iron latches standing silent guard.

Drawing a steadying breath to calm the flutter of unease in her chest, Arianna glanced behind her.

Nothing.

Saybrook paused and cocked an ear, straining to hear any sound from Girton's laboratory.

Was it only her imagination, or was that a faint moan?

Double, double toil and trouble . . . The words of Shakespeare's Scottish trio of witches cackled in her head. *Macbeth* had been a great favorite with her father. Perhaps because the themes of crime and guilt and punishment struck a chord—

A touch to her arm jerked her out of her momentary reveries. *Stay focused,* she chided herself, giving a quick nod to her husband's signal to advance and cover the right side of the doorway.

The sound came again, a little louder.

Saybrook darted into the laboratory and took cover behind a tall storage cabinet.

Pistol raised, Arianna watched for any flicker of movement within the shadows. All was still, save for the slight wavering of the lamp flame within its glass globe. The light was sitting atop a long, thin worktable set in the center of the large space. Counters crammed with bottles and scientific instruments lined the side walls, their shadows casting menacing patterns across the stained plaster. Above them were shelves crammed with books and ledgers. The sharp scent of chemicals hung heavy in the air.

Her husband took a small coin from his pocket and rolled it toward the table.

The tiny sound drew no reaction. He waited a moment longer and then moved to a new position by a wrought-iron rack of metal canisters.

The pistol butt began to feel a little slippery against her palm, despite the chillness of the room. Her blood was pounding in her ears, setting off a strange, spooky echo. Swallowing hard, she tightened her grip and made a quick check of the corridor behind her.

Sssssssssss. A ghostly sound seemed to flit through the shadows.

Her eyes flew back to the laboratory as a groan—one that sounded distinctly human—rent the air. It seemed to be coming from an alcove at the rear of the room.

"H-h-help me."

Saybrook flicked his pistol, indicating he meant to investigate.

Following his silent orders, Arianna slipped inside and took up a position to cover his advance. A veteran of the guerrilla conflicts in Spain, he needed no reminder from her that it could be a trap. Still, she felt as if her heart had leapt into her throat as he started forward.

No bullet, no blade flashed out of the gloom.

Inch by inch, the earl crept toward the sound. Without thinking, she eased up to a spot by the table, giving her a better angle into the alcove. Within the muddled shades of black, she thought she could make out a solid shape sprawled on the floor beneath a desk.

Saybrook suddenly stood and rushed over the remaining distance. He reached down, and his hand was swallowed by the shadows. "Bring the lamp here," he called after a moment.

Arianna grabbed it and hurried to his side.

In the pale, oily light, the slash of red across the man's throat looked like a spill of claret wine. The garnet-colored liquid was quickly soaking into the white shirt points.

A gurgling rattle indicated that he was still alive.

"Is it Girton?" she asked.

Crouching down, Saybrook leaned close to the man's fluttering lips. "Are you Girton?"

A feeble nod.

"Who did this to you?"

The professor's face spasmed as he tried to speak. "R-r-r . . ."

Was he trying to say Renard? wondered Arianna.

"R-royal . . ." A gasp. "In-inst . . ."

"Institution?" finished Saybrook.

Another nod.

"What's there?" prodded the earl.

"D-d-danger." The effort of speech brought a beading of blood to Girton's lips.

"From whom?"

The man's hand twitched against the floor.

"I think he's trying to draw something," said Arianna. She watched his finger trace three short strokes. "It looks like . . . a letter?"

Girton tried again.

"It might have been a 'P,' " said Arianna tersely. "Or a symbol of some sort."

"Girton." Saybrook leaned in closer, his long, windblown hair grazing the man's blood-soaked shirt. "Girton."

The professor lay as still as stone.

Her husband felt for the pulse point at the base of the man's jaw. "Damn," he muttered, letting his fingers fall away.

"We must have missed the murderer by mere minutes," said Arianna, staring down at the professor's lifeless body.

"Yes, Renard seems to have an uncanny ability to stay one step ahead of us," said the earl tightly. Wiping his hands on his coat, he began to search through the papers on the desk. "Let's see if we can spot anything of interest before we go."

"Are we going to summon the authorities?" she asked. "Or leave his colleagues to discover the body for themselves?"

"A good question. I'll decide shortly."

Leaving him to deal with the alcove, Arianna set to work in the main room. She made a methodical circuit of the outer counters, gathering every piece of paper that bore any writing.

I had better let Sandro and Basil decide what is important.

While even the most complex mathematical equations and theorems were child's play to her, she found the simplest scientific formulas baffling.

On the main worktable, several half-filled beakers sat by a small gas burner. A brass microscope was close by. She hesitated, not daring to disturb anything. "Sandro," she called. "Should we summon Basil? There's something here that he might wish to examine."

Her husband came out of the alcove and took a long look at the setup. "I'd rather not linger overlong here." He glanced up at the storage shelves. "I'll bottle the contents and seal them with beeswax."

"Be careful," she cautioned, stepping aside to allow him room to work.

"I dabbled in chemistry at Oxford, my dear," he replied, donning a pair of leather gloves that were lying beside the burner. "I've a healthy respect for the fact that potions and powders can maim and kill."

"But we are dealing with an unknown here," she pointed out, "and have reason to fear that it may be a very volatile explosive."

He leaned in cautiously and gave an experimental sniff. "Hmmph. Actually, there is no need to take it with us—one is simple sulfuric acid and the other nitric acid."

"You are sure?" she asked.

"Quite." He took a quick look through the microscope and seemed satisfied. "Yes, it's a standard experiment, used to instruct students who are just beginning to study chemistry. Girton was, after all, a teacher in addition to whatever darker pursuits he was involved with."

Arianna gazed at the crystalline powder in the glass vials and felt a shiver skate down her spine.

Eyeing the papers in her hand, Saybrook added an approving nod. "Well-done. Tuck them away inside your coat. I've found some things that may prove interesting as well. As soon as I fetch them—"

A gunshot suddenly rattled the windowpanes, followed by two more in quick succession.

"Bloody hell," he swore. "That's a Brown Bess—the standard military musket!"

"Basil!" Arianna snatched up her weapon from the table.

The earl raced back to the alcove to retrieve a folder of papers, then returned and grabbed her arm. "Hurry!"

Relying on speed, not stealth, Saybrook flew down the stairs. Rather than exit by the porter's door, he turned and sprinted down the corridor until he came to a portal opening out to the seaside lawns. "We'll skirt around the end tower and see if we can tell what is going on."

Pressing close to the stones, they crept to the corner of the building.

"Good God." Arianna drew in a hiss of air. The swath of grass was lit by a half dozen red-coated soldiers holding flaming torches. Another six, armed with muskets and fixed bayonets, had formed a line aimed at the porter's entry. Several more men were standing guard over . . .

"Basil!" she cried, breaking away from their hiding place and running for where their friend lay motionless on the ground.

Cursing in Spanish, Saybrook hurried after her.

"I must ask you to step back, Mr. Castellano." A black ripple stirred in the darkness, but as the figure stepped into the ring of torchlight, the flames lit the gold braid and medal adorning his scarlet tunic. "You are intruding on military business that does not concern you."

"The devil it doesn't," he replied, brushing past Colonel Stoughton's upraised arm without slowing a step. "You've just shot my colleague."

"Indeed?" Stoughton's face betrayed not a flicker of emotion. "Perhaps you would care to explain why he was skulking around the town with a firearm at this hour."

The earl ignored the question. Dropping down beside Arianna, he placed a hand on his friend's shoulder. "How bad is it?" he murmured.

Taking care not to look up, she replied in a low whisper. "A bullet to the shoulder. I think I've staunched the bleeding, but I can't tell whether any bones are broken. It needs proper care as soon as possible."

"The first order of treatment is a flask full of whisky," rasped Henning. His voice was weak but steady.

"And you shall have it," replied Saybrook. "Where shall we take you to be sewn up, Baz?"

A cough. "Murray. On Hope Street."

"Make a stretcher with your coats and muskets," he snapped at the soldiers. "And be bloody quick about it."

"I'll go along with them," said Arianna. He saw that she had had the presence of mind to hide her weapon. "To ensure that he is settled safely there."

Their eyes met for an instant. "Yes, a wise idea," he said softly.

"You are not the one giving orders here, Mr. Castellano." Stoughton approached with a leisurely stride.

"Call it a strong suggestion, Colonel," said the earl, not looking up from his friend. "I am sure that you and your government would not wish for an innocent man to perish because of this unfortunate incident. It might provoke trouble."

Stoughton hesitated for a half moment, then gave a brusque wave at his sergeant. "Take the man to the surgeon." A pause. "Post a guard there to ensure there are no further mishaps." To Saybrook, he added, "I shall, of course, wish to speak with your man in the morning."

The earl rose and stepped away, allowing the soldiers to ready Henning for the short trip. After pressing the pad of cloth torn from Henning's shirttails a little tighter to his wound, Arianna did the same, though she was careful to edge back out of the light. Her heavy cloak hid her shape, and she kept her head down so that the broad-brimmed hat blocked a view of her face.

They did not speak.

Henning remained stoically silent as the soldiers shifted him onto the makeshift stretcher. With a torchbearer leading the way, they trooped off into the night, Arianna at the surgeon's side, her hand protectively on his wounded shoulder.

Saybrook waited until the skirl of smoky light melted into the fog before turning to the colonel. "If you wish to do something useful, you will send the rest of your men to the laboratory on the first floor of the far tower. There's another body there to be carried away—though that one has no need for medical attention."

A glimmer of gold flickered as the colonel smoothed the braided cuff of his glove. After a long moment, deliberately drawn out, he barked an order to his remaining men.

"Now, perhaps you would be kind enough to explain what you and you friends were doing here, Mr. Castellano," said Stoughton, sarcasm shading the last few words.

"I think it's you who owe an explanation for your presence," countered the earl. "And for the fact that your men fired on an unidentified individual without provocation. Do you make a habit of shooting first and asking questions later? If so, it's no wonder the Scots wish to throw off the yoke of English rule."

"My, my, you sound as if you sympathize with the rabble," sneered Stoughton. "Force is needed to keep these Highland brutes in order. London has sent me here to ensure there will be no trouble from the north, and I do what is necessary to see that they have no cause for complaint."

"That doesn't explain what you and your men were doing here tonight," said Saybrook.

"We had word that there was a disturbance around the university." His flash of teeth was clearly not meant to be a smile. "Given that it's a hornet's nest of sedition, it was my duty to investigate."

"And yet, you are headquartered in Dundee. So unless the horses here in Scotland have sprouted wings, I fail to see how such news reached you—or how you were magically transported over such a distance."

The colonel shifted his stance, the gilded *clink* of his sword punctuating the scuff of his boots on the grass. "As a matter of fact, it was merely fortuitous coincidence that I was already here in St. Andrews. You see, I was coming to personally inform you of some unfortunate news. It is not within my power to deliver the prisoner whose release you requested."

"Then send to London for additional orders," said the earl.

"Alas, that won't help." A glint of gold-flecked malice seemed to spark in the colonel's eyes. "The fellow was shot dead while trying to escape."

The only show of emotion from Saybrook was the tic of a tiny jaw muscle. He stood, still and silent as stone, for several moments before saying slowly, "Ill luck seems to strike people who cross your path."

A careless shrug. "I would have thought that you, as a former officer, would understand that the best way to defeat one's enemies is to give no quarter on the field of battle."

"England is no longer at war, Stoughton."

"Not technically, perhaps. But from what I have heard, the diplomats and royalty gathered in Vienna care more about drinking, dancing and trading mistresses than they do about forging alliances or reordering borders. How long do you think peace will reign in Europe?"

"It isn't my duty to speculate on politics, either here or abroad. Nor is it yours," replied Saybrook.

A wink of starlight hung on the colonel's sandy lashes as he narrowed his eyes. "Quite right—my duty lies in keeping the powder keg that is Scotland from exploding. So it would be exceedingly helpful if you were to tell me why you wished to have a student revolutionary released."

"Sorry, but if Grentham did not choose to enlighten you on that matter, then I see no reason to reveal the information."

The colonel tapped his gloved palms together several times in succession, as if seeking to ward off a chill. "Ah, but the trouble is, when one hand does not know what the other hand is doing, it can result in dangerous misunderstandings. As you see from tonight, it really is in the best interests of you and your companions to keep me informed of what is going on." The taps grew a little louder. "By the by, was that your wife hiding beneath the masculine attire of breeches and boots?"

"My wife?" answered the earl very deliberately. "Your eyes must be playing tricks on you."

"If I were you, I would be very careful about how you—and she—go on here in St. Andrews. It's easy for those who are strangers here to stray into trouble."

"Thank you for the warning. My wife will certainly be on guard against any further mishaps. As will I."

Stoughton set a hand on the pommel of his sword. "A wise move." He paused. "Though I daresay you are making a foolish mistake not to share information with me. It always pays to have an ally when one is in enemy territory."

"I work best alone," replied the earl. "And as London entrusted me to handle this mission as I see fit, I shall continue to do so." He fixed Stoughton with a level gaze. "If I change my mind, I shall let you know."

"We're a far way from the civilized streets of London," said the colonel softly. "Horse Guards won't be sending the Oxford Blues galloping to your rescue if things go awry."

Saybrook's laugh was hardly louder than the wind ruffling through the gorse. "As I said at our previous meeting, I am very good at looking out for myself."

6

From Lady Arianna's Chocolate Notebooks

Chocolate-Dipped Dates Stuffed with Spiced Nuts

36 salted roasted almonds
2 teaspoons finely grated orange peel
1 teaspoon honey
½ teaspoon ground cinnamon
¼ teaspoon ground allspice
12 Medjool dates
¾ cup bittersweet chocolate chips

1. Toss 24 of the almonds, 1 teaspoon of the orange peel, the honey, and the spices in a small bowl.
2. Cut a slit in each date and remove the pit. Press 2 spice-coated almonds into each slit and enclose the nuts in the date.
3. Line a small baking sheet with foil. Melt the chocolate chips in a double boiler. Grasp the end of 1 stuffed date and dip three-quarters of it into the melted chocolate. Shake off

excess chocolate. Place the date on the foil. Repeat with the
remaining dates.

4. Sprinkle the remaining orange peel over the chocolate-
   dipped dates. Dip 1 plain almond halfway into the chocolate; place atop 1 date. Repeat with the remaining almonds
   and dates. Chill until the chocolate sets, 30 minutes.

At first the chill was just a tickle at the tips of her fingers, but
with each passing word it crept stealthily downward, turning her hands to ice.

"Basil's nephew is dead?" Arianna cupped the glass of whisky
between her palms, wishing beyond reason that its fiery copper
color could spark a note of hope in her voice. "Perhaps Colonel
Stoughton is mistaken and Angus was just wounded."

"Believe me, I pressed him for the details before taking my
leave," said Saybrook. "Granted, there is no body, for the lad
was supposedly fleeing along the cliffs and fell into the sea
when shot. But barring a miracle, Angus MacPhearson is buried
in a grave, no matter that it is a watery one." Her husband took
a long swallow of the spirits. The guttering candles darkened the
deep lines etched around his eyes, and his mouth pinched to a
grim line. "Despite the Christmas season, I don't see God giving
us such a gift," he added cynically.

"Oh, Lord," she whispered. "Basil is going to take the news
very hard. With his sister a widow, he considers it his responsibility to look after her and her family." Arianna edged a bit
closer to the hearth. Ever since crossing into Scotland, the cold
had been a constant companion—it seemed to have seeped into
her very marrow. "I . . . I can't help but wonder whether we
bear—"

"Don't," interrupted Saybrook roughly. "Don't second-guess
or let guilt gnaw at your innards. It does no good."

Regrets. Recriminations. Arianna had experienced enough of them on her own to know that his admonition made sense. But one's heart did not always listen to one's head.

"You may be right." She set aside her glass and pressed her fingertips to her temples. A dull ache pulsed against her flesh. *Sorrow, anger, exhaustion.* And some nebulous thrum she couldn't quite name. "And yet it doesn't make things any easier to bear."

"No," agreed her husband. His eyes were opaque, shutting her out from whatever emotion was swirling beneath the chocolate-dark surface. His grief must be sharp. He and Henning had been close friends for some years.

A fact that reminded her of how little she and Saybrook really knew each other. Death had brought them together in the first place, reluctant allies with little choice but to help each other fight against a cunning enemy. Their marriage had been spurred by equally pragmatic reasons. And while the relationship had grown from regard and respect to something far deeper, there was much left unsaid between them.

Biting back a sigh, Arianna slanted another look at Saybrook's brooding profile. At times it still felt as if the Grim Reaper were a silent, shadowy partner in their short marriage. A *ménage à trois,* she thought wryly, with murder and mayhem such a constant presence in their life that there had been little time to develop a conventional life together.

Not that either of us is remotely conventional.

Rubbing a hand to his stubbled jaw, the earl refilled his glass and drank it down in one swift swallow.

"What are you going to tell him?" Shaking off her own dark musings, her own niggling uncertainties, Arianna turned the talk to practical matters. Matters of the heart were an enigma, but they were both very good at solving practical conundrums.

"The truth," replied her husband. "Baz deserves no less."

"I agree," she said. "And yet, somehow I suspect that the truth isn't simple."

"It never is." The whisky had brought a strange glitter to his gaze. Or perhaps it was merely an optical illusion created by the flames as he picked up the candelabra and carried it to the side table.

"What is your impression of Stoughton? Do you think he is lying about Angus?"

Saybrook sat heavily in the armchair facing hers and tipped his head back to contemplate the ceiling. The chunks of burning peat in the fireplace gave off a smoky hiss, filling the small parlor with a pungent odor of burnt earth. "A difficult question. He could be simply an overzealous tyrant, whose position of authority has gone to his head. Power often brings out a latent streak of cruelty." He folded his arms across his chest. "Or he could be acting on Grentham's orders to double-cross us. Or he could . . ."

Her husband chuffed a harried sigh, his face looking gray with exhaustion in the hazy light. "Bloody hell, he could have his own nefarious reasons for what he did. At this point, it would be foolish to hazard a guess."

"Perhaps we will find something in the papers we took from Girton's laboratory that will give us a clue as to what is going on here in St. Andrews," she said. Mention of the papers suddenly reminded her of the small journal she had fished out from the ashes of the murdered professor's home hearth. With all the excitement, she had not yet had a chance to mention the discovery.

"It may be worthless, but just before we left Girton's house, I found a half-burned book buried in the coals of the fire." She shifted and felt the corner dig into her side.

Before she could take it from her pocket, Henning's friend Murray came into the parlor. "I've removed the bullet and sewn up his shoulder. His body is beginning te look like a lady's embroidery sampler, what with all the stitch marks te his hide. But I daresay he'll survive."

"Thank you," said Saybrook. "I am sorry for drawing you into our troubles. I hope you shall not suffer any consequences for helping us." He gestured toward the front entrance, where outside the door two soldiers were standing guard.

"Auch, it dunna matter. Basil is one of us, and we Scots look after our own." Murray absently wiped his hands on his tweed pants, leaving a tiny trace of blood on the wool. "I've dosed him with laudanum, so he'll sleep like a babe until morning. Best get some sleep yerselves." His gaze lingered for an instant on Arianna's breeches and boots, his face betraying a tiny tic of curiosity. But he looked away without comment.

"I'll see my wife back to our lodgings and then return, if you don't mind. I'd like to keep an eye on Baz, to make sure there are no further accidents."

"No need. I plan te sleep in a chair by his side." Murray took a pistol and a nasty-looking dirk from a wooden box tucked back on the bottom shelf of his malt cabinet. "And I won't be alone. If the residents close by hear a shot, they will be out in a flash, and the Sassenach soldiers know there will be a riot in the street. So I think Basil will be safe enough for now."

The earl nodded. "How long before he can travel?"

"At least a few days, and maybe more. The roads be rough this time of year, and I wuddna like te see the wound reopened."

Saybrook thanked him again and led the way out into the night.

Wincing as a gust of cold air slapped against her cheeks, Arianna couldn't decide which was worse—the prospect of staying in cold, cheerless Scotland or another interminable coach journey.

Damned if I do, damned if I don't.

The Devil was proving to have a perverse sense of humor.

Once in their rooms, her husband went through the motions of splashing water on his face and undressing without a word, his normally graceful movements stiff and awkward. Despite his earlier chidings, she guessed that he blamed himself for the shooting of both Henning and his nephew. The weak light from a single taper played over his bare back, making his olive skin appear as dark as bronze. His body was beautiful, the lithe contours reminding her of the engravings she had seen of classical Greek gods. *Mythic warriors, epic heroes.*

Yet tonight, his muscles were taut with tension. Arianna found herself longing to reach out and touch him. She lifted a tentative hand, wondering whether the press of flesh on flesh, heat on heat, would help dispel the knots.

But then he moved away, and she let the moment pass. When Saybrook retreated into himself, she wasn't quite sure how to follow. The path appeared daunting—deeply shadowed, guarded by thorns, its footing made precarious by the shards of sharp-edged stone.

Rather like the roads here in Scotland, she thought wryly. But then, her whole life had not been an easy journey. She was used to traversing treacherous stretches . . .

"Come to bed, Arianna." Her husband slipped beneath the eiderdown coverlet. "It's been a long, exhausting day, and we both need to keep up our strength."

She blew out the candle and watched the ghostly wisp of smoke dissolve in the darkness. "Yes, I know. I'm coming."

The page crackled, tingeing her fingers with soot. Shifting her chair closer to the window, Arianna picked up a book knife from the desk and gingerly turned another page.

"What secrets are you hiding?" she murmured, squinting at the spidery script through her magnifying glass.

Saybrook had gone to see Henning, saying that as the two of them had experienced death together on the battlefields, it was best for him to break the news about Angus MacPhearson alone. To keep herself distracted, she had decided to have a look at the half-burned journal.

"I wonder," she continued, "was it Girton or his murderer who sought to turn you into ashes?"

Either way, she felt there was a good chance that the little book contained some vital clue that would help with their investigation.

"Or perhaps I'm merely grasping at swirls of Scottish mist," added Arianna. So far, any tangible evidence had proved maddeningly elusive. Save for dead bodies, of course.

Frowning, she hunched closer in concentration, pencil and fresh paper close at hand for making notes. But after an hour of poring over the pages, her hopes of finding anything important began to fade. The writing seemed to be nothing but a daily log of mundane laboratory labors—microscope calibrations, notations on student performance, records of supplies used.

Pinching the bridge of her nose, Arianna sat back and stirred at her now-cold cup of tea. Perhaps someone more skilled in scientific study would see more. Her own formal schooling was spotty at best. A smattering of literature, learned in her father's lap on the rare nights when he wasn't submerged in a sea of brandy, comprised her education in English. And mathematics. Her father had been a genius, and apparently his knack for numbers had been passed on to her. They had spent hours playing complex games with equations, and the concepts came naturally.

But as for normal feminine skills, there had been no governess to oversee instruction in deportment and embroidery, no masters to teach the rudiments of art, music or dancing. Her classroom had been the hardscrabble streets of the Caribbean harbors, her instructors the few trusted friends she had made along the way.

In contrast, Saybrook was an erudite scholar, an expert botanist, a connoisseur of the classics, an avid reader of science and philosophy who had studied at Oxford. He had then been offered a military commission to serve as one of Wellington's intelligence officers for the war in Portugal and Spain because of his knowledge of the languages and customs.

Her grip tightened on the spoon as she recalled one of Grentham's nasty comments, made during one of their confrontations. The revelation that her husband had regular meetings with a reclusive female scholar was meant to cause pain.

I wasn't hurt—merely surprised, mused Arianna. Saybrook hadn't mentioned the arrangement. "Nor was he beholden to do so," she muttered under her breath. "I was no dewy-eyed innocent, with girlish illusions of making a love match." Theirs was a relationship of mutual respect and growing friendship. That was far more than most aristocratic couples had. As for the past, she and Saybrook had, by mutual consent, avoided discussing their private lives before their marriage. She assumed that he had taken lovers. He was rich, handsome, titled . . .

Forcing her thoughts back to the journal, Arianna carefully turned the page. But her mind kept wandering from the smoke-streaked paper. Was Saybrook regretting his impetuous offer, made to save her from bearing the brunt of Grentham's retribution? Did he long for a wife who shared his bookish knowledge?

Not long ago, he had, in the heat of battle, told her that he loved her. But the sentiment had never been repeated.

"Perhaps I only imagined it," she whispered. It might only have been the notes of a waltz drifting out from a Viennese ballroom, or the flutter of a starlit breeze dancing through the cobbled streets.

She stared, unseeing, at the scribbles of ink for several more minutes before admitting defeat. It must be the death of Henning's nephew that had her in such a strangely maudlin mood. She did not usually dwell on the past or fret over old mistakes.

"Damnation, I might as well try to do something useful." Exasperated, Arianna turned to put the book aside, but in her haste, it nearly slipped from her fingers, and the fragile pages fanned out, sending flakes of dark ash falling to the carpet.

"Damnation," she repeated, leaning down to brush away the specks. As she shifted the journal, it fell open to a spread near the back of the book. The ashes suddenly forgotten, she reached for her magnifying glass and read over the lightly penciled text.

The writing was so faint that it took several minutes to decipher the short message, and even then the string of letters was meaningless.

A code.

Putting down the glass, she quickly copied it onto her notepaper and stared at the sequence. A thrum of excitement tingled down her fingers. Dealing with emotions was like sparring with shadows. Here was something familiar. Something she knew how to attack.

Patterns, poppet. Look for patterns. Her father's jovial voice echoed for an instant in her head. A skill in mathematics was important in breaking a code, for working out patterns of repetition and frequency helped determine the actual message. There were, of course, all sorts of coding techniques, from simple shift ciphers to elaborate Vigenère squares. And if a text cipher was used—one based on a certain book page or passage that only the intended recipient knew—then cracking it was all but impossible.

Tapping her pencil to the tip of her chin, Arianna mulled over the myriad possibilities. *Tap, tap, tap.* Sometimes it was best to start with the simplest solution.

Lettering out the alphabet at the top of her notepaper, she flexed her shoulders and set to work.

"How did Basil take the news?" Arianna looked up at her husband's approach, knowing the query sounded absurd. "I meant . . ."

"I know what you meant." He sank into the chair by the hearth and ran a hand through his hair. "God in Heaven, I've performed difficult duties in the military, but never one so draining as that."

She rose and went to pour a glass of whisky. "Drink this. Your face is gray as ashes."

"I need more than a spark of Highland malt to warm my spirits," he muttered. "I need some flicker of light to help us see through the muddled mists of this Devil-cursed maze. It feels as if we are wandering blindly after an enemy who knows every twist and turn." The glass spun between his palms. "Which allows him to stay one step ahead of us with maddening ease."

Arianna wiped her soot-smudged fingers on her skirts. "I think I've found a small candle flame." She indicated the half-burned book on the side table. "I discovered several pages of pencil notations in the back section. They were written in code—a fairly basic one. Using a simple method of frequency analysis, I was able to decipher the message."

"Only a mathematical genius would call frequency analysis simple," he said with a tiny smile.

"As you know, I seem to have a natural aptitude for numbers," she said, handing him a sheet of paper. "Unfortunately, my formal education is sadly lacking, so the scientific data in the book is naught but gibberish. You and Basil will have to examine the material to see if there's anything meaningful."

"We need to pore over the documents taken from Girton's laboratory and his home as well. Assuming Baz has the stomach to continue," said the earl. "He is far more expert in the field than I am. However . . ."

He didn't need to go on.

Heaving a sigh, Arianna added another few squares of peat to the fire while Saybrook studied the decoded message.

" 'Greetings, my dear friend . . .' " Having finished skimming over it, her husband began reading the words aloud. " 'I fear that something very dangerous is brewing at RI. With HD away, one of his Bright Lights may be burning the candle at both ends. I suspect The Flame, but in truth, I don't know if any of them can be trusted, including TW. You must *not* reveal to them what Cayley and I have discovered. Too explosive, and if the plans got into the hands of England's enemies it would be devastating. I will explain more when I see you. In the meantime, I beg you to think of who among your government acquaintances we can warn.' "

"As you see," said Arianna. "It appears to be a draft of a letter. But whether it was sent is impossible to know."

The earl's brow was furrowed in thought. "Right," he replied absently. "Hand me your pencil, please."

She passed it over.

"HD and RI," he said, writing the two sets of initials below her transcription. "Given Girton's last words, I think it fair to assume 'RI' means the Royal Institution."

"I confess, I am a bit confused about all these 'Royal' organizations devoted to science. I would have thought that a man of Girton's abilities would be working with the Royal Society."

Founded in the late seventeenth century, the Royal Society was recognized as one of the oldest and most prestigious scientific organizations in the world. It funded numerous scholarly projects, including explorations of uncharted places around the globe as well as research in a variety of subjects. The membership was made up of the leading intellects in Britain—it was, in effect, an elite club of ideas and imagination.

"An excellent surmise, my dear," said Saybrook. "The society is indeed the best-known group in London. But for chemistry, the Royal Institution is the leading forum of experimentation, especially since Humphry Davy arrived there in aught-one."

"Humphry Davy—that is HD?" she asked.

"I think it has to be," he answered. A charismatic figure despite his diminutive size, the scientist from Cornwall possessed not only a brilliant mind but also an ebullient charm and boyish good looks, which had made him the darling of London Society. His lectures were always crowded to capacity—with both gentlemen *and* ladies.

"Davy has made chemistry a popular topic among the *ton*," he continued. "The headquarters on Albemarle Street has become a center for people who fancy themselves as the first wave of the future."

Arianna thought for a moment. "You mean, as a catalyst for change?"

"Well put," answered the earl. "The newly knighted Davy and his wife are away on a Grand Tour of Europe right now, and when he returns, he will serve as a professor emeritus, so who will serve as the institution's new leader is still undecided. Until Davy returns and helps make the final decision, Trevor Willoughby is serving as the acting director."

"TW."

He nodded. "His appointment was no surprise, despite his young age. I've heard him lecture, and like Davy, he's a charismatic showman. The institution was smart enough to realize that keeping in the public eye makes it easier to attract wealthy benefactors."

The paper crackled in his hands. "So, those first three guesses seem patently obvious. But as for the rest of the message . . ." He frowned. "Bright Lights can mean any of Davy's inner circle. Over the last few years, he has attracted quite a number of smart young scientists eager to work with the world's master of chemistry."

"What about Cayley?" asked Arianna.

He thought for a moment. "The name sounds vaguely familiar, but I shall have to do a little research on it."

Opening a notebook, Arianna began to make some jottings of her own. "Find out who Cayley is, then start compiling a list of those men who are acknowledged to be part of Davy's inner circle," she murmured. "It would also make sense to find out who were Girton's closest friends. We should be looking for someone he trusted, and someone who had connections to the institution. There can't be very many who fit that description."

"It's rather frightening how good you are becoming at organizing an investigation," said Saybrook.

"I have learned from an excellent teacher," she replied. "And I seem to have a natural skill at clandestine activities. It's far more interesting than the oh-so-proper hobbies a gently reared lady is allowed to dabble in."

"How fortunate for me that my wife prefers tracking down

murderers to playing the pianoforte." He said it with a hint of humor, but a momentary flicker in his eyes made her wonder . . .

Perhaps my odd habits are beginning to chafe against his skin.

Despite his eccentricities, Saybrook was an earl, with all the responsibilities and traditions that went with the noble title.

"And it seems imperative to marshal whatever expertise I have gained in order to help," she added quietly. "I fear you will be shorthanded for some time to come."

"I fear you are right," said Saybrook gravely. "Baz's injury will keep him out of action. A gunshot wound is always cause for concern."

"It's not just the physical injury that I worry about," she said. "I would hate to see the special friendship between you two suffer a mortal blow."

Shadows scudded over his face as he turned to gaze at the slate-colored windowpanes. Rain drummed against the glass like a martial tattoo summoning troops to battle. "I am aware of the danger, Arianna. It's a damnably difficult position when personal loyalties clash with duty to a higher cause." His dark lashes hid his eyes. "I hate that I've forced him into making painful choices. And yet, given what we had learned, and what we suspect Girton was up to, countless people will die if we aren't ruthless in our pursuit of Renard," he said bleakly.

War is a battle of moral imperatives as well as opposing armies, mused Arianna. As a former military intelligence officer, her husband must have faced such terrible decisions before.

"I understand, Sandro. In many ways, a general has a far easier job than you do. His mission is black-and-white—win or lose. The rules are clear and bloodshed is expected. While what Grentham has asked of us is shrouded in an infinite range of grays."

"An astute assessment," he said.

Her mouth quirked up for an instant. "But it doesn't make things any less wrenching."

The earl continued to stare out the window, though the world outside was reduced to naught but a watery blur. "No, it doesn't."

"On the field of battle, if a battalion has taken a beating, a general must improvise, correct? He must shift his forces and send in reinforcements," pointed out Arianna. "We shall just have to step up and cover the gap left by our injured comrade."

"Yes, I had come to that conclusion myself," mused Saybrook. "Though it stretches our ranks perilously thin. Baz is the real expert on chemistry, and without his help, we shall be left with our flanks exposed, so to speak."

"Well, we shall just have to shore up our weaknesses," she said. "Perhaps I can apply my knowledge of chocolate and experimenting with recipes to learning something about science."

As she had hoped, her words provoked a smile. "I don't doubt that you can do anything you set your mind to, my dear."

"As can you, Sandro. We shall find whoever murdered Baz's nephew and see that he is brought to justice. That will at least bring him some measure of satisfaction."

The earl smoothed at the page in his lap. "Still, I wish that Baz could have reviewed the papers we took from the laboratory. He might have spotted a clue that I will miss."

"It's not as if he's gone to the grave." *Assuming the close friendship between the two men wasn't dead.* "Or are you unwilling to ask because you think that Stoughton and Grentham have killed off any hope that Basil might aid England?"

"I—I haven't yet decided what to do."

The shadows around them suddenly seemed to shiver and darken with doubt.

"Don't worry." Arianna forced a show of certainty, despite her own misgivings on the mission. "Even without our friend's help, we shall outwit Renard and run him to ground."

"How is he, Murray?" asked Saybrook.

"Running a bit of a fever," replied Henning's friend. "I've

made him drink another dose of laudanum, so he'll be sleeping for some hours." He sounded tense, terse. "I wud rest easier mesself if those Sassenach soldiers weren't blocking me doorway."

"I shall try to see if I can get them withdrawn," said the earl. "But I cannot promise it."

"How soon before Basil can be moved?" inquired Arianna. She and her husband had decided that it would be best to get Henning away from St. Andrews as soon as possible. Stoughton's authority did not extend to Edinburgh. "We think it might be prudent to get him out of St. Andrews to ensure that no more unfortunate accidents take place."

Murray made a face. "A practical suggestion, and we Scots pride ourselves on being pragmatic. However, I dunna like the idea of him jostling over these rough roads. We must be cautious with a wound like this."

"Fever might not be the most serious threat to his well-being," said Saybrook softly. "My feeling is that recuperating at the home of his sister might be the best option."

"I suppose that a journey to Edinburgh will do no great harm. But I must advise against any further travel. He needs a long period of rest and quiet to ensure full recovery."

"Yes, I understand that a grueling trip to London would leave him sapped of strength," said Saybrook. "Let me pay a visit to the authorities now and see what I can arrange. I shall return in a few hours. There are some papers I wish for Baz to look at, assuming he feels up to the task."

"We'll see how he feels when he wakes," growled Murray. "But be warned, in this weakened state, he's in no condition to concentrate on papers. As I said, a gunshot wound is a serious injury."

But it's likely that the mental hurt is even more grave, thought Arianna grimly.

"I understand," replied her husband. "The last thing we wish to do is press him too hard."

1. Preheat the oven to 375°F.
2. In a medium bowl, whisk together the flour, baking soda, baking powder, salt, and cocoa. Set aside.
3. In a large bowl, beat the butter with an electric mixer until it is fluffy and lightens a bit in color. Beat in the sugars— the mixture should have a thick, frosting-like consistency. Mix in the eggs one at a time, making sure to incorporate the first egg before adding the second. Add the vanilla and mix until it is incorporated.
4. Add the dry ingredients to the wet mix in four batches. Stir a bit between each addition until the flour is just incorporated. At this point you should have a moist brown dough that is uniform in color. Stir in the espresso beans and chocolate chips by hand and mix only until they are evenly distributed throughout the dough.
5. Form the dough into balls using roughly 1 heaping tablespoon of dough for each one. Place on a cookie sheet with at least an inch between them so they won't melt together.
6. Bake for about 10 minutes on the middle rack. Don't overbake these cookies or they will really dry out. If anything, underbake them just a bit. Cool on racks.

"Welcome home, milady." Their butler, a taciturn Spaniard of unflappable demeanor, inclined a courtly bow as Arianna came into the entrance hall of their Mayfair town house. "Bianca has been busy in the kitchen since we received His Lordship's message that you would be arriving this afternoon. A pot of her special spiced chocolate is simmering on the stove, and platters of pastries fresh from the oven await you."

"Thank you, Sebastian," she said, untying the fastenings of her fur-lined cloak and gratefully handing it over. After breathing in the sweet fragrances of fresh-cut pine and melted sugar, she let out a long sigh. "The healing nourishment of chocolate will be most welcome. I feel as if every bone in my body has been bounced to Hell and back."

"I trust that the comforts of familiar surroundings will be a balm for your aches, and that the decorations of the season will restore a measure of good cheer," replied Sebastian. "The house has been hung with evergreens from your Somerset estate, and a lovely Yule log has been readied in the main drawing room hearth."

Oh, Lord—Christmas was only two days away, realized Arianna. She certainly wasn't feeling in a very festive mood at the moment. They had left Henning on the mend in body. But as for spirit . . .

The surgeon had read over the papers taken from Girton's laboratory, and while he had offered a few observations and suggestions, it was clear that his heart wasn't in the task.

No, we cannot look to the north for help in pulling England's goose out of the fire, she thought wryly. The dangerous flare of flames would have to be doused here in London.

"That sounds lovely," murmured Arianna, flexing her stiff shoulders. The cozy warmth from the blazing fireplaces was, in fact, already helping to dispel the pervasive chill of Scotland. "His Lordship and I will freshen up from our travels, and then refreshments in the library would be most welcome."

A short while later, Saybrook set his cup down with a contented sigh. "Remind me again of why I gave up a life of quiet scholarship to immerse myself in murder and mayhem."

"To begin with, you met me," answered Arianna. "I'm a bad influence on you."

"You are hardly to blame for these last few months." He reached for the chocolate pot and spun the *molinillo*, sending up tendrils of steam from the spout. "One almost wonders if Baz's outlandish suspicions about Grentham might have a grain of truth to them. It seems everyone close to me has been caught up in some dark intrigue."

A sidelong glance showed that worry had taken its toll on

him. Candlelight flickered on his taut features, accentuating the deep hollows beneath his cheekbones. The shadows looked like bruises.

An apt analogy, reflected Arianna, for he was letting the problems of this investigation fester beneath the skin. Being cooped up in a carriage for a long journey had offered too many hours for introspection. The earl had a tendency to brood, to blame himself when anything went wrong.

"Don't let your imagination run wild, Sandro," she said briskly. "This is real life, not a novel. You were the first to point out that the plotline suggested by Basil was too implausible to take seriously."

"I am also the one who often points out that truth is stranger than fiction," he quipped. "But point taken." He inhaled deeply, and the spiced aroma of the chocolate seemed to lighten his expression. "Let us keep our thinking confined to the practical considerations."

"Yes, let's," murmured Arianna, quickly reaching for her notebook and thumbing to a section near the middle. "Before we left Scotland, you got a list of Girton's possible confidants from Henning's friend Connery." She read off four names. "I assume you will begin seeking an acquaintance with them here in London."

He nodded. "Along with seeing what more I can learn about Sir George Cayley." Cursory questions around the university had elicited some interesting information. The baronet was a scientist with a broad range of interests—including ballistics and the design of ingenious mechanical devices.

"Sir George is certainly an intriguing figure," she replied. "Speaking of possessing an active imagination . . ."

"Perhaps *too* active." Saybrook poured himself more chocolate. "The mention that he is working on inventing some sort of engine that runs on a flammable liquid sparks a rather alarming concern," he added dryly. "He definitely merits further scrutiny."

"And while you deal with that scholar, we must come up with

a plan to get involved with the Royal Institution, in order to learn about the so-called Bright Lights." During the journey home from Scotland, they had decided that Girton's cryptic note had to be considered a compelling clue. And so it had been agreed that it was imperative to make friends with the group of intellectuals who made up the inner circle around Sir Humphry Davy and Trevor Willoughby.

But how to concoct a formula for doing so was another matter.

"Yes." Saybrook grimaced. "And yet I'm still puzzled on how to go about it. I'm confident that our involvement in both Vienna and Scotland were secret enough that Renard cannot know the full extent of our efforts. But he's not a fool—the fact that we were in Austria is enough to make him suspicious should we take a sudden interest in the Royal Institution lectures."

"I agree," said Arianna. "So I've thought it over and I think I've come up with a plan."

Her husband set down his cup. "I have the feeling that I'm not going to like this."

"Probably not," quipped Arianna. "But it will work."

He blew out his breath. "Go on."

"The institution lectures are popular with both sexes, so an eccentric foreigner, newly arrived in London, will not raise too many eyebrows."

"Arianna—"

"Come, you have to admit that I'm very good at accents and disguises," she said, quickly cutting off his protest.

"*Too* good," he growled. "*Dio Madre*, your masquerades have nearly gotten you killed three times since I met you . . ."

Ah, it was a good thing he knew nothing about her Caribbean capers.

"So how the devil do you think I feel about letting you take another such risk?"

"Not overjoyed," she said dryly. "However, personal feeling cannot be allowed to color our decisions. Renard and this chemical concoction are too great a threat. If we don't stop him, there's a chance that a great many innocent people will die."

The string of Spanish curses that followed told her that he knew she was right.

"Sandro, this time, the danger for me is not so great. My role will simply be to watch and listen. The institution attracts plenty of people who simply wish to rub shoulders with the intellectual elite. There's no reason for anyone to suspect that I have ulterior motives for seeking to be part of their circle."

His grunt was eloquent in its skepticism.

"I shall, of course, have to learn a little about chemistry," went on Arianna. "My lack of bookish knowledge may present a problem. But perhaps my knowledge of mathematics will help me hide my shortcomings and still attract the attention of the Bright Lights."

"Like Davy, Willoughby has become the darling of Society, and his lectures attract a huge audience of females who have, to put it mildly, no formal training in science," said Saybrook grudgingly. He was silent for a moment before a smile slowly curled at the corners of his mouth. "Trust me, they will be intrigued by your ingenious mind—as well as your more obvious endowments."

Arianna popped a small morsel of chocolate-studded cake into her mouth. "How very edifying that you think so. Though some ladies might be a trifle disturbed to hear their husband sound so cheery over the prospect of feeding his wife to the foxes."

"But not you," said the earl.

But not me. Arianna swallowed quickly, trying to keep a sour taste from coating her throat. Seeing as she had just encouraged him to view the investigation dispassionately, it was absurd to feel a tiny twinge of disappointment that he had not voiced a warmer response.

She waited, but he did not elaborate.

"I will check on the schedule of lectures," she announced,

making a notation in her book. "What with the Christmas and Boxing Day festivities, I imagine that things will be a trifle quiet for the moment. That will give me some time to read up on the subject."

Her tone must have had an edge, for he looked up from his cup, a small furrow forming between his brows.

Pretending not to notice, Arianna continue to write.

Saybrook cleared his throat. "You know, I, too, have been thinking . . . As we have remarked, Baz's absence leaves a hole in our ranks—a rather critical hole, as his expertise in chemistry was a key weapon in our arsenal." A rather strange expression pulled at his features. "So, like you, I've come up with an idea . . ."

"Yes?" said Arianna, a bit taken aback by his hemming and hawing. It was unlike him to beat around the bush. "Do go on, Sandro."

"Actually, I need to make a few inquiries first, to see if it's even feasible. But if all goes as I hope, I would like you to come to a meeting tomorrow afternoon."

"Of course," she replied. "Is it really necessary to be so mysterious?"

He hesitated for a moment. "Actually, I'd rather not say any more until later."

Biting back a sharper retort, she merely nodded, and murmured, "Very well." They were both tired, she reminded herself, and nerves were likely rubbed raw by all that had happened in Scotland.

"By the by, Bianca reminded me that it is a Christmas Eve tradition for your great-aunt Constantina to host the family for a fancy repast," she said, deciding to change the subject. "Your uncle and aunt are attending. She wants to know whether to send word to Constantina of our arrival."

"Yes, of course. I wouldn't dare incur her wrath by missing it," he replied with a wry smile. In truth, he was extremely fond of his elderly relative, whose tart wit and keen powers of observation were still as sharp as a tack. "In fact, she may be very useful in the coming months . . ."

Again, his words trailed off.

"Because of her connections in Society?" pressed Arianna. Constantina, the dowager Marchioness of Sterling, not only knew everyone in the *beau monde*, but also possessed a frighteningly accurate recollection of family histories, including past scandals and peccadilloes.

"If there is a skeleton in any attic, Constantina will know where the bones are hanging," said Saybrook.

True. The dowager had been a source of critical information during their very first investigation.

"But we shall have to be very careful in how we involve her in this," he went on. "Like you, she has a terrifying tendency to take risks with her own safety."

"Constantina is clever and resourceful—and she likes the challenge of being useful." Arianna sipped at her chocolate. "She says it keeps the blood pumping in her veins."

"Yes, well, I wish to ensure that her heart remains in full pumping order," he replied.

"I understand, but she's proven that she can be trusted to use good sense and discretion," said Arianna. "I think she deserves the respect of us allowing her to make certain decisions for herself about risk."

Saybrook made a face. "You have a point. I, of all people, readily acknowledge the equality of the feminine intellect. But it's still damnably difficult to let you ladies waltz into harm's way."

"I know that, Sandro. But short of nailing our dancing slippers to the parquet, you will simply have to accept our spins into danger."

He chuffed a low laugh. "Which means I shall just have to stay on my toes to make sure there are no slips along the way."

"Correct." She smiled. "But that said, you know that I'm just as concerned as you are about her safety. We shall be careful."

"Careful," repeated her husband. "We all must exercise caution. We are dealing with a cunning, ruthless adversary who has left a trail of dead bodies across half of Europe."

Arianna waited for his frown to relax before turning the talk back to matters of strategy.

"We don't know yet whether Lord Reginald was in any way connected with the Royal Institution," she mused aloud. The Duke of Lampson's youngest son had been part of Renard's nefarious plot at the Congress of Vienna. On his death, the British government had decided to keep the young man's betrayal of his country a secret, even from his family.

"That will be one of the first things for me to discover," went on Arianna. "But I would be surprised if there is not a connection." She thought for a moment. "Can you get a list of institution members? And perhaps one of regular attendees of the lectures?"

He nodded. "I've already made a note of it."

"We both know that the heart of this conspiracy has to beat here in London, within the highest circle of power and privilege."

Her husband tapped a silver spoon against his porcelain cup. "Agreed. Vienna and Scotland were roundabout routes through dangerous terrain, but I have a feeling that the journey will end here."

The tall case clock in the corner began to chime the hour, its echo muted by the carved oak bookshelves and leather-bound spines.

"We had better get some rest," he went on, gathering the tray of chocolate and rising. "We will need to keep sharp to negotiate the final twists and turns without a fatal mishap."

A damp wind, sour with the smell of the nearby river's low tide, cut across the parade grounds behind Horse Guards, its edge as sharp as a cavalry saber. Muttering an oath, Saybrook turned up his coat collar and quickened his steps, his boots beating a staccato tattoo across the dark stone tiles beneath the archway. A soldier stepped aside from the doorway, allowing him to enter the building and make his way up to Lord Grentham's offices.

"Back from Scotland so soon?" The minister set aside a sheaf of papers on hearing the earl's name announced. "I trust you have brought me some good news."

"As a Christmas *cadeau*?" said Saybrook, matching the other man's sardonic tone. "Alas, I come bearing no such gift." A none-too-gentle kick shifted the chair by Grentham's desk, allowing the earl to take a seat. "But I've not come empty-handed. I'm carrying a number of questions."

"You are the one who is supposed to be discovering answers," jeered the minister. "We had a bargain—"

"Which is now null and void."

Grentham's eyes narrowed, their pewter shade darkening to gunmetal gray.

"Your bargaining chip—Mr. Henning's nephew, Angus MacPhearson—was shot dead while trying to escape from Inverness prison," went on Saybrook. "I'm rather mystified at how a callow lad could contrive to slip out from a double-locked cell and through one of the most heavily guarded enclaves of the British military. Perhaps you could explain it to me?"

"Celtic magic? A Highland druid?" drawled Grentham. "The Loch Ness monster?"

"You might not be sounding so amused with a Scottish claymore wedged up your arse," growled Saybrook.

"You were the one there on the scene," countered the minister. "How should I, sitting here in London, have any idea what happened?"

"Don't insult me with such drivel," replied the earl.

A glint of malice lit in Grentham's gaze. "Stoughton's report did not explain how the young man escaped. It merely detailed that he was spotted running along the cliffs and was ordered to stop. When he did not respond, shots were fired."

"Did the colonel offer anything other than platitudes on why Henning was also shot?"

The minister's lashes flicked up a fraction, betraying a hint of surprise.

"Oh, did your minion neglect to add that little detail to his report?" said the earl. "How curious."

The minister remained silent.

"But then, I find much that is puzzling about the trip north. Such as how, just as we were closing in on a possible suspect, all hell suddenly breaks loose, leaving my quarry with his throat cut and my friend with a bullet in his shoulder." He paused. "One would almost think I was fated to fail."

"Good God." Grentham made a pained face. "Are we going to have to go through another round of asinine accusations? I thought we had settled the question of my loyalties."

Saybrook held the other man's gaze. "So did I. But as my wife so sagely points out, I can, on occasion, be wrong."

Sitting back, Grentham tapped his well-manicured fingertips together. "One must, of course, respect the Countess of Saybrook's pronouncements on intrigue. After all, she has such an *intimate* acquaintance with the sordid underbelly of life, and all its deceptions and betrayals."

The earl rose from his chair and braced his palms on the massive pearwood desk. "Indeed, having to survive by outwitting lying cheats, manipulative whoresons and other stinking piles of *merde* has taught her to be a very good judge of character."

Nostrils flaring, the minister turned white around the mouth. "Is there a purpose to this visit, other than to hurl insults?"

Saybrook slowly straightened. "Have you a dossier in your files on Sir George Cayley?"

"I don't have the department archives committed to memory," snapped Grentham.

"Might you have your clerk check?"

"Come back tomorrow morning," said the minister.

"I'll return this afternoon. Time is of the essence . . ." He put on his hat. "Assuming that you are as anxious as I am to capture Renard."

Steel flashed as Grentham put a new point on his quill with a penknife. "So far, for all your fancy words, Lord Saybrook, you've caught nothing but handfuls of air."

"Actually, thanks to me—and my wife—Lord Cockburn and Lord Reginald are no longer running tame within the highest echelons of the government. It's you, the head of state security, who have come up empty-handed, despite your fearsome reputation."

The minister ignored the pointed barb. "Are you of the opinion that the explosive chemical that sent you haring off to Scotland is, in fact, a real threat to England?"

A stride short of the door, Saybrook stopped and turned. "Henning's injury has severely compromised my ability to assess the danger. I have some expertise in chemistry, but my skills are not nearly as advanced as his are. That said, after perusing the paper we found in the suspect's laboratory in St. Andrews, I would say, yes, the substance is a very powerful substance, capable of great destruction in the wrong hands. If and how the enemy plans to use it are questions I can't answer right now."

Grentham set down his pen. "You must find someone to replace Henning," he said tightly.

"That—or perhaps I will simply walk away and leave the problem in your well-tailored lap. Snarls ring a little hollow when a dog has no teeth with which to back them up, Lord Grentham."

"You won't walk away," said the minister softly. "You are far too honorable. Your conscience wouldn't allow it."

"Ah yes. Honor." Saybrook drew in a deep breath. "No doubt a foreign notion to you."

"Let's not waste time in childish insults," retorted Grentham. "As I said, you need to find a trustworthy replacement for your friend."

"I believe that I have."

After waiting for a long moment for any further information, the minister huffed a harsh exhale. "But you don't intend to tell me anything more?"

"Let's just say that after what happened to us on the way north, I'm not inclined to entrust sensitive information to you and your inner circle," said Saybrook. "Secrets seem to leak out of your department faster than water flows from a sieve."

"What—" began Grentham, before catching himself and falling silent.

"What happened?" finished Saybrook. "Why not ask one of your spiders? You have them crawling around in every deep, dark crevasse of the kingdom, don't you?"

The minister's scowl pinched tighter.

"Our coach was attacked just south of the Scottish border," went on Saybrook. "The three men are now lying dead in some godforsaken ditch for their efforts.

"Be assured, Lord Saybrook. If I wanted to kill you, I wouldn't make a muck of it."

"Strangely enough, I am inclined to agree with you. The attack on us was badly planned and badly executed. Whatever else your faults are, you are smarter than that."

"High praise coming from you."

"It's not praise—it's merely a fact. Investigating a crime calls for one to set aside all emotion. Personal feelings tend to cloud one's judgment and make it harder to see the truth."

"Thank you for the primer on human nature," sneered Grentham. "Now kindly get out of my office and begin applying your own counsel to the task at hand."

8

From Lady Arianna's Chocolate Notebooks

Double Chocolate Walnut Biscotti

2 cups all-purpose flour
½ cup unsweetened cocoa powder
1 teaspoon baking soda
1 teaspoon salt
6 tablespoons (¾ stick) unsalted butter, softened
1 cup granulated sugar
2 large eggs
1 cup walnuts, chopped
¾ cup semisweet chocolate chips
1 tablespoon confectioners' sugar

1. Preheat the oven to 350°F. Butter and flour a large baking sheet.
2. In a medium bowl, whisk together the flour, cocoa powder, baking soda and salt. In another bowl beat together the butter and granulated sugar with an electric mixer until light and fluffy. Add the eggs and beat until combined

well. Stir in the flour mixture to form a stiff dough. Stir in the walnuts and chocolate chips.

3. Flour your hands. On the prepared baking sheet form the dough into two slightly flattened logs, each 12 inches long and 2 inches wide, and sprinkle with confectioners' sugar. Bake the logs for 35 minutes, or until slightly firm to the touch. Cool on the baking sheet for 5 minutes.

4. On a cutting board, cut the biscotti diagonally into ¾-inch slices. Arrange the biscotti, cut sides down, on the baking sheet and bake until crisp, about 10 minutes. Cool on a rack.

"Where are we going?" Curious, Arianna peered out the carriage window as the horses turned down South Audley Street. It appeared they were headed for the entrance to the park. "I hope it isn't far. My bum is still bruised from the Scottish roads."

"No, it's not far," replied Saybrook, once again evading the main question.

Repressing a sigh, she kept her attention on the bustle outside the glass panes. The fragrant scents of roasting chestnuts and fresh-cut evergreens wafted up from the barrows of the street vendors as they called out merry greetings to one another. Maids from the neighboring mansions of Mayfair hurried to fill their baskets with last-minute purchases for the holidays, while governesses sought to keep their young charges from gobbling down every morsel of warm gingerbread.

At the last minute, the wheels veered away from the park. Two quick turns brought them to a quiet side street. The carriage drew to a halt in the middle of the block.

"We're here," murmured the earl, unlatching the door.

Arianna descended in silence. No point in asking questions—the answers would be clear soon enough.

Saybrook offered his arm and led her up the marble steps of an elegant town house faced in pale Portland stone.

"Good afternoon, Lord Saybrook." An elderly butler answered the rap of the brass knocker and ushered them into an airy entrance hall painted in a soft shade of sage green. Gesturing toward the curved staircase, he intoned, "Tea is waiting in the West Parlor."

"Thank you, Miller." Her husband did not appear to be a stranger here. "You need not make the climb. I shall announce us."

"Very good, milord." The butler withdrew into the shadows, leaving the earl to lead the way.

In place of heavy, gold-framed paintings of ancestors, watercolor sketches of landscapes decorated the walls. They were unusual choices—bold, imaginative, assertive. And yet there was something feminine about the effect . . .

Arianna felt a strange prickling at the back of her neck as they started to climb the stairs.

"Do come in, Saybrook." The voice floating out from the half-opened door was low and a little liquid—like cool water flowing over smooth stones. "Have a care that you don't trip over the stack of books by the threshold."

The earl pushed the portal all the way open and stepped aside for Arianna to enter first.

"I hope your husband has warned you to check the chairs for cat hairs before sitting down. Sethos considers this his throne room."

Saybrook maintained a Sphinx-like expression.

"He neglected to mention it," replied Arianna. *Along with a number of other salient facts.* "But never fear; I am not one of those females who falls into a fit of megrims over finding a speck on my silks."

Their hostess rose from a work desk piled high with papers and open books. "I am glad to hear your sensibilities are not easily shocked, for precious little about my household conforms to convention." The tiny twitch of her mouth might have been a smile. "However, I shall defer to propriety enough to allow the earl to introduce us."

Saybrook cleared his throat with a low cough. "Arianna, this is Miss Sophia Kirtland. Miss Kirtland, my wife, Lady Saybrook."

Moving out from behind the stacked leather bindings and reams of paper and leather bindings, Sophia waved an ink-stained hand at the sofa. "Please make yourself comfortable. Do you prefer cream or lemon in your tea?"

So much for the usual exchange of polite flatteries.

Which was probably just as well, thought Arianna wryly. For at that moment, she was busy trying to keep her jaw from dropping down to her chest.

Hell's bells.

Sophia Kirtland was not at all what she had expected. Based on Grentham's snide comments, Arianna had envisioned a plain, unfashionable, middle-aged spinster with a tart tongue and bookish squint.

The tart tongue appeared to be accurate, but other than that . . .

"Cream," she managed to answer, hoping that her wide-eyed stare wasn't too obvious.

Tall and willowy, Sophia was dressed in a stylish gown of deep, dusky blue silk that set off her aquamarine eyes and honey-colored hair to perfection. Her face, while not conventionally pretty, was striking in its angular beauty. Wide cheekbones, full mouth, long Roman nose—together they created an oddly exotic beauty. As for age, Arianna guessed that her hostess was not much more than thirty.

"Would you care to try some of these walnut *biscotti*? I brought back the recipe from Italy, though I did not make them myself. Alas, I have no culinary skills." Her brows rose in a cynical arch. "The concoctions I create are not for human consumption."

"Thank you." Arianna accepted the plate of pastries.

The *clink* of china and silver punctuated the ensuing silence. Looking ill at ease, Saybrook took a seat in the facing chair and waited for a cup to be passed his way.

The ritual of serving tea finally over, Sophia leaned back and regarded Arianna through a scrim of steam.

"So we finally meet." The words seemed to hold a note of challenge. "I confess, you are not quite what I expected."

"Oh?" Lifting a brow, Arianna countered with matching coolness. "If it's any consolation, I was thinking just the same thing." After Grentham's nasty comment about her husband's involvement with another woman, Saybrook had explained about his regular meetings with Miss Kirtland. He had assured her that the long-standing acquaintance was based solely on shared scholarly interests—though he had confessed that his female friend had not approved of his sudden nuptials. Arianna hadn't pressed to know more at the time, feeling he owed her no explanation for his former life.

"I dare not ask what you imagined," went on Arianna after a small pause. "Sandro has indicated that you thought his precipitous marriage a big mistake."

"I am very outspoken and opinionated," said Sophia, her tone not overly apologetic. "Most people find that offensive."

"It sounds as if we might actually get along," answered Arianna after a fraction of a pause.

A low snort of laughter sounded, and though it was gone in an instant, it seemed to dispel a bit of the tension in the room.

The earl exhaled, the rigid set of his spine relaxing ever so slightly. "If we are finished with the introductions, perhaps we might get down to business."

"By all means." Taking up a small notebook and pencil from the tea table, Sophia glanced at the clock on the mantel. "I have a half hour, and then, as I told you earlier today, I must return to my laboratory. I have an experiment in progress and timing is crucial."

Ah, the pieces of the puzzle are beginning to fit together.

Arianna gave herself a mental kick for being so slow in figuring it out. "Of course . . . a chemistry expert to take Basil's place."

Saybrook turned and met her gaze. "Forgive me for keeping you in the dark. I thought it best not to go into details until I had asked Miss Kirtland whether she was willing to consider joining forces with us in a rather dangerous endeavor." He paused. "She is, but it is imperative that you agree to the arrangement before she is told the particulars."

"I take it you trust both her scholarly skills and her discretion," answered Arianna slowly. "Or you wouldn't be asking me."

"Correct," replied her husband.

"Then it goes without saying that I am in favor of the addition to our ranks."

"Excellent. Then let us move on." With that, Saybrook drew a sheaf of papers from his pocket and turned to Sophia. "Miss Kirtland, we have reason to believe that a French agent is working within the highest circles of the government . . ." He went on to summarize what had happened in Vienna, Henning's suspicions as to the dangerous substance's origins, and their subsequent travels to St. Andrews.

Sophia listened intently without interrupting, though Arianna saw her jot down some notes.

"So," finished the earl. "Here we are back in London, our scientific expert gravely injured, a cunning traitor still on the loose."

For a moment, the only sound in the room was the soft rustle of silk as Sophia leaned forward to pour herself a fresh cup of tea. "Perhaps anyone who scoffs that scholars live in ivory towers, far removed from the chaos of the real world, needs to revise their thinking," she quipped after adding a splash of cream. "I'm not very good with knives, but I'm an excellent shot with a pistol and a fowling gun. My father believed that a female should not be a helpless widget."

"I don't expect you to wage war against our enemy with anything other than your intellect," replied Saybrook. He shuffled through his papers. "We have a number of documents taken from Girton's laboratory. Henning has had a quick read through them, but I would like to have your opinion on their contents, and to know whether you see any clues that might help us uncover the identity of the enemy." He raised his gaze. "It goes without saying that these are highly confidential—and possibly dangerous to possess. They must be carefully guarded."

"I have a safe place to keep them," replied Sophia without batting an eye.

"If I may speak plainly, Miss Kirtland, what Saybrook means to stress is that this is not merely a cerebral challenge," said Arianna. "It will likely put you at risk of physical harm. Our enemy is ruthless and has no compunction about killing anyone who stands in his way."

"I do possess a brain, Lady Saybrook," replied Sophia tartly. "So that fact is rather clear to me."

The lady may claim she is not skilled with a knife, but she wields her tongue like sharpened steel.

"I was not questioning your intellect." Arianna tried to keep the edge out of her voice. If they were going to be working together, they could not be at daggers drawn. "But given the gravity of deciding to be a part of this, it would be remiss of me not to emphasize the risks." She paused. "Has anyone ever held a blade to your throat? Drugged you and threatened to snap your neck? Put a pistol to your temple and cocked the hammer?"

Despite her air of nonchalance, Sophia paled ever so slightly.

"I assure you, it's a terrifying experience," went on Arianna. "You want to . . . to . . ." Exhaling, she looked away to shadowed books and papers sitting atop the desk. "Suffice it to say, you should think very carefully about the consequences of joining us. Once you take the first step, there is no going back."

A sidelong glance showed that Saybrook looked torn between trying to intercede and letting nature take its course. Arianna was sorry to put him in such an awkward position. But it was best to see now whether this new partnership could run smoothly. Any friction would set off sparks. And sparks could be deadly dangerous.

As Arianna waited for the other lady's response, a cat appeared from behind the damask draperies and slowly sauntered across the carpet. Amber eyes flashed, and the candlelight caught a wide feline yawn and a glittering of needle-sharp teeth. Its jaws closed, and then, with a lazy leap, the animal landed in her lap. Tail twitching, it sheathed and unsheathed its claws before curling into a ball of brindled fur.

The throaty purring rumbled like distant thunder.

Does it presage a coming storm from the cat's mistress? wondered Arianna, scratching behind the animal's long, pointed ears.

"Sethos is an astute judge of character," said Sophia slowly. "He seems to like you."

The fate of England resting in the paws of an Egyptian cat?

The irony of it made Arianna smile. "I get along well with four-footed creatures. The same can't be said for people. I tend to be outspoken. Argumentative. Abrasive." She slanted a glance at her husband. "Saybrook will assure you that I often drive him to distraction."

"It would be most unfair of me to ask him to compromise his sense of gentlemanly honor," replied Sophia dryly. "So I will take your word for it."

"Cats," muttered the earl under his breath.

Arianna raised a brow. "I beg your pardon, Sandro?"

"Cats," he repeated. "Mysterious creatures. Quite impossible to read their minds."

"Yes, and unlike dogs, they can't be trained to do a man's bidding," she murmured.

Her husband chuffed a harried laugh. "*That* is putting it mildly. Obedience or intelligence—at times it's a bloody difficult choice as to which is preferable."

A smile tugged at Sophia's lips. "I do have some questions."

She consulted her notes. "Given the events in Vienna and Scotland, it would seem to me that this Renard fellow must be aware that you are after him—"

"Not necessarily," interrupted Saybrook. "You see, both his henchmen were killed during the confusion before the Carrousel in Vienna. We were able to leave the scene before anyone knew we were there, so I'm confident that he received no word of our involvement. As for Scotland, when I learned from Grentham that he had to inform an inner circle of trusted officials of our discovery, I demanded that he use a pseudonym for us when discussing the Austrian mission, as well as the trip to St. Andrews."

He allowed a small pause. "Given that we have reason to suspect a traitor has access to the most privileged information in Whitehall, it seemed the prudent thing to do. The group of advisers knew us only as Messrs. X, Y and Z—naturally I kept secret the fact that one of our party was a female. So our attackers knew they were striking at government emissaries but didn't know our actual identities."

"Assuming Grentham's word can be trusted," pointed out Arianna.

"Correct. But as of yet, I have no reason to think otherwise," answered the earl. "The minister tried to hide it, but he appeared surprised when I alluded to the attack."

"What about the contacts in St. Andrews?" asked Sophia, after a moment of mulling over what the earl had said.

An astute question, thought Arianna, grudgingly admitting that the other lady seemed to possess sharp analytical skills.

Still, I miss seeing Basil's rough-cut scowl and rumpled coat across from me rather than a coolly appraising stare and unruffled silk.

"Unless we were betrayed by Grentham, both Stoughton and Rollins were told I was a Spanish officer who had served with Wellington's staff on the Peninsula. Of course, it's known that the Earl of Saybrook is half-Spanish, but word has been spread that Arianna and I have been traveling home through Europe and only arrived in London yesterday from the Continent. That should cloud matters enough to keep them in the dark."

"All good explanations," mused Sophia. "But if I were Renard, I would be suspicious of why my plans keep going awry. So my guess is, he suspects that someone is onto his scent. And if he is as smart as you think he is, you and your wife have to be high on his list of suspects, regardless of alibis."

Arianna stilled the twitching of Sethos's tail. "It's a game of cat and mouse. We must make sure that we are the predator and not the prey. As to that, we have a few ideas."

"Any clue as to Renard's identity?" asked Sophia.

"Two." Saybrook went on to explain about Lord Reginald Sommers, the Duke of Lampson's youngest son. "Because of his father's title and connections, he moved within the highest echelons of Society. Seeing as he appeared to be in charge of the conspirators in Vienna, it seems logical to assume that Renard would be a member of his circle of friends here in London."

"We have no hard evidence of that," added Arianna. "However, both of us believe that it makes sense."

The other lady fixed her with a long look before shifting her gaze back to the earl. "And secondly?"

"In addition, we have Girton's dying words that warned of someone within the Royal Institution. Again, the words were cryptic, but given that we are after a dangerous chemical, it does make sense."

"A great many of your discoveries seem to be based on breaking the coded letters you found. How very fortunate that you possess such special skills in cryptanalysis—"

"Actually, it is Arianna who deciphered most of them," interrupted Saybrook.

Surprise shaded Sophia's face. "Indeed," she murmured.

The earl refolded his papers. "Are you still willing to be part of this? As Arianna pointed out, it is not a decision to make lightly, and once you read the first page, you will be committed to the very end."

"I am *always* careful about the decisions I make regarding my life, Lord Saybrook," replied Sophia. "They may be considered eccentric, but they are never unmeditated."

He acknowledged the statement with a tiny nod.

"That said, I am not intimidated by the dangers . . ."

Was that, wondered Arianna, a subtle challenge directed at her? *Damnation, this entire mission was getting more complicated by the moment.*

"It is imperative that Renard be stopped from causing more destruction and bloodshed in this world," went on Sophia. "If you think I can help, I shall gladly be part of your fight against him."

"Excellent." The earl placed the papers on the tea table. "Might we return tomorrow to begin a discussion of strategy?"

"Tomorrow is Christmas, Sandro," Arianna reminded him. "We have family commitments. As I'm sure does Miss Kirtland."

A faint flush colored Sophia's face. "I am not sentimental about holidays," she said curtly. "And besides, I haven't spoken to my relatives in years. My cousin, the present duke, finds my company intolerable." A pause. "The feeling is mutual."

"Perhaps . . . ," began Saybrook, then let his voice trail off.

"Perhaps you would care to join us for holiday supper. We dine with Saybrook's great-aunt, who is a very interesting female, so I don't think you will be bored."

Sophia hesitated, an odd flicker sparking in her eyes before she turned her head. "Thank you, but I have work to do." She pulled a folded sheet of paper from her notebook and made a show of smoothing it out. "I've a series of mathematical projections to calculate in support of my current experiment, and the equations are proving perversely complicated."

Arianna craned her neck for a look. "The problem is there," she said, tapping her teaspoon to a string of numbers. "Sandro, please hand me your pencil." To Sophia she added, "May I show you what I mean?"

Looking skeptical, Sophia passed over the paper.

For several minutes, the only sound in the room was the faint whisper of graphite scribbling over foolscap. "There, this new equation should simplify the process of calculating the algorithms.

"Good Lord," murmured Sophia, her eyes widening just a touch as she looked over the complicated equation. "I wasn't aware that you are good with numbers."

"Arianna isn't merely good with numbers—she is a mathematical wizard," said Saybrook.

"I have no formal training," she said quickly. "The knack seems to come naturally."

"That is a remarkable gift to have."

Arianna shrugged. "My father had it as well. Though he chose to use it for less than admirable purposes."

Sophia allowed a fleeting frown and then glanced at the clock. "Is there anything else we need to discuss right now? I have perhaps five minutes more before I must excuse myself."

"As a matter of fact . . ." Perhaps she was being a trifle thin-skinned about things, but Arianna found herself feeling a little nettled by the other lady's attitude.

You could *say thank you.*

"As a matter of fact . . . ," she repeated, taking care to avoid meeting Saybrook's eyes. This was not part of the original plan, but in battle one often had to improvise. "There is something we ought to mention, before you make a final commitment. Your help in analyzing the scientific data is, of course, key. But it would be equally important if you would agree to play a more active role in the investigation."

The mathematical paper crackled softly as Sophia fisted her hands.

"You see, it's critical that I become friends with the inner circle of the Royal Institution—that is, the followers of Humphry Davy and the interim director, Mr. Willoughby. I assume you attend the lectures there regularly, so if you would agree to introduce me, it would save a great deal of time."

"Why do *you* need to gain access to the group?" asked Sophia a little sharply.

"Because I'm good at seducing secrets out of people," she shot back. "I have a great deal of experience in sorting out lies from truth, and I'm not afraid to use an arsenal of unladylike skills to beat a cunning criminal at his own game." A pause. "Theoretical knowledge is all very well, but we will also have to be willing to strip off our kidskin gloves and get our hands dirty, if need be."

"I see," replied Sophia slowly.

Two could toss down a gossamer gauntlet of challenge, thought Arianna, carefully observing the other lady's face for her reaction. To her credit, she masked her emotions rather well. Other than a slight thinning of her mouth, her expression did not alter.

"Miss Kirtland," interceded Saybrook. "Be assured that neither of us expects you to take any real risk—"

"There is an old saying—in for a penny, in for a pound," drawled Sophia. "I said I would help—but only if I am treated as a full member of the investigation, not some delicate glass beaker that must be wrapped in cotton wool to protect it from cracking."

"Women," muttered the earl. "I swear, the fairer sex will badger me into an early grave."

"I sincerely hope that *all* of us will survive to lead long and happy lives," said Arianna, trying to blunt her husband's ire with a bit of dry humor. "I know you are not happy about any of this, Sandro, but Miss Kirtland is right. She must be fully involved. Half measures will only cause unnecessary confusion and make it more dangerous for her."

He did not retort, which in itself was an acknowledgment that her words were true.

"Excellent. Then it's settled," said Sophia crisply, giving him no chance to reconsider. "When do you wish to start?"

"As soon as possible," replied Arianna. "I have checked the

schedule of lectures. Willoughby is speaking on the twenty-eighth and then hosting a party afterward, with a holiday punch and a pianoforte recital by one of the institution members. It seems a perfect opportunity to introduce me."

"Let us plan to meet beforehand and go on to the lecture together."

"One other thing," counseled Arianna. "I won't be appearing as myself. As you pointed out earlier, Renard may be suspicious if Lady Saybrook develops a sudden interest in science. So for the duration of this investigation, I shall become . . . someone else." She switched to a different accent. "A rich widow from America, who has decided to return to her homeland now that the wars are over. I am curious about science—but most of all, I'm curious about people. I'm vain, volatile, and clever at learning the little secrets that can stir up trouble." A casual wave emphasized the assertion. "Along with a number of other malicious little habits."

Sophia blinked. "But it is not easy to become an entirely different person, and one slip of the mask will give away the investigation. How can you be sure that you can pull it off?"

"Because I've done it a number of times before." Arianna allowed a tiny smile. "It won't be the first time that London Society sees me slide into another skin."

Saybrook confirmed her words with a quick nod. "Arianna is a master of disguise. She's fooled a great many people. Including me."

"Though not for long," she conceded.

"Your wife appears to be a female of many unusual talents," said Sophia slowly.

"Yes," murmured the earl. "She is."

"Well, then, given all our eccentricities, the three of us should make a very formidable force indeed."

"Yes." Arianna ran her fingers through the cat's fur. "I think that Renard may finally have met his match."

9

From Lady Arianna's Chocolate Notebooks

Dark Chocolate–Cherry Ganache Bars

1½ cups all-purpose flour
¾ cup confectioners' sugar
¼ cup unsweetened cocoa powder
½ teaspoon fine-grain sea salt
¾ cup (1½ sticks) cold unsalted butter, cut into ½-inch chunks
1 teaspoon vanilla extract
2 tablespoons cherry jam
12 ounces bittersweet chocolate (at least 62% cocoa)
⅔ cup heavy cream
3 tablespoons kirsch, rum, brandy or other spirit
½ teaspoon fleur de sel, for sprinkling

1. In a food processor, pulse together the flour, sugar, cocoa powder and fine-grain sea salt. Pulse in the butter and vanilla until the mixture just comes together into a smooth mass. Line an 8-inch square baking pan with parchment or

wax paper. Press the dough into the pan. Prick all over
with a fork. Chill for at least 20 minutes and up to 3 days.
2. Preheat the oven to 325°F. Bake the shortbread until firm
to the touch and just beginning to pull away from the sides,
35 to 40 minutes.
3. Cool in the pan for 20 minutes on a wire rack. Brush the
jam over the shortbread's surface and let cool thoroughly.
4. Place the bittersweet chocolate in a heatproof bowl.
5. In a saucepan, bring the cream to a simmer. Pour the cream
over the chocolate and whisk until smooth. Whisk in the
kirsch. Spread over the shortbread. Sprinkle with the fleur
de sel. Cool to room temperature; cover and chill until
firm. Slice and serve.

"Come along, gel, and walk with me to the library before
the bell summons us to our Christmas feast." Constantina, the dowager Marchioness of Sterling, set down her glass of
sherry and waved a bejeweled hand at Arianna. "I have a lovely
little book there that I wish to fetch for Sandro to see."

"You could send a footman," pointed out the earl.

"Yes, but then I wouldn't have a chance to gossip in private
with your lovely wife," shot back his great-aunt. "And seeing as
the two of you have been gone for months, I am sure that there
are a number of delicious scandals for her to tell me about."

Charles Mellon, Saybrook's uncle and a senior diplomat with
the Foreign Office, chuckled. "As they were in Vienna, I imagine
that Sandro could write a book about royal peccadilloes as well
as one on the history of chocolate."

"Oh, do tell us, is the Russian Tsar as much of a rake as is
reported in the newspaper?" asked Mellon's wife, Eleanor.

Arianna bit back a harried laugh. Given that his name had
become entangled in a treasonous plot, Mellon had never been
told the real reason for their recent trip to the Austrian capital. He

and his wife thought the earl had wished to study the collection of early manuscripts from the New World held at the Emperor's famous rare book library.

"Alexander loves fine wine, rich food and beautiful women," answered Saybrook with a small smile. "He was very attentive toward Arianna. They became . . . well acquainted."

"The Tsar is a glutton for pleasure," added Arianna. "Though I assure you that from me he got only tiny morsels of friendship." A pause. "To his credit, he has some redeeming qualities."

"And what about Prince Metternich?" asked Mellon. "It is said—"

"Come along, my dear," said Constantina, punctuating the command with a sharp rap of her exotic cane.

Arianna dutifully offered her arm to the elderly dowager. "When did you start needing to walk with the aid of a support, Constantina?" she asked in concern, once they were in the corridor.

"Oh pish! I haven't slowed a step," responded the dowager with an evil grin. "Lord Gambrill brought this stick to me from Constantinople. Like me, it's an antique, and I enjoy looking at the filigree gold work and jewels of the handle." Humor glinted in her pale gray eyes. "Besides, it's rather fun to wave it at everyone and see them scamper out of arm's reach."

"Ah." Arianna laughed. "I am glad to hear that your body is keeping pace with your wit."

"Thank God my mind seems as sharp as ever," replied Constantina. "At my age, one worries about sinking into permanent decline, but I intend to go down kicking and screaming." As they entered the library, the dowager directed her Turkish cane at the sideboard, where a bottle of champagne was sitting in a silver cooler. "Pour me a glass of bubbly and let's have a comfortable little talk together before rejoining the others."

Over the cheerful fizz of the wine, Arianna amused her elderly great-aunt by marriage with anecdotes from their Austrian sojourn, taking care to omit any mention of the darker reasons for their travels. No one, save for Grentham and his inner circle, knew of the trip to Scotland.

"Hmmph. Given all the excitement of Vienna, with its glittering celebrities and late-night revelries, it's no wonder you look a little peaked." Arching her silvery brows, Constantina lifted her quizzing glass and looked Arianna up and down. "You're not increasing, gel?"

"Only with chocolate," quipped Arianna. Though she appreciated the dowager's blunt frankness, this particular question made her a little uncomfortable. She slowly spun the glass between her fingers before adding, "In all seriousness, Constantina, I don't know if I can . . . bear children. I did warn Sandro of the possibility . . ."

The cane whapped against sofa pillows. "Sandro looks *quite* satisfied with the state of his marriage." The dowager spoke lightly, but a spark of sympathy lit in her eyes. "Besides, some women need a long time to conceive. You simply must let nature take its course."

For an instant, Arianna couldn't help but picture Sophia Kirtland, who possessed such an intriguing face and erudite mind.

Suddenly anxious to change the topic of conversation, she nodded and quickly said, "Actually I have another delicate subject to discuss. Might we discuss it now, before rejoining the family? I should prefer that Sandro doesn't overhear what I am about to say."

"I am very liberal minded about many things, my dear," murmured Constantina. "But bear in mind that I am exceedingly fond of my great-nephew. So if you are about to confess to some marital scandal, I am not sure I can lend a sympathetic ear."

Arianna smiled. "No, no, the scandal does not involve me, but the old earl—Sandro's father." She watched the candlelight play off the faceted crystal before drawing a deep breath and going on.

"Has Sandro told you he has a sister?"

Constantina nearly choked on a sip of champagne. "A *sister?*"

"A *half* sister," amended Arianna. "Who may or may not be legitimate." She went on to explain about how Saybrook had discovered the existence of a sibling when going through his late father's papers. "The girl—her name is Antonia—is currently at a school in Shropshire. Charles is using his diplomatic connections to make discreet inquiries in Spain about whether the old earl was, in fact, married to Antonia's mother."

"I confess, this is quite a great surprise."

"Not an unwelcome one, I hope," said Arianna. "For you see, regardless of the circumstances surrounding her birth, Sandro would like to have Antonia come live with us and make a proper come-out in Society."

"It could be done," mused the dowager. "Not easily, mind you. But with a concerted effort to cultivate the right support from influential members of the *ton* during the winter months before the Season begins, she could receive invitations from most everyone who matters."

"I was hoping you would say that," replied Arianna. She knew that Saybrook was reluctant to draw Lady Sterling into their dangerous mission, but in thinking over the situation, she believed that she had come up with a clever compromise. "Naturally, I will need to learn a great deal about the inner workings of Society in order to help. I hope that I may turn to you for guidance."

"But of course! In truth, it will be great fun." A martial gleam lit in the dowager's eye. "Ha! Just let any of the high sticklers try to whisper a nasty word about the gel."

Arianna quickly stilled a twinge of guilt. *Experience has taught me that one sometimes has to be devious and duplicitous for good to triumph over evil.* This strategy would allow her to ask Lady Sterling a good many probing questions without telling the elderly dowager the real reason.

"Ha!" echoed Arianna, hoping her laugh didn't sound too

forced. "I can't imagine anyone having the courage to cross verbal swords with you. Even Lord Grentham does not care to test his steel against yours."

Lady Sterling tapped the handle of her cane against her palm. "Actually, I rather hope he does." Her eyes narrowed. "Has he been pestering you?"

"Not really," answered Arianna. "I did exchange some barbs with him at the Marquess of Milford's house party several months ago, but it's nothing to worry about."

Tap. Tap. The dowager waggled a brow. "Somehow, I have the feeling you are not telling me everything, gel."

"I—"

"Nor do I expect you to," went on Lady Sterling. "Whatever you are up to, you can count on my help." *Tap, tap.* She set down her glass. "Now, we had better return to the others and sit down to supper, before Cook burns the Christmas goose."

"How do I look?" Stepping away from the cheval glass, Arianna fluffed her skirts and turned in a slow circle.

Saybrook pursed his lips and studied her with a critical eye. "I hate to admit it," he said after several moments. "But I'm not sure I would recognize my own wife if we passed on the street."

"Then there should be no worry about anyone connecting Mrs. Greeley, newly arrived from Boston, with the Countess of Saybrook." She cast another glance at her reflection. A henna wash had added rich red highlights to her dark hair, and kohl had darkened her eyes, subtly changing their shape. Lip color made her mouth look fuller and wider, while her bosom and hips had been padded, giving her willowy form a lusher shape.

"There is a certain benefit to being something of a recluse," she murmured, smoothing at the ruffles edging her bodice. "Most of the people attending the institution lectures have never met me, which makes a masquerade like this far easier to pull off."

The earl's gaze remained riveted on her enhanced décolletage. "What do you use to create such curves?"

"Never mind," replied Arianna. She batted her lashes at him. "Feminine secrets," she drawled, practicing her American accent. "Bianca's cousin is a very skilled modiste, and combined with my experience in theatre costumes, we came up with a whole new wardrobe." The colors and embellishments were deliberately brighter and bolder than her usual style. "I trust that you will send the bill to Grentham."

"I should like to see his face when he opens it," quipped the earl.

"Fine silks and fancy accessories are expensive, and Mrs. Greeley must appear fashionable enough to move in the highest circles of Society." She picked up her reticule. "The gowns have been delivered to the house on Half Moon Street." Saybrook had rented a town house to serve as the American widow's residence, and two servants from their Shropshire estate had come up to serve as a makeshift staff.

Yet another costly expenditure—but then, justice was worth any price.

"The minister would likely fall victim to a fit of apoplexy if you asked him to pay," she said.

"Then I shall be sure to pass him a bill. Well padded—like your false chest."

Arianna made a face at him before tying the ribbons of her new bonnet. "I must be off. Needless to say, you can't be seen with me."

"There is a chance that you may be spotted entering or leaving from here on in, so we need to—"

"Yes, yes, I've been giving that careful consideration. From now on, I shall dress at the Half Moon house. It's far easier for a street urchin to slip through the back alleys of Mayfair without anyone noticing," said Arianna. "But today, I shall sneak out with the modiste, wearing one of her assistant's cloaks, and ride in her carriage to the shop. From there I will go out the front door and hail a hackney to take me to Miss Kirtland's residence."

Saybrook nodded, finding no fault with the plan. However, after a slight hesitation, he cleared his throat. "Arianna, you are exceedingly clever. But so is Renard. We have been lucky in our two previous encounters with him, yet we both know that luck can be fickle. Do *not* make the mistake of underestimating his cunning."

"I won't," she promised. "I've a lifetime of experience in eluding predators, so I'm very aware that I can't let down my guard for an instant if I wish to survive."

Her words only deepened his frown. "Rather than reassure me, such a statement only reminds me that you are taking all the risks, while I sit with my nose buried in books and papers."

"Learning more about Cayley and Girton's friends is important—you know that. Not to speak of learning the truth about why Basil's nephew was murdered, for I can't help but believe that it is in some way related to Renard," she replied. A tug straightened the hem of her glove. "I really must be going. It wouldn't do to be late."

The circuitous route finally brought Arianna to Miss Kirtland's town house. Sophia was waiting in the entrance hall, facing a mirror and fidgeting with the strings of her bonnet. As she turned around, Arianna heard the breath catch in her throat.

After a sliver of silence, Sophia seemed to recover her composure. "You should have kept the hackney waiting. My footman will now have to summon a fresh one," she said, somewhat belligerently. "I don't bother with the extra expense of keeping a carriage, as I so rarely go out."

"I'm sorry," murmured Arianna. "We must learn more about each other's backgrounds and habits."

"Why?" challenged Sophia.

"Because," she explained carefully, "if we are to present ourselves as friends, we must be able to carry it off. Ignorance might cause one of us to make a critical mistake."

"I see."

"Think of it as soldiers going into battle," continued Arianna. "The more you know and trust your comrades, the more you will know intuitively how they will react in the heat of the fight. That may make the difference between life and death."

"That makes sense," conceded Sophia. Lapsing into a stiff silence, she turned to the side table and began gathering up her gloves and notebooks.

The servant returned and escorted them out to the waiting hackney.

As the wheels clattered over the cobbles, Arianna heaved an inward sigh. She couldn't help but wonder whether this plan was going to work. Fighting a skilled enemy was going to be hard enough—to be constantly skirmishing with an ally . . .

A brusque cough interrupted her reflections. Shifting uncomfortably against the squabs, Sophia slanted a sidelong look her way. "You . . . you appear awfully conversant with the art of disguise."

"You mean deception?" said Arianna dryly. "Yes, I am. Has Saybrook not mentioned anything to you about my background?"

Sophia shook her head. "Your husband and I discuss science, not personal subjects."

Deciding to take the bull by the horns, she turned to face her companion. "Yet you offered your advice on his decision to marry. That seems a *very* personal topic."

A flush of red ridged Sophia's cheekbones. "I warned you that I was outspoken and opinionated."

"I appreciate both qualities. But you also need to be honest with me, if we are to have any chance of success." Arianna fixed her companion with a level gaze. "Miss Kirtland, are you, perchance, in love with my husband? "

"G-g-good God," sputtered Sophia. "In l-l-love . . . *No!*"

"Not that it would present an insurmountable obstacle to our working together. However, it would be far less awkward to have it out in the open. That way we can find a path around it."

"I consider Lord Saybrook a friend, nothing more. Indeed, I have no amorous interest in *any* man."

"Ah." Arianna thought for a moment. "Do you prefer females? It's not for any prurient reason that I ask. Nor am I making any moral judgments. But a fact like that is important for me to know."

Her companion's face was now completely beet red. "That is *not* what I meant. It's simply . . ." She sucked in a sharp breath. "Damnation. I'd rather not discuss my past." Her chin tilted up a notch. "I fear you would be shocked by certain revelations."

"I highly doubt it," replied Arianna. "Very little shocks me. My own life has not, to put it mildly, followed a pattern card of propriety." A quick glance through the grimy windowpane showed they were nearing their destination. "But further discussion of our backgrounds should probably wait for another time. Tell me more about Willoughby. I have read a few articles on Humphry Davy's early life and his scientific achievements, in order not to make a fool of myself when claiming to be interested in chemistry. But I've not yet had a chance to learn much about the interim director. I should like to hear your impressions of the man."

Sophia shifted her reticule in her lap.

"Assuming I haven't frightened you off with my bluntness."

A low laugh, barely audible above the rattle of the mullioned glass. "To take umbrage at your plain speaking would be rather like the pot calling the kettle black. I like to think of myself as an objective, rational person who can look at a problem dispassionately and use logic to solve it. You have explained clearly why certain things must be done, and I am willing to defer to your experience. There is no reason why we can't make this work."

An oblique way of saying we need not like each other to fight side by side, thought Arianna.

"Good," she said aloud. "Now, about Willoughby. Is he really the showman he's made out to be in the newspapers?"

"Yes," answered Sophia without hesitation. "He's nearly as

brilliant as Davy. And many of the ladies find him even more attractive. Sir Humphry is quite short—barely five feet in heeled boots—while Willoughby cuts an imposing figure. He stands over six feet tall and deliberately cultivates a dramatic image." Her mouth quirked. "Lord Byron once mentioned that Willoughby reminded him of a corsair, so the director now wears his hair tied back in a queue with a black velvet ribbon and sports an earring in one lobe. According to rumor, he has a large box full of precious baubles sent by his female admirers."

"Perhaps he should be treading the boards at the Drury Lane theatre, rather than the stage at the institution," said Arianna dryly.

"No question he enjoys playing a role," said Sophia. "But as I said, he has substance as well as style."

"But it sounds like one can appeal to his vanity."

Sophia considered the statement. "Yes. He's definitely not immune to flattery. I've heard whispers that beneath the show of affable charm, he's highly ambitious and secretly aspires to take over Davy's place permanently."

"Interesting." Arianna made mental note of the weakness. Perhaps it could be wielded as a weapon.

The hackney turned onto Albemarle Street and lurched to a halt, putting an end to the discussion of strategy.

"Now, remember," she cautioned as Sophia reached for the door handle. "I am Mrs. Greeley, a widow from America. We met at Hatchard's bookstore and discovered we had a mutual interest in chemistry."

"Yes, yes," murmured Sophia. She sounded calm, but to Arianna's eye, a telltale flush of heat on her cheeks betrayed a hint of nerves.

"One last thing. It's known that you are . . . not overly sociable. So don't try to act out of character. Introduce me to one or two members of the inner circle and then step back and let me take charge. If I need further help, I shall contrive to find you and let you know."

True to her word, Sophia did not take offense. "I understand."

"Take several deep breaths, and relax," she counseled. "I'm sure you played charades as a child. So think of this as a game—a challenge to your wits—and it will go fine."

Lost in thought, Saybrook stepped into the path of an oncoming high-perch phaeton as he turned down Whitehall Street.

"Bloody hell!" swore the irate driver as his team of matched chestnuts shied away. "Are you looking to get yourself killed, man?"

The earl waved an apology and quickened his pace toward Horse Guards. "Get myself killed," he muttered under his breath. "No matter which way I turn these days, Death seems to be shadowing my steps." So far, he hadn't made much headway in identifying Girton's London friend. The men suggested by Connery had all seemed unlikely candidates. However, following a lead he had just gleaned from talking with a fellow member of the London Scientific Society, he had decided to head straight to the military headquarters of the Home Guard.

Rather than proceed through the archway and take the stairs up to Grentham's offices, the earl ducked through a side door and cut though to the warren of rooms next to the stables.

"Is Colonel Greville in?" he asked the adjutant standing guard at the door. "Tell him De Quincy wishes to see him."

The young man returned shortly. "This way, sir."

"Sandro!" The colonel pushed aside a stack of dossiers and rose from his desk. "Or must I now tug at my forelock and call you Lord Saybrook?"

The earl responded with a rude oath. "I just heard you had been posted back here from Paris. When did you arrive?"

"Last week. Wellington doesn't need a flock of intelligence officers around him in France, now that peace reigns in Europe." The colonel made a face. "The only thing I have to decipher these days are a cursed cartload of supply and troop movements.

Have you any idea how complicated it is to move an army from one place to another?"

"I'd rather not know," quipped Saybrook. "Actually I would rather discuss a military matter, if you don't mind." He glanced around to make sure the door was shut. "Might I ask you a few questions concerning your work in the Peninsula? In confidence, of course."

"Of course." Greville signaled for him to have a seat. "Trust me, I much prefer to talk about war than barrels of moldy biscuits."

Saybrook shifted a stack of ledgers. "You helped handle the question of ballistics for Wellington's invasion of Spain, correct?"

"Yes," answered the colonel. "There were a great many challenges—bridges to blow up, mountain passes to clear, city walls to breech during the sieges."

"I've recently heard some rumors that the government enlisted the help of a number of scientists here in England, including Sir Humphry Davy, to secretly work on creating new explosives."

Greville cleared his throat. "May I ask why you are interested?"

"Let's just say I've been asked to do a little informal investigation for a department within Whitehall. I can't tell you more, except to say that it's important—and it's imperative for you to keep the fact that I'm asking you this in the strictest confidence."

His old comrade nodded. "You can trust me to keep mum."

"I wouldn't be here if I thought otherwise." The earl rose and began pacing back and forth across the well-worn carpet. "So tell me about Davy."

"He was engaged in a project to develop an explosive far more powerful than gunpowder," replied Greville. "I believe the work began around 1808. The research was so secret that he didn't work in his regular laboratory at the Royal Institution but had a special place in Tunbridge." The colonel pursed his lips.

"It turned out to be a bloody dangerous job. He nearly lost an eye when a tiny grain of the stuff blew up in his face."

"So he invented a substance that worked?"

"Yes. But it proved unstable. We didn't dare use it except for the really difficult jobs. Understandably, Davy himself became a bit skittish after that about continuing with his experiments. However, he did continue to do some theoretical work on the subject. He's a brilliant chemist."

"Yes, I know." Saybrook took another turn. "Were there any other scientists involved with him to do the practical testing?"

Leaning back in his chair, Greville rubbed at his jaw. "Damned if I can remember. Can you not ask Davy?"

"Davy is in Europe at the moment, making a Grand Tour with his wife and assistant Michael Faraday to celebrate his recent knighthood. Time is of the essence, and besides, the subject isn't one that can be discussed in a letter. Try to remember, and if it comes to you, trot along in person to my town house. I'd prefer that you don't commit any message to paper." The earl allowed a pause before asking, "What about a fellow named Cayley? Do you know if he ever was brought in to consult with Davy?"

The colonel's chair hit the floor with an audible thump. "Ye God, Sandro. You are touching on some *very* sensitive stuff here."

"So the rumors are true," he mused.

"Yes. For a time, the two of them were looking at certain . . . possibilities. If feasible, they would have revolutionized warfare."

"As if we aren't adept enough at killing," muttered Saybrook.

His former comrade nodded grimly. "Yes, but this . . ." Greville blew out his cheeks. "In any case, after much study, the plans were still merely theoretical and I was shifted to other work. I assumed that the project was abandoned. And now that peace has come . . ."

The words trailed off, leaving a speculative silence.

"We soldiers know that peace can be a very fragile thing," murmured Saybrook.

"Good God, is there a new threat looming? I thought those fancy diplomats in Vienna were making some progress in their negotiations, despite all the partying and philandering. Everyone here at Horse Guards assumes that with Wellington taking over as the head of England's delegation, the other leaders will snap to attention and quickly finish up the last little details of restoring world order."

"Sorry, Grev. I'm not at liberty to say more." The earl paused to regard a large map of Europe that hung on the wall. "Like you, I wish to see the peace conference live up to its name. But just in case there is a hawk lurking among the doves, I wish to be ready to clip its wings."

10

From Lady Arianna's Chocolate Notebooks

Rosemary Olive Oil Cake

¾ cup spelt flour
1½ cups all-purpose flour
¾ cup plus 2 tablespoons sugar
1½ teaspoons baking powder
¾ teaspoon kosher salt
3 eggs
1 cup olive oil
¾ cup whole milk
1½ tablespoons fresh rosemary, finely chopped
5 ounces bittersweet chocolate (70% cocoa), chopped
into ½-inch pieces

1. Preheat the oven to 350°F. Rub a 9½-inch fluted tart pan with olive oil. Alternately, use a 4½ x 13–inch loaf pan lined with parchment paper.
2. Sift the flours, ¾ cup of the sugar, the baking powder and the salt into a large bowl, pouring any bits of grain or other ingredients left in the sifter back into the bowl. Set aside.

quarry was holding court by the punch bowls. Introduc-
were made, and with a few silky hints and smiles, Arianna
o trouble having her name added to the guest list for the
gathering.

Now let me look for Bartlett," said Sophia, once they had
d past a decorative plinth holding a large urn of fresh-cut
, "I—"

Oh, Miss Kirtland, I was hoping you would be here." A
y but painfully thin lady dressed in pale green silk broke
 from her two escorts and gave a cheery wave. "I have the
 you lent me on nitrous gases." A small volume bound in
worn cloth appeared from inside her reticule. "I fear it was
advanced for me, but I made copious notes of my questions,
heus has promised to explain them."

hen I daresay you will have no trouble in grasping the es-
ls of the subject," answered Sophia. "Your brother is not only
ledgeable but also explains things clearly and concisely."

He says the same thing about you." The lady smiled shyly
ianna. "Forgive me for interrupting. My enthusiasm some
 leads me to forget my manners."

ophia had already returned to scanning the crowd. "Hmmm?"
eplied distractedly. "Oh." A brusque cough. "Mrs. Greeley
s Lady Urania Mortley. Lady Urania, Mrs. Greeley, newly
ed from Boston."

How wonderful! I think that travel must be a very educa
l experience, but unfortunately my circumstances keep me
 venturing far from home," exclaimed Lady Urania, looking
le wistful. "So I must live vicariously through the adven
 of others." A soft sigh punctuated the statement. "Bosto
d to be a very interesting city."

Not as interesting as London," said Arianna, hoping to dis
age a spate of questions. She had learned enough about th
 England port during her years in the West Indies to fee
dent about carrying off her deception, but it was alway
to avoid discussing too many details.

3. In another large bowl, whisk the eggs thoroughly. Add the olive oil, milk and rosemary and whisk again. Using a spatula, fold the wet ingredients into the dry, gently mixing just until combined.

4. Stir in two-thirds of the chocolate. Pour the batter into the pan, spreading it evenly and smoothing the top. Sprinkle with the remaining chocolate and run a fork along the length of the cake so that the batter envelops the chocolate just a bit. Sprinkle with the remaining 2 tablespoons sugar.

5. Bake for about 40 minutes, or until the top is domed and golden brown, and a skewer inserted into the center comes out clean.

The last words of the summation were still echoing through the decorative colonnading when a thunderous applause rose up to fill the lecture hall.

Smiling, Trevor Willoughby acknowledged the crowd with a graceful bow. "Thank you, thank you." He managed to inflect a note of boyish surprise into his voice—a charming artifice, thought Arianna. And quite effective, she noted, taking a surreptitious look at the people seated near her. The men were regarding the professor with undisguised admiration, while the ladies . . .

The ladies were staring in adoration.

She bit back a cynical smile. Willoughby was as skilled as any actor at playing his audience. His performance—tone, gesture, posture—had been very impressive.

"Isn't he *magnificent*?" gushed a buxom blonde to her companion. Both ladies tittered behind the waving of their painted fans.

Somehow Arianna doubted that they were commenting on the content of the lecture. As to its quality, she didn't feel qualified to judge—indeed, it had seemed incomprehensible at times.

But despite the theatrics, she assumed his reputation was built on more than hot air.

"Was he good?" she murmured to Sophia, once the people surrounding them had filed out to the adjoining hall.

"Very. His research on voltaic batteries is quite advanced." Lowering her voice to a whisper, Sophia added, "Just say, 'Oh, what an interesting observation on the reaction of potassium,' and you will impress any of the members."

"Thank you," replied Arianna.

Sophia was already heading for the doorway. "Come, I saw that Lord Chittenden is here. He's someone you should meet."

Several large refreshment tables draped in crimson damask had been set up at one end of the room. There was champagne punch, served in large crystal bowls, along with silver platters of sultana cakes and gingerbread. At the opposite end, a pianoforte sat on a raised platform, and a balding gentleman with a beak of a nose was gamely playing a Mozart sonata.

But no one appeared to be paying particular attention to the music. Even with the lecture over, Willoughby was still the center of attention. He was surrounded by well-wishers, all eager to get a word with him.

"Has the professor invented some magical love potion that exerts a captive hold on his audience?" murmured Arianna.

Sophia suppressed a smile as she scanned the room. "If he has, he could make a fortune bottling and selling it to the *ton*."

"Looking for someone, Miss Kirtland?" A sandy-haired gentleman wearing an exquisitely tailored coat approached them. "I couldn't help but see that you and your friend are without a cup of good cheer." With a flourish, he offered two glasses of punch.

"How kind," said Sophia, hesitating just a fraction before accepting the drink. "Mrs. Greeley, allow me to introduce you to Mr. Henry Lawrance. Mr. Lawrance, this is Mrs. Greeley, a friend recently arrived from America."

Lawrance lifted Arianna's gloved hand to his lips. "Enchanted, Mrs. Greeley. And what brings you to our Sceptered Isle?"

"Curiosity," answered Arianna. "A wish to broa
zons."

Light winked off his lashes as he looked up. "B
able qualities in a scientist. Are you interested in c

"I should like to learn more on the subject," she
it seems as if I have come to the right place. Willo
servation on potassium was quite interesting."

His brows notched up. "It seems you are being fa
about your abilities. I daresay few ladies here would
what the professor was talking about." He looked
"Present company excluded, of course."

Arianna noted that her companion-in-intrigue a
glance.

"Ah, there is Chittenden," announced Sophia. "Do
Mr. Lawrance."

The rules of etiquette left the gentleman no choice b
aside. "Will you be staying in London long, Mrs. Gr
asked in parting.

"That depends," said Arianna coyly.

"On Mr. Greeley?"

"No, I am a widow," she replied. "Which leaves
make my own decisions."

"Then I do hope you will favor us with a long vis
the city won't disappoint you." Lawrance bowed
look forward to furthering our acquaintance."

There had not yet been an opportunity to hay
discussion on who was—and wasn't—importa
mused Arianna. That was the next order of busines
meeting was over. The so-called Bright Lights nee
an individual shine.

As if reading her thoughts, Sophia leaned in a
"Chittenden holds a weekly soiree for the scienti
stitution's inner circle are all regulars, so an invi
you entrée into their group."

Edging through the crowd, they made their

"I believe that one of the oldest universities in America is located there." Undeterred, Lady Urania chattered on. "Har . . . Harworth?"

"Harvard," corrected Arianna. "Indeed, it is *the* oldest and is considered a very fine institution of higher learning."

"I take it you are interested in intellectual pursuits, Mrs. Greeley, seeing as you are here."

"Yes." One of her father's friends in Jamaica had been a wealthy American trader in cacao and spices, and she quickly decided to adopt him as her own. *Forgive me, Papa, but the truth is, Josiah Hammond was far more a model parent than you were.*

"Very much so," replied Arianna. "My late father was a trustee of the university. Growing up, I was often exposed to conversations on literary and scientific topics."

"What subject did he teach?" asked Lady Urania.

"He was not a professor, but a merchant of spice and coffee— in America, working for a living in trade has no stigma attached to it."

"I think that a *very* wise philosophy," said Lady Urania resolutely. "It is very important to be useful, and not merely an indolent idler."

One of the lady's escorts turned away from his own conversation and came over to join them. "My dear Rainnie," he murmured, brushing a light touch to her arm. It was a subtle gesture, more protective than possessive. "Have a care not to frighten Miss Kirtland's guest with your radical views."

Two hot spots of color bloomed on the lady's pale cheeks. "Miss Kirtland isn't intimidated by my ideas."

He crooked an apologetic smile. "Yes, but others may not be quite so tolerant of how forcefully you express them."

"I assure you, I am a firm believer that people should feel free to speak their minds," said Arianna. "It is through disagreement and debate that we challenge our own preconceptions."

Lady Urania's chin rose a notch. "You see, Theus? I haven't offended anyone."

"You need not try to rein in your sister's passions on our account, Lord Canaday," added Sophia. "I always enjoy a frank expression of opinion, as does my friend."

He inclined a small bow. "You are kind to encourage Rainnie in pursuing her interests. Most of Society thinks intellectual endeavors are very unladylike."

"I am well aware of the *ton*'s petty-minded opinions," replied Sophia tartly. "We are considered unnatural, eccentric. Ape-leaders, bluestockings—and those are just some of the kinder monikers."

"Does it bother you?" asked Canaday.

"Not particularly," answered Sophia.

It was interesting that Sophia Kirtland seemed uncomfortably sharp with everyone, noted Arianna. *So perhaps I should not take it personally.* Reminding herself that Saybrook's female friend was not her primary concern, she forced her attention back to her new acquaintances.

"Once again, I am forgetting my manners," murmured Lady Urania. "Mrs. Greeley, please allow me to formally introduce you to my brother, Viscount Canaday."

"Are you interested in science, Lord Canaday?" asked Arianna. "Or are you only here out of fraternal affection, to serve as your sister's escort?"

"Theus could be a brilliant scholar, if only he would apply himself," answered his sister.

"Fondness for her wayward sibling leads Rainnie to exaggerate. I do find science fascinating . . ." He flashed a roguish wink at Arianna. "But alas, I have not her monkish devotion to books."

Lady Urania's flush crept across her cheekbones. "Oh please, Theus, you will have our new friend thinking that I subsist on naught but bread, water and parchment."

In truth, the lady looked like she lived on air and a few lettuce leaves.

Arianna regarded the fragile, birdlike bones and had to quell the urge to offer a recipe for spiced hot chocolate, thickened with sweetened cream. Her research had discovered that throughout history, cacao was often prescribed as a nourishing medicine for the weak and infirm. But Mrs. Greeley must be careful to show no interest in botany . . .

Instead she merely said, "What an unusual name you have."

"My father was a classical scholar, with an expertise in Greek mythology," explained Lady Urania. "I am named after one of the Muses." Her eyes rolled. "I wish it had been Clio or Calliope. They are so much more cheerful. I mean, Rainnie sounds rather gloomy, does it not? It reminds me of the old nursery rhyme—rain, rain, go away."

Arianna smiled. "And you, Lord Canaday?"

"I, too, am saddled with a tongue-twisting ancient moniker," he answered wryly. "As you see, we have both chosen to shorten them into some semblance of English."

Before Arianna could inquire as to what that name was, the viscount was called away by a friend to answer a question about an upcoming auction of horses at Tattersall's. It was probably just as well, she decided. No doubt he had endured a great deal of teasing at school. Children could be cruel—sometimes more so than adults.

"Will you be attending the Mayfair Scientific Society meetings with Miss Kirtland?" inquired Lady Urania. "Our members are mostly female, but I think you will find that the lectures are not frivolous."

"I have not yet settled on how long I shall be staying in London," she replied evasively. "So I am not sure what my plans will be."

"Of course." Twisting the fringe of her shawl around her fingers, Lady Urania retreated into her brother's shadow. "Well, I mustn't keep you from meeting the other guests. I do hope we shall meet again."

"An odd pair," murmured Arianna, once they had rounded a display of potted palms. She paused beneath the gently swaying fronds, savoring the whisper of a breeze that stirred the overheated air.

"I suppose the same could be said for most people in this room," muttered Sophia. "Polite Society prefers females to be brainless widgets and men to be debauched wastrels."

"So aside from attending scientific lectures, you prefer the company of your cat to that of humans?"

"In general, yes," said Sophia somewhat testily. "But I thought you just asked about the Mortley siblings, not my personal proclivities."

"Please go on," said Arianna.

"Lady Urania is, as you see, very earnest, while Canaday is, shall we say, the livelier of the two."

"He seems pleasant. Is he well liked among his peers?"

Sophia gave the question careful consideration. "Quite," she answered. "As you see, he has an easy manner, a dry wit and an excellent mind when he chooses to be serious." Her lips pursed in thought. "He's very kind and protective of his sister."

"It sounds like I should cultivate an acquaintance with him and his sister. He appears to be well connected, and though she is quiet, his constant presence near her will provide me the opportunity to chat about the institution and its members."

"I see that one does have to possess a devious mind to do this," mused Sophia.

Was that a deliberate barb, or merely a blunt observation? Arianna didn't know her companion well enough to decide.

"It's a matter analyzing the problem at a hand," she replied. "Solving questions of human nature is not all that different from solving conundrums in chemistry or mathematics."

Sophia's brow furrowed.

"One must use cold logic in both," she added. "So I prefer to see it as possessing an ability to be both rational and creative."

"Hmmm."

Again, the sound was impossible to interpret.

"I agree that Canaday may be useful, but he's only on the fringe of Davy's inner circle," said Sophia. "Come and meet

Bartlett. He spins within its very center. As does Wrighthall, who's just joined him."

Willoughby, Lawrance, Chittenden, Canaday . . .

The new faces were already beginning to blur together. Squeezing her eyes shut, Arianna pressed her fingertips to her brow, trying to ease the ache pulsing against her skull.

"Lud, what a tangle," she muttered, pulling the brim of her tattered hat a little lower. The coming weeks were going to be a daunting challenge, what with the constant masquerades and the delicate dealings with Saybrook's elderly aunt and prickly female friend.

"Somehow, I must dance along a razor's edge," she went on, wiggling through a hole in the alleyway fence. Dressed as a street urchin, she was making her way back home from the residence rented for the phantom Mrs. Greeley. "One tiny slip and the blade's bite could prove lethal."

As if I need a reminder of how dangerous a path lies ahead.

Ducking into the shadows of the mews, Arianna quickly made her way to the back entrance of the town house and slipped inside. The thought of Henning brooding over the murder of his nephew made her even more determined to keep her footing on the treacherous steel.

"What is that stench?" Saybrook put down his cup and turned around from the kitchen worktable as she entered.

"You don't want to know." She peeled off her filthy jacket and tossed it into one of the storage pantries. "The disgusting odor discourages anyone from getting too close."

The earl blew out a breath through his nose. "Wash your face. Then come have some of Bianca's spiced chocolate."

"That feels *much* better," she said a few minutes later, returning from the scullery in a clean shirt and freshly soaped skin. Shaking loose the pins from her tightly wound hair, she heaved a sigh and watched a curl of steam rise from the chocolate pot. "That smells ambrosial."

"How did it go?" asked Saybrook as he poured her a cup.

Like the rich brew, the question swirled with subtle nuances. Arianna took a sip before answering. "Quite well, all things considered."

Click, click, click. He stirred his drink, the silver spoon tapping softly against the fine porcelain.

"I'm glad that I had a chance to hear Willoughby speak, for I am now beginning to understand how science can have a magnetic effect on people. In addition, I made some interesting acquaintances at the reception and have an invitation to attend a soiree later this week, which many of Davy's inner circle are expected to attend." She went on to give a more detailed account of the lecture and reception.

Click, click, click. "No problems with Miss Kirtland?"

"None to speak of. She was a little nervous beforehand but carried off her role very well." Arianna tried to read his expression through the scrim of steam, but the hazy light and the dark fringe of his lashes made it impossible. "Is there a reason she is so skittish around men?"

Her husband pursed his lips. "I have the feeling that she's suffered a bitter disappointment at some point in her life. However, I have never asked."

"No? And yet, the two of you clearly have a friendship—" Arianna immediately regretted her words. They sounded so . . . shrewish. "But then," she quickly amended, "I am hardly one to talk about guarding intimate secrets from the past."

He shifted uncomfortably on his stool. "Arianna, Miss Kirtland and I meet to discuss science, not personal matters."

"I am merely trying to understand her," she responded tartly. "If we are to work together, we must know each other's strengths and weaknesses."

"I am aware of that." Saybrook expelled a long breath. "Trust me, I am no happier than you are over the fact that we've had to improvise and draw in new allies. I would much prefer to work alone, but we don't have that choice if we hope to unmask Renard before he creates mayhem."

He sounded tense, tired, and she felt a little guilty on realizing how much he must miss Henning. The two of them had been close comrades for years and had gone through many battles together.

"I'm sorry, Sandro," murmured Arianna, suddenly aware that her own relationship with the earl was the shortest of all. "I know how much you trust and value Basil's counsel. And his friendship." She waited a moment before going on. "Just as I know that it means we must not only trap Renard, but also learn the truth about why Basil's nephew was murdered. It won't bring the boy back, but it will allow the wound to heal in time. Uncertainty will only make it fester."

Saybrook took a long sip of his chocolate. "Yet another challenge to add to the list."

"I'm sorry," she repeated. "Trust me, I know that his absence makes things much more difficult for you."

"You are the one facing a greater challenge." He fixed her with a searching stare. "There are definitely dangers to working with a stranger—"

"I've discussed that with Miss Kirtland, and to give her credit, she is wise enough to see it. So we've agreed to address the problem."

"You have?" A wary note had crept into his voice.

"Don't sound so worried—we are not about to square off in a bout of fisticuffs or draw pistols at dawn."

Saybrook chuffed a harried laugh. "Thank God."

"We have arranged to meet for an early-morning walk in the park several days a week—it's perfectly respectable, so if anyone notices, it shouldn't stir any attention. In fact, we plan to begin tomorrow."

"As which female will you appear?" he inquired.

She smiled. "I did mull that over and decided to be myself.

There is always the chance for making a mistake that might give away the masquerade, especially given the need to travel back and forth between residences. So I think it's prudent to limit Mrs. Greeley's appearances to scientific gatherings."

"You don't worry that Renard may grow suspicious on seeing Miss Kirtland friendly with both you and the newly arrived widow from America?"

"Now that Miss Kirtland has introduced me—that is, Mrs. Greeley—to the Royal Institution, I don't really need her to be seen with me in public anymore. So the connection will appear slight."

Saybrook started to protest, but she waved him to silence and hurried on. "In battle, a general must always assess the risks and decide which is greater. I have an idea on how she may be more useful to us in another role."

He frowned.

"But I want to think it over a bit more before discussing it with you."

"Very well." He leaned forward, propping his elbows on the scarred oak planking. The lamplight flickered, catching the toffee-gold highlights in his dark eyes. "I trust that you will be careful and won't do anything to put yourself at greater risk."

"You have my promise on that."

A ripple stirred in the depth of his gaze. "Thank you."

She reached out to touch his cheek. "You've learned something—something that's put you on edge."

He nodded. "So far it's naught but vague bits and pieces of information that may or may not fit together as a whole."

"But if they do?"

"Then the danger to England—and indeed, to all of Europe—is beyond our wildest imagination."

Arianna felt a chill snake down her spine. "Good heavens, you are the most down-to-earth person I have ever met, Sandro. I confess, I am surprised that you are letting your fears fly away with you."

Saybrook gave an odd little laugh. "I assure you, I'm not." He drew in a deep breath, and she noted that his olive complexion had turned a little ashen in the uncertain light. "I've confirmed with a former comrade that Humphry Davy was working on developing a chemical explosive far more powerful than gunpowder for the British military. It was never fully developed for regular use, but the laboratory tests showed it to be terrifyingly effective."

"We suspected the existence of such a substance after what we discovered in Vienna," she pointed out. "And Girton's notes pointed at Davy and his followers. So the news shouldn't be a great shock."

"No, *that* part isn't."

A strange flutter stirred in her chest, as if butterflies were beating their gossamer wings against the cage of her ribs. "You are beginning to frighten me."

"Good, because I confess that I am scared witless."

Arianna swallowed hard.

Saybrook's voice dropped to a taut whisper. "Earlier this afternoon, I heard some disturbing rumors about Sir George Cayley and a joint secret scientific project involving Davy. I was tempted to dismiss them as too far-fetched, but when I asked my former comrade, he admitted that the talk was true."

She could stand the suspense no longer. "What in the name of Lucifer is Cayley working on?"

"Lucifer is an apt expression," he replied darkly. "In addition to his other inventions, Cayley has been working on the designs for a flying machine. One that can be used to carry a powerful bomb and drop it on a specific target."

Her brows winged up. "That's absurd . . . isn't it?"

Saybrook lifted his shoulders, a gesture eloquent in its uncertainty.

"I mean, the French were quick to explore the use of balloons in warfare soon after the first manned flight, but I thought the air quickly leaked out of the idea." She thought for a moment. "I seem to recall that Napoleon formed a corps of aeronauts and took them with him on his Egyptian campaign in 1798. However, as the balloons were at the mercy of the winds and proved impossible to steer, they were abandoned as useless for military purposes, save for the occasional reconnaissance flight."

"Yes," he replied. "For a time at the turn of the century, the Royal Society, which as you remember is England's most prominent general scientific group, was worried that Napoleon was going to launch an airborne invasion of England. I believe it was the American Benjamin Franklin who warned that five thousand balloons, each carrying two soldiers, could transport an army of ten thousand across the Channel in a matter of hours. But when it became clear that balloons could not be controlled well enough, the threat seemed to die."

His long fingers began to drum softly on the wood. "You are right about Napoleon disbanding his Compagnie d'Aérostiers as impractical. Indeed, the public's fascination with balloon flight deflated over the years. The early launchings used to attract huge crowds—Lunardi, the first man to fly in England, drew over one hundred fifty thousand spectators to the Artillery Grounds in London, including the Prince of Wales. But these days, it's just a handful of scientists laboring in obscurity who keep experimenting with different types of gases and steering mechanisms for the inflatable behemoths."

"So what has changed?" she asked slowly.

A breath of air stirred the candle flame by the chocolate pot.

"Apparently Cayley's machine isn't a balloon . . ."

11

From Lady Arianna's Chocolate Notebooks

Blueberry Chocolate Tonic

2 cups cold blueberries
2 tablespoons unsweetened cocoa powder
1⅓ cups cold almond or oat milk
2 teaspoons flaxseed oil
3 teaspoons honey

1. Place all the ingredients in a blender and blend on high for about 30 seconds.
2. Drink immediately or the pectin in the blueberry seeds will make a pudding rather quickly. For extra health benefits, add 1 teaspoon licorice root powder.

~

"You must remember to relax your hands, milady. Horses can sense when you are nervous, and it makes them skittish as well."

"Thank you, Jorge." Arianna loosened her grip on the reins

and urged her mount through the entrance to the park. "I think I shall manage better now that we are off the streets." Fog swirled through the trees, obscuring the lawns and bridle paths in a sea of silvery mist.

"Would that I were seated on the teak taffrail of a schooner and not a dratted leather sidesaddle," she muttered under her breath. She had little riding experience and was worried that at any moment the jarring trot was going to bounce her off her precarious perch. "How embarrassing if I were to land on my arse in front of Miss Kirtland."

The groom came abreast of her and pointed out a mounted figure approaching at a canter. "Is that the lady you are meeting?"

Arianna squinted through the early-morning shadows and couldn't help admiring the effortless grace of the rider. "Yes, I believe so," she answered as the big gray stallion came closer.

"Good morning." With a casual flick of her wrist, Sophia reined her mount to a walk.

Not a hair out of place, not a fold in a twist. Arianna slanted a baleful look at the other lady's stylish attire and suddenly regretted agreeing to a mounted rendezvous. From the pert little military shako framing the wheaten curls to the frogged jacket and tailored skirt, Sophia presented a picture of elegant refinement.

Despite her eccentricities, Miss Kirtland is at home in the English world of privilege, while I . . .

"Good morning," she replied rather curtly. "I trust that I haven't kept you waiting."

"I came early," replied Sophia, patting her horse's lathered neck. "Early morning is the only time a lady may indulge in a good gallop without setting Society's tongues to clucking."

"I see." Arianna turned to her groom. "You may stay here, Jorge. Miss Kirtland and I will just circle through the nearby bridle paths and return shortly." The rules of propriety demanded the presence of a servant, but now that they were in the park, it was permissible to take a short interlude of privacy. "Perhaps you would care to lead the way, Miss Kirtland. I am not as familiar with the terrain as you appear to be."

They rode on for several minutes, the rhythmic thud of the hooves and the whisper of leather and brass the only sounds between them. Arianna felt her mouth thin to a wry grimace. Mouthing polite pleasantries was not something she was very good at either.

"You don't ride very well," observed Sophia critically as they turned into a copse of trees. "It's odd—you carry yourself with confidence on the ground, and yet sit in the saddle like a sack of grain." She took another long look. "Square your shoulders, lift your chin . . . don't stare down at the reins, but ahead, at where you are going."

"Damnation," muttered Arianna, trying to do as she was told. "I grew up around water and ships, not meadows and large, sweaty animals—at least not the four-footed kind."

Sophia stifled a snigger.

"So I haven't had much practice."

"Why didn't you say so? We could have walked instead," said Sophia.

"Because," she answered through gritted teeth, "I should like to practice my riding. I . . ." *Should I admit the real reason?* After all, if they were to get to know each other, they both must be willing to let down their guard.

"If you must know, I should like to surprise Sandro. He is, of course, a superb horseman, and it would be nice to be able to join him on occasion without embarrassing myself."

"Ah." They continued on for a moment as before, and then Sophia suddenly swung her stallion around and came up on Arianna's other side. "Hold your hands a little lower." She reached out and adjusted the angle of Arianna's fists. "And for God's sake, unclench your fingers. You're not about to throw a punch."

"Right," muttered Arianna.

"Now, drop your leg just a touch, so it hooks more firmly

around the pommel. And sit up straighter—correct posture is very important."

"But it feels so awkward."

"I know it feels odd at first," replied Sophia. "But trust me, you will be far better balanced."

Drawing a deep breath, Arianna tried to do as she was told.

"And lastly, try to move in rhythm with your horse's gait. Fighting against the natural motion is what makes you bounce around like a rag doll."

The path suddenly seemed to smooth out beneath her horse's hooves.

"Better?" asked Sophia.

"Much." Arianna no longer felt in danger of tumbling from the saddle. "Thank you."

A hint of wintry sunlight peeked through the clouds, setting off sparkles in the lingering frost.

"Once you become comfortable, we can progress to a trot." Sophia watched a little longer and then gave a nod of approval. "You learn fast. Most females are helpless when it comes to physical skills."

"I had little choice—it was either sink or swim."

"Right—you did mention water and ships." Sophia's expression turned curious. "I take it you did not grow up along the English coast. Otherwise horses wouldn't seem so foreign to you."

"Correct. I was raised in the West Indies."

"Oh? Was your father a plantation owner?"

"No, he was a scoundrel." Arianna made a wry face. "A charming scoundrel, but his partners in crime did not find some of his other qualities very endearing, so like many wayward sons of the aristocracy, he was forced to flee England and take refuge in the New World."

"I—I am sorry. I did not mean to pry," said Sophia a little stiffly.

"No apologies are necessary. As I mentioned the other day,

we must get to know each other." Arianna paused. "Did Sandro really tell you nothing about my background?"

Sophia shook her head. "Lord Saybrook is rather reticent about personal matters."

A burble of laughter escaped Arianna's lips. "*That* is a bit of an understatement."

For an instant, Sophia appeared offended, but then her pinched expression curled into a grudging smile. "I am not sure who is more stone-faced—the Sphinx or the earl."

"He is not easy to read," Arianna agreed.

The air was growing warmer and a light breeze ruffled through the fallen leaves, slowly dispelling the mist. Snorting, the stallion tossed its head and tugged at the reins, impatient to pick up the pace.

Steadying the animal with an expert hand, Sophia cleared her throat with a brusque cough. "Might I ask how you came to return to England and met Lord Saybrook?"

"That, I fear, is a very long story. However, I won't bore you with all the gory details. Suffice it to say, my father was murdered by his former partners, leaving me orphaned at the age of fourteen. I did not care to accept the innkeeper's offer of trading my body for his protection, so I decided to fend for myself."

Arianna closed her eyes for a moment, remembering the years spent drifting through countless hellhole harbors and rum-drenched taverns. "I learned a number of very useful skills, like picking pockets, cheating at cards, acting in a traveling theatre troupe, and cooking."

"The one thing Lord Saybrook did tell me was that you were very knowledgeable about chocolate," said Sophia.

"Our local housekeeper was not only a cook but also a renowned healer, so I gleaned a lot from her about esoteric plants and herbs—as well as how to use knives and cleavers." A pause. "Just ask Sandro."

Sophia's eyes widened.

"In any case," went on Arianna. "Along with learning the fine points about cuisine, I was also cooking up a plan to punish my father's killers. Working as a cook for the crew of a merchant ship, I earned my passage back to England and embarked on my quest for revenge. But to quote my father's favorite poet, 'the best laid plans of mice and men'. . ."

"Which is to say, things did not go as planned?"

"Indeed, they did not. I was soon jumping from the frying pan into the fire. If not for a fortuitous encounter with Saybrook, I might have been burned to a crisp."

"And?"

"And as the earl had his own reasons for wanting to pursue the men I was after, we decided to join forces, so to speak. The rest is . . . Well, I'm afraid that I'm not at liberty to divulge the details, other than to say we both were satisfied that justice was done."

"Good heavens, have you considered writing a novel?" quipped Sophia.

"Unlike you, I have no formal education, no fancy bookish learning," answered Arianna. "My literary skills are completely unpolished."

"Yet your story is far more interesting than mine." Sophia bit back a sigh. "I've led a very staid life. It won't take but a minute to tell you about my background."

"Nonetheless, it will have to wait until next time." They had reached the end of the path and Sophia was already turning her stallion to return to the waiting groom. "I need to tell you about Sandro's latest discovery." She quickly went on to explain about Cayley and his secret work with Sir Humphry Davy.

Sophia let out a low hiss of air. "A flying machine? If it's not a balloon, what does the thing look like?"

"I have no idea," answered Arianna. "I haven't seen a sketch."

"Mmmph." Gazing up at the clouds, Sophia said, "I know that a number of chemists were experimenting with different gases to provide lift for balloons, for at one point it was thought that altering pressures during flight could help control direction.

But the efforts seemed to fizzle out. As intriguing as the idea of air travel was, the potential seemed impossible to harness." A gust of air set the feather in her shako to dancing in the pale light. "If Cayley has indeed come up with a new type of flying machine, the invention would be revolutionary."

"Earth-shattering," said Arianna. "Quite literally."

The dreamy expression disappeared from Sophia's face. "Yes, of course. The application of such an invention to warfare would be terrible. I was thinking of the theory, not the reality."

"The reality is, the plans for this flying machine, combined with a powerful new chemical explosive, could be used to wreak unimaginable destruction both here and abroad. An army possessing both would be unstoppable."

"So how do you plan to stop the enemy before he gets off the ground?"

"Attending Chittenden's soiree takes on an even greater importance. I need to work myself into the good graces of the institution's inner circle as quickly as possible."

"How can I help—"

"You can't," said Arianna. "Not there, that is. We need your help in another way." Knowing full well how dangerous desperate men could be, she was loath to draw an inexperienced person into the heart of the fray. "We must not forget to explore the other clues we have concerning Renard. Lord Reginald Sommers was heading his network in Vienna, so we must take a closer look at his friends and family."

A twitch tugged at the corners of Sophia's mouth. "I—I don't move in those circles."

"But you could, given your family connections," said Arianna softly. "You've known many members of the *ton* since childhood. I haven't, which is a distinct drawback. I've enlisted Sandro's great-aunt to help me. But it would be a great asset to have you as well. You are close in age to Lord Reginald and his friends, so I imagine that you have some idea of their character."

It might have been a quirk of the clouds, but her face seemed to darken for an instant. "You mean that you want me to dance through the mansions of Mayfair, attending frivolous balls and soirees given by shallow, superficial aristocrats?"

"Yes," answered Arianna. "I know it's a lot to ask."

Sophia turned to watch another early-morning rider galloping toward the Serpentine.

"So if you would rather remain in your laboratory and serve as a technical consultant, Sandro and I will certainly understand."

Though fashioned of velvet rather than chain mail and leather, a gauntlet had been tossed at the other lady's feet.

Would she accept the challenge?

Sophia stiffened her spine and squared her shoulders. "You and the earl are certainly doing your fair share of distasteful tasks. Seeing as I have agreed to be a partner in this, I can hardly refuse to do my part."

"Thank you," said Arianna, grateful that she had won a quick surrender.

It was her hope that keeping Sophia and Constantina engaged with Society would remove them from the direct line of fire.

"This monster must be stopped before he murders more innocent people."

Arianna eyed her husband's friend, taking in the strong, sculpted lines of her profile and the resolute jut of her jaw. "I hope you aren't regretting your involvement. This investigation may be even more dangerous than we feared."

Sophia expelled a rueful laugh. "My life has been a bit boring of late. I could use a spark of excitement."

Muttering yet another curse—this one in Spanish—Saybrook shuffled the pile of papers into order and began rereading his notes. "Something is eluding me, though I am not sure what is it is."

He reached for the chocolate pot and slowly spun the *molinillo* between his palms. The liquid, now lukewarm, swirled inside the porcelain, its whisper teasing, taunting . . .

The sound was suddenly drowned out by the thumping of steps in the corridor.

Frowning, the earl released his hold on the polished ebony handle. "Bloody hell, Sebastian knows better than to admit visitors at this hour."

Unless . . .

The door flew open. "Auch, I hope ye have some decent malt close at hand, laddie," rasped Henning. "My throat is dry as a bone after traveling all night."

Saybrook regarded his friend for a long moment before allowing a tiny smile. "I may be able to rattle up a bottle. Have a seat by the fire while I have a look."

"Make it more than a wee dram," said Henning. Heaving a sigh, he dropped into the leather armchair and propped his scuffed boots on the fender. "Much as I hate to admit it, it's good to be back in London—despite all the Sassenachs crowding the streets."

"I thought you were under orders to keep your mangy carcass in Scotland for the next few weeks," said Saybrook as he handed the surgeon a generous measure of whisky.

"Since when have I ever obeyed orders?" Henning took a long swallow. "Ahhh, that tastes nearly as good as yer wife's chocolate." He looked around the room. "By the by, where is Lady S?"

"Out," replied the earl.

"Not getting into trouble, I hope."

"Hope springs eternal," quipped Saybrook.

"I trust that yer bottle does the same." The surgeon held out his glass for a refill. "Any further progress in the investigation?"

"We'll talk about that in a moment. But first, I want to hear your news." His gaze slowly traversed Henning's rumpled figure. His clothes were in worse disarray than usual, the wrinkled wool and frayed linen hanging off his gaunt body like rags on a scarecrow. "You look like something the Devil dragged out of the deepest pit of Hell."

The surgeon raised his glass in mock salute. "It's lovely te see you too, laddie."

Pinching back a smile, Saybrook crossed his arms and assumed a stern scowl. "Have you had your head up your arse? As a medical man, you know that a patient has to keep up his strength in order to recover quickly. And yet you look like you haven't had a decent meal in weeks."

The surgeon dropped his eyes and stared into the glowing coals. "I didna have much of an appetite fer food. Or fer life." His mouth thinned to a grim line. "But then my sister decided to visit relatives in Skye, to get away from home during the painful holiday season, and I got to feeling useless, just sitting and brooding. So I decided I might as well come back to London and help you trap a fox. But make no mistake, it's fer you and Lady S, not for that bloody English bastard Grentham and his Whitehall coterie."

"Damnation, Baz, I know how hard it must have been for you, having to break the news to your sister. But if there is any blame to be shouldered, it's me who should bear the brunt. Bringing you into my investigation put your family at risk."

Henning answered the statement with a rude sound. "We both know that Angus was involved with the Dragons of St. Andrews long before that." He blew out his cheeks. "I thought I could be clever enough to save him, but I failed."

"If it's any consolation, I don't think Grentham doublecrossed us. He appeared surprised to hear of the shooting."

The surgeon chuffed a skeptical snort.

"I haven't forgotten about Stoughton," said the earl. "You have my promise that I'll press to learn what really happened, and if I can prove that he violated any military rule, I'll see that he's punished."

"I don't give a bloody damn about the military's rules, Sandro," growled Henning. "We Scots adhere to a more primitive code."

"It's the best I can do."

"I know that, laddie. I don't expect *you* to break any laws."

"Baz—"

"Enough said on the matter." Setting his empty glass aside, the surgeon leaned back and let his eyes fall half-shut. "Now tell me about what you've discovered before the whisky and the warmth of yer hearth put me to sleep."

"I'll allow Arianna to recount her progress, but as for me, I've been following up on the names in Girton's coded letter."

"And have ye learned more about the chemical explosive?"

"A little," answered Saybrook. "But there may be an even greater threat hovering on the horizon . . ."

Wincing, Arianna gingerly descended the stairs. "Why anyone enjoys riding is beyond me," she mumbled, rubbing at her sore bum. "But then, I find the rolling motion of a ship in rough seas exhilarating, while others are puking over the larboard side."

One man's pleasure is another man's poison.

There was a deeper, darker truth lurking within the sardonic humor of the old adage, she reminded herself. The elemental differences in human nature could be stark. Like good and evil.

"Yes, and whoever invented a sidesaddle was *truly* evil," she said under her breath.

"Did you say something, my dear?" Saybrook poked his head out of the library.

"Nothing important," answered Arianna. "How is Basil? Sebastian told me he arrived just a short while ago."

"Sleeping," replied the earl. "Let's not wake him. He looks exhausted and has lost far too much weight."

"I've asked Bianca to prepare some of his favorite foods. She will soon have him fattened up."

"Chocolate will help nourish his body, but we shall need to find a tonic for his spirit as well," mused Saybrook. "He's still bitterly resentful of the British government."

"Can you blame him?"

"Of course not. But I worry that he might have his own motives for wishing to rejoin the investigation. He spoke obliquely about revenge."

"A sentiment that I understand well," she said dryly. "Let us not start imagining specters. We have enough real demons to face."

The earl quietly closed the door behind him and led the way to a parlor overlooking the back garden. "How did your walk go?" he asked, once they had settled in the chairs by the bank of diamond-paned windows.

"I think Miss Kirtland and I are making some headway," she replied carefully.

"That sounds ominously vague." He said it lightly, but a shadow of concern hung beneath his lashes. "If you feel that the two of you cannot march in step together, it would be best if we come up with another plan. A stumble will only put both of you at risk."

"I know that, Sandro. Just as I know that it would put you in peril, as well as Basil and Constantina."

Patterns of light and shadow played across his profile, dipping and darting along the chiseled planes of his face. She saw a tiny muscle in his jaw twitch.

"What's bothering you?"

"Other than the fact that some fantastical chariot of fire may at any moment streak through the heavens and drop devastation on the Earth?"

"My question was not well phrased," said Arianna.

"Sorry." He ran a hand through his hair. "There is something unsettling about this investigation. I feel as if I am walking blindfolded through a nest of vipers. I feel their coils brush against my boots, but every time I reach down to grab one, it slithers out of reach."

Arianna repressed a shiver. "We dealt with snakes before and always managed to catch them and then cut off their heads."

"This feels different," he said softly. Uncertainty shaded his voice. "And I can't explain why."

"Then I understand your concern. Your instincts must be trusted, so we have to be even more careful."

A sigh seeped out. "Not a word I normally associate with you."

"This mission has forced me into a number of odd new associations," she said dryly. "As you know, I am very good at improvising."

He acknowledged the remark with a gruff nod. "True. But if anything were to happen to you—"

"Good God, do you think that I don't worry about you, Sandro?"

The question forced him to silence.

"We must accept that fear will be an elemental ingredient in our emotions. As in chemistry, we will have to find a way to balance its volatility."

The earl rose and went to stand by the windows, his gaze fixing on the bare branches of the elm trees lining the far wall of the garden. "There is no going back, so we must look ahead. What is your next move?"

"Chittenden's party," she replied. "Tomorrow night. And then Constantina has secured invitations to a ball given by Lord and Lady Brodhead. Their son was friendly with Lord Reginald Sommers, and he is expected to be in attendance."

Saybrook clasped his hands behind his back.

"Miss Kirtland has agreed to come too," said Arianna.

He turned around abruptly, surprise etching a furrow between his brows. "She hates going out in Society."

"As do I," she replied calmly. It was hypocritical to feel any hurt at his reaction. Miss Kirtland had little experience in playing a role other than a recluse, so it was natural that he comment on it. "But we must put aside our own personal preferences if we are to trap Renard."

A grunt.

Arianna made a show of pleating the folds of her skirts before explaining her reasons for distancing Miss Kirtland from the Royal Institution's scientific circle.

"You seem to have given this a great deal of thought," was his only comment.

"You are not the only one who senses danger. I am trying to plan everything carefully," she answered. "But even with the best-laid plans, one must be prepared to make spur-of-the-moment changes."

12

From Lady Arianna's Chocolate Notebooks

Chocolate-Dipped Hazelnut Caramel Squares

2 cups all-purpose flour
1 cup packed light brown sugar
¼ teaspoon salt
¾ cup (1½ sticks) plus 6 tablespoons chilled unsalted butter,
cut into ½-inch cubes
⅔ cup granulated sugar
6 tablespoons heavy whipping cream
¼ cup honey
2 teaspoons finely grated orange peel
5 ounces hazelnuts, coarsely chopped
¼ cup chopped candied orange peel
8 ounces bittersweet chocolate (not exceeding 61% cocoa), chopped

1. Preheat the oven to 350°F. Line a 13 x 9 x 2–inch metal baking pan with foil. Mix the flour, brown sugar, and salt

in a food processor for 5 seconds. Add ¾ cup of the butter.
Pulse until a coarse meal forms.

2. Transfer to the pan; press firmly and evenly onto the bottom of the pan. Bake the crust until golden, about 20 minutes.

3. Bring the remaining 6 tablespoons butter, granulated
sugar, cream, honey, and finely grated orange peel to a boil
in a small heavy saucepan, stirring until the sugar dissolves and the butter melts. Boil until a candy thermometer registers 230°F, about 6 minutes. Stir in the nuts and
candied orange peel.

4. Spoon the hot nut mixture evenly over the crust in the pan.
Return to the oven and bake until the entire surface is bubbling, about 10 minutes. Cool for 20 minutes.

5. Using the foil as an aid, lift the cookie from the pan. Carefully peel the foil from the edges. Cut the warm cookie
into 1½-inch squares. Cool the cookies completely.

6. Line a rimmed baking sheet with parchment paper or
waxed paper. Melt the chocolate in a small metal bowl set
over a saucepan of simmering water until warm to the
touch. Remove the bowl from over the water. Dip the corner or edge of each cookie in the melted chocolate and
place on the prepared baking sheet. Chill until the chocolate is set, about 1 hour.

Arianna made a last check of her reflection in the glass before descending from the elegant carriage. Working with
their usual quiet efficiency, Saybrook's country servants had
taken charge of things and quickly arranged for all the outward
trappings of wealth. Mrs. Greeley now appeared to be just what
she claimed—a worldly lady of means, intent on residing in
London for an indefinite period of time.

Approaching the front steps of her destination, she paused

and looked up at the town house. The draperies in the drawing room were drawn back, allowing the blaze of the crystal chandelier to shimmer through the leaded windows.

Bright lights.

She would have to match that brilliance with some fire of her own.

"Mrs. Greeley, how lovely that you could join us tonight." Her host flashed a gracious smile as a servant escorted Arianna through the double doors at the top of the staircase. "There are light refreshments set up in the side parlor, and a champagne punch can be found in the music room. Please be forewarned that it is all very informal here. Everyone simply circulates as they wish, for the main purpose of the gathering is to talk and exchange ideas."

"Thank you," replied Arianna. "Don't worry about me. I am quite capable of managing on my own."

"Indeed, don't fret about our new American friend feeling adrift among foreign faces, Chit." Henry Lawrance, whom she had met at the Royal Institution reception, suddenly appeared by her side. "I shall be sure Mrs. Greeley is introduced properly to the other guests."

"There is no need for you to trouble yourself, Mr. Lawrance," said Arianna quickly.

"Oh, it's no trouble at all," he answered politely.

Damnation. She turned, hoping a cool response might discourage his misplaced gallantry. The last thing she wanted was company. "I'm sure you have come to mingle with your own friends, sir. For me, part of the allure of travel is feeling independent, so I am not at all intimidated by having to navigate foreign waters on my own."

"It's clear you are a lady who is interested in exploring both intellectual and physical boundaries." Lawrance smiled, seemingly oblivious to her hint. "You have my admiration, for it cannot be easy, given the prejudices against those of your sex."

"Indeed, it can be very trying at times," said Arianna tartly.

For someone who supposedly possesses a modicum of intelligence, your brain appears as thick as granite.

Without further word, she walked off.

"The music room is the first door on the left," he said, sticking close to her side. "Shall we get a glass of punch?"

"How kind." Spotting Willoughby holding court close by, she stopped just inside the doorway and fanned her cheeks. "I shall wait for you here."

As he headed for the refreshment table, Arianna sidled closer to the group of men gathered around the institution's acting director. They were discussing some arcane point of chemistry, and though she couldn't follow the technical talk, she listened carefully to the exchange, watching the faces and making careful note of who spoke up to challenge Willoughby. The dangerous spark among the Bright Lights would be an individual who was both clever and confident.

"Do you have a special interest in potassium?" murmured Lawrance as he returned with two glasses.

"I am not very familiar with the subject, but I am always curious to learn about new things."

He fixed her with a measured look. "What is your particular field of interest, Mrs. Greeley?"

"Oh, since I am among such experts, I just wish to listen and see what sparks my imagination," she said coyly.

His gaze sharpened, though his tone matched her teasing note. "Sparks can be dangerous in chemistry."

Arianna gave a light laugh. "Yes, of course—thank you for the reminder. I see that I shall have to be more careful with my choice of words." She took a sip of her drink and felt its effervescence prickle against her tongue. "And you, sir? What draws you to science?"

"Echoing your sentiments, I find a variety of topics fascinating."

Before he could go on, a portly gentleman with ginger sidewhiskers and a large, intricately enameled stickpin decorating his cravat approached from the side salon. "I say, Lawrance, I have found the answer to that question you were asking me about lighter-than-air gases." Suddenly aware that he was interrupting, the stranger inclined an apologetic nod to Arianna. "Forgive me, madam. I didn't realize my fellow member was already engaged."

"Please don't apologize. The enthusiasm shown by all you scientists is most refreshing."

"Ha! How nice of you to say so. Some of my colleagues think I'm filled with naught but hot air."

"Are you?" drawled Arianna.

"Ha, ha, ha! I confess, sometimes I do get carried away in talking about my specialty."

She turned slightly to allow someone to pass, and once again her gaze fell on his cravat. "That is a very unusual stickpin. Does it have some special significance?"

"Indeed it does! It is a replica of the first manned balloon launched by the Montgolfier brothers. You see, my field of study is aeronautics."

"How interesting." Arianna slanted a quick glance at Lawrance, who seemed to have fallen oddly silent. "Aren't you going to introduce me to your colleague?"

He reluctantly did so. "Mrs. Greeley, this is Mr. Brynn-Smith—who does tend to expend a great deal of wind talking if you allow him to go on and on."

Brynn-Smith accepted the needling with a good-natured laugh. "I try to rise to the occasion when I am asked about my work. And seeing as you asked some very arcane questions, you ought to be glad of it."

Lawrance's gaze clouded for just an instant.

"Come around to my lodgings tomorrow. I've made copies of the papers you inquired about," continued Brynn-Smith. "Oh, and if you have further questions on flight, there is a new tea shop on Montague Street that has become quite popular with the aeronauts who lift off from the Artillery Grounds. The proprietor is a Spanish woman who serves a variety of exotic coffee and chocolate drinks." He looked at Arianna and explained, "One tends to get chilled at high altitudes, so a hot beverage serves to warm the bones after several hours aloft."

"I can imagine," she murmured. "Do you soar through the skies as well, Mr. Brynn-Smith?"

"Alas, only occasionally," he answered. "My work is mostly confined to the laboratory, as I like to experiment with the types of gases that allow the balloons to defy gravity."

"So without you, no one would get off the ground?"

Brynn-Smith beamed. "I suppose you could say that. Though I did not, of course, invent hydrogen, I am trying to see if a new element might be added to make balloons more maneuverable." Pulling a pocket watch from his waistcoat, he checked the time. "Dear me, if I don't fly off this instant, I shall be late for another engagement. It was a pleasure to make your acquaintance, Mrs. Greeley. I hope we have a chance to talk further at some later date."

"I look forward to it."

Bobbing a quick bow, Brynn-Smith hurried off.

"What an interesting fellow," she remarked, curious to draw a reaction from Lawrance. He did not seem happy about the interruption, and she wondered why. "The members of the Royal Institution are engaged in *such* intriguing projects. I can see that I shall enjoy my stay here in London."

"What other plans do you have for your visit?" he asked. "Perhaps you would allow me to escort you to the theatre some evening?"

"Actually, I don't care for playacting," said Arianna. Flicking a curl of faux hair from her cheek, she refused to be diverted from talk of flight. "Tell me, do you fly balloons, Mr. Lawrance?"

"No," he replied. "The information is merely for a friend."

A glib response, given just a little too quickly, she decided. He definitely merited further scrutiny.

"What about you, Mrs. Greeley? Do you aspire to soar through the heavens?"

"It must be a unique experience, to see the world from such a perspective. Everything must look very small and insignificant." Arianna deliberately drew out a pause. "I wonder if, like Icarus, one feels a great sense of power and freedom from constraint."

"Icarus crashed back to Earth in a fiery ball of flames," said Lawrance slowly.

"Oh, yes, he did, didn't he?" She smiled. "Ah well, so much for dreams of power and glory." Anxious to move on and observe the other guests, she pointedly looked around. "I hope your friend appreciates the effort you have made to help him. Now, if you will excuse me, I think I shall go sample some of Mr. Chittenden's refreshments. I am feeling a little . . . How do you English say it . . . peckish?"

"Yes, peckish—like a bird," replied Lawrance with an enigmatic smile. "Come, the parlor is this way."

Like a cocklebur, he seemed determined to stick to her skirts. Was he merely an incorrigible flirt who liked to attach himself to a lady? Or was there some other reason she couldn't shake him off?

Ignoring his attempts to talk about London's landmark sights, Arianna kept pondering the questions. Perhaps Miss Kirtland knew more about his background. If not, Saybrook could make some inquiries . . .

Spotting Lady Urania and her brother near the platters of cheese and shaved ham, she put aside the pesky thoughts of Lawrance to concentrate on them.

Once her self-appointed companion returned from the tables with a plate of food, Arianna asked, "Does Lady Urania ever venture out from her sibling's shadow?"

Lawrance eyed the pair over the rim of his wineglass. "I suppose there is a special bond between twins that the rest of us cannot fathom."

"Twins?" Arianna hadn't been aware of the connection and made a mental note to ask Miss Kirtland why it had not been mentioned. Details like that were important.

"Yes, and I believe that she is the eldest," went on Lawrance. "Which may explain why she fusses over him like a mother hen."

"In truth, the opposite appears the case to me," she replied pensively. "To my eye, it is Lord Canaday who seems solicitous of his sister's welfare. He looks like he feels beholden to protect her."

As Arianna watched, the lady in question took hold of her brother's arm, as if to steady a momentary tremble. Smiling, he shifted slightly in order to place his hand at the small of her back.

"Many men would resent the duty of playing constant guardian to an invalid sister," she mused. "And yet he seems quite good-natured about it."

"Indeed, he is a paragon of virtue," said Lawrance, though there seemed to be a slight shade of sarcasm to his voice.

"Are you friends with His Lordship?"

"We move in the same circles, so yes, we are quite well acquainted."

The reply, noted Arianna, did not really answer the question she had asked. For a moment, she debated whether to retreat, in hope of shaking off Lawrance and returning a little later on her own. However, given that time was of the essence, the chances of missing the siblings seemed too great a risk to take.

"Well, I do hope that I shall have a chance to get to know both of them better. I find his sister very bright and interesting to talk to, so if you will excuse me . . ."

His smile seemed to tighten ever so slightly, and yet Lawrance fell in step beside her.

Quelling her irritation, Arianna approached the siblings with a cheerful greeting. "Lady Urania, Lord Canaday, how lovely to encounter you again."

"Ah, Mrs. Greeley." The viscount turned and lifted her gloved hand to his lips. "How are you enjoying London?"

"Very much," she replied. "Though I confess, I have spent a good deal of time in frivolous amusements like visiting the Tower Zoo and taking in a performance of the acrobats at Astley's Amphitheatre."

"Work must be balanced by play," replied Canaday, a mischievous twinkle flashing in his eyes. "Astley's is an experience no visitor to our fair city should miss."

"It was most impressive. But on the whole, I do prefer more serious entertainments."

"Then you must be sure to attend the next meeting of the Mayfair Scientific Society," said Lady Urania. "We have a special lecturer visiting from Scotland. I am hosting it at Mortley House, as Professor McClellan will be staying with us during his visit."

Arianna's ears pricked up at the mention of Scotland. "What is the subject of the professor's talk?"

"Metallurgy," said Lady Urania. "I believe he has been analyzing some of the ancient iron found in Viking burial mounds and has some very interesting discoveries to recount."

"I will be sure to attend," she said. "I just heard Willoughby discussing the topic of his next lecture, and it, too, sounds fascinating. It is very impressive how active the London scientific community is."

"Which reminds me . . ." Canaday gave an apologetic shrug. "I'm afraid we have another event to attend." He glanced at his sister. "Are you ready to leave, Rainnie?"

"I . . ." Lady Urania drew a ragged breath and to Arianna it appeared that her eyes had an unnatural brightness—a febrile glow matched by two hot spots of color ridging her cheekbones. "I fear that I may have to let you go on without me."

"Are you feeling ill?" Canaday sounded a little alarmed.

"No, just a bit tired is all."

"Good heavens, why didn't you say so? I would have taken you home earlier," said her brother tightly.

"I do not always wish to ruin your evenings with my weaknesses." For all her fragility, Lady Urania managed to muster a note of command. "I insist you go about your evening as planned, Theus. You may drop me at Mortley House on your way to Lord Taft's gathering."

He reached down to rearrange her shawl. "I shall be happy to stay at home and read to you," he murmured.

"I won't hear of it," insisted his sister.

Canaday fixed Arianna with a rueful grimace. "What is your opinion, Mrs. Greeley? Am I a selfish sybarite to abandon her at home and go dashing off to another entertainment?"

"I think," said Arianna slowly, "you would be wise to respect your sister's wishes. She is not a child—and besides, it seems to me that she is stronger than she looks."

"There, you see!" said Lady Urania triumphantly. "Thank you for your stalwart support, Mrs. Greeley."

"Ah, I see I shall have to bow to feminine logic." As the viscount looked up, he flashed a wink from beneath his golden lashes. "Or feminine wiles." His voice dropped to a near whisper. "Like most men, I find it impossible to ignore the request of a beautiful woman."

"You are a true gentleman," said Arianna with a smile. "And a kind brother."

"Dare I hope that you will reward me with a waltz at Lady Brodhead's ball?" he asked.

"Unfortunately, I won't be able to attend the event, as I have a previous commitment." *To appear there as the Countess of Saybrook.*

"Perhaps some other time."

"Perhaps," she murmured. "Though to be honest, I am not very fond of dancing." *I am required to spin through enough fancy footwork as it is.*

Lawrance watched the twins move away through the archway and into the shadows of the corridor before quaffing the rest of his champagne punch in one quick swallow. "What a charming fellow, eh? I daresay he puts the rest of us gentlemen to blush with his sensitive nature and soulful smiles."

"Indeed. A female appreciates it greatly when her opinion is solicited and then given proper respect." She smiled sweetly. "It happens so rarely."

At long last Lawrance seemed to get the hint, for when she turned a few moments later to leave, he did not follow.

"We saved you some chocolate and hazelnut confections, Lady S." Henning lifted his whisky glass in salute as she entered the library. "Though perhaps you are not hungry. Scientific soirees usually feature a great deal of food, as scholars tend to get lost in their work and forget to eat during the day."

Still clad in her urchin garb, Arianna moved to the hearth and warmed her hands over the dancing flames. "In truth I am famished. The refreshments were unpalatable—dry cheese, bland ham, stale cakes." She rubbed at a crick in her neck. "But the company provided much food for thought."

Saybrook poured her a glass of port and set out a plate of salted Marcona almonds on the side table by her favorite armchair. "Sit down and have some sustenance before you tell us what you learned."

"Thank you." She sank gratefully into the soft leather and heaved a sigh. "I must be getting old. This constant changing of personas is proving a trifle fatiguing." A wiggle of her toes sent up tiny puffs of steam from her wet boots. "Ouch—Mrs. Greeley's evening shoes are one size too small."

The surgeon stifled a snort. "When you get to be *my* age, then you may grouse about sore feet or stiff necks. At the moment I have precious little sympathy."

"Wretch," she responded. "Speaking of which, how is your shoulder?"

Henning lifted his arm and waggled it back and forth. "Nearly good as new," he said, carefully masking a grimace.

"You are nearly as good an actor as I am," she said dryly.

Her husband perched a hip on the arm of her chair and helped himself to a handful of the nuts. "Your recovery would no doubt progress more quickly if you would stay here for a while longer. God only knows what noxious forms of molds and lichens are growing in your living quarters."

"I don't charge them rent, so they have agreed to leave me in peace," retorted Henning. "And remember, the ancient Greeks believed that a healthy body required a healthy mind—"

"Actually, it was the other way around," murmured Saybrook. "But I take your point."

"My point is that my patients need me, and keeping busy will prevent other things from festering." The surgeon reached for a pastry. "Though I will miss your chocolate creations."

"I shall make sure you don't starve," said Arianna.

Her husband crunched an almond. "Whenever you are ready, I wouldn't mind being fed some information."

She took a last sip of port and then set it aside. "I've a plateful to offer. To begin with, what do you know of a Mr. Henry Lawrance?"

Saybrook drew his brows together. "Nothing to speak of."

"He's tall and a bit of a macaroni, with well-tailored clothing that whispers of money," she went on. "I first met him at the institution reception, and he was there tonight—and I couldn't seem to shake him from my skirts. It was . . . suspicious."

"There are reasons other than espionage that a gentleman might want to attach himself to you," pointed out the earl dryly. "Especially as Mrs. Greeley pads her already considerable charms."

"That may be. But when that same gentleman is approached by a balloon expert and told that the research he requested on lighter-than-air gases is ready to be picked up, one tends to think that amorous activities are not his primary reason for being at the gathering."

"You are sure?" asked her husband.

"Quite. And he seemed a little unhappy that I overheard the exchange," replied Arianna. "Another thing—I was introduced to him by Miss Kirtland, and my impression was that they knew each other."

Saybrook's frown deepened. "I shall pay her a visit in the morning to ask about—"

She cut him off. "I think it would be more efficient for the investigation if you pursue information through your other sources while I speak with Miss Kirtland about Lawrance. She and I are, after all, trying to learn to work together."

He rose and went to refill his glass with Spanish brandy. "Very well. That makes some sense."

Was she only imagining the note of reluctance in his voice? Fatigue—along with the faint hiss of the coals—was muddling her judgment. "That's not all," she hurried on. "The balloon expert, a man by the name of Brynn-Smith, mentioned that the aeronauts from the Artillery Grounds have taken to gathering at a new tea shop on Montague Street that serves up special coffee and chocolate drinks. Its proprietor is a Spanish woman."

"Interesting," mused her husband. "It certainly sounds worth a visit."

"Aye," said Henning. "But will it stir suspicion if ye are seen sniffing around men who are involved in flight?"

"My interest in chocolate is no secret," said the earl.

"Still, Renard is a cunning varlet, and the coincidence may be too great," insisted the surgeon.

"Basil raises a good point," said Arianna. "But what about me? I could strike up a friendship with the proprietor over chocolate recipes. Two females discussing cooking would draw far less attention. For all of Renard's cleverness, he can't know about my exploits in our first two investigations, so he's likely to underestimate a woman."

"I take it you are suggesting the Countess of Saybrook become a regular visitor to the shop."

Arianna let out a chuckle. "Despite my skills at deception, even I would be hard-pressed to carry off a third persona."

"Thank God," quipped her husband. "Two of you are already causing me twice my usual worries."

"Don't fret about me. I shall simply be sitting in a snug little shop, enjoying hot chocolate and pastries while trying to pick up any useful morsels of information," she retorted. "Leaving you free to find the most important piece to this puzzle. It seems to me that it's imperative for you to locate Sir George Cayley." No one in London seemed to know the baronet's present whereabouts. "Any further luck in trying to track him down?"

The earl shook his head. "Not yet. But I have a meeting tomorrow evening with another source that may prove helpful."

"While I am attending a ball with Constantina and Miss Kirtland," said Arianna, "in order to learn more about Lord Reginald's family."

Henning levered to his feet. "I'll make a few inquiries among my friends," he said vaguely.

"We would rather you rest and recover," said Arianna. "Sandro and I can manage."

The surgeon waved off the suggestion. "I'm not about to desert the field of battle because a bit of my blood has been shed."

Arianna watched the lamplight flicker over his gaunt face. It wasn't Henning's physical wound that was cause for concern, she thought. Since coming back from Scotland he had been . . . different. *Distant. Detached.* As if his nephew's death had cut a chasm between him and Saybrook, no matter their years of friendship.

"No one questions your courage or your resolve, Baz. But keep in mind that victory is rarely achieved by a commander who takes the fight personally," counseled Saybrook.

"I don't need a lecture on tactics, laddie," replied Henning. "If you want to win the war against a cunning enemy general, ye'll need to destroy not only him but all his field officers. So while you concentrate on Renard, I'll do some reconnoitering of my own."

13

From Lady Arianna's Chocolate Notebooks

Intense Chocolate Mousse Cake

10 ounces bittersweet chocolate
9 tablespoons unsalted butter
6 large eggs, separated
Pinch of salt
¾ cup granulated sugar
2 tablespoons brandy
1 teaspoon confectioners' sugar

1. Preheat the oven to 350°F. Cover the outside of a 9-inch springform pan with a double layer of foil. Using a microwave oven or double boiler, melt the chocolate and butter together; set aside to cool.
2. Using an electric mixer, whisk the egg whites and salt until thick. Add ¼ cup of the granulated sugar, and continue to whisk until stiff and shiny but not dry. Set aside. In another bowl, whisk together the egg yolks and remaining ½ cup granulated sugar until pale, frothy and increased

in volume. Whisk in the brandy. Fold in the cooled chocolate mixture.

3. Place a kettle of water over heat, and bring it to a boil. Fold
about ½ cup of the whisked egg whites into the chocolate
mixture to lighten it. Gently fold in the remaining whites,
being careful not to let the mixture deflate. Pour the mixture
into the prepared springform pan, and place the springform
pan in a roasting pan. Add boiling water to the roasting
pan to come halfway up the side of the springform pan.
Bake for 45 minutes; the top of the cake will be hard and
the inside will be gooey.

4. Remove the cake pan from the water, and place on a rack
to cool completely. Unwrap the foil and remove the side of
the springform pan. Place the cake on a serving platter.
Just before serving, dust the top with confectioners' sugar
passed through a sieve.

"Well, this is *quite* a crush." Lowering her quizzing glass,
Constantina gave a tiny nod of satisfaction at the
crowd funneling into the ballroom. They had taken momentary
refuge in one of the shallow alcoves created by the decorative
colonnading that ran along one of the walls. "As I suspected, no
one wanted to miss the festivities. Lord and Lady Brodhead are
known for serving sumptuous suppers and superb wines."

Arianna drew in a lungful of air, its warmth already sticky
with the lush scents of hothouse flowers and expensive perfumes.
"I have never understood why the word 'crush' is considered
such an accolade by Society."

"Kindly refrain from any further sarcasm tonight." Constantina waggled a warning brow. "I know your opinion of the *ton*,
but remember, if you wish to begin cultivating friends and allies
to help with Antonia's come-out, it's best to use honey, not vin-
egar."

"Don't worry. I can ooze sweetness when I choose." Arianna flashed her great-aunt by marriage a conspiratorial wink. "After all, I got your nephew to bite."

Constantina stifled a snort of amusement. "He prefers tartness to a mouthful of sugar."

"I trust you are not implying that I am a *tart*."

Another laugh. "I have no doubt that a good many interesting nouns apply to your former life. But be that as it may, tonight you are a countess." The dowager's gaze lingered for a moment on Arianna's stylish ball gown, fashioned in a subtle shade of smoke-tinged emerald silk. "A lady of supreme elegance and refinement."

The teasing was helping to unknot her nerves. She had avoided going out in Society, so the glittering opulence of the occasion was a little intimidating. "Never fear. If I can play the role of a street urchin, I can play the role of an aristocrat." Lifting her chin a notch, Arianna assumed a pose of regal hauteur. "Though I admit that I feel a little out of place in such gilded grandeur."

"As do I," muttered Sophia.

A wink of light sparked within the recessed niche of the colonnading as the dowager once again raised her gold-rimmed quizzing glass. Magnified by the faceted lens, the pale gray eye took on an accentuated clarity.

Age had not diminished its sharpness, thought Arianna, as the orb subjected the earl's friend to a thorough scrutiny. "Remind me again why you are accompanying us tonight, Miss Kirtland?"

"Moral support," said Arianna quickly, before Sophia could answer. "We have become friends through Sandro—Miss Kirtland is a very accomplished scientist. So he thought I would be more at ease if I had the company of a kindred soul."

"Hmmph." The jeweled walking stick tap-tapped on the polished parquet. "An odd choice." The dowager took another moment to study Sophia. "You are the Duchess of Brentford's granddaughter, aren't you?"

"Yes."

"You remind me of your grandmother, gel—you've got her strong bones and lively eyes. And from what I hear, your intelligence is not lacking. So it surprises me that you've spent years holed up in your little lair, afraid—"

"I'm *not* afraid," said Sophia tightly, her voice barely more than a whisper. "I—I loathe the artifice and snobbery of Polite Society and choose to show my disdain by avoiding it."

"Well, if you really care about changing its prejudices, you're going about it all wrong," said the dowager bluntly. "You ought to come out occasionally with your head held high. Show your disdain by being yourself and forcing the tabbies to accept you."

Sophia inhaled sharply, the short, staccato rasp echoing off the fluted marble.

"It's not easy, I know. If you feel a little shaky, simply imagine whoever you are looking at naked—that usually strips away all pretenses." A glint of mischief hung on Constantina's silvery lashes. "Just don't look at the Prince Regent—the thought of seeing his pizzle would make anyone fall into a dead faint."

Biting her lips to keep from laughing, Arianna slanted a look at her companion. If one wasn't used to the dowager's rapier tongue . . .

To her credit, Sophia showed some mettle. "I doubt one could catch a glimpse of his pizzle beneath all those rolls of fat. Unless, of course, he were allowed to retain his corset. Still, not a pretty picture."

"That's the spirit," murmured the dowager with a flourish of her walking stick. "Now, I don't know what you two are up to, but I wager it's something interesting. What a pity that I'm not allowed to know the details."

"Aunt Constantina—" began Arianna.

"Oh pish, I understand. Sandro is probably quaking in his high-top Hessians, fearing that I would get myself into trouble." *Tap, tap.* "When he gets to be my age, he will understand that the prospect of trouble is rather exciting."

"I'll explain as much as I can, but . . ."

The music started, and Arianna paused for a moment to watch the gentlemen and ladies spin by, the swirl of jewel-tone silks and glittering gems a colorful contrast to the coal black evening coats and starched white cravats.

Pomp and privilege dancing with treachery and treason.

"But I, too, am concerned," she finished softly. "So you must allow me to go slowly."

"Fair enough." The dowager fingered the rope of pearls looped around her neck. "Is there anyone in particular you wish to meet?"

Arianna hesitated. "Whoever knows the social connections of the *ton*'s leading families and likes to gossip."

"Hmmph." Turning a basilisk stare on the crowd, Constantina tapped her stick in time to the music. "Very well, I have some ideas. Now, both of you square your shoulders and come along. We have work to do."

Moving along the perimeter of the dance floor, the dowager stopped every few steps to exchange greetings with the other guests.

"Lady Sterling seems to know *everyone* here," murmured Sophia, observing yet another gentleman insist on dipping a courtly bow over the dowager's hand. "But I'm not sure this experiment of bringing me along is going to work. I don't think anyone knows me from Adam." A pause. "Or Eve."

Despite her sardonic words, the earl's scholarly friend did not go unrecognized, noted Arianna. The flicker of surreptitious glances and low whispers followed their progress through the milling crowd.

"Miss Kirtland?" A sandy-haired gentleman with a saber scar cutting across his left cheek flashed a hesitant smile. "Good heavens, it *is* you! How nice to see you."

Sophia looked a little surprised at the warm greeting. "M-Mr. Bellis," she stammered, inclining her head a fraction. "H-how are you?"

"Oh, a little worse for wear," he said wryly, touching the puckered red slash. "But quite happy to have exchanged my sword for a plow. Father shuffled off his mortal coil last year, so I am now running the estate."

Recalling her manners, Sophia quickly made the introductions. "Lady Saybrook, this is Michael Bellis, a childhood friend from Somerset."

"I heard quite a lot about your husband during the Peninsular campaign, milady," said Bellis politely. "He was quite the hero."

"And so, it appears, were you," said Arianna, eyeing his scar.

Bellis colored. "Oh, no, not at all. I simply stumbled into the path of flying steel." Looking uncomfortable, he quickly changed the subject. "Might I engage you for the next set of dances, Miss Kirtland? George and Charles would be delighted to make their greetings, and you remember my cousin Suzanna . . ."

Arianna gave Sophia a discreet nudge to remind her of the reason they were both here.

Friend and foe—we must find a way to discern who was whom.

"Do go on," she urged. "I see Constantina waving her walking stick at me. No doubt there is another distant relative I must meet. We shall meet up again later."

The dowager was indeed tapping a summons, and for the next hour, Arianna found herself marched around the room and introduced to a select group of Society gossips.

Apparently males gabbled just as much as females, reflected Arianna, for several gentlemen were included. After dutifully dancing with several partners, she finally managed to rejoin the dowager and catch her breath.

"Lord Bertram is even a worse dancer than I am. I have several squashed toes to prove it."

"My feet are aching a bit too," replied Constantina. "So if you will excuse me, I think I will go have a seat with the Dragons . . ." She gestured to a group of turbaned matrons sitting next to a large marble urn festooned with flowers. "And catch up on the latest *on-dits*."

"By all means," replied Arianna. "I shall make my way to the refreshment table. My throat is parched from so much talking." The blaze of the chandeliers, the clink of crystal, the trill of laughter, the kaleidoscope of colors—all her senses were feeling a bit overworked.

How people spin through this night after night is a mystery to me—the superficiality would soon squeeze the life out of me.

"Ah, but I've a far more pressing mystery to solve," she said under her breath. She stilled her steps for a moment to watch the dancers twirl into a waltz. More and more of the faces were looking familiar . . .

A flash of scarlet caught her eye but just as quickly disappeared in a swirl of blues and greens. Shifting her gaze, she saw Sophia at the far end of the dance floor, partnered by Henry Lawrance.

Ha.

With an inward smile, Arianna edged through the crowd and positioned herself to intercept the couple as soon as the music ended.

Two can tiptoe through a dance of deception, Mr. Lawrance.

"Oh, there you are, Miss Kirtland." Arianna waited for the last trilling of the violins to fade before feigning a note of surprise. "I was hoping that I might find you."

"Lady Saybrook," acknowledged Sophia. Maintaining a mask of bland politeness, she asked, "Are you acquainted with my partner, Mr. Lawrance?"

"I don't believe we have been introduced," murmured Arianna.

"Mr. Lawrance, allow me to present the Countess of Saybrook."

"Charmed, madam." Lawrance stared for a moment before bowing to brush his lips to her hand.

Over his tousled curls, Sophia quirked an inquiring brow.

In silent answer Arianna gave a tiny nod at a shadowy recess behind an arrangement of potted palms.

"How odd that our paths have not crossed before, Lady Saybrook," he said on rising. "Being the frivolous fellow that I am, I rarely miss a party here in Mayfair, and yet I've never seen you among the guests."

"How can you be so sure?" she countered, deciding to test his *sangfroid*.

Lawrance leaned in a little closer. "Because I don't easily forget a beautiful lady."

"A very disarming answer." Arianna slid back a step. "Are you always so clever?"

"How should I answer that?" he asked. "If I say yes, then I appear a pompous ass. And if I say no, then I appear a witless fool."

"Then perhaps it is wise to remain silent," answered Arianna coolly. "Now, if you don't mind, I wish to speak with Miss Kirtland."

Lawrance smiled but didn't budge. "Not at all."

"In private," she added, batting her lashes. "We have some feminine matters to discuss."

At that, he had no choice but to gracefully withdraw.

"Tell me, how well do you him?" asked Arianna, drawing Sophia behind the screen of swaying fronds.

"Lawrance? I've known him since we were adolescents, riding neck and leather over the hills of Somerset." Her face screwed in thought as she considered the question more carefully. "As you see, he has an easy manner and tends to play the role of careless fribble. But beneath the *bon mots* and bantering flirtations, I think he is a good deal sharper than he lets on." The slivered shapes of the leafy shadows made her eyes appear to narrow. "Why do you ask?"

Arianna quickly explained about the encounter at Chittenden's soiree, and her chance discovery of Lawrence's interest in aeronautics.

"You think he may be Renard?"

"I am not leaping to any conclusions yet," she replied. "However, I do think he merits careful scrutiny. Sandro is making inquiries through his contacts. Now that you are aware of our concerns, it would be helpful if you could see what information you can tease out of him."

Was that a frown flitting across Miss Kirtland's face? The uncertain light was making it difficult to gauge her reactions.

"Lawrance seems to like you," went on Arianna, "so he may be coaxed into making a slip of the tongue."

Sophia looked away. "Nonsense. We are simply familiar with each other; that is all."

"It's more than that," she pressed. "I am used to reading the subtle shifts of expressions on a man's face—at times I depended on that ability to save my life. Lawrance admires you. And though you may think me callous or conniving to suggest it, that is something a female may turn to her advantage."

"Y-you may possess that skill," said Sophia in a halting voice. "I certainly don't."

"Trust me, you have far more power than you imagine, Miss Kirtland."

"I doubt—" Sophia suddenly broke off in midsentence, the shadows accentuating the fact that in the space of a heartbeat, her face had gone as pale as ashes.

"What is it?" Arianna turned to see what had caught Sophia's eye.

A tall, broad-shouldered officer in a scarlet tunic dripping with gold braid had just joined a trio of ladies standing at the edge of the dance floor, and his elaborate greeting set off a flutter of fans and a tittering of giggles.

Clearly enjoying the attention, he threw back his head and joined in the laughter.

Bloody hell. Arianna sucked in her breath.

It was Sophia who whispered the name. "Stoughton."

"You know him?" asked Arianna.

Her companion continued to stare straight ahead in unblinking silence.

"Miss Kirtland . . . Sophia."

Sophia finally turned her head, but a glassy look still glazed her eyes.

Shaking off her own shock, Arianna took Sophia's arm and drew her back through the archway and past the card room.

"This way," she ordered, turning down a dimly lit corridor. "Let us find the withdrawing room and splash some water on your face."

Sophia stumbled along unresisting, as if in a daze.

Spotting a half-opened door, Arianna stopped to peek inside. It appeared to be some sort of game room—there were several backgammon boards stacked atop a storage chest, and a chess set was arrayed on a black-and-white checkered table, waiting for someone to come along and make the first move.

"In here," she ordered, pulling the door shut behind them and turning the key in the lock.

"W-what . . ." The fog seemed to be clearing from her companion's head.

Arianna shoved her down into one of the leather armchairs and rushed to the sideboard, where she quickly poured a large measure of brandy.

"Drink!" she ordered.

Sophia obediently gulped down a long swallow. "Arrgh!" The color came rushing back to her face as she sputtered a choked cough. "Good God, that is *ghastly* stuff."

"Yes, but it clears the cobwebs from your head." Picking up a poker, Arianna stirred the banked fire to life. "Feeling better?"

"Yes, much." Sophia took a tiny sip this time, and it seemed to go down more smoothly. "Thank you."

"De nada," she murmured in Spanish, then added an unlady-

like oath in the same language. "Whenever you are ready, would you kindly explain what the devil that was all about?"

* * *

Getting no answer to his soft knock, Saybrook eased the latch open and let himself inside the surgery. All was still inside, save for the usual creaking of the ancient beams and the scurrying of mice within the woodwork. The silence seemed to indicate that Henning was asleep. And yet, on approaching the building, he had seen the hint of a candle burning behind the window draperies, which stirred a flicker of unease. An untended flame could so easily tip over in the breeze, and with the assortment of chemicals lying around . . .

He moved quietly over the stone tiles of the entrance hall and down the short passageway to the private parlor. Sure enough, there was a faint spill of light showing from beneath the closed door. Pressing his hand to the rough planking, he gave a small push.

"Sandro!" Henning spun around in his chair, a look oddly akin to guilt spasming across his features. "I didna hear you come in."

"I should have knocked louder," said Saybrook. "But I didn't wish to wake you if you were sleeping." He glanced at the other man half-hidden in the surgeon's shadow. "I didn't mean to interrupt your meeting. I'll come back another time."

"Nay, nay." Henning gave an airy wave. "William was just leaving."

The earl couldn't help but notice that with the other hand, the surgeon was surreptitiously sliding some papers from his blotter into his desk drawer.

"Gud night te ye, Major." The man gave a ragged salute as he sidled by and melted into the darkness.

"One of the riflemen from the Third Regiment of Foot Guards," explained Henning with a smile that seemed a trifle forced. "Needed a salve for a boil on his leg. Nasty things, boils are, especially if left untreated."

The floorboards groaned as the earl shifted his stance. "Indeed," he answered blandly, taking a packet from his coat pocket. "I, too, have medicines to dispense. Arianna sends an assortment of chocolate wafers and almond confections. She and Bianca are concerned that you don't starve during your convalescence."

"Tell Lady S that I—and my bread box—are always happy to receive her prescriptions." The surgeon shifted uncomfortably in his chair. "But I would guess ye didna come here at this hour simply to deliver chocolate."

"Correct," said Saybrook. "I thought you might be interested in accompanying me on a late-night visit to a man of science." He dropped the packet on the desk. "But never mind. I can see that you have other concerns on your plate."

"Hold yer water, laddie." The surgeon rose and hastily tugged his rumpled coat into place. "As if a bloody scratch would keep me from lending ye a hand."

"I don't want to tax your strength, Baz."

Henning dropped his gaze and began rooting through the pasteboard boxes piled on his desk. "Auch, I'm tough as nails." A coil of string and a small scalpel went into his pockets, followed by a pocket pistol and an extra charge of powder and bullets. "There—best to be prepared for trouble whenever I venture out with you."

The earl didn't smile at the jest. "On second thought, it might be best if I went alone."

Their eyes met.

"I've drawn you into enough trouble," Saybrook added softly. "I need to pursue this lead, for it may bring me closer to Renard. But be assured I haven't forgotten your nephew or the fact that his death is a mystery that needs to be resolved."

A gruff exhale stirred the air between them. "Trouble is rarely simple, laddie, or rarely black-and-white. It wasn't your fault Angus made decisions that put him into danger. Ye must, in good conscience, do yer job. As must I."

"I trust that those two things are one and the same, Baz. And that we will do them together."

Henning remained silent.

"Patience, Baz," counseled Saybrook. "As for tonight, I don't expect trouble—"

"Aye, but ye never know when it will creep up and try to bite ye on the arse," replied his friend. "So ye need someone ye can trust to be watching yer back."

Saybrook lifted a dark brow.

Ignoring the implied question, Henning added a narrow roll of linen to the other items, then blew out the candle. "Let's be off."

The scuff of their steps was quickly lost in the scrabbling sounds of the back alleyways. The earl led the way through a series of narrow streets to a small square of shabby but respectable buildings grouped around a small, unpruned garden.

"Who are we here to see?" asked Henning, gazing around at the darkened windows.

"A chemist by the name of Brynn-Smith. He works on gases used to propel the big balloons used for manned flight."

The surgeon chafed his hands together as a frigid gust swirled through the night. "Is he working with Cayley?"

"That," answered Saybrook, "is what I intend to find out."

14

From Lady Arianna's Chocolate Notebooks

Coffee Crunch Bars

2 cups all-purpose flour
½ teaspoon baking powder
¼ teaspoon salt
1 cup (2 sticks) plus 2 tablespoons unsalted butter,
at room temperature
1¼ cups firmly packed dark brown sugar
2 tablespoons instant espresso powder
½ teaspoon almond extract
1 cup semisweet chocolate chips
½ cup sliced almonds

1. Preheat the oven to 325°F. Whisk the flour, baking powder, and salt in a medium bowl to blend.
2. Using an electric mixer, beat the butter and sugar in another medium bowl until blended, about 2 minutes. Add the espresso powder and almond extract; beat 1 minute.
3. Stir in the flour mixture in 3 additions, mixing until just

absorbed after each addition. Stir in the chocolate chips
and almonds (dough will be thick).

4. Turn the dough out onto an ungreased, rimmed baking
   sheet. Using your hands, press the dough into a 12-inch
   square. Pierce all over with a fork at 1-inch intervals.

5. Bake until the edges are lightly browned and beginning to
   crisp, 45 to 50 minutes. Cool on the baking sheet for 1
   minute. Cut into 48 bars. Immediately transfer to a rack to
   cool. The bars will crisp as they cool.

"Devil," repeated Sophia. She swallowed hard. "That is an
apt word for such a . . . creature from Hell."

Arianna remained silent, waiting for her to go on at her own
pace.

"Though perhaps I am maligning Lucifer." Sophia gave a
sardonic grimace. "For the Devil makes no bones about who he
is, while Stoughton cloaks his evil behind an array of gaudy
medals and gold braid."

"Would you like some more brandy?" Arianna asked, for in
the guttering light of the candelabra, it seemed that her companion's face had once again gone as cold and white as Carrara
marble.

"No." A sigh. "I—I have never talked about this with anyone."

"If you would rather not . . ."

"You did say it was important to know each other's vulner-
abilities." Sophia's mouth quirked. "On second thought, perhaps
I do need another small splash of brandy to loosen my tongue."

Arianna wordlessly refilled her glass.

Lifting it to the red-gold flames, Sophia slowly spun it between her fingers, watching the slivered shades of amber dance
across the darkened wall. "Oh, it is hard to know where to begin.
I was a fool, I suppose."

"Aren't we all at times?" said Arianna. "If it makes you feel any better, I have done more than a few things that would make your cockles curl."

Sophia flashed a wry smile. "Do females have cockles?"

"I haven't a clue." Arianna grinned back at her. "Look, why not just spit it out? Whatever it is, I promise you that I won't fall into a fit of megrims."

"Very well." Another sigh, another swallow of spirits.

Arianna was beginning to wonder whether she might have to find a footman to help carry her companion out to the carriage.

"To make a long story short, when I was seventeen I fell in love," began Sophia, "with a young man my father deemed beneath our family's notice. He wanted me to marry money, a title— all the trappings that would give him the power and prestige he thought he deserved. You see, he had squandered his own inheritance, and my grandfather refused to go on paying for his profligate spending. Younger sons were expected to make their own way in the world, but my father thought that grossly unfair."

"This is, you know, an oft-told tale," murmured Arianna.

"Yes, I know. And my story follows the usual plot of a horrid novel—I surrendered my virtue to my true love, and we made plans to elope to Scotland. Indeed, we were nearly at the border when my father caught up with us." Her voice tightened. "He had bribed the local militia commander to accompany him—and to keep the affair silent."

"Stoughton?" asked Arianna, though she was certain of the answer.

"Stoughton," confirmed Sophia. "Who proceeded to knock Edward from the perch of our rented gig and slowly, methodically, *gleefully* thrash him to a bloody pulp." Her eyes squeezed shut. "It was horrible. Neddy was barely more than a boy. He was slight and slender—a gentle-natured poet who planned on going into the Church. While Stoughton was a big-muscled brute who clearly took pleasure in inflicting pain." The dregs in the glass swirled slowly, silently. "My father dragged me back home, cursing all the way about damaged goods. I learned that Neddy died within hours of the beating."

"I'm so sorry."

"To add insult to injury, Stoughton had the nerve to suggest to my father that he take me off my father's hands." Sophia shuddered. "Though God knows why. I had only a modest dowry, and the fact that my grandmother was leaving me a generous bequest was not yet known."

Arianna found it interesting that Sophia seemed unaware of her striking looks and their effect on men. But she didn't know her well enough to broach such a personal subject. Instead, she merely pointed out a more mundane fact of life. "A duke's influence could be important for an ambitious military officer."

"His motive didn't matter. Needless to say, I refused—and informed my father that I had no intention of marrying anyone. Ever."

Ah, youthful pride.

Sophia lifted her gaze. "So now you know my sordid little secret."

"There is nothing sordid about being young and desperately in love," replied Arianna gently. "Now is not the time, but at some point I shall share some stories that will assure you I know what 'sordid' truly means."

"Oh." Setting the glass down on the chess table, Sophia plucked at the folds of her skirts, as if smoothing the silk could put her emotions back into order. "I hope that I have not stirred unhappy memories for you."

Arianna shook her head. "I am slowly learning to live with my mistakes—not to say that it is easy. It isn't. But it helps to keep moving forward, rather than to allow your feet to remain mired in the past."

"Wise words," said Sophia thoughtfully. After a moment of meditation, she pressed her palms together. "How is it that you know Stoughton?"

"Because he is the murderous bastard responsible for the

death of Basil Henning's nephew. Sandro had several confrontations with him." Arianna clarified the details of the Scottish trip.

"Why is he here in London?" mused Sophia.

"A good question. I mean to find out, for along with trapping Renard, I intend to learn the truth of why Basil's nephew was shot. It seems too great a coincidence to be merely a random act of fate." She looked over at the black-and-white chess figures ready to square off in combat on the checkered field of battle. Pawns and knights, rooks and queens . . .

Ah, the most powerful figure is a female.

"I've an idea." Arianna rose and began to pace back and forth in front of the hearth. "First, let me help you down to the carriage so José can drive you home—"

"Bollocks," exclaimed Sophia, her chin taking on a mulish jut. "I'm not going anywhere. I may not be as experienced as you are in intrigue, but I can learn."

"Miss Kirtland, you've suffered a severe shock." A shade of amusement crept into Arianna's tone. "Not to mention the fact that you're a trifle foxed."

"I'm not foxed. I'm just pleasantly tipsy." A pause. "Just because you know all manner of clever tricks to deal with men doesn't mean I should be trundled off to bed like a helpless child."

The momentary truce seemed over as Sophia's prickliness reasserted itself.

Like me, she does not like letting anyone get too close.

Heaving an inward sigh, Arianna said, "I wasn't implying any such thing. The choice is, of course, yours."

Her companion's scowl softened.

"If you stay, it will mean facing up to your Devil. Are you sure you are ready for that?"

"Yes," answered Sophia stoutly. "It's time for me to finally take a stand and fight back."

"You need not throw any punches this evening," replied Arianna. "We are simply going to reconnoiter, so to speak. All I need for you to do is introduce me to Stoughton. He caught only a glimpse of me dressed as a male, so I doubt he'll recognize me in my present persona." She took another turn in front of the fire. "I should be able to learn what has brought him to London."

"But once he sees Saybrook, he can't help but realize that it was the two of you who were overseeing Lord Grentham's investigation in St. Andrews."

"You're right. However, for the moment we hold the advantage of surprise, so I mean to use it. If we have to change tactics later on, so be it. Sandro has stressed to me that a good field general always remains flexible."

"I am looking forward to hearing more about the art of warfare." Sophia slowly clenched and unclenched her hands. "Will you . . . will you help me learn how to strip off my gloves and get my nails dirty?"

"If you will help me learn how to structure a more formal course of education. I should like to put together some reading lists, on subjects like literature and philosophy."

Sophia quirked a rueful smile. "I think you will have the harder of the two teaching tasks."

"Don't be so sure of it. I have a feeling you have a natural aptitude for clandestine intrigue." With a flick of her finger, she knocked the black king from the chessboard. "Shall we return to the ballroom and make the first move in this game?"

"Ye know, it would be nice if we could ever pay a visit to someone at a civilized hour," groused Henning as he blew out a puff of vapor and followed Saybrook's careful circuit of the garden's wrought-iron fence. "Lud, it's colder than a witch's tit out here."

"You are welcome to come back with me and warm your gizzard with hot chocolate when we are done here," said the earl. "But for now, stubble the bellyaching."

"Let us hope that we're not going to find another dead body," said the surgeon mournfully. "Though that is likely wishful thinking."

Saybrook stopped to count the doorways. "It's that one," he said, pointing to a dark portal topped by a classical pediment carved out of marble. Moonlight fluttered over the stone, showing that soot had darkened it to a dingy gray. "Look, if you've no stomach for the task, there's no need to come any farther. I simply wish to talk with Brynn-Smith without anyone knowing of the visit." He made a wry face. "And as we know, night covers a multitude of sins."

A frosty grunt was the only reply.

"Perhaps I should abandon the idea of writing a book about chocolate in favor of one about the locks of London," muttered the earl as he slid a steel probe from his boot.

"I know a number of people who would eat that up," quipped the surgeon. "I trust you would include diagrams for those who can't read."

"Very humorous." *Click.* "Our quarry's rooms are up one flight and at the back, overlooking the alleyway."

The landing was muddled in shadows, and Saybrook took a moment to strike a lucifer match.

"Oh, bloody hell," swore Henning under his breath as a flame sparked to life. The flare showed that the door to Brynn-Smith's rooms was slightly ajar. No light was visible through the crack.

"Hand me your pistol and stand back," whispered Saybrook as the match fizzled out.

"The devil I will." The surgeon slipped both the firearm and the scalpel from his pocket. "You go in first with the bullets, and I'll back you up with my blade."

Taking the weapon without argument, the earl crept forward, with Henning right on his heels. He was only a few steps from the threshold when the door banged open and a dark shape came barreling out.

As a lowered shoulder slammed into his gut, Saybrook twisted and threw out an arm to shove Henning clear. The force of the impact knocked him down, but he scrambled to his knees just as the assailant regained his own footing and leapt for the stairs.

The earl's lunge caught the man's coattail, spinning him off balance. Snarling, he lashed a kick at Saybrook's head, forcing him to let go of his hold.

Ducking low, the earl made one last desperate grab as the attacker stumbled, but his fingers snagged only a pinch of fabric.

A curse, echoed an instant later by the hiss of a fresh match igniting.

Wrenching free, the man tore off, leaving Saybrook holding a scrap of silk.

"Ye all right, laddie?" Pushing up to a sitting position, Henning held the lucifer aloft.

The earl sucked in a deep breath and nodded. "Did you get a look at him?"

"Just a wee glimpse. Not quite your height . . . lean . . . fair hair showing beneath his hat." He bit back a grunt as he gingerly got to his feet. "And his coat looked expensive."

"Not much to go on," muttered Saybrook. He looked down at the strip of fabric in his hand, then tucked it into his pocket and bent down to retrieve the dropped pistol.

Grimacing, Henning flexed his injured shoulder. "Sorry. Yer shove knocked me arse over teakettle, and I'm not moving as fast as usual these days."

"Let us check the rooms," said the earl after a long moment. "Though I fear we shall find Brynn-Smith in no condition to talk."

"Auch, there's a chance he was out for the evening."

A sudden hiss of phosphorus swallowed the match light, leaving them in the gloom.

Saybrook rubbed his fingers together. "Seeing as our assailant's coat was wet with blood, I highly doubt it."

A quick inspection of the chemist's rooms confirmed the

grim surmise. Brynn-Smith—for now they assumed it was him—lay faceup on the carpet, a knife protruding from his chest. His sightless eyes still held a look of mild surprise.

"Merde," muttered the surgeon after checking for a pulse. "He's not been dead for long. The flesh is still warm."

"There doesn't appear to be any sign of struggle," said Saybrook after checking the dead man's hands for scrapes or flesh embedded under the nails. "I would guess that he knew his assailant."

"Who wanted to be very sure that certain information remained a secret," said Henning slowly. They had lit an oil lamp, and the yellowish light showed that the parlor and bedchamber had been ransacked.

"So it would seem." The earl sat back on his haunches. "A theft could be done while Brynn-Smith was out, so we must also assume that the chemist needed to be silenced. I wonder whether he had made a discovery, or whether he was just privy to someone's research."

"Well, it's too late to ask him," said Henning sourly. "Now what?"

The earl rose and took a quick look through the other two rooms. On returning, he answered, "There's little more we can do tonight. I was going to ask Brynn-Smith if he knew Cayley's present whereabouts . . ." He absently wiped his hands on his trousers. "It seems even more imperative that we locate the inventor."

"Aye," grunted Henning. "Before someone else gets to him first."

"Take several deep breaths. It helps calm the nerves," counseled Arianna as they paused several steps away from the entrance to the ballroom.

"I won't fall into a fit of megrims," assured Sophia. They had decided on a strategy to confront Stoughton, but it demanded that she keep her composure. "Indeed, I am looking forward to playing my part."

"Don't overdo it," replied Arianna. "Let us position ourselves to attract his attention. Given his hubris, I am sure he will say something to you. You will have to improvise in order to pique his pride, and that will allow me a chance to intervene."

"I understand."

"Excellent. Then let us proceed."

A last fluffing of skirts, and they rejoined the crowd. The atmosphere had grown even thicker—cloying scents, sweaty heat, a cacophony of music and laughter. Arianna slanted a sidelong look at Sophia to see whether her resolve was in danger of wilting.

As if sensing the scrutiny, Sophia lifted her chin a fraction and calmly surveyed the room. Spotting the colonel's scarlet coat, she veered off in his direction and deliberately chose a position to watch the dancers just steps away from him.

"Well, well, what a surprise to see you here, Miss Kirtland." It was only a matter of several capering piano chords before Stoughton turned slowly and smiled, his arrogant mouth curling into the shape of a scimitar. "I had heard that you had retired from Society."

"Apparently your information is inaccurate, Colonel Stoughton," replied Sophia coolly. "Mine must be too, for I was under the impression that you were assigned to guard duty in some spot in the far north. The Hebrides, was it? Or the Orkneys?"

Arianna was impressed by her companion's outward *sangfroid*. Sophia was a good actress. *And with my tutelage she will get even better.*

Flushing slightly at the barb, Stoughton stiffened and drew himself into a more martial bearing. Chin up, chest out—the subtle change set the medals to whispering against the scarlet wool, observed Arianna.

"Actually, I am in command of the greater part of Scotland," announced the colonel, exaggerating an officious sneer.

Arianna saw her chance and seized it. "How impressive. That sounds like a position of great responsibility," she interjected.

"Indeed, madam." He shifted his attention to her, his chest swelling like a Montgolfier balloon filling with hot air. "It requires constant vigilance to keep the Scots under control."

Really, men like Stoughton were so laughably predictable—it took only a bit of overt flattery to inflate their hubris to monstrous dimensions.

"We are fortunate to have military officers who are so dedicated to keeping England safe from its enemies," said Arianna. She looked at Sophia and added a not-so-subtle chiding. "All of Society ought to appreciate their efforts, Miss Kirtland."

Her mouth pinching to a sulky pout, Sophia gave an ungracious nod.

Emboldened, Stoughton responded to the flattery with a wolfish grin. "Does that include you, madam?"

"But of course, sir." Allowing a flutter of a pause, she added, "I do hope that your arrival in London is not reason for any of us to be alarmed?"

"Not at all, not at all." He laughed softly and continued to fix her with a speculative stare. "Do introduce me to your charming companion, Miss Kirtland."

Sophia hesitated before acceding to the request. "Colonel Stoughton, allow me to present the Countess of Saybrook."

At the mention of her name, Stoughton's smile flickered into a more wary expression.

So he wasn't such a fool after all, observed Arianna.

"So what *does* bring you to London, Colonel?"

"Routine talks with Whitehall," he replied slowly, aware that several other onlookers were following the exchange. "On what new measures are needed to suppress the rabble-rousing radicals who are looking to foment dissent."

"Oh, is there trouble at the moment in the North?" asked Arianna innocently. "Now that peace reigns on the Continent, I would have thought that the radicals in Scotland were no longer such a threat."

"Politics is not quite so simple as it may seem, Lady Saybrook," he said a little brusquely.

"Oh, well, naturally I defer to your greater experience in these matters."

"That would be wise," replied the colonel. "Now, if you will excuse me, I see an old family acquaintance who I must greet."

"For all our clever planning, we didn't learn much from him," commented Sophia, once they had strolled to a more secluded spot.

"On the contrary, the colonel revealed a great deal," replied Arianna. "The mention of the Saybrook name put him on guard."

"Ah." Sophia looked thoughtful.

"It's important to pay attention to little details like gestures and expressions," Arianna went on. "They often say far more than words."

"I see that I have much to learn."

"You did very well."

"D-did I?" Sophia seemed surprised by the praise. "To be honest, my insides were quaking like *blancmange*."

Seeing her companion's shoulders start to slump, Arianna quickly sought a distraction to keep shock from setting in. Time enough later for brooding—Sophia had suffered a nasty surprise, and while it was only natural to experience a delayed reaction once the blood had cooled, she would rather it didn't happen here in the ballroom.

"We need to find Constantina and see if she has gleaned any interesting gossip from the Dragons."

Seeing them approach, the dowager rose from the circle of turbaned matrons and regripped her walking stick. "All this talking has worked up quite a thirst," she announced. "Come along, gels, and let us find a glass of Lord Brodhead's excellent champagne."

"This way," said Arianna, offering an arm to her great-aunt.

"By the by, seeing as you asked about . . ." Constantina's words trailed off as she stopped to squint at the main entranceway, where a late arrival to the festivities was just passing through the portals. "Good God, I wonder what brings Grentham here. He rarely appears at such frivolous entertainments."

Arianna stared as well, allowing her lips to curl up at the corners. "Perhaps we should go and find out."

15

From Lady Arianna's Chocolate Notebooks

Pecan-Mocha Meringues

⅓ cup packed light brown sugar
1 tablespoon unsweetened cocoa powder
⅓ cup egg whites (from about 3 large eggs)
¼ teaspoon coarse kosher salt
⅛ teaspoon cream of tartar
⅓ cup granulated sugar
2 teaspoons instant espresso powder
1 cup finely chopped toasted pecans
½ cup semisweet or bittersweet chocolate chips (optional)
18 untoasted pecan halves

1. Preheat the oven to 300°F. Line a large, heavy baking sheet with parchment paper. Press the brown sugar and cocoa powder through a sieve into a small bowl to remove any lumps; whisk to blend.
2. Using an electric mixer, beat the egg whites, salt, and cream of tartar in a medium bowl until very soft peaks begin to form. With the mixer running, gradually add the

granulated sugar, then the espresso powder; beat until medium peaks form. Beat in the brown sugar mixture by the tablespoonful. Continue beating until the meringue is very stiff and glossy, 2 to 3 minutes.

3. Fold in the chopped pecans and chocolate chips, if desired. Drop the mixture by rounded tablespoonfuls onto the prepared sheet, spacing the meringues about 1 inch apart. Place 1 pecan half atop each meringue, pressing very lightly to adhere.

4. Bake the meringues until dry but still slightly soft when pressed with a finger, about 25 minutes. Turn off the oven. Cool the meringues in the oven with the door closed until crisp, about 1½ hours.

"**I**s that Lord Percival Grentham?" asked Sophia. The figure had shifted into the deepest recess of the shadows.

"Yes," replied Arianna. "You know him?"

"Not really. He was acquainted with my late father." A pause. "I don't believe they were bosom bows."

"That's not a surprise. Grentham doesn't get along with *anyone*," Arianna replied dryly. "He prefers poking out eyes and pulling out fingernails to dancing and flirting." Seeing Sophia's puzzled expression, she added, "He is Minister of State Security. A fancy title for having *carte blanche* to terrorize people in the name of keeping England safe from its enemies."

"I hadn't heard that," mused Sophia. "But then, I don't pay much attention to Society tittle-tattle."

"I would wager that he's one of the most feared men in all of England—and knows it. His department at Whitehall wields a great deal of power and influence."

"It's like one of those silly men's clubs on St. James's Street," remarked Constantina.

A thought suddenly popped into Arianna's head—a childish

one, perhaps. But she assured herself that it actually might result in some useful information.

"I suggest we form our own little club, dedicated not to drinking and telling bawdy jokes but to needling the minister."

"You mean you wish to persecute 'Persecute'?" asked Constantina. The play on Grentham's Christian name, Percival, was often used in London Society, though nobody ever dared say it to his face.

"Exactly," replied Arianna.

The dowager chortled. "Sounds like fun. He needs a few pokes to his self-importance."

Sophia's reaction was much more uncertain. "Isn't that asking for trouble?"

"Trouble needs no invitation to find me," quipped Arianna. "Grentham takes special pleasure in trying to make my life miserable. I am simply returning the favor."

Her expression remained doubtful, but Sophia refrained from further protest.

As they came abreast of the archway, it was Constantina who fired the first salvo. "Is that you, Percy?" An intimate friend of the minister's mother, she had known him since he was in leading strings. "Why are you skulking in the corner?"

Grentham turned his head slightly and looked down his well-shaped nose at them. "I prefer to call it 'observing,' Lady Sterling."

"Yes, the minister likes to peep, Aunt Constantina," murmured Arianna. "He watches a great deal of what goes on here in London. I daresay he recognizes our companion, despite having never formally met her."

Grentham's eyes narrowed.

"What do you mean?" asked Sophia, her voice sharp with surprise.

"Oh, it was Lord Grentham who so kindly informed me of your private meetings with Saybrook," Arianna explained. "He seemed to know all the details, including those concerning your looks."

Sophia's face tightened in outrage. "You *spied* on me, sir?"

"I doubt that he did the dirty deed himself," answered Arianna. "He has minions who do that."

Flames flared in Grentham's gaze. She could almost hear the hiss of smoke and crackle of brimstone.

"Percy, allow me to formally introduce you to Miss Kirtland." Constantina intervened before the sparks could set off a conflagration.

Dangerous. Arianna reminded herself that it was dangerous to play with fire. As an experienced chef she should know that.

The minister inclined a nod to Sophia. "I was acquainted with your father. He drank and gambled to excess."

"Those were the least of his flaws," shot back Sophia.

He blinked.

It was almost comical, thought Arianna wryly. The minister—a man much feared throughout England for his cold-blooded cleverness and ruthless tactics—appeared outgunned by a trio of females. *Steel versus silk.* And for a moment, the delicate flutter of their words seemed to have him on the defensive.

"You probably have the rest of them written down in one of your dossiers," Sophia went on. "Though why my father's personal failings should be of any interest to the government is beyond me."

"Hmmph." Like all men, Grentham seemed to feel a masculine grunt somehow disguised the fact that he had no other answer to make.

Again, Constantina intervened. "You have come to a ball, Percy. So why don't you ask my niece to dance?" The dowager punctuated the suggestion with a rap of her walking stick.

He looked as if he had just been asked to press an asp to his chest.

"Normally I wouldn't be any more eager than Lord Grentham to take a twirl together across the parquet," said Arianna softly. "But in fact, I have a few questions to ask him, and a waltz affords a bit of privacy."

His jaw tightened, but Grentham offered an arm, perfectly angled, as proscribed by the gentlemanly rules of deportment. To give the Devil his due, he had faultless manners to go along with his exquisitely tailored evening clothes.

Spin, slide, sidestep—Arianna was concentrating so hard on not squashing the minister's toes that the first figures of the dance passed in grim silence. Dancing was a newly acquired skill and she somehow felt that making a misstep would cede the advantage to her partner.

"Is this merely an exercise in futility?" Grentham finally asked. "Or is there really a reason you wished to speak with me?"

She raised her eyes from his well-shod feet. "Actually there is. I see that Stoughton is in London and I wish to know why."

For an instant, he looked tempted to tell her to dance her way straight to Hell. But then he relented—a fact that must mean he had his own reasons for sharing information, thought Arianna. The minister was not motivated by altruism.

"The colonel came here to complain about the investigator sent to St. Andrews by my office. He claims that Mr. Castellano was actually in league with the radicals and quite likely murdered a scientist for—as he put it—reasons as yet unknown."

"His reaction earlier this evening to Saybrook's name was suspicious. It shouldn't have meant a thing to him, but I was watching his face carefully and it did," she mused. "I wonder . . ." A frown tugged at her lips. "My husband said you used only a pseudonym for him in arranging the mission. So no one within your circle of advisers knew his true identity, correct?"

Crystalline shards of light dipped and darted over his features as they passed under one of the massive chandeliers, blurring with the swirling shadows cast by the other couples. "Not precisely."

"It's a simple question, sir," she countered. "And so is the answer—yes or no."

"Oh, come, Lady Saybrook, don't pretend to be so naïve. You, of all people, know that things are never so neatly black-

and-white. The edges fuzz; the shades muddle into an infinite range of grays." A small smile. "Granted, some are darker than others."

"If I want a lecture on art, I shall visit the studio of Thomas Lawrence."

"And what *do* you want? Information?" With a firm hand and agile step, he guided her to a less crowded section of the floor. "Very well, I was going to inform your husband of the fact tomorrow, but you might as well save me the trouble of a meeting. The fact is, I did drop his name to one person within the group."

"In other words, you used us as bait to draw out Renard."

He shrugged. "I had every confidence that you and the earl could defend yourself if it came to that."

"Who?" she asked.

"Lord Mather."

Arianna thought for a moment. She had met the viscount at one of the diplomatic parties given by Saybrook's uncle. Her only recollection was that of a portly man with thinning gray hair and a passion for collecting violins.

"You think him Renard?"

"No," answered Grentham decisively. "But I recently uncovered information that made me suspect he was involved in some sort of illicit activity in Scotland. The attack on you seems to confirm it."

"Yet my husband seemed to think you were surprised that our coach had been waylaid."

A low, humorless laugh sounded close to her ear. "I was. It seemed such a crude, ill-conceived plan, which doesn't fit with Renard's usual sophistication. Which is why I've ruled out Mather as our fox."

"I agree," she mused. "So how does all of this fit together?"

"That, my dear Lady Saybrook, is what you and your husband are supposed to be finding out."

The music was fast rising to its final crescendo. "I'll pass all this on to Sandro. But I'm sure he'll want to speak with you."

The minister let out a martyred sigh. "Unfortunately, you are probably right. However, tell him I prefer not to do it at Horse Guards."

She nodded.

As the violins trilled their last notes, he drew his gloved palm away from the small of her back. "Now that we've had our charming *tête-à-tête*, allow me to return you to your friends."

"You need not keep looking daggers at Miss Kirtland," murmured Arianna. She had noticed Grentham's interest throughout the dance. "She's proving a great help in analyzing the chemical data we discovered, so you really shouldn't be trying to bully or frighten her just because she stood up to you."

His mouth compressed to a hard line as they approached the archway. "I, too, have some advice to offer," he said very softly. "Be careful about making presumptions. This case—"

A rap of Constantina's cane cut him off.

"Come, Percy. It is only polite that you now partner Miss Kirtland for the coming set."

"I hate to disappoint you, Lady Sterling, but I did not come here simply to dance attendance on the ladies. I have some business to deal with, so must beg off from further frivolities." The minister inclined a sardonic bow to Sophia. "I am sure that the lady will suffer no disappointment."

Thump. The stick hit the floor with surprising force, and its rebound came perilously close to whacking him across the bum. "Good God, Percy, try to unbend and have a little fun sometime. It would do you a world of good."

His lips twitched, and in the shiver of shadows, it appeared . . .

No, impossible, decided Arianna. Grentham was not really holding back a chuckle.

"Enjoy the rest of the evening, Lady Sterling. And do try not to kill anyone with that lethal weapon."

"Ha." A touch of bemusement played over Constantina's face as she watched him walk away. "That was rather interesting."

Arianna agreed, but given all the discoveries of the last few hours, there wasn't time to dwell on the minister's revelations. Time enough later to go over everything with Saybrook.

"Indeed, but let's forget about Grentham for now"—she noted that Sophia's scowl was still firmly in place—"and concentrate on the reason we came here in the first place."

"Who else are you looking to meet, my dear?" asked Constantina.

"Your introductions to the gossips of the *ton* were a great help, but I was wondering, do you perchance see any relatives or close friends of the Sommers family?"

"The Duke of Lampson, eh?" The dowager's gaze took on a speculative edge, but to her credit she didn't ask any more questions. After a quick scan of the room, she shook her head. "You've already made the acquaintance of Colonel Stoughton—"

"*Stoughton.*" Arianna felt her insides give an unpleasant little lurch.

"Why, yes, his father and the duke were cousins, so the colonel is second cousin—or is it third?—to the duke's sons. I seem to recall that he is the same age as the youngest . . . you know, the unfortunate Lord Reginald, who was recently murdered in a robbery attempt somewhere on the Continent."

Tap, tap. The dowager turned and signaled a footman to bring more champagne. *Tap, tap.*

Arianna drew in a deep breath. *Perhaps the pieces of the puzzle were finally falling into place.*

"How was your evening?"

"Eventful," murmured Arianna, tossing her shawl and reticule on the kitchen worktable. "And yours?"

He looked up from the mortar and pestle, where he was grinding several dried ancho chili peppers into a fine powder. "The same."

A kettle of water was simmering on the hob, and silvery skirls of steam drifted across the table, muddling with the shadows—but not quite enough to obscure his face.

"Is that a bruise on your cheek?" she asked.

"The one on my ribs is far worse," he replied with a lopsided smile.

"Good God, what happened?"

"We discovered, as Baz so bluntly puts it, another dead body."

"Dio Madre." Her hands froze on the chocolate pot. "Brynn-Smith?"

A nod confirmed the surmise.

"But if he was dead, how did you come to have such bruises?"

"The killer had not yet left the room," replied Saybrook. "Unfortunately he had the elements of darkness and surprise working in his favor. I reacted a step too slowly and he got away."

Arianna washed the bitter taste of fear from her throat with a quick swallow of hot chocolate.

"If you wait a moment, I'm almost ready to add some spice," he said. "By the by, have you seen where Bianca put the vanilla beans?"

"I would rather have mine sweet tonight." She spooned a generous helping of sugar into her cup and was mortified to see that her hands were shaking. Over the last few months, her husband had come within a hairsbreadth of death more times than she cared to count. The margin for error was too small to keep tempting fate.

"So," she murmured, trying to keep her voice flat. "We've no clue as to the killer's identity?"

"Baz caught only a fleeting glimpse in the flare of a lucifer. The man was tall and lean, with fair hair—not an overly helpful description." The earl took out a scrap of silk from his pocket and placed it on the table. "However, I did manage to tear off a piece of his waistcoat as we were wrestling on the floor."

The slubbed fabric, patterned in alternating stripes of mulberry and navy, tickled against her fingertips. "I'm not sure that this is much of a clue either."

"There are some benefits to being a lordly aristocrat who patronizes the fashionable tradesmen of Town. Baz got the impression from the man's coat that he was a gentleman, and this silk is certainly expensive. So in the morning I shall visit my tailor and show him the remnant. As you see, there is a bit of stitching left at the seam. There's a good chance he'll be able to identify the maker."

Her hand suddenly stilled. "Mr. Lawrance is tall and fair-haired. And he favors stylish clothing."

"I shall ask Weston who fashions his wardrobe."

Arianna took another sip of her sweetened chocolate. "You will have to be making one other visit tomorrow," she said. "You will be wanting to meet with Grentham, but he doesn't want to do it at Horse Guards."

"Why—that is, why do I want to meet with the minister, and why must it be at a clandestine location?"

"Because Colonel Stoughton is in London." She went on to tell him all she had learned from the minister. After watching her husband's reaction—naught but a mild twitch of his brows—she added, "You don't seem overly surprised by his using us as bait."

"I'm not. I suspected that Grentham might be considering such a move. In his place, I would have done the same thing." He grimaced. "Good God, what a frightening thought that my mind is starting to work like his."

"Speaking of surprises, I have several more," said Arianna. "First of all, Miss Kirtland has a history with Stoughton."

That elicited a grunt.

"Not a good one, but I'm afraid I don't feel at liberty to disclose the details. She confided the story to me while she was . . . upset. If you wish to know it, you will have to ask her yourself."

"I—"

"Secondly," she went on before he could interrupt, "Stoughton is related to Lord Reginald Sommers. A second or third cousin, but still, the connection is there."

Taking a pinch of the dark red pepper powder from the stone

mortar, Saybrook slowly rubbed the spice between his fingers. Light licked across his hand, the candle flames turning the spice's hue to the color of fresh-spilled blood.

"Stop that," she snapped, then quickly expelled an apologetic sigh. "Sorry. My nerves are a little on edge."

"Understandably so." There was an oddly hesitant hitch to his voice, which seemed to linger in the air as he dusted his fingertips on his trousers. "It is not just our enemies who are keeping secrets from us, but also our friends."

Is he upset over the fact that Miss Kirtland has not shared her past with him?

Arianna tried to read his expression, but he had turned to add the pepper to the chocolate pot. The strands of his hair fluttered, forming a shimmering, silken curtain of midnight black.

An apt metaphor, she thought a little sourly, seeing as her husband still had deeply private places within himself that she was not invited to enter.

Was anyone else?

But after a moment of petty brooding, it suddenly sank in that his words could have a different shade of meaning. "Why isn't Basil here?" she asked abruptly. "It's unlike him not to accompany you back here for a council of war after such a deadly encounter." She hitched in a breath. "Did he suffer a new injury?"

"No more than a few bumps when I shoved him aside," replied Saybrook. "As to why he's not here, it appeared to me that he was occupied with other concerns."

"What other concerns?"

"I don't know." He explained about the interrupted meeting and the furtive hiding of papers.

"Damnation," swore Arianna. "What do you think he is planning?"

"Nothing good," said the earl glumly. "His friend was a fellow Scot, so I fear it may be some sort of revenge or retaliation for his nephew's death. However, there is no use speculating."

"True." She sketched a small circle on the tabletop, intimately aware of the nicks and scars cut into the wood. "There are more accurate ways of gathering information."

Their gazes met over the flicking flame.

"True," he echoed. "But we already have enough conundrums to solve. We need to attack them first."

An oblique way of saying that he drew the line at spying on close friends.

"Then we had better devise a battle plan for doing so. This latest murder is yet another reminder that time is of the essence."

"Tomorrow I will deal with the tailors and Grentham," said Saybrook. "What about you?"

"I am meeting with Lady Urania to attend Willoughby's evening lecture at the Royal Institution. But in the afternoon, I plan to pay a visit to the new chocolate shop and see what I can learn about the corps of aeronauts stationed at the Artillery Grounds."

"Let us hope that some new lead arises from our efforts." Steam hissed as he added boiling water into the chocolate pot and began to spin the *molinillo* between his palms. "I am growing heartily sick of feeling that I'm chasing naught but my own tail."

"Then come to bed, Sandro," she whispered, feeling the churning of her own doubts and frustrations. "It does no good to exhaust yourself running in circles. In the morning, we will renew the hunt."

16

From Lady Arianna's Chocolate Notebooks

Chai-Spiced Hot Chocolate

4 cups low-fat (1%) milk
¾ cup bittersweet chocolate chips
10 cardamom pods, coarsely cracked
½ teaspoon whole allspice, cracked
2 cinnamon sticks, broken in half
½ teaspoon freshly ground black pepper
5 tablespoons packed light brown sugar
6 quarter-size slices fresh ginger plus ½ teaspoon grated
peeled fresh ginger
1 teaspoon vanilla extract, divided
½ cup chilled whipping cream

1. Combine the milk, chocolate chips, cardamom pods, all-spice, cinnamon sticks, black pepper, 4 tablespoons of the brown sugar, and the ginger slices in a medium saucepan. Bring almost to simmer, whisking frequently. Remove from the heat; cover and steep for 10 minutes. Mix in ½ teaspoon of the vanilla.

2. Meanwhile, whisk the cream, the remaining 1 tablespoon brown sugar, the grated ginger, and the remaining ½ teaspoon vanilla in a medium bowl until it forms peaks.

3. Strain the hot chocolate. Ladle it into 6 mugs. Top each with dollop of ginger cream.

The door—an ornate confection of jewel-tone leaded glass set in a frame of dark mahogany—opened, and Arianna was immediately enveloped in a cloud of warm, sugar-scented air. Stepping inside the chocolate house, she inhaled deeply, the heady mix of sweetness and spices a piquant reminder of a childhood spent in the West Indies.

Yes, definitely the smell of the tropics, she thought wryly, detecting a whiff of rum mixed in with nutmeg and cacao beans.

Whisky and brandy also teased at her nostrils. A glance at the crowd explained why. Big, muscled men were lounging at the tables near the hearth, smoking cheroots and tossing back pewter tankards filled with hot chocolate—well fortified with spirits. On the wall pegs hung fur-lined hats, sheepskin coats and an assortment of leather gauntlets, all emitting tiny tendrils of vapor as they dried in the heat of the fire.

Aeronauts, aviators, *aérostiers.* Whatever moniker they went by, the men who defied gravity in their flying balloons were a boisterous, cocksure flock of daredevils—as was made clear by the rising volume of their raucous shouts and good-natured teasing.

"May I help you, *señora*?"

Arianna turned to find a slender, dark-haired female eyeing her over a tray of freshly washed mugs.

"I have heard much praise for the quality of your chocolate beverages and should like to sample a taste," she responded. "Are ladies permitted to patronize this establishment?"

A throaty cackle answered the inquiry. "If you can tolerate

the mayhem and foul language, you are welcome to sit." Setting down the tray, the woman gestured at several tables by the bow front window. A display case of pastries set them slightly apart from the main room. "Be forewarned, if the cursing becomes too offensive, it is you who will have to leave. They have rough manners, but they spend freely."

"My ears are not easily scalded," replied Arianna.

"*Bueno.* Then I am happy to take your money as well." The woman brushed back a bit of lace from her cheek. She was wearing a black mantilla, a traditional Spanish head scarf that spilled over her shoulders from a high, carved comb perched at the back of her head. Her thick black lashes and prominent nose made her look a little like a raven, an impression accentuated by her high-neck black gown and beady-eyed gaze. "I have a variety of flavored chocolates. Would you like to try one of my exotic spices, or does your English palate prefer a plain brew?"

"If you are using *criolla* beans, I should like to try something with a sweet spice like cinnamon or nutmeg to complement their subtle delicacy. If the choice is *trinitaro* beans, I would rather have a more robust brew, based on achiote peppers and cochineal."

"You appear to know something about *Theobroma cacao,*" said the woman with an appraising glance.

"Yes," answered Arianna. Switching to Spanish, she introduced herself and explained how she was translating the notes and recipes collected by the earl's grandmother.

"Recipes?"

She had deliberately mentioned them, hoping the woman would bite. "*Sí.* Some are from the very early days of chocolate's introduction to Spain. I find them fascinating."

The woman's reserve melted a little. "I am Señora Delgado, the proprietor of this shop. Sit, and allow me to serve you one of my favorite mixes, which is based on a batch of my special *criollas.*" She cleared her throat with a tiny cough. "Perhaps, if you find it to your taste, on your next visit you will share one of yours."

"Gladly." Taking a chair that afforded a good view of the main room, Arianna quietly smoothed her skirts and peeled off her gloves. A book appeared from inside her reticule, along with a pencil. But under the guise of reading, she kept her ears and eyes open to what was going on among the other occupants of the shop.

The aeronauts were discussing—quite loudly—the different methods of creating hydrogen, the light gas that was used as an alternative to hot air in their balloons. There were eight of them, and as names and technical terms flew through the air, she jotted some notes in the margins of the open page. Oddly enough, it was the smallest, slightest fellow of the group who seemed to command the most respect.

Señora Delgado reappeared to deliver a porcelain pot of her special chocolate and then once again retreated to make another round of drinks for her other patrons.

Ambrosial. The complex aroma tickled at Arianna's nostrils, giving a hint that the proprietor understood the nuances of *Theobroma cacao*. Distracted, she took another sniff, and then a sip of the frothed beverage, nearly missing the faint tinkling of bells as the shop door swung open.

Henry Lawrance entered and quickly made his way through the tables to join the pair of burly men seated closest to the hearth. They seemed to know one another and, after a quick exchange of casual quips, fell into a more serious conversation.

Oh, to be a fly on the wall, thought Arianna. Unlike the others, the trio had dropped their voices to a discreet murmur.

Whatever they were discussing, Lawrance looked unhappy with what he was hearing. His face furrowing in a frown, he drummed his still-gloved hands on the table and appeared to ask a series of short questions, which elicited naught but negative shrugs from his companions. He didn't stay long—after several minutes, he rose abruptly and headed for the door. It was only as he cut around the pastry case that he noticed her.

Arianna quickly lowered her gaze, but not before noticing his look of surprise. She heard his steps stop, as if he were perusing the selection of fruit tarts beneath the glass, but she had a feeling his gaze was on her.

Damnation. Her skill at disguises was excellent, but a discerning eye might begin to notice an uncanny resemblance between the Countess of Saybrook and Mrs. Greeley, the recent arrival from America.

Shifting, Arianna reached for her reticule and began to search through its contents. After a long moment, Lawrance moved off, and the soft *snick* of the latch falling shut signaled his departure from the shop.

"Are you enjoying your chocolate?" Señora Delgado paused for a moment by her table after dispatching a serving girl to the aeronauts with their drinks.

"Very much so. The hint of sweet vanilla is a perfect complement for the earthy roast of the *criollas*," she replied. "Might I have another pot?"

The proprietor bobbed her black-shrouded head. "Ah, it is a pleasure to serve someone who appreciates my artistry." Lowering her voice, she added, "These balloon men have their heads in the clouds—I could serve them mud if it were laced with enough brandy and they wouldn't notice."

"I daresay they don't notice if you inflate the bill," drawled Arianna, "so you may make sure that you are paid handsomely for your skills."

"A lady who understands business as well as chocolate. I think we shall become good friends, Lady Saybrook." The raven-like cackle was interrupted by the approach of the aeronaut leader.

"Madam Delgado, might we trouble you for an extra measure of rum? The morning flight was a bit brisk, and the fellows need a bit more heat to chase the chill from their toes."

"Will a cup do?" asked the proprietor.

"You had best bring the bottle." The aeronaut winked at Arianna. "My friends are rather large men."

"It must take a great deal of muscle to work the ropes and

stoke the fires of your flying balloons, sir," said Arianna as Señora Delgado retreated to the kitchen. "And a great deal of courage, of course. I am quite in awe of those who dare to fly. The
views must be heavenly."

"They are indeed spectacular," he replied with a friendly
smile. "One feels like . . . like an eagle, soaring through the
skies." His arms flapped a little. "It's hard to describe the sensation in words. But it's a marvelous feeling."

"Oh, I imagine it is!" she exclaimed.

His smile stretched wider at her obvious enthusiasm.

"I am curious," went on Arianna quickly. "How do you control your direction, sir?"

"There are a number of ways . . ."

Seeing the proprietor reappear with the rum, Arianna waved
a hand. "Please bring another bottle for these brave gentlemen,
and put it on my bill." With a flutter of her lashes at the aeronaut,
she added, "I do hope you will allow me to express my admiration by offering a toast to your impressive exploits."

His blue eyes lit up. Her guess appeared bang on the mark—
adventurers rarely were plump in the pocket.

"With pleasure, ma'am." He bowed. "James Sadler, at your
service. I and my fellow aeronauts would be delighted to explain
the fine points of flying."

"I should love above all things to hear about it, Mr. Sadler."

"If you can stand our coarse manners, you are welcome to
join us while you finish your chocolate."

"Oh, I can endure a great deal in the quest for knowledge,"
answered Arianna.

"Ah, a lady with an adventurous spirit!" Another wink. "Ho,
lads," he called out. "I think we have a kindred soul in our midst.
Now, mind that you devils keep a civil tongue in your heads
while we answer a few of her queries on aeronautics."

"If you wish to know the fine points of flying, you've come
to the right place, madam," called one of the men. "Sadler here
is the finest aviator in all of Europe."

"As you will soon learn, flyers are prone to exaggeration," murmured Sadler.

"Ha! Who else could make an emergency landing smack in the sea, and then relaunch his balloon from the storm-tossed waves?" piped up another of Sadler's fellow aviators.

Arianna felt her eyes widen. "You managed that feat?"

Sadler's ruddy face turned a touch pinker. "My flight had been driven off course, and I was hoping to be picked up by a passing boat. But the captain seemed fearful of tangling his rigging in my lines and wouldn't approach." A self-deprecating shrug. "So I improvised and dumped my ballast."

"Don't be fooled, madam. That was no simple task," said the largest of the aeronauts. "Sadler then went on to drop into the sea a second time—in the near dark, I might add—and had a more daring ship maneuver to run its bowsprit through his balloon's lines to keep it from sinking."

"How intrepid, sir!" enthused Arianna.

"That was three years ago, and my father was trying to cross the Irish Sea," offered a young man who looked barely old enough to shave. "It would have been the longest flight ever completed in the British Isles, and in truth he flew more than three hundred miles in trying to catch the right current."

"Now, now, Windham, don't be boring our guest with ancient history," said Sadler, looking even more embarrassed. "Especially as the attempt was a failure."

"Oh, I assure you, this is all fascinating," protested Arianna. "You believe there are currents in the sky, which can be used to navigate?"

"Actually, I do," began Sadler.

"Father has a theory about oceanic air currents," said Windham Sadler. "He believes that fixed patterns exist at different altitudes, all flowing in different directions, and that it's possible to map them, just as seamen have charted the seas."

"Please forgive the lad," murmured Sadler. "He tends to get a little carried away by the subject."

"As I said, I truly am interested in the subject of flight." Pausing for a sip of her chocolate, she considered what she had just heard. "Tell me, does that mean you think it's possible to get from one place to another simply by using the winds?"

Sadler smiled. "Science is rarely simple, milady. Yes, I do think that one can navigate quite well by using valves on the balloon to alter altitude and thus catch prevailing currents. However, I have yet to prove my theory—and even if I do, there is no denying that fickle gusts would make any map merely a useful guide rather than a route that could be relied on."

"So, to ensure a precise journey, an aviator would still need to have some controls over his flying apparatus—like movable wings or rudders?"

"Well, yes. That is the ideal, though in reality we have yet to invent a reliable way to steer. Those suggestions you just made, along with a great many others, have been tried," answered Sadler.

"And failed," chorused his fellow aviators.

"For the present, we are forced to rely on the very imperfect art of adding or subtracting air to our balloons," added Windham.

"Or hydrogen," pointed out one of the men who had been talking with Lawrance. "It all depends on what sort of balloon you choose to fly."

Arianna frowned. "There are differences?"

"Oh, yes," exclaimed Windham. "You have the traditional Montgolfier balloon, which is named for the brothers who invented the balloons used for manned flight. It uses hot air. The Charlier balloon, which is more favored by the French, gets its buoyancy from hydrogen gas."

"A theory first suggested by the *English* chemist Joseph Priestley," said one of Sadler's tablemates. "Though we favor the Montgolfiers, as they are easier to adjust to the barometric pressure of the changing breezes."

Hydrogen gas, oceanic currents, barometric pressure. Though her head was starting to spin with all the technicalities of flying, Arianna concentrated on making mental notes of the discussion. "I can understand the exhilaration of seeing the world from a bird's-eye view," she said slowly. "But from what you are saying, it sounds like ballooning serves more for entertainment than for any practical purpose."

"Not so, milady," said Sadler. "It has a number of serious scientific purposes. Luke Howard has created a comprehensive catalogue of cloud types, and Francis Beaufort has created a system for measuring wind velocity. In addition, high ascents have provided valuable data on barometric pressure and other phenomena. Why, the French chemist Gay-Lussac established that man cannot breathe above the altitude of twenty-three thousand feet. Is not that fascinating?"

"Indeed," replied Arianna. "Though I cannot say it is a fact that affects our daily life."

"Ballooning serves as an inspiration," said Windham. "It uplifts our aspirations, our spirits, no matter our everyday drudgeries." The young man drew in a deep breath. "As the poet Wordsworth says,

> *Away we go!—and what care we*
> *For treason, tumults, and for wars?*
> *We are as calm in our Delight*
> *As is the crescent-Moon so bright*
> *Among the scattered stars.*"

Sadler gazed fondly at his son, then turned to Arianna. "Youthful exuberance," he said half-apologetically. "But I believe all of us aviators share that sense of wonder. There are risks, to be sure, but they are far outweighed by the rewards of being pioneers."

"Aye, we've learned a thing or two about safety since Blanchard and Jeffries made the first flight across the Channel," said the man who had been conversing with Lawrance. "Ho, what an adventure that was . . ."

Nearly three-quarters of an hour passed before Arianna took her leave from the chocolate shop, having garnered a great deal more arcane information about balloons and an open invitation to join one of their flights. But even more intriguing was the fact that over the last several months, Lawrance had become an avid aficionado of aeronautics and was now a frequent visitor to the Artillery Grounds.

"That should give Sandro some new food for thought," she mused, climbing into her carriage. And with any luck, the evening lecture at the Royal Institution would also serve up some useful tidbits of information.

"Let us hope," she added to herself, "that at long last, we may finally be getting this investigation off the ground."

"Do you, perchance, recognize this, Mr. Stutz?" asked Saybrook.

The tailor took a moment to examine the scrap of silk. "Aye. It is Indian, milord, a very distinctive weave from Jaipur. One can tell by the nubbiness of the texture and the richness of the colors."

"Is it one of your exclusive fabrics? I was told the stitching was done by this shop."

Stutz looked up. "Dare I hope you are thinking of switching your allegiance from Weston to me?"

The earl smiled. "Alas, no. I am very happy with my current wardrobe, so it would be disloyal to desert a man who has served me so well."

"I can't find fault with that sentiment, milord—though it was worth a try," replied Stutz, still caressing the silk. "The material is indeed mine. Might I ask why the interest in it?"

"I am hoping you might tell which of your clients have had a waistcoat made up out of it."

The tailor fingered his chin. "Hmm, let me think . . . The pattern and colors are a bit out of the ordinary, so I believe we only had a few orders . . . Hmmm, there was Lord Glastonbury, an

Irish peer here on a visit from Dublin; Mr. Thornwood, the Earl of Bridport's youngest son . . . oh, and Mr. Lawrance, Baron Blight's heir." He pursed his lips. "Yes, yes, I'm quite certain that only three were made."

"Thank you," replied Saybrook. "That's very helpful."

Stutz watched him tuck the scrap back into his pocket and let out a mournful little sigh. "I take it one of them is damaged beyond repair."

The earl didn't answer directly. "I would prefer that this conversation remain confidential." He put a fat leather purse on the counter. "It is a private matter."

"But of course, milord."

Tipping his hat, Saybrook took leave of the fancy shop and turned his steps toward a less elegant part of Town.

A brisk walk brought him to Henning's surgery, where he hesitated for a moment before entering in his usual manner—without a knock.

"Sandro!" Henning fumbled to shove a handful of papers into his desk drawer as he spun around in his chair. "What brings ye here at the crack of dawn, laddie?"

"It's well after noon, Baz," replied the earl dryly.

"Is it?" The surgeon scratched at his unshaven chin. With his red-rimmed eyes and uncombed hair, he looked as though he had just crawled out from under the bedcovers.

"Indeed." Saybrook eyed the surgery counter, a tiny frown pinching his features as he took in the jumbled disarray. In contrast to Henning, the instruments of his trade were always arranged in an orderly fashion. "Having spent the morning chatting about threads and fabrics, I believe that I've discovered the identity of our assailant. It's Henry Lawrance, and I thought you might care to join me in paying him a visit." He shifted his stance, the faint scrape of his boots punctuating the pause. "But I can see that you are otherwise occupied."

"Nay, nay." Henning rose and ran a hand through his disheveled locks. "Lady S would have my guts for garters were I to let you go off on yer own." Opening the bottom desk drawer, he took out a pocket pistol and quickly tucked it into his coat.

"A new acquisition?" asked the earl softly.

"Yes, a recent patient bartered it for my services," replied Henning without blinking an eye. "I'm ready," he announced, quickly changing the subject. "And be advised that I expect an ample breakfast after we're done."

"Bianca will be happy to serve up your favorite creamed herring. But first, we have another fish to fry."

As they headed west in a hired hackney, Saybrook explained what he had learned. "After making some discreet inquiries, I've also discovered that Lawrance has an appointment with the Royal Society's librarian this afternoon. He wishes to read over some of Antoine Lavoisier's chemical experiments from the last century."

"Lavoisier," repeated Henning. "A Frenchman whose brilliance rivaled that of our current English genius, Humphry Davy." The wheels *clacked, clacked, clacked* over the cobblestones, as if echoing the turning of his mental gears. "How interesting that Lawrance would be so curious about a scientist who performed so many experiments with explosives and propellants for flying balloons."

"It seemed so to me as well."

"So we shall find him in one of the private study rooms?"

"Yes," replied the earl with a smile of satisfaction. "A perfect venue for an intimate little chat, don't you think?"

Henning cracked his knuckles. "Auch, my fists are feeling awfully garrulous today."

"I thought you didn't believe in violence."

"In science, one is always putting theory to practical tests, laddie," came the cryptic reply.

"Baz—" began the earl.

"Save yer breath te cool yer porridge, Sandro. I don't need a lecture on the moral triumph of turning the other cheek."

"I wouldn't presume to be such a pompous windbag," answered the earl. "I'm simply concerned that the desire for revenge doesn't cloud your normally clear-eyed vision. Just ask Arianna how its prism can distort the view of the world."

Pursing his lips, the surgeon slanted a long look out the grimy window glass.

"We're here," announced Saybrook, breaking the uneasy silence. "For now, let us turn our gaze to a more immediate challenge."

17

From Lady Arianna's Chocolate Notebooks

Lemon–Olive Oil Banana Bread

1 cup all-purpose flour
1 cup whole wheat flour
½ cup dark Muscovado or dark brown sugar
¾ teaspoon baking soda
½ teaspoon kosher salt
1 cup coarsely chopped bittersweet chocolate
⅓ cup extra-virgin olive oil
2 large eggs, lightly beaten
1½ cups mashed, very ripe bananas (about 3 bananas)
¼ cup whole-milk yogurt
1 teaspoon freshly grated lemon zest
1 teaspoon vanilla extract

For the glaze:

½ cup sifted dark Muscovado or dark brown sugar
½ cup confectioners' sugar
4 teaspoons freshly squeezed lemon juice

1. Preheat the oven to 350°F. Place a rack in the center. Grease a 9 x 5–inch loaf pan or equivalent.
2. In a large bowl, whisk together the flours, sugar, baking soda, and salt. Add the chocolate pieces and combine well.
3. In a separate bowl, mix together the olive oil, eggs, banana, yogurt, zest, and vanilla. Pour the banana mixture into the flour mixture and fold with a spatula until just combined.
4. Scrape the batter into the prepared pan and bake until golden brown, about 50 minutes. Do not overbake or the bread will be dry.
5. Transfer the pan to a wire rack to cool for 10 minutes. Turn the loaf out of the pan to cool completely.
6. While the cake is cooling, prepare the glaze. In a small bowl, whisk together the sugars and the lemon juice until smooth. When the cake is completely cool, drizzle the glaze on top of the cake, spreading with a spatula to cover.

"I'd like for you to distract the porter while I take a peek at the guest log," said the earl to Henning as they climbed the front steps of the Royal Society's headquarters in Somerset House. "It would be best if our interest in Mr. Lawrance remains a secret."

A few innocuous questions regarding an upcoming exhibit served the purpose and they were once again out on the Strand. But rather than seek a hackney, they lit up cheroots and strolled around past the side portico, lingering near one of the delivery entrances until they were able to slip inside unnoticed. A back stairwell led to the rear of the central wing, overlooking the Thames, where the book and manuscript collections were housed.

"Lawrance is in Room Three, at the end of the corridor," said Saybrook, pausing to check the connecting entryway. There was no sign of life, and aside from the creaking of the floorboards, it was quiet as a crypt. "Check the priming of your weapon, Baz. I don't expect you will have to use it, but we've seen that he's a slippery devil, and on no account do I intend to let him get away from us this time."

The hammer cocked back with a low *snick*.

"That said, aim for his knee and not his heart." He made a wry face. "I need to have one of our adversaries stay alive long enough for me to question him."

"Don't worry, my bullet won't kill him." *Snick, snick.* "But it will be painful enough that he will wish he were dead."

The door latch released with the same muted metallic sound, allowing them entrance into a small, windowless study room. The only source of illumination was a single Argand lamp set on the corner of the worktable, its oil-fed circular wick casting a halo of mellow light over the sherry-colored paneling and Lawrance's hunched shoulders. His back was to them, head bent so low that only a glimmer of fair curls showed above the broad curve of his navy coat.

Engrossed in his work, Lawrance appeared unaware that he was no longer alone.

The earl eased a knife from his boot and moved stealthily across the patterned Turkey carpet, Henning shadowing his steps. The thick weave swallowed the sound of their approach, and it wasn't until the steel point kissed up against Lawrance's neck that the scratch of his pen abruptly stopped.

"I would advise against any further movement," said Saybrook, watching a tiny bead of blood well up just below the other man's ear. "Another flinch and you might sever your carotid artery."

Lawrance remained motionless. "May I be permitted to turn around?" he asked calmly. "If I am to be executed, I prefer to face my killer."

"Slowly," allowed the earl. "And keep your hands away from your pockets." He kept the blade poised a scant inch from Lawrance's throat. "I see you have chosen a more subdued waistcoat for today. A wise move, though a trifle too late to save you from your own hubris."

"I didn't realize you had an interest in fashion, Lord Say-brook," said Lawrance coolly.

"Only when I can follow a thread that leads me to a vicious murderer." Saybrook set the razor-sharp blade to the pulse point located beneath Lawrance's chin. "Let us not bother with embroidering any more false pleasantries, shall we? Who sent you to kill Brynn-Smith?"

Lawrance tightened his jaw, but to his credit he reacted with admirable *sangfroid*. "Is this attempt at distraction and dissembling meant to confuse me into spilling my guts?"

"Nay, laddie," answered Henning. "It is *I* who will mince yer intestines into wee little chunks to use for Scottish haggis. That is, when we have no more use for yer miserable carcass."

The prisoner turned a little green around the gills. "I've no doubt that I will die, and likely quite in a hideous manner. But you are wasting your time trying to extract information from me."

"Brave words," commented Saybrook. "Yet in my experience, most men turn quite talkative once the blade starts carving at their liver. You can, of course, avoid bloodshed by telling us what you know now."

"Ah, is that what you promised Brynn-Smith before you shoved the blade into his heart?" countered Lawrance.

"Me?" The earl frowned as he considered the question. "As you say, any ham-handed attempts at dissembling are insulting. None of us here is a fool."

"Yet it was a foolish move to return to the murder scene," countered Lawrance.

"Why would I do such a thing?" asked the earl. "Assuming, of course, that I killed him."

"Good God, I have no idea how your devious, traitorous mind works." Lawrance let out a bark of laughter. "I suppose you must have remembered some telltale clue that would have given you away. A pity that I had not yet found it before you came back to cover your tracks. But be that as it may, we are tightening the noose on you and your circle of conspirators, Saybrook."

The earl heaved a sigh. "Must we keep spinning round and round through these pointless bluffs, Lawrance? It is getting us nowhere."

"Then go right ahead and kill me. It doesn't matter a whit. I've left a dossier of detailed notes, and another will take my place." Lawrance raised his chin in a show of bravado. "As I said, I was closing in on you, just as I was closing in on Lord Reginald Sommers. I'm heartily sorry that he fell victim to a cutpurse in Vienna. I would have preferred to see him exposed as the treacherous snake that he was."

Lawrance paused to draw a deep breath. "I admit, you were the cleverer of the two. I hadn't pegged you as part of their group until the other night." A sneer curled at the corners of his mouth. "Your uncle is so damnably proud of you and your heroic service to God and country. He will be devastated to learn that in reality, he's been nursing a viper at his bosom."

As Lawrance finished his statement, Henning suddenly tossed a small leather purse at his head. Reacting instinctively, he threw up his right hand to catch the missile.

"Oh, bloody hell," muttered the surgeon.

Saybrook fixed him with a questioning look.

"While ye were checking the bedchamber, I made a cursory examination of the body," explained Henning. "Brynn-Smith was killed by a left-handed thrust. And as we see, both of ye are right-handed."

"You did not think that important to mention before now?" growled the earl.

"I . . . I assumed ye were going to arrange it with Grentham that I got a full examination of the body."

"*Grentham?*" Lawrance couldn't hold back his surprise. "B-but . . ." His voice trailed off in confusion as he eyed his captors.

"Let me guess," said the surgeon sardonically. "Ye are working for the Home Guard—no, no, on second thought, they would choose a former military man. So it must be—"

"The Foreign Office," finished Saybrook. "They are the most obsessive about keeping secrets from the other branches of government, so it makes sense that they would have their own network of spies."

"I am *not* a spy," said Lawrance, mustering a show of dignity. "I am an investigative agent for the Crown."

The surgeon uttered a rude sound. "Auch, a rotten fish by any name smells—"

"Baz," warned Saybrook.

"What a devil-damned cock-up," said the surgeon. "The government has an itch on its arse, and no idea which of its arms is moving to scratch it." His expression brightened somewhat as he went on. "Grentham will be mad as a newly gelded stallion to hear that another department is treading on his turf."

At the second mention of the minister's name, Lawrance's scowl turned a trifle tentative. "Are you claiming that you work for Lord *Grentham*?"

Saybrook pinched a grim smile. "Would you believe me if I did?"

Lawrance shifted slightly in his chair, careful to avoid the sharpened steel still poised perilously close to his throat.

"We're not the enemy, laddie," said Henning.

"No?" Eyes narrowing, their prisoner fixed Saybrook with an uncertain look. "Then why was your wife at a chocolate shop frequented by the Artillery Grounds aeronauts? It couldn't have been a coincidence."

"She was seeking information," said the earl. "If you were there, I presume you were doing the same."

"You allow your wife to participate in such a dangerous, dirty business?" said Lawrance disbelievingly.

"I don't 'allow' my wife to do anything," replied the earl dryly.

Henning's rumbled chuckle seemed to throw Lawrance into deeper confusion.

"Did you perchance discover any clue as to where Sir George Cayley is?" asked the earl.

"Assuming you haven't murdered him too?" shot back Lawrance, though the challenge lacked any real force.

"I'm as anxious as you are to find him alive." The earl suddenly shoved his knife back into his boot. "And keep him and his inventions out of the hands of the French."

"W-what inventions?"

"Ye had better flap yer arms a bit faster, laddie, if ye wish to fly with us," quipped Henning.

Saybrook had edged closer to the desk and was riffling through the documents on the blotter. "You are on the right track to be looking at Lavoisier's chemical experiments from a quarter century ago. However, it's Davy and his acolytes who you need to be scrutinizing."

Lawrance shifted again against the slatted back of his chair, his discomfort even more pronounced than before.

"By the by, what put the Foreign Office onto the scent of Renard in the first place?"

"I—I am not at liberty to divulge that."

"They had to be aware of his existence for months," pointed out Henning, "seeing as our friend here knew about Lord Reginald's betrayal." The surgeon uncocked his pistol. "Don't worry, laddie, the fellow's demise was no random act of fate. He was called to task for his betrayals, though his family and the public have been told a different story."

"H-how—" Lawrance bit off his stammer.

"It would make sense to share our knowledge and work together, seeing as time is of the essence," said the earl. "Assuming we could deal with the small matter of trust."

The lamp flickered, and the silence seemed to quicken the hide-and-seek play of shadows over their faces.

"Any suggestions for how that might be accomplished?" asked Lawrance tentatively.

"Grentham is coming to my town house this evening for a secret meeting. We've decided to avoid Horse Guards for the moment, seeing as we don't wish to alert the traitor as to how close we are coming to unmasking the conspiracy. Will the Minister of State Security's word be good enough to vouch for my credentials?"

Lawrance nodded.

"The back garden gate will be unlocked, and I imagine that you have the skills to slip inside unnoticed," went on Saybrook. "The minister will arrive around ten. He will, of course, need to verify your assignment with whoever you are working for."

"Mory," replied Lawrance after letting out a slow hiss of breath. "I report to Lord Mory."

The earl nodded. "A competent man in his own right. But as my wife will tell you"—a wry smile tugged at his lips—"too many cooks can spoil the broth."

"I—I don't see what cooking or your wife have to do with state treason," muttered Lawrance.

"Oh, trust me, laddie," said Henning. "Yer eyes will be opened soon enough."

"Thank you for saving me a seat." Arianna slid into the spot next to Lady Urania. "My, what a crush. I hadn't expected a lecture hall to be as popular as a ballroom for the *ton*'s evening's festivities."

"Actually, they have more in common than you might think, Mrs. Greeley," replied Lady Urania, a twinkle dancing in her eyes. "Most of the people are not here for the science. They come to see and be seen, to ogle the latest darling of Society, and to appear . . . more intelligent than they really are."

Arianna bit back a laugh.

"I do hope that I haven't shocked you by sounding too cynical."

"Not at all," she assured her companion. "I appreciate plain speaking, especially when it is bang on the mark."

Looking a little relieved, Lady Urania replied, "I had a feeling that you might understand." She smoothed a finger along the ribbon trim of her bodice, "You seem a very pragmatic sort of person."

"I daresay I . . ." Arianna was distracted by a wink of reddish gold flashing from beneath the curl of pale satin. "Why, what an unusual locket," she remarked, catching a glimpse of an ornately engraved oval hanging by a delicate filigree chain.

Lady Urania hesitated, her hand pressing over the disc for an instant before slowly lifting it up from the folds of her gown. "Theus designed it for me. It was a present on the birthday when we came of age."

An intricate pattern of sinuous, swirling lines was cut into the precious metal. *Are they meant to be leaves, or merely an abstract arabesque?* wondered Arianna, leaning in for a closer look. The word inscribed in the center was equally puzzling. Set vertically, the letters spelled out . . .

"Is that Greek?" asked Arianna, squinting to see whether she was making out the letters correctly. Her father had enjoyed reading the *Iliad* in the original, but her own knowledge of the ancient language was nonexistent.

"Yes. Its meaning is something of a family jest," replied Lady Urania, but she did not elaborate.

"No matter its meaning, the design is quite lovely." A single bloodred ruby, set inside the first letter, "Λ," added an extra accent of interest.

"My brother had it made up as a watch fob for himself, and several of our relatives who share his sense of humor."

"He is a very skilled artist as well as a scholar," said Arianna.

"Theus has a great many hidden talents," replied Lady Urania with a small smile.

"Do I hear my name being taken in vain?" Canaday had found a spot in the row behind them and was now cocking an ear to the conversation.

"Your sister was showing me her locket," said Arianna, half turning to face him. "You've a lovely imagination."

He laughed. "Perhaps too much so." Catching Urania's reproving look, he made a moue of contrition. "As I've said before, Rainnie thinks I need to be more disciplined in my endeavors. What do you think, Mrs. Greeley?"

"Life requires a balance of the disparate elements of our nature," she replied.

"How very wise," intoned the viscount, softening his serious tone with a boyish wink at her.

Arianna ducked her head to hide a smile. It was hard not to respond to his breezy charm, but she quickly stilled the quiver of her lips, reminding herself that she was not here to be amused.

"Speaking of wisdom, I was wondering something." She made a slow, sweeping survey of the audience. "In your opinion, who are the most gifted of Humphry Davy's followers?"

"An interesting question," answered Canaday. "Is there a specific reason you ask?"

"Call it curiosity. I find it is always wise to know the leaders of a group to which I belong."

"Wise indeed." He tapped a finger to his chin. "Hmmm."

"I should say Chittenden," ventured Lady Urania. "His intellect may not be as sharp as some, but he's got connections in Society and has established himself as an important host for the institution. Davy does like to rub shoulders with the *haut monde*."

"An astute observation," agreed her brother. "I would add Brynn-Smith to the list. Just before he left for his tour of the Continent, Davy had great praise for the fellow's creativity in chemistry."

Arianna made no mention of the man's murder. For now, Grentham had ordered that the death be kept a secret.

The viscount pursed his lips. "And Michael Faraday can't be ignored, despite his odd quirks of character."

"Faraday?" Arianna pricked up her ears at the unfamiliar name.

"A strange young man. He's served as Davy's assistant for a while and is presently in Italy with him. I daresay there will be tension between him and Willoughby in the future, as our temporary head will be loath to relinquish the stage once Davy returns."

"Ah." Arianna wasn't particularly interested in the internecine squabbles of the group. "What about Mr. Lawrance?"

Canaday's expression didn't alter, but to Arianna it appeared that the planes of his face hardened ever so slightly. "Lawrance?" he repeated. "No, I wouldn't say he holds any influence with the institution." His voice dropped a notch. "In truth, I think he's a bit of a shallow, superficial fribble, more inclined to pay attention to the social interaction of the members, rather than the scientific work." A smile lightened the assessment. "But then, I imagine a lot of people think the same about me."

"How can you say such a thing!" scolded Lady Urania. "You have written several highly praised papers. While Mr. Lawrance has contributed little to our gatherings, save for a steady stream of flirtations."

"That is perhaps a trifle harsh," said Canaday. "Be that as it may, I would join with my sister in advising you to avoid a more intimate acquaintance with the fellow. He does not hesitate to toy with people."

"Thank you," said Arianna. "I appreciate the warning." But before she could add anything more, a bell called the audience to order and Professor Willoughby strode out onto the stage.

18

From Lady Arianna's Chocolate Notebooks

Orange-Scented Brownies with Dried Cranberries, Pistachios and Ginger

½ cup (1 stick) unsalted butter, diced
3½ cups bittersweet chocolate chips
2 ounces unsweetened chocolate, chopped
2 large eggs
½ cup granulated sugar
½ cup packed dark brown sugar
¼ teaspoon coarse kosher salt
1 tablespoon finely grated orange peel
¾ cup all-purpose flour
½ cup dried cranberries
⅓ cup shelled unsalted natural pistachios
¼ cup chopped crystallized ginger
2 ounces high-quality white chocolate, chopped

1. Preheat the oven to 350°F. Line a 13 x 9 x 2–inch metal baking pan with foil, leaving overhang. Butter the foil.

2. Place the butter, 1 cup of the chocolate chips, and the un-sweetened chocolate in a medium metal bowl set over a saucepan of simmering water. Stir until the mixture is smooth. Remove from over the water and cool to room temperature.

3. Using an electric mixer, beat the eggs, sugars, and coarse salt in large bowl until light and fluffy, about 4 minutes. On low speed, gradually beat in the chocolate mixture, then the orange peel. Add the flour and beat just until blended. Fold in 1½ cups of the chocolate chips. Spread the batter in the pan.

4. Bake the brownies until a tester inserted into the center comes out with moist crumbs attached, about 20 minutes. Remove from the oven. Sprinkle evenly with the remaining 1 cup chocolate chips. Let stand for 2 minutes to allow the chips to soften. Spread the chips evenly over the brownies. Sprinkle on the cranberries, pistachios, and ginger.

5. Melt the white chocolate in a double boiler and stir until smooth. Drizzle the chocolate over the brownies. Chill until the topping sets. Using the foil overhang as an aid, lift the brownie sheet from the pan and cut into squares.

❧

"Would you care for a cup of chocolate, my dear?" asked Saybrook.

Arianna made a face as she entered the kitchen and peeled off her floppy urchin's hat, along with the canvas jacket. "Thank you, but no, I've already drunk an ocean of it today—and quite likely gained several pounds in the bargain. I swear, these breeches are beginning to feel uncomfortably snug." Several hairpins pattered against the chopping block as she loosened the tight twist of her hair and let the coiled curls spill over her shoulders. "I think I shall brew a pot of chamomile tea instead."

"Any extra curves would only make ye look even more fetching, Lady S."

She turned abruptly as Henning's voice floated out from the shadows. "I didn't realize we had company, Sandro."

"Aye, we've a right cozy little party in progress," quipped the surgeon, nodding at the worktable near the stove.

Damnation. It was only now that she noticed the two additional figures standing at the far end of the knife-scarred slab of maple.

Saybrook gave an apologetic shrug. "There have been some new developments in the investigation, and we needed to meet in a place where the walls don't have ears."

There may be no unwelcome ears lurking within the well-scrubbed wood and plaster, she thought wryly, *but two sets of eyes appeared glued on her tight breeches and light linen shirt.*

"Really, sirs. You need not gawk like virgin schoolboys," she muttered as she walked past Grentham and Lawrance to fetch a glass from the cupboard. "I assume you've both seen a female's bum and legs before."

The minister quickly submerged his stare in the goblet of Spanish brandy cradled between his palms. Lawrance, on the other hand, began to chuckle.

"Kindly stubble your hilarity," snapped Grentham. "This is serious business."

"We were just discussing possible suspects for the Bright Lights mentioned in Girton's letter," explained her husband. "I will explain the details later, but it turns out that Lawrance is an agent of the Foreign Office, and he, too, has been working to track down Renard. We have agreed to join forces."

Lawrance inclined a small bow. "At your service, milady. I hope your visit to Señora Delgado's establishment proved fruitful. I understand from His Lordship that you possess an expertise in chocolate."

"Among other things," replied Arianna coolly. She was feeling tired, testy and in no mood for bantering with him. The basic information on balloon aeronautics had been interesting, but as yet, she was still digesting it all and had not decided whether it had any relevance to the case.

"On second thought, I think I'll have port instead of tea." Reaching for one of the bottles by the stove, she poured herself a small measure of spirits. "What names have been mentioned?"

"Mr. Lawrance was just about to share his thoughts with us," said Saybrook. "I've made little headway in the matter, but seeing as he's spent a goodly amount of time mingling with the institution members, I hope he may have some useful information to share with us."

"I believe I do, sir," said Lawrance. "There is one person in particular who has drawn my attention . . ."

Grentham set down his glass and crossed his arms.

"A Mrs. Greeley, who claims to be a widow recently arrived from America."

Henning drowned his snort of mirth in a mouthful of whisky, while Saybrook confined his skepticism to a mere arching of his brows.

"I beg you not to dismiss the suggestion simply because she is a woman," said Lawrance defensively. "Look at history—the female brain is capable of great cunning and ruthlessness." He slanted a look at Arianna. "No offense, Lady Saybrook.

"None taken," she murmured. "However, I can assure you unequivocally that Mrs. Greeley can be crossed off the list of suspects."

"H-how can you be so certain?" he demanded.

"Because *she* is *me*," answered Arianna. Switching to her nasal American accent, she added, "I apologize for being prickly at the recent soiree, Mr. Lawrance, but you were a damnable nuisance, clinging like a cocklebur to my skirts."

His jaw dropped slightly.

"Don't feel badly. I've a knack for disguises and have fooled a great many men over the years, some of them far more conversant with ruses and subterfuge than you are."

"True," confirmed her husband.

"Before these theatrics descend into farce, is there any *useful* name to be mentioned?" snarled Grentham.

The lamplight caught the flush of color creeping across Lawrance's cheekbones. "I had hoped to learn more from Brynn-Smith, but our adversary was a step ahead of me."

"What about Chittenden?" asked Arianna.

Lawrance considered the question for a long moment and then shook his head. "No, I'm quite sure he's innocent of any plot, save to curry favor with Davy and his social set. He was one of the first people I scrutinized, so I spent time shadowing his daily movements, as well as contriving to have a look at his private papers."

"I'm not sure that I should have a great deal of confidence in your judgment, given how easily Lady Saybrook pulled the wool over your eyes," growled the minister.

"Actually, I have to agree with Mr. Lawrance's assessment," said Arianna, feeling a twinge of sympathy for him. "My intuition tells me Chittenden is not devious enough to be part of this plot."

"Ah well, I bow to *your* expertise in that matter," said the minister with mocking politeness.

"Naturally," she replied. "For you are clever enough to recognize a kindred soul."

Henning gurgled another malty chuckle. "On that note, I will have to excuse myself from this discussion. It doesn't appear that we'll be making any further headway tonight, and I have a previous engagement." Gathering up his hat and coat, he waved at the earl to remain seated. "Don't bother seeing me out, laddie. I'll slip out through the mews."

Grentham ignored the interruption. "Any other suggestions, Mr. Lawrance?"

"Has anyone looked into Willoughby's background?" asked Arianna before he could answer. "We know he's brilliant, and when you add hubris and ambition to the mix, it's a recipe for possible trouble. He's just the sort of man who could be seduced into betraying his country."

The minister speared Lawrance with a steely stare. "Well?"

"As a matter of fact, I *have* taken a close look at him, and so far have uncovered nothing that sparks concern. But there are records I've not yet been able to access." He countered Grentham's gaze. "Perhaps you could use your influence to obtain information on his financial transactions."

"That won't be a problem. Do you know who serves as his bankers and man of business?"

A sip of brandy seemed to have settled Lawrance's nerves, noted Arianna. He rattled off several names without hesitation.

"What is your impression of Lord Canaday and his sister?" she asked, watching a skirl of smoke waft around a brace of candles.

"An interesting pair," he replied slowly. "A study in contrasts—he has a free and easy charm while she is shy and reserved. They are twins, as you well know"—he gave a wry grimace—"having pumped me like a leaky frigate for information."

"Sorry," she murmured.

"Don't be. I learned a valuable lesson about looking more closely at a beautiful woman."

"In the netherworld of intrigue and espionage, one must view everyone with a healthy skepticism," put in Saybrook. "Assuming one wishes to live to a ripe old age. Witness Brynn-Smith."

"Yes, that was a graphic reminder." Lawrance tipped the glass to his lips and drew in a mouthful of the amber-dark brandy. "There are a good many distasteful things about conducting an investigation like this. The need to turn over every stone along the way and examine the dirt clinging to its bottom means you uncover secrets that might cause ruin for those innocent of any involvement of the case."

Arianna stopped picking at a thread on her cuff. "I take it you've found something unpleasant about the brother and sister."

"Perhaps," said Lawrance. "One of the old family retainers hinted that the twins are not the actual children of the late viscount, but rather the by-blows of his younger brother. He and his wife were childless for nearly twenty years before returning from a Grand Tour with two lusty infants and a dying brother." Another swallow. "It's said that the fellow died of syphilis, and was a mad, raving lunatic at the end."

"The story, if true, would mean that Canaday has no claim to the title or the lands he's been brought up to think of as his own," mused Arianna. "Nor would his sister have any standing in Polite Society."

"Correct," said Lawrance tightly. "He's a pleasant fellow, and her genteel life revolves around the institution and its members. So it seems somehow sordid to pursue the matter."

Saybrook shrugged. "Their personal history doesn't appear to have any relevance to our interests."

Arianna glanced at Grentham, whose gimlet gaze didn't betray any reaction.

But no doubt he is filing away the information in that dark, dank place he calls a brain.

As for her own feelings on the twins . . .

"The Bright Lights are not the only people we need to focus on," said Saybrook, interrupting her musings. "I'm even more concerned about Sir George Cayley. The more I learn, the more I'm convinced he's the lynchpin—however unwitting—of the current conspiracy."

Lawrance nodded, and yet his expression pinched to a frown. "I agree, but I'm not sure why that is so. What the devil is he working on?"

"We have reason to know that Renard has access to a powerful new explosive," went on the earl, after a tiny nod from the minister signaled permission to explain. "And I fear that Cayley may be perfecting a flying machine that will allow an aeronaut to target specific locations with an aerial bombardment. If that's true, then God help us all if the French get hold of him and his plans."

In spite of the heat from the stove and the simmering kettle, Arianna felt a chill skate down her spin.

"But I've spent weeks around the big balloons and their aeronauts. I would be willing to wager my life on the fact that they can't be steered with such precision."

"It isn't a balloon," said Saybrook curtly. He turned to confront the minister. "Lord Grentham, now that you've raked Lawrance over the coals, what about your own investigative efforts? You've supposedly been using your resources to try to locate Cayley. Any joy in that quarter?"

"It has, as usual, been maddeningly slow to rattle any information out of the military's chain of command," said the minister. "However, I've just learned that Cayley has been sequestered in a remote enclave near our naval base in Middlesbrough for the past few months. Apparently the wind patterns are suitable for the experiments he is conducting for a newly established secret unit of the Home Fleet."

"Do we know that he is, in fact, still there?" demanded the earl. "We need to put him under special guard until Renard has been captured. But we can't afford to rush off on a wild-goose chase." Under his breath he added, "I'll be damned if I subject myself to yet another hellish carriage journey, only to find he's flown the coop."

"I've given the question top priority. My most trusted courier is already en route to verify the information," answered Grentham. "The fellow is tough as steel and rides like the Devil. We should have an answer by tomorrow afternoon."

"Let us hope it isn't too late," muttered the earl.

In response, the minister pulled a pocket watch from his waistcoat and flipped open the engraved case. "We've wasted nearly an hour dithering over your so-called Bright Lights. Do you have any other leads to follow, Mr. Lawrance, or do I need to assign one of my own men to take over the task?"

"I don't think that would be a wise move at this point, milord. It would require far too much time for a new member to establish himself at the Royal Institution," replied Lawrance stiffly. "I've a morning meeting with Willoughby's secretary and expect to turn up some new leads."

A wink of gold, a snap of metal, sounding overloud in the grim silence. "Then it seems any further talk here is pointless," said Grentham. "Let us hope tomorrow provides an opportunity for decisive action. So far, you all have been moving"—he slanted a sneer at the crocks of spices and condiments—"slower than molasses."

"Why, bravo, sir. You actually recognize some of the contents of a kitchen," murmured Arianna.

The flick of her husband's dark lashes semaphored a clear message—*bite your tongue*. She looked away. "Speaking of which, is anyone else feeling peckish? The refreshments at the institution were inedible."

"Thank you, but no. As the minister says, it is late, so I'll join him in taking my leave without further delay," said Lawrance.

"It's best that you don't leave together," replied the earl. "If Lord Grentham would kindly wait here for a few moments, I will show you the way out through the mews."

The minister chuffed an impatient grunt, but as it was obvious that Saybrook wanted a private word, he remained where he was.

"Would you care for some of my chocolate pastries, Lord Grentham?" The door to the larder swung open. "The ancient Aztecs considered *Theobroma cacao* a very healthful substance," she added. Her first encounter with the minister had come when she was the prime suspect in the poisoning of the Prince Regent. That she, a lone female, had evaded his network of operatives still seemed to stick in his gullet—a fact that she couldn't resist jamming down his throat.

"I don't care for sweets," he answered curtly.

"Aunt Constantina seems to think you weren't so sour in your youth." A low laugh echoed the rasp of the storage tin popping open. "Were you ever young, sir?"

"No—like Athena, I emerged fully formed from the forehead of Zeus."

The quip took her by surprise. She must have betrayed her ignorance because Grentham was quick to add, "It is one of the core tales of Greek mythology, Lady Saybrook. Athena is the goddess of wisdom . . . and war."

"Th-that sounds contradictory," she said, carefully placing several pastries on a plate.

"The ancient Greeks had a keen understanding of human nature. It's one of the reasons that we study the classics"—he allowed a tiny pause—"in our youth."

Feeling a little off balance, Arianna drew in a steadying breath. *I must be weak with hunger to allow Grentham to put me on the defensive.*

"I did not attend Eton, or any fancy English school, sir," she replied, trying not to sound snappish. "My education was of a more pragmatic bent."

"Ah yes, that's right—you were taught far more practical skills by your swindler father."

"Really, sir, such juvenile taunts ought to be beneath you."

His response was another jolt to her equilibrium. Rather than fling further insults at her head, Grentham reached for the brandy bottle and poured a little more into his empty glass. "That is rather the pot calling the kettle black, is it not, Countess?"

His words struck home harder than she cared to admit. "True. But one of the lessons I learned very early in life was that I could either be intimidated by a bigger, stronger opponent—and therefore be crushed—or I could take the offensive and throw the first punches. A show of fearlessness is often a far more powerful weapon than actual force."

"An interesting philosophy."

"It wasn't philosophy; it was necessity," replied Arianna tartly.

"You appear to have led a rather serendipitous life."

"No, I have led a desperate life, Lord Grentham." She sliced one of the sultana-studded pastries into quarters. "Have you ever been hungry—truly hungry? Or so cold that you would have gladly sold your soul to the Devil if Hell would have warmed the ice from your bones?"

He stared at her unblinking.

"Well, now that we're sharing intimacies with each other, I am curious, sir." He had made her feel vulnerable and she wished to pay him back in kind. "Were you or weren't you ever married? Saybrook seemed uncertain when I asked him."

"Yes, I recall overhearing your question at Lord Trumbull's house party. As you no doubt intended."

He was right. She had, of course, made some highly unflattering speculations in querying her husband.

"Allow me to satisfy your curiosity. I *was* married," said Grentham softly. "My wife died in childbirth, along with my newborn son."

"A-and you are heartbroken?" she replied, covering the clench of her insides with a sardonic sneer.

"Precisely," he answered, mimicking her tone. "Ah, but we are both forgetting—I don't have a heart."

Arianna wasn't quite sure how to answer.

He rose and straightened the pleats of his trousers. "I am surprised you and your husband haven't yet questioned whether I have *cojones*."

"Why, Lord Grentham, you shock me." Her mouth twitched in grudging acknowledgment of this new dimension to his character. "It seems you *do* possess a sense of humor. I shall have to inform Constantina."

"While you are at it, you may tell the old dragon that if she ever threatens to burn my bum again, I shall lock her in a Newgate dungeon with no sweets for a month."

"You wouldn't dare."

"No." The minister turned at the sound of footsteps in the corridor, hiding his expression in the swirl of shadows. "Probably not."

Saybrook halted in the doorway, as if the strange sparks of tension in the room had sent up a warning flare. "What wouldn't the minister dare?" he growled at Arianna.

"To cross swords with Constantina," she replied lightly. "Which shows he possesses at least half a brain."

"You wished to discuss something with me, Lord Saybrook?" demanded the minister. "For however entertaining it is to hear your wife's opinion of my intelligence—or lack thereof—I've other work to finish this evening."

"I won't keep you long," said the earl. "I simply wanted to ask whether you are satisfied with Lord Mory's explanation of the Foreign Office's independent investigation."

"I was not unaware of the fact they have their own agents. I have dealt with Mory on several occasions and have no reason to doubt his integrity," answered Grentham. "Is there a reason you ask?"

"Merely to consider all the possibilities, however remote. The thought did occur that maybe it's not an individual we are up against but a group of people. Maybe a faction within the Foreign Office is betraying the government," suggested the earl.

"A cabal within Whitehall? Good God, you are even more suspicious than I am." Grentham gave a thin smile. "But the answer is yes, I've thought of that too, and have done enough probing to feel confident that the threat is not coming from that quarter."

"How very terrifying that my mind might spin in the same direction as yours." Saybrook perched a hip on the worktable and watched Arianna cut one of the pieces of her pastries into bite-size morsels. "Is that your new recipe for sultanas and orange peel?"

"Yes. I let the textures and flavors mellow for a few days.

Here, have a taste and see what you think," she said, lifting a nibble to his lips.

Saybrook opened his mouth and she placed the chocolate on his tongue. Their eyes met, sparking spontaneous smiles.

Out of the corner of her eye, Arianna caught Grentham watching them share the moment. His expression was impossible to read.

"Mmmm." The earl swallowed thoughtfully. "Excellent, though I think it could do with a teaspoon or two less sugar. That would let the orange peel have a little more bite."

"I think you are right," she murmured.

"Would that the two of you would devote as much attention to cooking up a recipe to catch Renard," said the minister, reaching for his hat.

"We are doing our best to assemble the ingredients, Lord Grentham. We can't crack eggs until we can add your courier's information to the mix."

"Which way out shall I use?"

"Follow me."

As the sound of their steps receded, Arianna propped her elbows on the scarred wood and inhaled deeply. Maybe the exchange with Grentham had her unsettled, but all at once the smells of the kitchen—caramelized sugar, fragrant spices, steam infused with the sweet scent of chocolate—stirred sharp memories of her childhood. Tropical colors and voodoo shadows, lilting laughter and pitiful screams, languid days and frenzied nights.

Life. Past and present seemed to bubble up from the copper cauldrons and wash over her, an ocean of memories surging, swirling, spinning. Strange, how her schemes now had a purpose, her relationships now had meaning. In years gone by, she had deliberately avoided commitment, caring only about surviving from day to day.

"I traveled wherever the whim took me," she murmured. "Light as a feather, free as a sea breeze."

Coals crackled in the stove.

"I've more substance, more depth, which I suppose is for the good." Her mouth pinched in a rueful grimace. "But things back then were easier. Simpler."

Love—love was oh so complicated, a coil of conflicting feelings twisting in her gut. A part of her resented the loss of emotional freedom . . .

"Ah, but would you rather be adrift on an ocean of loneliness, with no anchor to humanity?" Arianna asked herself. Freedom was not simple either.

Loss and compromise were part of both worlds. *Ebb and flow.* Like the sea, life had an elemental rhythm to it. And like the sea, there were shifting tides, dangerous rip currents, hidden shoals, ready to wreck the unwary sailor.

"Are you all right?"

Arianna looked up. She hadn't heard Saybrook return.

"Just thinking."

He bent down to pick up the knife that had slipped from her fingers. "About what?"

"Did you study Greek mythology?" she asked evasively.

"Of course. Every schoolboy does."

"Tell me one of them."

Saybrook raised his brows. "Murder, betrayal, rape—they aren't exactly the most soothing of bedtime stories."

"Nonetheless, I wish to become familiar with them," insisted Arianna, feeling sharply aware of the void in her formal learning. Most of his friends—including Miss Kirtland—possessed a classical education.

"Very well, let me think of where to begin . . . Ah, let us start with the one about light. An apt subject for our present predicament." He offered his arm. "But if you don't mind, let us retire to more comfortable quarters."

19

From Lady Arianna's Chocolate Notebooks

Chocolate-Dipped Shortbread Cookies

½ cup butter, softened
¼ cup brown sugar
1⅛ cups all-purpose flour
4 ounces semisweet chocolate, finely chopped
¼ cup heavy cream

1. Preheat the oven to 300°F. Beat the butter with an electric mixer until creamy. Gradually add the brown sugar, beating until light and fluffy. Slowly add the flour, beating until blended. Chill for at least 1 hour.
2. Roll the chilled dough to ¼-inch thickness between sheets of parchment paper. Remove the top sheet of parchment paper. Cut the dough into desired shapes using a cookie cutter. Remove excess dough.
3. Place the cookies with the parchment paper on a baking sheet. Bake for 18 to 20 minutes, or until lightly browned. Remove immediately to a wire rack to cool.
4. In a small bowl set over a saucepan of hot water, melt the

semisweet chocolate with the cream. Stir until smooth and keep warm.

5. When the cookies have cooled, dip one half of a cookie in the chocolate and return it to the cooling rack so the chocolate can set. Repeat with the remaining cookies.

"Lift your hands." Sophia's breath formed pale puffs of vapor against the early-morning gloom. "You are allowing your horse to control you rather than the other way around."

"Sorry." Arianna straightened in the saddle and tried to keep her attention from wandering.

"You look tired. If you would prefer to curtail our ride, I know a shortcut back to your groom."

"No, no, I could do with a bit of fresh air to clear my head." She squeezed at the reins, still finding the sensation felt very awkward. "Besides, there have been a number of new developments that you ought to hear."

Sophia listened in silence, waiting until the summary was done before letting out a low a whistle. "Henry Lawrance an agent for the Foreign Office? I suppose I must give him credit for being more than a foppish fribble."

"So it would seem," murmured Arianna, wondering whether there was a reason other than the biting chill that her companion's cheeks were now a vivid shade of crimson.

"Exotic chocolates and daredevil aviators, a secret explosive and a missing inventor." Sophia shook her head. "How does it all fit together?"

"I don't know yet," admitted Arianna. "One tiny piece of the puzzle eludes me right now. What's frustrating is that I've a feeling that I've got it in my grasp"—she gestured to punctuate her point—"I just haven't recognized it."

Her horse shied at the sudden jerk on the reins.

Arianna lurched forward. Losing her grip on the leather,

she ducked low and grabbed a handful of her mount's glossy mane.

"Damnation," she muttered, determined not to suffer an embarrassing fall. "I—"

The rest of her words were lost in a pelter of pounding hooves as a dark shape exploded from behind a thicket of holly bushes.

A frightened whinny, a skittish veer. The ground began to spin and suddenly everything was happening so fast that all Arianna could see were bits and snatches of the whirling action. *A flash of steel, a foam-flecked stallion charging straight at her.*

Abandoning the fight to keep her seat, she threw herself sideways, hoping against hope to roll free of the slashing strides of the big bay. Her heart was galloping faster than the oncoming beast. The chances were slim—she would likely be squashed like a bug.

Sophia reacted in a flash. Urging her mount forward, she cut off the attacker's angle and forced the stallion to alter its path. Mere inches perhaps, but just enough that it raced harmlessly by.

Tucking into a tight roll, Arianna bounced over the hard, cold ground, dead leaves crunching loud as cannon fire in her ears. She looked up to see the stallion trying to wheel around, but Sophia had set her spirited gray flank to flank with the bay, and the two animals were jostling and kicking up great clots of earth.

Expelling a vicious oath, the rider threw up an arm to shield his masked face from the flurry of blows from Sophia's crop.

"Watch out! He has a knife!" called Arianna.

Deaf to the warning, Sophia redoubled her attack, elbows flying like a whirling dervish as she added a barrage of slaps and punches with her other hand.

Scrambling to her feet, Arianna snatched up a rock and hurled it at the prancing bay. It hit square against the stallion's withers, and with a frightened snort, the big beast danced back.

Between the bucking horseflesh and the thrashing rain of whip leather, their assailant lost his weapon. A last, strangled snarl, and he turned his mount and spurred away into the thinning mist.

"Good God, are you hurt?" cried Arianna between gasps for breath. Catching hold of the gray's bridle, she ran a calming hand along its sweating neck.

Sophia blinked, and it took a moment for the blank look to clear from her face. "I—I don't think so," she said. "J-just a bruise or two." The air leached from her lungs. "What about you?"

"The same," answered Arianna. "Thanks to your intervention. Is Boadicea, the warrior queen of Britain, among your family forebears?"

"Not that I know of." Her shrug ended in a wince. "Nor can I explain what came over me. It was like a haze—"

A question cut through the fog. "Does this horse perchance belong to you?"

Arianna turned slowly at the sound of the all-too-familiar voice. She had lost her shako, and smears of mud streaked the disheveled folds of her riding habit. "Yes, it does, Lord Grentham," she said tersely.

The minister looked down his long nose, and then at Sophia, whose hair was hanging down in lopsided tangles from beneath the battered brim of her once-stylish high-crown hat. "Your mastery of eccentric skills does not appear to extend to equestrian pursuits, Lady Saybrook."

Sophia huffed an indignant snort.

"You don't appear to be much more comfortable in the saddle, Miss Kirtland."

"Do forgive our unladylike appearance, sir," said Sophia acidly. "Alas, fending off an attack by a knife-wielding military man requires such an *untidy* amount of exertion."

His features immediately sharpened. "You were attacked?"

"By a man mounted on a big bay stallion," replied Arianna. "Did you not see anyone riding off?"

Thinning his lips, Grentham flicked a hard stare off into the distance.

Ignoring the minister for a moment, she turned back to Sophia. "What makes you say he was a military man? A cloak and a mask covered most of his person."

"I got a good look at his eyes when my crop cut a rip in the silk. It was Stoughton."

"You are sure?" demanded Grentham.

"Absolutely," answered Sophia without hesitation. "I would recognize his God-benighted orbs anywhere. Not to speak of the small scar that I put above his left brow the last time he attacked a companion of mine."

The minister frowned.

"If you doubt me, track him down. I struck a solid blow to our assailant's right eye." Her voice was edged with savage satisfaction. "I'm quite sure it will be swollen shut."

"I noticed that the horse had a white blaze on its forehead, and a stocking of the same color on its hind leg—" Arianna sucked in a sharp breath on spotting a small dark circle spreading just below the epaulette of Sophia's claret-colored riding jacket. "Good Lord, you *are* hurt, Miss Kirtland!"

Sophia touched a gloved hand to her shoulder and looked in quizzical bemusement at the smear of blood on the kidskin. "Oh."

"Dismount this instant and let me take a look at you."

Grentham swung around. "I'll summon help."

"No! The last thing we want to do is attract attention to the attack." Arianna grabbed the reins of Sophia's gray and handed them to the minister. "Let's get ourselves into the shelter of the bushes so that I can take a look at the wound. Then we can decide how to proceed."

Taking Sophia by her uninjured arm, Arianna marched her to a secluded spot screened by the leafy branches. "Sit down," she ordered, grateful to find a rock outcropping. Without further ado, she began peeling back the layers of fabric.

"Have you a handkerchief, Lord Grentham?"

The minister pulled a snowy white square of linen from his

pocket and handed it over. "Surely we must summon a surgeon," he said tightly.

"Not necessary," said Arianna, folding the handkerchief into a thick pad. "It's just a flesh wound. A bit of pressure will staunch the bleeding. Once I get Miss Kirtland home, I'll have Mr. Henning come bandage it properly. But I doubt it will require stitches."

Sophia swayed slightly.

"You are doing quite nicely, Miss Kirtland. Is this the first time you've been knifed?"

"Yes," answered Sophia faintly. She glanced down at the makeshift bandage and blanched. "I can't say that I wish to make a habit of it."

A growl rumbled in Grentham's throat.

"No, indeed not," said Arianna quickly before he could comment. "I can assure you the experience does not improve with repetition." Seeking to keep her companion distracted, she recounted several of her dockyard tales from the Caribbean. "The Malay captain was quicker than a snake. I thought I'd escaped his blade when I swung away on the rope, but he nicked my bum just as I cleared the ship's railing."

Sophia started laughing. "Do you have a scar?"

"Shaped like a half-moon." She darted a glance at the minister, who was standing rather stiffly by her side. "Sorry if we are shocking you, sir."

Scowling, he muttered something about "deucedly odd females."

"Seeing as we offend your sensibilities, sir, you may feel free to leave," said Sophia.

"Indeed, you ought to be pursuing that cur Stoughton, not wasting precious time with us," added Arianna.

"But I can't very well rush off and leave you two ladies here on your own," exclaimed Grentham. "What if you were to . . . faint?"

Arianna and Sophia each fixed him with a coldly disdainful stare. "I've never fainted in my life," they snapped in unison.

Looking uncertain, Grentham cleared his throat with a defensive cough. "Hmmph. Shock often sets in as a delayed reaction."

"I'm well aware of that, but as far as shocks go, this one is really quite mild," said Arianna. "There was a time off the island of Guadeloupe . . . Oh, but never mind that now."

"I assure you, there is no need to kick up a dust, sir," said Sophia, shooing him away with a wave of her bloodstained glove. "We are quite capable of managing on our own. I have every confidence in Lady Saybrook's ability to patch me up and get me home without making a fuss about it."

Seeing Sophia's pale face, Arianna did not blame the minister for looking unconvinced.

"Speaking of making a fuss, how is it that you were here on the scene, Lord Grentham?" demanded her companion. "Are you still spying on us?"

His nostrils flared. "I was taking a shortcut through the park to my office at Horse Guards." He paused for just an instant. "As I do every day."

"At this early hour?" scoffed Sophia.

"I am often at my desk by this time in the morning." A thin smile pinched at his mouth. "Trouble waits for no man."

"Or woman," quipped Arianna, wiping her hands on her skirts. "Saybrook is not going to be happy about this—"

"Oh, let's not tell him," exclaimed Sophia. "He'll demand that we stop investigating."

Arianna hesitated. Her thoughts were running in much the same direction, so she was sorely tempted to agree. However, a glance at Grentham slowed her scheming to a halt. "I'm afraid we can't count on the minister not to spill the beans. With him, logic often seems to fall on deaf ears—he has a very low opinion of females and will probably do it simply out of spite."

The minister's cheeks turned a mottled red. She guessed it wasn't because of the chill wind.

"You ladies aren't frightened?" he demanded.

"We are not ninnies, Lord Grentham," retorted Arianna. "Of course we are frightened. But that doesn't mean we intend to flee and relinquish the field of battle to the enemy. We must fight and win."

"And we can't do that effectively if we are told to sit at home and work on our embroidery," chimed in Sophia.

His brows rose. "You embroider?"

"Oh, for God's sake, I did not mean it literally. Must you always be such a . . . a . . ."

"A martinet?" suggested Arianna.

"I was thinking of a far less ladylike word, but that one will do," snapped Sophia.

Eyes narrowing, Grentham regarded them for a long moment, his lidded gaze lingering on the slash in Sophia's spencer before looking down at his glove and smoothing a wrinkle from the pristine leather. "And if I agree to keep silent, what do I get from you in return?"

"Renard's pelt to hang in your trophy room," suggested Arianna.

"You are very sure of yourself, Lady Saybrook."

"Does that frighten you, Lord Grentham?"

A pale blade of sunlight cut though the mists for a fleeting moment, catching the curl of a smile. "Like you, I'm not easily frightened."

She raised her chin. "So do we have a deal?"

A heartbeat passed, and then another, the thrum of her blood tickling against her ribs.

"Very well," he said softly. He looped the reins of the two horses over a branch. "I trust you won't make me regret it."

Saybrook marched through the door a half step ahead of the minister's secretary.

"Milord, I did try—" began the harried young man.

"You may leave us, Jenkins," said the minister, cutting off the apology. "Close the door behind you."

"I take it that 'urgent' means your messenger has arrived back from Middlesbrough?" said Saybrook once they were alone.

"No." As the earl started to protest, Grentham raised a hand. "His information doesn't matter anymore," he explained coolly. "I've just obtained a new whole set of revelations which should finally allow us to run the clever fox to ground."

"And how did you suddenly obtain them?" asked the earl, a touch of skepticism shading his voice. He gestured at an ancient Greek urn set on the bookshelf. "Did the Oracle of Delphi suddenly decide to grant our wish for answers in this case?"

"I haven't been talking with mythical seers or prophets," replied Grentham a little smugly. "I have just come from a private chat with Colonel Stoughton, who decided to tell me a story—a rather long story—in return for a reprieve from the hangman's noose."

Saybrook took a seat in the proffered chair. "I'm listening."

"I shall, however, endeavor to keep it short. To begin with, it was Stoughton who arranged the ambush on you as you traveled to Scotland, but not for the reasons we suspected. He's been running a highly profitable business stealing naval supplies that land at Inverness harbor from Scandinavia, and then reselling them to the fleet at Middlesbrough for an obscene profit. His partner in the scheme is Lord Mather."

"Who works here in your department," mused Saybrook.

"Yes. He's privy to naval movements in the Baltic, and used that information to target the convoys carrying costly goods. With Stoughton in charge of the military, it was an easy matter to arrange the theft of materials."

The earl tapped his fingertips together.

"I had been suspicious of Mather for a while but unsure what he was up to," went on Grentham. "So I included him in the secret meeting about sending you North. It was he who passed your name to Stoughton."

"And yet I can't help but wonder—why bother attacking me? I wasn't going to Scotland to investigate military corruption. The odds were quite good that I'd not stumble on their scheme."

A sour smile appeared on the minister's face. "Two reasons. Firstly, I was deliberately vague on the reasons why I was dispatching an investigator to Scotland. They couldn't afford to take a chance that you weren't already alerted to their misdeeds." He rose and went to stand in front of the mullioned windows. Backlit by the silvery winter light, his profile was dark. Impossible to read.

"But more importantly, they couldn't afford to have Mr. Henning's nephew go free from the prison," he went on. "You see, Stoughton uses the inmates as slave labor to repackage the stolen goods and move them to various warehouses around the Highlands. Even if you weren't aware of the scheme, Stoughton knew that the young man would ruin everything by telling what he had seen."

"Bloody hell," muttered Saybrook. "What a cursed coincidence. So Angus MacPhearson's death had nothing to do with Renard."

"Actually, that's not precisely true," said Grentham.

"Ah." The earl grimaced. "I should know better than to think anything is clear-cut when *you* are involved."

The minister ignored the barb. "Stoughton arrested men as a favor to his cousin, Lord Reginald Sommers. He knew something sinister was afoot, but he was happy to take money for his favors and not ask questions. He's admitted to arranging several executions and kidnappings for his cousin. However, he swears that he knew nothing about a conspiracy to betray the country. For him, Renard was simply the code name of Lord Reginald's associate in London."

"You believe him?" asked Saybrook.

"Let's just say, my men in the Horse Guards interrogation rooms are quite persuasive."

"Be that as it may, I have several questions of my own to ask of Stoughton," replied the earl. "Let me talk to him as well."

"I'm afraid the colonel is in no condition to receive visitors," said the minister.

Silence shrouded the room, as if mirroring the dark, rain-thick mist that had suddenly swirled up against the window-panes.

"How did you finally unmask him?" asked Saybrook, after thinking over what he had heard. "Stoughton must have done something to give himself away."

Grentham moved away from the window, an odd expression tightening his features. He picked up a pen from his blotter and inspected the nib, as if looking to find a carefully worded reply engraved on the steel. "I can't tell you that. I'm sworn to secrecy," he finally growled. Tossing the pen aside, he gave an impatient wave. "The informer's identity isn't important. What matters is that on account of his dealings with Lord Reginald, Stoughton was blackmailed by Renard into arranging the abduction of Cayley, who was taken two days ago from the outpost near Middlesbrough."

Saybrook swore. "Is he still alive?"

"According to Stoughton, the answer is yes. He says there is no plan to kill Cayley. On the contrary, the inventor is being held captive at an abandoned watchtower near Dover and the plan is to take him to France, though Stoughton claims not to know when or how."

The earl shot to his feet. "Then we haven't a moment to lose. I take it you have the exact location of the place."

Grentham pulled a piece of paper from his document case. "The directions are written down here."

"I don't suppose you were able to extract any other details about Renard or how Stoughton contacted him."

Grentham shook his head. "All messages between them were

passed through a system of blind drops. Our fox has been very careful to cover his tracks, but even the most canny creature cannot run forever without making a stumble. This time, I trust we are finally close—close enough to snap our teeth shut on his traitorous tail."

The tic of a tiny muscle tightened Saybrook's jaw. Shifting his stance, he asked, "Have you a map of the area where Cayley is being held?"

The minister handed over a leather portfolio of large-scale military sketches. "One last thing," he said as the earl flipped open the covers. "Mather is not the only member of my department that I've been watching. One of the troubling aspects of this investigation is the fact that at times it feels like we are dealing with two different enemies."

"You've just explained why," cut in the earl.

"Perhaps, but I'm not yet totally satisfied that it answers for all the anomalies. So I placed a bit of bait out at a meeting I had with the man several days ago—a hint that Mr. Brynn-Smith had requested a meeting with me over concerns of suspicious activity at the Royal Institution."

"Damnation." The earl looked up. "Why the Devil didn't you tell me this before now?"

The minister's face might have been carved of marble for all the emotion it showed. "Because, Lord Saybrook, like you, I don't care to share all of my methods or thoughts with others." He brushed a mote of dust from his immaculate sleeve. "Suffice it to say, I'm pursuing the matter. Interestingly enough, the man in question has a mistress . . . I'm not yet ready to reveal any conjectures, but it may prove relevant."

"You and your prurient speculations," muttered Saybrook. "I will leave the peeping into bedchambers to you, while I deal with Cayley." After poring over the details of the map, the earl tapped a finger to a stretch of woodlands edging the cliffs. "As a precaution, I want you to dispatch a force of your men to take up position here. They are to stay well hidden along this ridge and wait for my signal to move in."

"I'll give you twenty-four hours, Saybrook," said Grentham after eyeing the mantel clock. "After that, I can't risk the chance of having Renard spirit Cayley away. The orders will be to storm the ruins."

"No matter who gets caught in the cross fire?"

"Cayley cannot—I repeat, *cannot*—be allowed to fall into the hands of the French. When you returned from Vienna, you blistered my ear with a wild story about Napoleon planning to escape Elba and retake his throne. If that is true, well, use your imagination . . ."

"Fair enough," agreed Saybrook after a long moment.

"Do you wish to have Lawrance accompany you? Or some of my most skilled operatives? I have men who are experts with knives and hand-to-hand combat."

"I'll take Henning with me," he replied. "We are used to working together, and I plan on depending on stealth, not force, to free Cayley."

"Always the altruist," sneered Grentham.

The earl tucked the map and directions into his coat pocket. "Unlike you, I take no pleasure in crawling through the cesspools and muck of the espionage world."

"Mock me all you want," countered the minister as Saybrook turned for the door. "But for all your noble speeches and squeamish sentimentalities, we are more alike than you think."

20

From Lady Arianna's
Chocolate Notebooks

Chocolate Nut Chews

1½ cups sugar
¼ cup cocoa
½ cup evaporated milk
⅓ cup butter
⅓ cup peanut butter
1 teaspoon vanilla
1½ cups quick rolled oats
½ cup salted peanuts

1. Mix the sugar, cocoa, milk and butter in a heavy 2-quart saucepan. Stir over medium heat until the mixture bubbles. Boil and stir 2 minutes more. Remove from the heat.
2. Stir in the peanut butter until melted. Add the vanilla, uncooked quick rolled oats, and nuts. With 2 teaspoons, drop on waxed paper. Let stand until set.

Uncurling the cat's tail from the around the crystal decanter, Arianna poured a measure of sherry and carried it to the sofa. "Drink this," she ordered, placing the glass in Sophia's hands, "while I dispatch a servant to fetch Mr. Henning from his surgery."

"There is really no need for that," protested Sophia. "I have a well-stocked medicine chest. A sprinkling of basilicum powder and a clean bandage is all that is required . . . and you seem as skilled as any medical man in treating wounds." She took a swallow of the wine. "Not to mention the fact that Mr. Henning might feel morally obligated to tell the earl."

"Basil's scruples are a trifle flexible on certain things, but you have a point," conceded Arianna. "Slip off your jacket and let me have a better look at you before I decide."

The chest was brought in, along with a basin of hot water, and for the next few minutes, Arianna worked in methodical silence, cleaning bits of dirt and dried blood from the jagged cut. "The blade didn't cut in too deeply," she announced, setting aside the sponge and tweezers. Rising, she made another quick trip to the sideboard.

"I would prefer to keep a clear head," murmured Sophia, eyeing the bottle in Arianna's hands. "Besides, I *hate* brandy."

"Grit your teeth. A splash of spirits is good for warding off infection."

A sharp hiss leaked from Sophia's lips as the brandy doused the raw flesh, but other than that, she remained stoically silent as a bandage was fastened into place.

"Well-done, Miss Kirtland—"

"Oh please, won't you call me Sophia?" Smoothing at the torn edges of her chemise, she gave a tentative smile. "Considering all we've been through together in the last little while, it seems rather absurd to stand on formality."

"I would be happy to." In England, calling someone by her given name was a mark of intimate friendship. "But only if you will do the same."

"Agreed . . . Arianna."

"Finish your sherry, and then I imagine you will wish to change into some fresh clothing and lie down for a nap—"

"Be damned with a nap," swore Sophia. "We need to have a council of war. Stoughton is a filthy swine, especially when it comes to women, but I don't think he would be stupid enough to risk attacking us for purely personal reasons. He *must* be involved with Renard. So while Grentham goes after him, we must figure out how to pursue the Fox."

"The scent has been maddeningly hard to pick up," said Arianna. "Even Saybrook and Lawrance feel that despite all their sniffing, the trail remains elusive."

"Surely we can be clever enough to think of new ground to cover," insisted Sophia.

"I confess, I have tried, but at this point I feel a little lost as to which way to turn."

Talk of the hunt seemed to have brought a touch of color back to Sophia's cheeks. Raising herself from the pillows, she flexed her shoulder and reached for her discarded riding jacket. "Well, then, we have to retrace our steps and look more closely . . ."

Her words stopped abruptly.

"What is it?" asked Arianna.

"I—I'm not sure." Frowning, Sophia extracted a small object snagged in the fold of the woolen cuff. "How odd," she murmured, leaning in for a closer look at it. "It must have caught on the metal button when I was punching at Stoughton's gut." A wink of gold. "Hmmm, it's a fob of some sort . . . I wouldn't have thought the colonel had any interest in the classics, but this is written in Greek."

"Greek?" repeated Arianna. She felt a sudden spark of excitement flare to life.

"*Lumos,*" translated Sophia. "That means 'lamp.' "

"And a lamp gives light." She felt a burning in her chest. "May I see that, if you please?"

Sophia handed it over.

The red flash of the ruby confirmed her suspicions. "Lady Urania and Canaday wear identical designs."

Their gazes met. "The Bright Lights," whispered Sophia, echoing the whirring of Arianna's own mental gears.

"It seems a logical deduction," she agreed. "Though there still are a number of shadowy questions to answer." A flicker of the candles, stirred by the cat's movement on the sideboard, suddenly set off a thought. "*Dio Madre,* just last night, Saybrook was telling me the Greek myth about how man received the gift of fire."

"The story of Prometheus is a core tale—"

"Theus!" exclaimed Arianna. "Good God, do you know the viscount's full given name?"

"No," answered Sophia. "But I've a copy of *Debrett's Peerage* in the library."

A quick check of the book revealed the sought-for entry halfway down page ninety-two—

PROMETHEUS PERICLES MORTLEY, VISCOUNT CANADAY,
OF OXFORDSHIRE . . .

"Eureka," intoned Sophia, staring at the black-and-white image for a long moment. "Now what?"

"This certainly changes everything." Arianna thought for a moment. "Get dressed quickly. We need to hurry to Grosvenor Square. Saybrook may still be at home."

The earl nearly collided with Henning as he darted inside the entrance to the surgery.

"Sandro!" His friend shifted the leather rucksack from hand to hand. "I was just going out for a bit."

"So I see." Saybrook thinned his lips. The butt of a pistol was poking out from beneath the buckled flaps. "Baz . . . ," he said tightly. "I speak as a friend, not as a lackey of Whitehall, when I say you are—"

"Indulging in the Scottish penchant for holding a grudge?"

"I wouldn't put it that way."

"Auch, neither would I."

The earl let out a harried sigh. "Look, Baz, I've some important news to tell you."

But before he could go on, Henning countered with a humorless laugh. "As do I, laddie. I was just on my way out to collect one last piece of evidence from a friend who arrived late last night from Inverness. And then I was coming to see you."

"Me?" Saybrook's voice held a note of surprise. "I had the distinct feeling you had been doing your best to avoid me of late."

"I didna want to tell you what I was doing, for fear that you would think my wits addled by grief. I wanted to have proof, and now I've got it. Proof that the high-and-mighty Stoughton has been running a thieving ring for several years. A treasonous one, for stealing supplies from the navy hampers the war effort and is considered a crime against King and country. He's murdered other prisoners, not just Angus, and this will ensure that he pays for those crimes."

Saybrook opened his mouth to speak.

"Nay, hear me out. I've documents and sworn statements, and incriminating letters in the colonel's own hand. Ye might have thought I was deaf to yer counsel that justice is the best form of revenge, but I was listening. I dunna have to pull a trigger to put a period to the smarmy weasel's existence. This packet of proof"—he gave the rucksack a little shake—"will have the government do it for me, all right and tight."

"I know, Baz. Grentham arrested Stoughton this morning and convinced him to confess to his misdeeds."

It was Henning's turn to evince surprise. "Well, I'll be a blue-faced Pict. How did he come to suspect the colonel?"

"The minister wouldn't tell me," answered the earl with a wry grimace. "He said he had made a promise."

"To the Devil, no doubt."

"I don't know whether Grentham is on intimate speaking terms with Lucifer, but he certainly had a lengthy discourse with Stoughton. Or rather his inquisitors did. Never fear, justice will be served." Saybrook paused. "In addition we also now know that Cayley has been abducted, by order of Renard, and is being held near Dover while they arrange to have him smuggled over to France."

"Merde," muttered Henning. "Any idea precisely where?"

"As a matter of fact, yes." Saybrook cocked a nod at the sack. "I'm glad to see you are carrying a firearm, for I was hoping to enlist your help in freeing Cayley. The minister has granted me twenty-four hours to do it. After that, he will send in an armed force to ensure that no one makes the trip across the Channel to France."

"This pistol is part of my proof," said the surgeon, pulling a face. "It bears the crest of the Swedish Royal Armory and was meant as a gift for the Admiral of the North Sea Fleet stationed at Middlesbrough. Stoughton kept it and was foolish enough to have his own initials engraved on the silver cap."

"Let us put it to better use," replied the earl. "Assuming you are willing, there is no time to waste."

"Give me several minutes to exchange these papers for my knives, laddie, and then let's be off."

"Gone?" said Sophia. "Gone where?"

"Sandro doesn't say." Arianna reread the hastily scribbled note. "He just writes that Grentham seized Stoughton and discovered that Cayley has been abducted and is in danger of being taken to France. He's rushed off to find Mr. Henning and see if the two of them can rescue the inventor."

Sophia bit at her lower lip. "Surely we must tell someone."

"Tell them what?" she responded. "I've seen how the wheels of bureaucracy turn—with a leaden slowness that often crushes what is in its path." Pacing to the parlor window, she stared out at the scudding gray clouds. "Renard will move quickly once he—or she—knows about Stoughton. But the question is, what will he do?"

A patter of raindrops tapped against the leaded glass, the watery blur catching the reflection of Sophia's grimace. "Well, we can't very well stroll into Canaday's drawing room and politely ask him and his sister what their little group of conspirators is intending to do."

The casement creaked in the gusty breeze.

Arianna turned slowly, a smile taking shape at the corners of her mouth. "Actually, that's exactly what we are going to do."

"I—I was jesting!"

"But I was not." She hurried to one of the breakfront cabinets and pulled open the bottom drawer. "We are indeed going to pay the twins a visit, but it won't be a purely social call. However, for my plan to work, you are going to have to be willing to play a dangerous game."

"Just tell me what I have to do."

"Simply be yourself," answered Arianna. "I want you to pay a morning call on the Mortleys and keep them occupied while I sneak in through the rear of the house and have a look around their private quarters."

"But—"

"Follow me to my dressing room. I'll explain as I change into more comfortable clothing."

Sophia watched the rapid transformation from elegant lady to tattered street urchin in wordless wonder. "How do you do that?" she finally asked as Arianna tucked her coiled hair under a floppy wool cap.

"Through years of practice." She flexed her knees. "Breeches and boots are much more practical for movement than yards of flapping fabrics."

Peering into one of the open bandboxes, Sophia let out a wistful sigh. "I used to borrow breeches from our youngest groom so I could ride astride. It was very . . . liberating."

"Yes, isn't it?" Arianna slid a slim-bladed knife and several picklocks into the hidden sheath of her boot. "I think men are desperate to keep it a secret from our sex. Allowing such physical freedom might encourage us to shed our mental corsets as well. And that has them quaking in their Hessians!"

Sophia smiled as she fingered the napped wool.

Eyeing her companion's figure, Arianna quickly picked out a full set of men's clothing and rolled the garments into a tight bundle. "Better take these with us, just in case things take an unexpected turn."

As they hurried out to the mews, where a carriage was being readied, she explained what she had in mind.

"Once we're close to Canaday's town house, we'll leave the carriage on a side street and proceed on foot. You will march right up to the front steps and knock on the door, as befits a perfectly ordinary social call, while I will get into the back garden from the alleyway and find a window or door to force open."

She gestured for Sophia to climb into the small, shabby cabriolet. "As you see, we keep several nondescript vehicles for moving around Town unnoticed."

"Wh-what if you're caught?" asked Sophia.

"I won't be," assured Arianna. "I'm very good at moving around quickly and quietly. And if worse comes to worst, I daresay I can outrun any servant."

Sophia gave a nervous little tug at her sleeve. "I wish I felt as confident as you do."

"All you have to do is stay calm. Don't worry about me—just be yourself. After all, there's nothing unnatural about stopping by the residence of a fellow scientist to borrow a book."

"I . . . Oh Lud, *what* book?" A blank look came over her face. "I—I can't think of a one that Canaday might have that isn't in my library."

Arianna held back a huff of impatience. "Any book will do. In fact, it's better to pick a common one. Then you improvise. Say you spilled a chemical on your copy and are in need of a quick replacement to finish your experiment."

"What ex . . . Oh, right. Improvise." Sophia blinked. "You are frightfully good at thinking on your feet."

"As I said before, I've had years of practice." Arianna peeked through the window draperies, then let them fall back into place. Shadows wreathed her companion's face, but she could sense the tension coiling through her body.

"Have you been to visit Lady Urania before?" she asked, seeking to keep Sophia's nerves from growing too tight.

"Yes. Several times."

"It would be helpful if you remember anything about the layout of the rooms."

There was a whispering of wool as Sophia stirred against the squabs. "Let me think . . . They share a study. It's the center room at the rear of the house, and each has a small separate workroom on either side."

"Excellent," murmured Arianna. "It's likely that only one or two trusted servants are permitted to clean there, so at this time of day, I should be safe enough." She checked that the small pocket pistol was snug in her waistband. "Relax. You've shown a great aptitude for clandestine activities. Just do your best to prolong the visit. Cough. Complain of the chemicals making your throat scratchy, and perhaps Lady Urania will offer you tea."

"Improvise, improvise," repeated Sophia, as if she were reciting a prayer.

"Trust your instincts," murmured Arianna. The curtain twitched as the wheels clattered to a halt. "Ready?"

The wintry shadows, a chill gunmetal gray that reminded her of Grentham's eyes, hid her movements through the garden. Hugging close to the overgrown ivy vines, Arianna crept along the perimeter wall, surveying the back of the town house for the best point of entry. The ground-floor windows were guarded by heavy iron grilles—Canaday looked to be taking security seriously—and for a moment, she feared that her plan was all for naught.

But a closer study revealed that the decorative facing of pale Portland stone provided perfect footholds for someone used to climbing through the rigging of a West Indies schooner.

Her gaze followed the carving up to the second floor, where the diamond-paned glass stared out, unprotected, at the leafless trees.

Ha, she thought grimly. It appeared that Prometheus Mortley, the self-styled god of fire from the Greek myths, had an Achilles' heel.

Moving lightly over the last few yards of half-frozen turf, Arianna made her way up to the window ledge. A stealthy peek showed the room was empty, and her blade made quick work of releasing the lock. Leaving it open just a crack for a quick escape, she took shelter behind an ornate pearwood desk and considered how to proceed. From the corridor came the sounds of conversation drifting out from the drawing room. *So far, so good.* But Sophia could only be expected to occupy Lady Urania for at most a half hour. Twenty minutes was more likely.

"Not much time to gather proof of a perfidious traitor," she whispered wryly. But with the hounds snapping at his tail, Renard may have gotten a little careless.

Keeping one ear cocked for the fall of footsteps, Arianna began a search through the desk drawers and the papers piled on the leather blotter. *Nothing* . . . until small map of the southern coast caught her eye. Hidden beneath a copy of a sporting journal, it was marked with a snaking red line leading from Dover to Calais. *Strange.* The route was not the shortest distance, but rather a helter-pelter twisting that made no sense to her. *A route through the perilous currents and tides, perhaps?* The Channel waters were notoriously dangerous for any sailor unfamiliar with them.

She made a quick tracing of the map and put it back in place, then moved on to the book cabinet by the arched door connecting the study to one of the side workrooms. It held only a variety of chemistry books and glass beakers filled with liquids and powders that gave off a faintly noxious smell.

"Damnation." She mouthed a soundless mutter. "What did I expect? A beribboned diary detailing the recipes of their many betrayals?"

Closing the cabinet, Arianna circled the room, checking all the obvious hiding places—a wooden humidor, a bust of Socrates, a classical red and black krater.

Perhaps this visit had been an impetuous decision.

A wiser move might have been to wait until night offered the chance for a more thorough search of the premises. But too late now for misgivings, Arianna told herself, hesitating in front of the connecting door and listening for any whisper of movement. Nothing but silence; however, Lady Urania's brother might very well be reading . . .

The hurried click of steps and then a snatch of conversation drifting down from the drawing room forced a decision.

"Forgive me for interrupting, Miss Kirtland." It was Canaday's voice, unruffled as always. "But may I draw my sister away for a brief moment?"

Easing the latch open, Arianna ducked into the workroom.

"Could it not wait?" hissed Urania as the pair entered the study.

"No." The viscount's silky voice was now turning a little rough around the edges. "Stoughton has been hauled off to Horse Guards, and I fear he will crack like an egg."

Silence.

"Cayley—" he began.

"Forget Cayley," said his sister decisively. "As we've discussed before, there are times when we must cut our losses. We have the papers—the plans and the formulas. Those are the ultimate prizes."

But where are they? Holding her breath, Arianna pressed closer to the door.

"If we get away with them to France," went on Lady Urania, "then all of our efforts will have been worthwhile."

"Having Cayley in our control would be an even greater achievement," protested Canaday. "There is time, if we move quickly."

Lady Urania seemed to hesitate. "No. I know you wish to leave England in a blaze of glory, my dear. But we must be smart."

Another tiny silence. "We'll dispatch Grimmaud to do away with Cayley. Even if there are other drawings of his invention tucked away somewhere, they will be of little use to Britain without the formula for the explosive. And we've ensured that the chemists involved have taken its secret to the grave. So let us not risk ruining our ultimate achievements. Le Chaze is waiting to take us across to Calais. We must go now."

"Now?" echoed her brother. "But that will mean a nighttime crossing."

"I fear that Lord Saybrook and his she-bitch have been sniffing around a little too closely at our activities," said Lady Urania. "Their presence in Vienna had a plausible explanation, but Stoughton did not mention their visit to Scotland until yesterday. Otherwise I would have acted sooner."

There was a rattle of wood and metal that Arianna couldn't identify.

"It's the one mistake I regret—but let us not dwell on that. We have to assume that the colonel's planned attack on the countess never materialized, as Miss Kirtland is here."

"A coincidence that is rather hard to swallow," muttered her brother.

"Indeed," said his sister. "So we can't afford to tarry, and with the British navy in control of the Channel waters, we run too great a risk trying to go by boat." A rustling of paper. "Le

Chaze knows the air currents and has the nerve to fly in the dark. Even if the English somehow get wind of our flight, their aeronauts will not dare follow."

Balloons! thought Arianna. *Of course—they had meant for Cayley to disappear into thin air!*

A soft laugh. "As always, my dear sister, you think so clearly, and boldly. I shall regret giving up our game of twisting the inner circle of Whitehall around our fingers. But with this final secret in our grasp, we can soon make a triumphant return to London."

"Let us not gloat just yet. We still have much work to do," cautioned Lady Urania. "Gather the papers while I get rid of our guest."

So the papers were here. Arianna eased the pistol out from her waistband.

"Perhaps I should simply use my stiletto," said Canaday in a low voice. "That Miss Kirtland rides in the park with Lady Saybrook must mean she is somehow involved in forcing our hand."

"She can't hurt us now," mused Lady Urania. "However, you have a point. Like Icarus, she ought to suffer the consequences for trying to soar too close to the Sun."

"And the heavenly planets, my dear sister, the muse of the starry skies."

Good God, the two of them were sounding more and more unhinged.

"Your glow is all the brighter for being set against the midnight-black sky." His voice dropped to a dreamy whisper as he quickly recited some lines of poetry.

> *Descend from Heav'n Urania, by that name*
> *If rightly thou art call'd, whose Voice divine . . .*

"*Paradise Lost*—Milton's epic is an apt choice, as we find ourselves forced to leave our home by inferior beings," replied Lady Urania when her brother was done. "But this time, we shall be a grand part of helping noble Lucifer triumph in his rebellion against the Powers That Be."

One bullet, two villains. Arianna eased the hammer of her pistol to full cock. *But how many servants loyal to their nefarious scheme?*

She had only an instant to make a decision.

"Go ahead," said Lady Urania. "But be quick about it."

Kicking the door open, Arianna took dead aim at Canaday's chest. "Not so fast."

21

From Lady Arianna's Chocolate Notebooks

Sparkling Ginger–Chocolate Chip Cookies

½ cup turbinado sugar
6 ounces bittersweet chocolate
2 cups whole wheat or regular pastry flour
1 teaspoon baking soda
4½ teaspoons ground ginger
½ teaspoon fine-grain sea salt
½ cup (1 stick) unsalted butter
¼ cup unsulfured molasses
⅔ cup fine-grain natural cane sugar, sifted
1½ tablespoons grated fresh ginger, peeled
1 large egg, well beaten

1. Preheat the oven to 350°F with racks in the top and bottom third of the oven. Line a couple of baking sheets with unbleached parchment paper and place the turbinado sugar in a small bowl. Set aside.

2. Finely chop the chocolate into ⅛-inch pieces.
3. In a large bowl whisk together the flour, baking soda, ground ginger, and salt.
4. Heat the butter in a saucepan until it is just barely melted. Remove from the heat and stir in the molasses, sugar, and fresh ginger. The mixture should be warm but not hot at this point. If it is hot to the touch, let it cool a bit. Whisk in the egg. Pour over the flour mixture, and stir until just combined. Fold in the chocolate.
5. Form the cookie dough into small balls (the size depends on how large you like your cookies!). For each one, add a sprinkling of the turbinado sugar you set aside earlier to your hand and roll each ball between your palms to heavily coat the outside of each dough ball. Place the cookies a few inches apart on the prepared baking sheets. Bake for 7 to 10 minutes, or until the cookies puff up, darken a bit, and get quite fragrant.

The viscount fell back a half step in surprise but quickly composed himself with a rumbled laugh. "A dashing disguise, a gleaming pistol—dear me, it appears that you have been reading too many horrid novels in the solitude of your fancy town house, Lady Saybrook."

Arianna smiled grimly in return. "I'm glad you find me amusing, sir. It will likely be your last laugh for quite some time."

Lady Urania stood as still as a statue, her face pale, devoid of expression. Like cold marble.

"Is it?" he jeered. "You have only one puny bullet and there are two of us. Apparently you aren't very good at mathematics."

"I can add up the fact that a shot through your heart leaves me to go *mano a mano* with your sister. So, given her frail form, I'm willing to wager that the numbers favor me," she replied.

"Lady Urania, you will be so good as to tell me where those papers are, else your brother is a dead man."

"She's bluffing," said Canaday calmly. "Even if she has the nerve to pull the trigger, the shot will likely sail far wide of the mark."

"I'm quite experienced in handling both pistols and knives, as the unfortunate Lord Reginald would tell you. That is, were he still alive."

His face darkened, whether in anger or uncertainty was hard to tell.

Arianna adjusted her aim just a hair. "I won't ask again, Lady Urania."

"They are in the cabinet to your left," said Canaday's sister.

"I already looked in there," she countered. "It contains naught but books and vials of chemicals.

"Oh come, you don't think I would be stupid enough to leave them lying in plain sight," said Lady Urania. "They are hidden in a false book at the back of the bottom shelf."

"Step away from your sister, Lord Canaday." A curt gesture indicated a spot out of arm's reach of the desk and any implement that might serve as a weapon. "Call in Miss Kirtland, Lady Urania. And do it nicely, without raising any alarm. I am easily spooked when I'm nervous. You wouldn't want my finger to twitch on the trigger and extinguish Prometheus's flame."

"Oh, aren't you the clever one," murmured Canaday while his sister shot her a venomous look.

Nonetheless, Lady Urania performed the request exactly as ordered.

"Now move clear of the door, if you please." Arianna was careful to choreograph every little movement. She did not underestimate their cunning or their quickness.

A moment later, Sophia stepped cautiously into the room, a dainty little cake fork grasped in her hand. "Oh, thank God. I feared things had gone awry."

"No." Arianna curled a quick grimace. "A good thing, seeing

as that is not good for attacking anything other than spun sugar."

"I thought it a better choice than the butter knife," replied Sophia.

"Indeed. Now, please circle behind Lord Canaday and come stand by me. His sister is about to retrieve a cache of documents from its hiding place and hand it over to us."

Lady Urania had not yet moved a muscle.

"What made you, two scions of pampered privilege, betray your homeland?" demanded Sophia.

Arianna bit back a cynical comment. She had long ago given up asking villains to justify their actions, for the self-serving answers were usually as worthless as horse dung. However, given the complex cleverness of the pair's conniving, it might be possible to learn some practical information about how they gathered state secrets, if they could be goaded into a response.

"Oh, don't bother asking, Sophia. In my experience, it's not noble idealism but filthy greed that motivates most traitors." She shot the twins a contemptuous look. "How much are you being paid to sell out your country?"

"*Our* country?" The viscount's voice quivered with emotion. "Britain be damned! My father hated the snobbery and arrogant self-importance of the English aristocracy. He renounced his family during his first year at Oxford and moved to Paris, where he embraced the radical republican ideals of France. As Citoyen Mortley, he joined the common people in rejoicing when they sent their king and queen to the guillotine."

"Keep your hands by your side, sir," warned Arianna. The pistol maintained its unwavering aim. "So, I take it your mother was French?"

Glowering, Canaday clenched and unclenched his fists.

It was his sister who answered. "Yes. The revolution empowered intelligent women. My mother served with Robespierre in creating a new France, a better France. One based on merit and equality—"

"One bathed in blood," said Arianna.

Lady Urania shrugged. "Change requires sacrifice."

"It's easy to sound so cavalier," snapped Sophia, "when the head that is rolling is not yours."

The pale eyes remained opaque, emotionless. "You think I speak lightly of death and suffering?" Lady Urania glanced at her brother. "Theus and I were made orphans by my priggish uncle, who could not bear to think of his family tree blighted by a republican. He hired an English adventurer who was spiriting French aristos out of the country to kidnap my ailing father and us." The words were coming out as a monotone drawl—she might have been reciting a shopping list for the butcher and greengrocer. "My mother tried to stop the men who broke into her home. They shot her dead."

A muscle jumped on Canaday's jaw. He started to reach for his sister, but Arianna's order stopped him short.

"Don't move, sir."

"It was all for our own good," went on Lady Urania, ignoring the brief interruption. "Or so our aunt assured us when she revealed the full the secret of our background on our sixteenth birthday. She expected gratitude, I suppose."

"What she got was a draught of hydrogen cyanide," said Canaday with a chilling smile. "We both were already very skilled in chemistry. Our so-called father followed her to the grave soon after."

The foul odor from the cabinet was beginning to make Arianna's stomach queasy. "A sad tale, but it's no excuse for your actions. Because of you, many innocent people have already died." She flicked an impatient gesture at Lady Urania. "Get the papers."

A flutter of pale blue silk stirred, its soft hue looking deceptively innocent against the dark-grained wood.

At the same instant, Canaday slid a hand toward his boot.

"Stop!" cried Arianna.

Both of the twins froze.

"Unknot your neckcloth, sir and toss it over here." Her eyes had strayed for only a fraction of a second. "Now turn around and put your hands behind your back."

To Sophia she said, "Take the linen and bind his hands. Tightly and double the knots." Once the viscount was well and truly trussed, she would have Sophia search for the hidden knife. "Have a care that you stay to the side—"

Too late.

Sophia, in her haste to help, had moved directly into the line of fire. Sensing her position, Canaday reacted with a serpent's slithering quickness. Spinning around, he whipped out his weapon with one hand while the other snaked out to catch Sophia and pull her close to shield his own body.

"Run, Rainnie."

A wild blur of movements, a sudden shattering of glass as liquid, hot and stinging, splashed against her cheek. Steeling her focus, Arianna drew a steadying breath and calmly pulled the trigger.

Canaday let out a bellow of pain as he fell back. Seeing that Sophia had scrambled out of reach, he clasped his bloodied hand to his breast and darted out into the corridor.

The door slammed shut, the *snick* of the key turning in the lock punctuating his muffled shout.

"Froissart! Grimmaud!"

"That answers my earlier question about whether the servants are in league with their masters." Tossing aside the spent pistol, Arianna hurried to the massive oak desk. "Quick, help me push this to block the entrance."

Between the two of them, they managed to maneuver the weighty piece of furniture into place. "That will hold them, but only for a bit." Arianna wedged in a few chairs and shoved the cabinet to reinforce the barricade. "Here, cut off your skirts at the knees." Taking the book knife from the blotter, she tossed it over to Sophia. "We'll have to climb down from the window—"

"Wait!" Sophia grabbed for a vase of flowers.

"For God's sake, we haven't time to smell the roses," shouted Arianna.

Tossing the blooms on the carpet, Sophia splashed the water over Arianna's face.

"Wh-what the Devil—" she sputtered.

"Acid—sulfuric by the smell," answered Sophia. "Lean back and let me rinse it off. It's a diluted mixture, but it can burn your flesh badly. You're lucky. If it had struck a scant inch higher, you would be blind in one eye."

Arianna huffed a grunt as the pounding of boot heels clattered on the stairs. Fending off further ministrations, she said, "Let us try to ensure that our luck holds. The window, without delay."

"Wh-what about the papers?" ventured Sophia.

"A ruse, seeing as she fled without taking anything from the cabinet," answered Arianna, throwing open the casement. "I suspected as much, but I thought it worth the chance."

"Sorry," muttered Sophia.

"We all make mistakes. The key is to live and learn," she replied, inching out onto the ledge. "Give me your hand."

"Not necessary," said Sophia. "I spent my youth climbing in and out of my bedchamber windows so I could accompany my older cousins on their nocturnal escapades."

"Excellent." Heavy thuds were hammering against the door. "I suggest you put such skills into action."

Splinters flew up as one of the panels split with an ominous *crack*.

"Now!"

Hands scraping over the chiseled stone, Arianna scrambled down the carved façade. "Follow me," she called, hitting the ground and setting off at a run. She doubted that Canaday would risk attracting attention by firing a shot. Still, she kept low and wove a path in and out of the holly bushes, ignoring the jagged slap and tear of the sharp leaves at her clothing.

The tripping steps and ragged gasps told her that Sophia was keeping pace.

Banging a shoulder into the back gate, she popped it open.

"This way," called Arianna as the gate yielded to a hard shove. Cutting through the winding alleyways, she led them to the side street where their carriage stood waiting.

"To Horse Guards?" wheezed Sophia, fighting to catch her breath as she tumbled into the cab.

Slamming the door shut, Arianna rapped on the roof for the coachman to spring the horses. A moment of mental calculation led her to discard the idea. "By the time we talk our way into the minister's inner sanctum and convince Grentham that we shouldn't be whisked away to Bedlam, it will be too late."

"B-but we can't hope to discover which way they have fled. From the drawing room window I saw Canaday's curricle waiting right outside the town house. By now, they could be headed anywhere."

"No need to give chase." She patted at her coat to make sure the piece of paper was still safely tucked in her pocket. "I know exactly what route they are taking. And how."

As the carriage careened around a corner and raced along the Strand, Arianna thumped another signal—this one to halt. Taking pencil and paper from one of the side compartments, she scribbled a note and then called out the window to one of the street urchins sweeping horse droppings from the crossing.

"Can you carry this to Horse Guards without delay?" She held up a shilling.

"Oiy." The lad held out a grubby hand.

"Don't let the guards stop you. There will be a gold guinea for you if you get it into Lord Grentham's hands without delay." She saw his eyes widen to the size of tea saucers. "Tell him it's from the Countess of Saybrook."

Snatching the paper and coin, he set off at a dead run.

"You had better change into these." Arianna tossed Sophia

the bundle of men's clothing, then fished a chamois cloth from beneath the seat and began blotting the moisture from her coat.

"Where are we going?" asked Sophia. "Or don't I want to know?"

"I wouldn't blame you for deciding that you have had your fill of adventure. If you choose, I can drop you here and continue on my own."

As she wriggled into her breeches, Sophia responded with a word that made Arianna blink.

"Very well. Seeing as you seem determined to continue, we are headed for the Artillery Grounds."

"I'm not sure cannons are going to do us much good . . ." The remnants of her gown fell to the floorboards as Sophia twisted around. "Can you cut the cursed strings of this corset? Whalebone stays are *not* conducive to physical exertion." Once free of the constricting garment, she pulled on the shirt. "So unless there is a secret weapon there—"

"No, it's not secret," said Arianna. "But let us hope it's *highly* effective." Seeing Sophia's questioning look, she added, "Balloons."

"Balloons!"

"And the men who fly them," she explained. "The military allows a company of experienced aeronauts to keep their equipment there and use the fields for ascents and landings. Their flights along the coast provide valuable mapmaking information."

Realization suddenly dawned on Sophia's face. "Are you saying the twins intend to make an *airborne* escape?"

"I overheard them making their plans. They know of Stoughton's arrest and have decided to make a run—metaphorically speaking—for France with Cayley's sketches and the formula . for the explosives."

"Y-you think we have a chance of stopping them?"

"I'm willing to follow them to Hell and back to see that we do," vowed Arianna.

* * *

"This way." Saybrook dropped down from his vantage point and pointed to a small gap in the crumbling wall surrounding the castle ruins. "There's a light in the tower's top window, but the rest of the building appears deserted."

"My guess is Renard may be running out of people he can trust," said Henning.

"Stoughton said that he only left two men to guard Cayley, but he wasn't sure whether reinforcements were being sent down from London."

"No sign of any new arrivals," observed the surgeon as they made their way along the perimeter of the grounds to where the stable sat silent and shrouded in shadows by the rutted dirt cart path.

Drawing his pistol, the earl ducked inside. "Naught but two horses in the stalls," he murmured, reappearing a few moments later.

"So it's two hired ruffians against the pair of us." Henning gave a whispered laugh as they circled through the trees to approach the back of the castle. "Poor devils. Do ye care whether we take them alive?"

"I always avoid mindless bloodshed when possible," answered Saybrook tersely. "That is one of the things that separates us from the evil ones." He stopped to survey the surroundings from the shelter of the unpruned privet hedge. "God knows, there are far too many things we have in common."

"Feeling a twinge of conscience, laddie? If ye plan te keep doing Grentham's nasty work for him, ye had better toughen up yer tender sensibilities. Nobility is all very well in theory, but sometimes, ye must strip off yer fancy principles and drop into the filth, to fight these miscreants on their own turf."

Saybrook shaded his eyes from the setting sun as he stared at the stone tower. "You know, I'm not afraid of getting my hands dirty, Baz. But I don't like dragging my friends into the muck along with me."

The surgeon dismissed the oblique apology with a rude sound. "I told ye before, I don't hold you to blame fer Angus. The lad made his own choices. If anything, I should have seen the trouble and done something to steer him clear of the danger before he got in over his head."

The earl shifted to sweep his gaze along the rugged sea cliff. "Those who are closest to us are often the hardest people to guard from danger," he said softly.

"Auch, is that what's eating at yer insides? That ye can't wrap yer wife in a sweet little apron and keep her locked in a kitchen?" A grunt. "No wonder she took a carving knife to ye the first time ye met."

For an instant, a flicker of wry amusement softened the grim set of his mouth. "I am learning to compromise. But what of friends who have less experience with the sordid side of life? To draw them into our affairs is a little like dropping a dab of butter into a red-hot frying pan."

"Ye are worried about—"

"Ssssshhhhhhh." A hiss from the earl warned him to silence. With a groan of the rusty hinges, the back door opened and a big man in a greasy canvas coat came out, holding a chamber pot at arm's length.

"Cor, we ought te be paid double for having te be bloody maids to a addlepated lunatic as well as his captors." Stomping down the footpath, the guard tossed its contents perilously close to where Saybrook and Henning were hidden in the shrubbery. "Rattling on about flying and such," he grumbled. "Let the madman sprout sodding wings and try to make his escape. Ha, ha, ha . . ."

As the guard turned, still snorting nasty chuckles, the earl slipped out and whipped the butt of his weapon against the man's temple. He dropped like a sackful of stones, the empty basin rolling away into the tangle of tall, winter gray fescue.

"Let's carry him inside," whispered Saybrook. "We'll leave him locked in the pantry, trussed and gagged, for Grentham's men to deal with."

After securing the prisoner, they found his tallow candle still burning on the kitchen table, a plume of oily black smoke curling up from the guttering flame.

"Hoy, Jock!" A shout reverberated overhead. "Move yer lazy carcass and bring that jug. I'm thirsty."

Saybrook pointed wordlessly to a narrow passageway. A set of slitted windows at the far end let in just enough of the fading sunlight to illuminate a rough-cut circular staircase winding up to floors above.

Henning hooked an earthenware jug from the table and signaled for them to proceed.

"Leave it to me to draw the varlet out," he said under his breath, edging forward to take the lead. They crept up the stone steps, following the earthy scent of a peat fire to the top floor.

On the landing, Henning stopped and let the jug fall to the floor.

"Oiy!" The muddy *thunk* of it shattering into tiny shards drew an outraged bellow from inside the room. "Ye bloody clumsy ox!" Boot steps, hard and heavy, punctuated the curse. "I swear, I'll drop ye and yer thick skull from the window here—"

"I think not." Saybrook caught him with a hard right cross to the jaw as he barged through the doorway. Like his cohort, the man dropped like a boneless bag of rocks.

"They must be Stoughton's choices," said Henning dismissively. "Renard's personal network of skilled operatives appears to have disappeared."

"We have eliminated some of his best men," said Saybrook grimly. "Now let us hope we are close to catching him by the tail." He nudged the fallen guard. "Can you handle locking him away with his cohort while I check on Cayley?"

"Aye, leave him to me," said the surgeon. "I'll make sure he gets enough bumps and bruises on the way down to keep him quiet until morning."

The earl edged his way into the tower chamber, alert for any other guard who might be lurking inside. But the only body he saw was wrapped in a thick blanket and huddled in front of a meager fire.

"Sir George?" he said softly.

The man turned, blinking his bleary eyes. "If you're another one of those ruffians sent to shake information out of me, you can go to the Devil." His voice, though weak, bristled with defiance.

"I'm not." The earl lowered his weapon. "Whitehall sent me. I've come to take you away from here."

Cayley squinted in suspicion. "Hmmph. That's what the others said. How do I know I can trust you?"

"A good question." Saybrook squatted down by the inventor and gently cut the ropes binding his wrists. "To begin with, my friend and I coshed your two captors over the head, so that should help allay your fears."

Wincing, Cayley rubbed weakly at the chafed skin. "Point taken."

"Secondly, I served with Colonel Greville in the Peninsula. He's a great admirer of the work you and Davy were doing for the army, no matter that the project was put aside," said the earl. "By the by, I'm Saybrook. My companion is Henning, a military surgeon who also served with the colonel."

"Dashed good fellow is Grev." The scientist ran a hand along his unshaven jaw. "I—I suppose if you know about our work, you must have access to Whitehall's inner sanctum."

"Unfortunately, so does our enemy. You are right to be cautious." Spotting a glass of water on the windowsill, he brought it over and offered the scientist a sip.

"Bloody hell," muttered Cayley, after a grateful slurp. "I wasn't careful enough. The dastards have stolen all my plans and sketches!"

"Is there enough information for them to build a working model?" asked the earl.

"Alas, I fear so. There are detailed diagrams, exact dimensions, mechanical specifications, rudder designs . . ." He grimaced. "In the hands of a competent man of science and a skilled craftsman, the material will provide very clear step-by-step instructions for building my flying machine."

"I suppose an even more important question is, does it actually work?" said the earl.

"There are still some things to work out," replied Cayley. "Right now, the flying machine must be carried aloft by a balloon, and then launched at the right altitude. It's dangerous work at that point and requires a skilled pilot, but we have proved it can be done on a regular basis."

Henning returned from downstairs, bringing with him a plate of cheese and cold gammon, along with a loaf of bread and a fresh jug of brandy. "Anyone else hungry?"

"Sir George looks likes he's been kept on thin rations."

The inventor's eyes lit up at the sight of the cheddar and meat. "Food would be most welcome. I've had nothing but gruel for days."

"Our friend here was just explaining his invention," Saybrook said to Henning as Cayley wolfed down a bite. "It must be launched from a balloon, and then . . ."

"And then once my machine is airborne," went on Cayley after a quick swallow, "the long wings allow it to glide like a hawk through the skies, and a series of movable flaps can control the direction. With a good man at the rudders, the flying machine can ride the air currents and home in on a specific target quite easily."

Henning blew out a low whistle.

"So the answer is yes, by Jove, it *does* work," finished Cayley with some pride. A sigh then deflated his smile. "Save now that it's fallen into the wrong hands, I wish I had never invented it."

"Science is a two-edged sword," murmured Saybrook. "Good and evil—it's a choice that has faced man since Adam and Eve."

Cayley nodded. "Now I have a question for you, sir. Who the Devil took my drawings? And what does he intend to do with them?"

"An English traitor, working for the French, is responsible for kidnapping you and your plans, Sir George," answered Saybrook. "As for the reason . . . right now it is mostly conjecture."

"But why would King Louis want to steal my work? As far as I know, he has no interest in science—only fine wine and rich food."

"You are correct. The present monarch, like his Bourbon predecessors, has little interest in chemistry or technological advancements. But Napoleon Bonaparte does."

"Aye, the former Emperor has a keen interest in science; I'll give him that." Cayley looked even more quizzical. "But Napoleon has been exiled to the isle of Elba, a tiny speck of rock off the coast of Tuscany."

Saybrook expelled a long breath. "Yes, but I fear he's not planning to stay there for very much longer."

22

From Lady Arianna's
Chocolate Notebooks

Chocolate Soufflé

Butter for greasing the molds
Granulated sugar for coating the molds
⅓ cup half-and-half
3 ounces bittersweet chocolate, chopped
½ cup unsweetened cocoa powder
⅓ cup water
8 large egg whites
½ cup granulated sugar
Confectioners' sugar for dusting

1. Preheat the oven to 375°F. Use a pastry brush (or your fingers) to coat the inside of four 1½-cup soufflé molds with softened butter. Fill the molds with granulated sugar. Pour out the excess.
2. Pour the half-and-half into a saucepan and heat over medium-high heat until bubbles begin to form around the edge of the pan. Remove from the heat and make a ga-

nache by adding the chopped chocolate. Stir well until combined and all of the chocolate has melted.

3. Place the ganache in the top of a double boiler, add the cocoa powder and water, and whisk until very hot. Remove from the heat and set aside.

4. Place the egg whites in a large mixing bowl and whip on medium speed until foamy. Increase the mixer speed to medium-high and make a French meringue by adding the granulated sugar 1 tablespoon at a time and whipping the whites to stiff but not dry peaks. Do not overwhip the egg whites! You can tell the egg whites are overwhipped if they start to separate and resemble scrambled eggs. (Been there, done that.)

5. Use a rubber spatula to gently fold about half the meringue into the warm chocolate mixture. Then fold the chocolate mixture into the remaining meringue, being careful not to deflate the batter. The soufflé mixture should be homogeneous in color, but if you still see streaks of meringue in the batter, that's okay.

6. Use a large spoon to gently place the soufflé mixture in the buttered and sugared molds. Fill to about ¼ inch below the rim of the molds. Run your thumb around the rim to remove the excess butter and sugar.

7. Bake until the soufflés have risen to about 1½ inches over the rim and start to brown on top, about 12 minutes. Remove from the oven and dust the tops with confectioners' sugar. Serve immediately.

Arianna and Sophia entered the shadowy warehouse. The pungent smells of old smoke and oiled leather permeated the chill air, mingling with the sweeter scents of straw and beeswax.

"Halloooo!" Arianna's call echoed through the cavernous

space. In answer came a snuffled snort from one of the horses stabled at the rear of the building.

"Maybe they have all gone home for the day," said Sophia, craning her neck to look up at the massive iron hooks and pulleys hanging down from the crossbeams. "Good heavens, look at all these implements—they look like something out of the Spanish Inquisition."

"I don't think the doors would have been left unlocked if the men had left," said Arianna as she walked along a rack holding giant coils of ropes as thick as her wrists. "Perhaps there are storage rooms or an office behind the stable area."

"Hear, hear now!" Holding a lantern aloft, James Sadler stepped out of the gloom. "This is no place to be larking about, lads"—the beam moved up from Arianna's boots and breeches to the curling hair spilling over her shoulders—"er, that is, ladies."

His brows rose even higher as Arianna ducked clear of the oversize loops of cordage and into the ring of light. "L-Lady Saybrook?"

"Yes, Mr. Sadler." She flashed a smile. "You did invite me for a ride, did you not."

"I—I don't think this is quite the most opportune time, milady. Perhaps if you came back tomorrow."

"I'm afraid we can't wait."

Sadler darted a quizzical look at Sophia. She had cut a square of silk from her ruined gown and tied it in a bandana to hold back her hair. With the flickering light sharpening her features, the look gave her a slightly menacing, piratical air.

"I realize this appears a trifle odd, but allow me to explain." He cleared his throat with a cough. "By all means, do."

"We need your help. Or rather, Britain needs your help. A pair of traitors are seeking to escape to France with vital documents. A man named Le Chaze is to fly them across the Channel in his balloon. They must be stopped . . ." She went on to explain as many of the details as she deemed safe to disclose.

Though Sadler listened in silence, his expressions ran the gamut of emotions—surprise, disbelief, consternation, concern.

Perhaps he thinks me mad.

"I don't blame you for wondering if my wits have gone wandering," added Arianna as she watched him mulling it over.

"Even to my own ears the story sounds more outrageous than Mr. Walpole's book *The Castle of Otranto*," interjected Sophia. "Nonetheless, it's all true."

"I am acquainted with Le Chaze. He occasionally comes to watch our maneuvers," said Sadler, finally rousing himself to speech. "We all find him a rather irritating, arrogant fellow. Always boasting about how, as opposed to us, his countrymen do things with Gallic flair."

"He said English aeronauts are afraid of the dark," murmured Arianna.

Sadler let out an indignant huff. "Ha, the impertinent Frog! Le Chaze is showy, but there is little substance beneath his bravado. I would like to see *him* try to navigate at night—he probably doesn't know Venus from Mars."

"I hope not. The quicker we can catch him, the better," responded Arianna. "Speaking of which, there's not a moment more to lose. We need to inflate your balloon and launch now."

Sadler shook his head. "I am just as afire to go after them as you are, Lady Saybrook. But the sad fact is that we can't."

"Why not?" demanded Arianna.

"The other aeronauts have all left for the day, and Windham has gone to the neighboring village to pick up a fresh batch of pine tar. It's impossible for me to get the balloon ready by myself, so we are grounded until he returns. And even if I could manage it, I need to have an assistant to stoke the fire for a trip of this length."

Arianna and Sophia exchanged a look. "*We* can serve as your assistants," they both chorused.

"Good heavens, I don't think . . . Surely you can't mean . . ."

He shook his head. "Not to be indelicate, ladies, but the job requires, er, muscle."

"Mr. Sadler, I am tougher than I might look," replied Arianna. "And I've a great deal of experience in handling ropes, having crewed on smuggling ships in the West Indies."

"And I've driven an open phaeton from London to Gretna Green, which requires both muscle and stamina," added Sophia. "We're not afraid of soiling our lily-white hands." She held up her scraped palms and smiled sweetly. "See?"

He blinked several times in rapid-fire succession, and the air seemed to leak out of his protests. "Make no mistake, it will be hard work," he cautioned.

They nodded.

"And very dangerous."

"That goes without saying," replied Arianna.

He pursed his lips. "One last thing. Once we catch up to them, how do you intend to stop them?"

"I'll shout a warning, and order them to descend."

His brows winged up in skepticism.

From her coat pockets, she carefully drew out the expensive dueling pistols she had brought along from the carriage. "These are deadly accurate, and I know how to use them."

"In that case, we may also want this." Sadler marched over to a nearby cabinet and took out a short-barreled rifle. "And this." He added a large pair of iron tongs to the sack containing bullets and gunpowder.

"What's that for?" asked Sophia.

"Heating the lead to a red-hot glow over the fire before we load our weapons," he answered grimly. "Le Chaze flies a Charlier balloon, which is filled with hydrogen—an extremely flammable gas."

Arianna had once witnessed a dockyard explosion. She forced herself not to recall the smells of singed canvas and charred flesh. "An excellent suggestion," she answered coolly. "The traitors cannot be allowed to reach France."

"Then we had better start putting your nautical experience to the test, Lady Saybrook." Sadler gestured at Sophia. "Your companion—"

"Miss Kirtland," supplied Arianna.

"Miss Kirtland had better gather up some additional clothing for the flight." His hand flicked to a line of pegs on the wall, from which hung an array of heavy leather garments. "Windham is not too much larger than you are. Help yourself to some of his flight gear—and be sure to take gauntlets and fur-lined helmets. It's going to be bloody cold up there."

Without further ado, he maneuvered the cart holding the balloon's gondola basket under the huge pulley. "We need to attach the top of the balloon to this heavy line," he explained, lowering the hook with a few slow turns of a winch. "I'll need you to spread the guidelines out while I ratchet the fabric up a few notches. That will allow the balloon to inflate when I stoke up the fire."

Arianna eyed the dimensions of the warehouse double doors as she hurried to perform her duties. "But surely it won't fit through the opening?"

"I'll fill it just enough to keep the fabric and lines from getting into a hopeless tangle before taking it out to the launching field. Normally we do this whole procedure outdoors, but it takes a full crew of fliers, so I thought I had better improvise."

That the aeronaut was quick-thinking and flexible was a stroke of luck—Arianna imagined that they would be called upon to react with lightning speed in the coming hours.

"Miss Kirtland, please fetch one of the horses from the stalls. We'll need to move the cart in a matter of minutes."

Sadler started a fire in the metal stove and continued to bark out a series of orders, directing his new crew members on how to guide the balloon through the doors and peg out the ropes so the huge sack could begin to inflate to its full dimensions.

Slowly, slowly, the undulating fabric began to take its proper shape.

"Get the horse and cart inside, then hurry back," called Stadler over the din of the flapping ropes and rattling metal. "The wind is rising! We need to cast off quickly!"

Arianna helped Sophia into the wickerwork gondola basket, then made a rather inelegant entry as a sudden lurch sent her sprawling headfirst into the interior. Righting herself, she tugged at the lines, giving Stadler a hand in releasing the knots.

With a last little shudder, the balloon shimmied sideways before steadying its sway and rising up, up, up toward the heavens.

"Someone is coming," said Henning in a low whisper. He set down his cup and cocked an ear.

A brush of wool, barely audible, on stone.

The earl heard it too and pinched out the candles, leaving the room lit by only the banked coals in the hearth. Pressing a finger to lips, he signaled Cayley to take shelter in the small alcove behind the fireplace.

Another sound, this one the faint scuff of leather. The intruder was at the top of the stairs.

Henning had taken up a position beside the doorway, his back pressed against the rough wall. The earl was just creeping up to the other side of the half-open portal when a flash of fire and deafening blast erupted from the landing.

A deadly hail of buckshot splintered the table and shattered the window glass. With the echo still reverberating against the stones, the intruder flung the door wide and let loose with a second volley that peltered the hearth with a rain of lead.

Henning lashed a hard kick that knocked the double-barreled coach gun from the intruder's hand. Snarling, the man spun away and whipped a pistol from his waistband.

Sparks flashed; a plume of pale smoke shivered in the aftershock of the bang.

The man dropped his arm and then fell face-first to the floor.

"At this rate, my surgery will be filled with enough cadavers for dissection to last into the next decade," Henning quipped, watching a dark stain spread between the corpse's shoulder blades.

"Be grateful one of them isn't yours," said the earl. Brushing grits of gunpowder from his fingers, he turned. "Sir George?"

"All in one piece, Lord Saybrook." The inventor peered around the corner. "This Renard fellow seems to have changed his mind about carrying me off to France."

The earl began to reload his pistol. "So it would seem." He looked up at Henning. "Stoughton's arrest must have spooked him into flight."

"Aye." The surgeon made a face. "Taking with him the detailed plans of the flying machine."

"Can't we stop him?" asked Cayley.

"Not unless you can conjure up a flying carpet," growled Saybrook. "There are countless coves along this coast, and countless smugglers willing to make a trip across the Channel, no questions asked. I would be willing to wager a fortune that the Fox is already sailing toward France."

Steadying herself on the rail of the basket, Arianna felt her pulse quicken as she gazed out at the scene unfurling beneath her feet. The views were absolutely breathtaking. Off in the distance London rose in spiky splendor, glimmers of gaslight winking amid the pale stone spires and towers. She could just make out Westminster Abbey, St. Paul's Cathedral and the silvery, snaking water of the river Thames.

"Oh, I can see the appeal of this," she murmured, lifting her face to the wind. The setting sun was painting the clouds in muted hues of orange-gold streaked with pinks and purple. "It is wondrous."

The sense of silence was otherworldly—

"Kindly take a step back from the rail, Lady Saybrook. You are throwing the balance off," called Sadler. Moving with an unconscious grace, he circled the centered burner, carefully adjusting the position of the ballast bags within the rigging.

"Please explain what you are doing," said Arianna, "so I can help you."

"The basket must be kept at an even trim to fly properly. Allow a tilt and a gust of wind might tip it over and send us plummeting to our death." He indicated a maze of cording attached to cleats, spaced at various intervals around the basket. "We must constantly adjust the sandbags that serve as ballast. This changes the altitude and lets us catch currents or avoid turbulence. The key is to gauge the winds properly. A downdraft can cause a crash."

She sucked in a lungful of air. "I will do my best to follow your orders, sir."

He patted at the series of valves on the burner. "We also adjust the flow of hot air to control our rise and fall."

Sophia was already on her knees, stoking the flames with chunks of fuel, as she had been shown.

"I may have to be a little brusque," he warned both of them. "Here in the heavens, one can't afford to stand on ceremony—not when there's naught but swirling air beneath your feet, ha, ha, ha."

"Ha, ha, ha," echoed Arianna, brushing a wildly dancing hank of hair from her cheek. "You warned us that we were not here as pleasure passengers." Another gust buffeted her face. "Hmmph, you were right," she said, plucking an errant curl from her mouth. "It *is* a little chilly up here."

"And it's going to get a great deal colder," replied Sadler. "But don't worry. You two will keep plenty warm with all the shoveling required to keep us aloft."

"Speaking of which," she said dryly, squatting down to exchange places with Sophia. "It's my turn to feed the fire."

"Thank you." Rising slowly, so as not to rock the gondola, Sophia blotted the sweat from her brow. "I, too, have some questions. How do you judge your altitude and direction? I have been looking around for a compass."

"It's here," answered Sadler, tapping at a binnacled instrument fastened to a block beneath the lip of the railing. "One tends to bump into things when the winds get a little rough. As for altitude . . ." He produced a beautifully crafted barometer from a padded leather case strapped to one of the gondola's struts. "This precision instrument measures atmospheric pressure and thus serves as an altimeter." His fingers drew a fond caress along the length of glass. "It was a gift from the great Dr. Samuel Johnson, who bequeathed it to me after hearing how I lost all my scientific implements in an early balloon crash."

"Let us hope it helps us avoid a similar fate," quipped Sophia, looking a little uneasy. Though at home on the back of a galloping horse, she seemed far less comfortable with the constant rocking motion of the gondola.

"I always fly with it, and consider it a good luck talisman," said Sadler. He made a quick reading, then put it back in its holder. "Besides, I am very good at what I do."

"So I have heard," said Arianna. "I'm told that no one has ever duplicated your feat of relaunching a balloon from the sea."

"The conditions happened to be just right," he said modestly.

Sophia cast a scientist's critical gaze over the rigging and the canopy overhead. "I would imagine there is a limit to the weight we can carry in relation to the size of the balloon."

"Indeed, there is." A twinkle lit in Sadler's eye. "I daresay you are both too young to remember the first ascent of a female in a balloon. It happened in 'eighty-five."

"I vaguely recall my governess telling me about it," answered Sophia. "Her name was Mrs. Sage, was it not? She was . . . an actress?"

"Indeed," said Sadler. "And she put on quite a performance. The great Lunardi had a flair for showmanship and he had decided that a female aeronaut would bring out crowds for the planned ascent. So he and a wealthy young man by the name of

George Biggin invited Mrs. Sage to be part of the group." He paused to look up and check the set of the rigging. "However, the actress had fibbed about her weight and the balloon couldn't lift off."

Sophia stifled a laugh. "Honestly, he should have known better than to ask any female to be truthful about her weight or her age."

A grin twitched at his mouth. "Ever the gentleman, Lunardi jumped out and allowed Biggin and Mrs. Sage to fly off. However, he omitted to lace up the door. The actress realized the danger and had to scrabble about on the floor to fix the matter"— his grin grew more pronounced—"which set off a great deal of speculation on whether the couple had engaged in, shall we say, amorous activities while in the air."

"It's a good thing I didn't drink any more of Señora Delgado's rich chocolate drinks," said Arianna, once her chuckling had died down. "Else you might have had to leave me behind."

"They are quite marvelous," said Sadler. "As are her confections. I am a baker by trade, and her creations are most unusual. I would never have guessed that chocolate could be eaten in solid form."

"You and I are going to have some interesting conversations, once we are at leisure to discuss the subject," said Arianna. "But let us not stray from the topic of balloons."

"I am curious. Are there any females who possess an expertise in flying?" asked Sophia.

"Very few," replied Sadler. "I can't think of any, save for Blanchard's wife. He is the renowned daredevil aeronaut who made the first crossing of the Channel. She is equally daring, seeing as she specializes in aerial fireworks displays."

Despite her heavy gloves, Arianna could feel the heat of the fire prickling at her hands. "I would call that dangerous, as well as daring," she mused.

"Yes, well, like men, some women appear drawn to danger." The pattern of the rigging, a crisscrossing of dark on dark lines,

cut across his face, hiding his expression in the fading light.
"Like a moth to a flame."

"There's a difference between being willing to face danger
and feeling compelled to create it," said Arianna slowly.

"Sometimes it's a fine line between the two."

Sadler was very perceptive, she realized. *Perhaps too much so.*

"I suppose, sir, that your eye is attuned to see the smallest
nuances. A tiny flutter of wind, a slight drop in temperature, a
change in the texture of the clouds—such things can mean the
difference between life and death for an aeronaut."

"Yes," he replied. "One must be observant."

"You think we will be able to spot our quarry in this vast
expanse of sky?" At the mention of the word "observant," Sophia looked around doubtfully. "It seems akin to trying to find a
needle in a haystack, especially with night coming on."

"I know where Le Chaze keeps his balloon." Sadler reached
into a leather pouch secured beneath the railing and pulled out a
small brass telescope. Snapping it open, he began scanning the
heavens. "Trust me, we'll see him and your pair of *renards*.
Darkness will not afford them any cover for escape. The moon
is full tonight, and besides, there are prevailing air currents. He
doesn't have a great many choices."

"Damn, I nearly forgot—the map!" Arianna quickly exchanged places with Sophia. "I found this on the traitor's desk."
She handed over the copy she had made of the coastlines and the
squiggling red line. "It made no sense to me, but I figured it
must have some meaning."

Stadler studied it for a moment, a small smile slowly wreath-
ing his face. "It does indeed. This helps us conserve our fuel, as
we need not circle up and down the coast looking to pick up his
trail. According to this, he's going to use the western route."

Arianna watched the burnt gold glow hovering on the horizon begin to fade. "What if Le Chaze changes his mind?"

"I doubt that he will, given the earlier barometer reading.
We'll continue on this course for another quarter of an hour. If

we don't see anything, we'll double back and cruise to the east."

Shifting her stance, she slapped her palms together, trying to contain her impatience. Waiting always set her nerves on edge.

"Halloo, I've just spotted the Fox!" Stadler shifted several bags of ballast, the starlight catching the gleam of excitement in his eyes. "Add another twist of straw to the fire. The chase is on."

23

From Lady Arianna's Chocolate Notebooks

Chocolate Almond Bark

½ cup sugar
1 tablespoon unsalted butter
1½ cups roasted Marcona almonds (not in oil)
1 pound good-quality dark chocolate (62% to 70% cocoa),
finely chopped
Coarse sea salt (for sprinkling)

1. Line a baking sheet with a silicone baking mat or foil. Combine the sugar with 2 tablespoons water in a small saucepan. Stir over medium-low heat until the sugar dissolves. Bring to a boil and cook, occasionally swirling the pan and brushing down the sides with a wet pastry brush, until the caramel is dark amber, about 5 minutes. Remove from the heat.
2. Immediately add the butter and whisk until melted. Add the almonds and stir until well coated.
3. Transfer to the baking sheet, spreading out to separate the nuts. Let cool. Break up any large clumps of nuts. Set aside one-quarter of the nuts.

4. Stir the chocolate in a medium bowl set over a saucepan of simmering water until melted. Remove from the heat, add the nuts from the baking sheet, and stir quickly to combine. Spread the chocolate-nut mixture on the same baking sheet, keeping the nuts in a single layer. Top with the reserved nuts; sprinkle with the salt. Chill until the chocolate is set, about 3 hours.

❧

"Let's be off. Grentham's men must be in position by now and we can signal them to come take charge of the prisoners." Saybrook struck a flint to the candles and glanced around the room. "Have you any belongings to gather up, Sir George?"

The inventor shook his head. "No," he answered mournfully. "They stripped me of all my books and sketches, right down to the last stump of pencil and scrap of paper."

"Come along, then," said the earl. "I'm anxious to return to London."

Henning finished a cursory search of the room. "Nothing of interest here," he said. "I'm sure we'll find that the guards are simply ruffians from the London stews." To Cayley he added, "Grab one of the cloaks hanging by the door, Sir George. It's quite chilly outside, now that the sun has nearly set."

Trooping out to the castle's perimeter walls, they made their way around to the wall facing the wooded hillside. The earl lit a small shuttered lantern and flashed out the prearranged signal. It wasn't long before they were joined by several hard-looking men carrying the latest-model Baker rifles.

"No need to storm the place, Mr. Brewster," said Saybrook. "The captive has been rescued unharmed. There are two prisoners locked in the pantry and a body to dispose of."

Looking a bit disappointed, the leader of Grentham's force cocked a nod at his companions. "Go bring the rest of the men down," he ordered. "It appears we have naught but charwomen's duties to perform."

"I would suggest that . . ." The earl's words trailed off as a ghostly shape moving overhead caught his eye.

Brewster let out a grunt of surprise. "What the Devil!"

"Lucifer be buggered," intoned Henning, watching the big balloon pass high overhead. "You don't think . . . Nay, I'm letting my imagination get carried away."

Saybrook said nothing. For a moment he stood still, squinting up at the sky, then expelled a low oath.

"Have you a spyglass?" he barked at Brewster.

The man reached inside his coat and handed over a small brass cylinder.

"Damnation," muttered the earl, after a sweeping survey of the heavens.

"What do you see?" demanded Henning.

"A second balloon," answered Saybrook tersely. "They are both too far away to make out any details."

"May I have a look, milord?" asked Brewster. Snapping the lens into focus, he studied the sailing spheres. "The closer one is Sadler's balloon. I recognize it from the Artillery Grounds."

"You are sure?" snapped the earl.

"Yes. Balloons are bloody big things, sir, and each one has its own unique design." Brewster handed the spyglass back to Saybrook. "Why in the name of Hades are he and his fellow aeronauts out flying at this hour?"

"A good question," murmured Henning. "Isn't Sadler the fellow Señora S met yesterday?"

In answer, Saybrook swore again. "Brewster, I'm leaving you and your men to escort Sir George back to London. He's to be taken straight to Horse Guards and held in seclusion until Grentham gives you further orders." His gaze darted back to the sky for an instant. "I'll need to borrow your rifle as well."

The weapon and ammunition pouch quickly changed hands,

the burnt orange light limning the blackened steel barrel. "Baz, come with me."

"Can't we go any faster?" Sophia peered through the rigging. "They seem to be getting away."

"No need to be alarmed." Sadler made a series of adjustments with the heating valves. "Le Chaze is riding a gust that will die at the rise of that hill. As the heat from the sun dissipates from the ground, the breezes will calm down. And for all of his braggadocio, his Charlier balloon is much slower than my Montgolfier. That's because he's never bothered to tune his rigging to its optimum performance."

Their gondola made a sharp drop in altitude, and to Arianna the dark-fingered tops of the trees looked uncomfortably close. "Are you sure you wouldn't like to take another look at your barometer, sir?"

A chuckle rumbled in the shadows. "Nay, nay, I know every bump and jog along this coastline, so I'm flying on instinct right now. Just watch; in another moment we'll rise swiftly."

Sure enough, with wind chattering through the wickerwork of the gondola, the balloon shot up, gaining speed as it hurtled along the snaking line of the sea cliff.

"Mmmph." Sophia was thrown back by a rocking jolt.

"Here, now." Sadler gave her a hand up. "We'll be riding the currents, so you can take a rest from fueling the fire."

"How is your shoulder?" asked Arianna, experiencing a rush of guilt on realizing she had forgotten all about her companion's injury.

"Fine," said Sophia. "It looked a lot more gruesome than it feels." Seeing Sadler's brows shoot up, she explained with a casual shrug, "I was stabbed this morning."

It was said as if a slashing blade was served every day, along with her breakfast tea and toast.

"You two ladies are, er, rather more intrepid than the usual female," said Sadler.

"A fact that we must ask you to keep a secret," replied Arianna. "Indeed, I am sure that Lord Grentham will ask you to swear an oath of silence concerning this entire affair. The government won't want a word leaking out."

"Y-you deal with Grentham?" Sadler blanched at the mention of the minister's name. "I assure you that my lips will be sealed tighter than the seams of my balloon. I've no desire to stir his wrath."

A wise fellow, thought Arianna. *Wiser than me.*

"You are right," she suddenly said, catching sight of their quarry as they emerged from a skirl of drifting mist. "We appear to be gaining on them."

Up ahead, the balloon carrying Canaday and Lady Urania did seem to be losing speed.

"Look! Several cords have snapped!" cried Sophia.

A scudding of moonlight showed Le Chaze scrambling furiously to repair the damage.

"Serves the lazy bugger right," said Sadler with a savage smile. "We have him now. He'll be forced to turn back and land. Only a reckless fool would attempt to fly over water in that state."

Sadler's surmise, however, proved wrong. Le Chaze dropped down from the ropes and suddenly the big Charlier balloon veered out over the Channel.

"Well, I'll be a flightless dodo—he's going to make a run for Calais after all!"

"We have to stop him," said Arianna. "Can you get us any closer?"

More fiddling with the valves and shrouds gave their balloon an extra burst of speed.

As they came closer to the Frenchman's balloon, Arianna could see Canaday and his sister huddled in one corner of their gondola, while the French aeronaut worked the lines in the opposite one. She grabbed up the speaking trumpet and shouted a warning. "Turn back and land. Else we'll have no choice but to shoot you down!"

In answer, a flash of light winked out of the gloom. An instant later she heard a bullet whistle through the air and pierce their balloon with a sharp *thwock*.

"Why, the scurvy varlet is shooting at my Monty!" Sadler climbed up in the rigging and shook his fist. "Hoy! I'll—"

"Get *down*, Mr. Sadler!" Arianna grabbed his coat and pulled him back into the shelter of the gondola as another bullet pinged against the burner. "Is there anything you can do to force him back over land? If not"—she checked the priming on her pistols—"I shall have to fight fire with fire."

"I can try cutting off his angle and giving him a good thump," said Sadler. "Our balloon is bigger and heavier than theirs, so I might be able to knock out enough of his hydrogen gas to force a descent. But to get that close will bring you ladies into danger."

"Don't worry about us. I'll keep Canaday's head down with a steady stream of shots. Sophia can help me reload," replied Arianna. "What about the damage to our balloon?"

"We would have to take a lot more hits before it becomes serious." Sadler's expression turned grim. "There is also the option of using red-hot shot on him."

"We'll give them one last chance to land before resorting to that."

"Very well." He thrust several handfuls of fuel into the burner. "Off we go."

Crouching low, he made a quick round of the cleated lines, fine-tuning the tension. A valve snapped open, giving them a lift in altitude. *Snap, snick, snap*—another flurry of metallic sounds and the big Montgolfier balloon altered course.

"Canaday is taking aim," warned Sophia.

"Yes, yes, I see him." Arianna carefully squeezed off a shot, giving thanks for the lethally lovely precision of the beautiful dueling weapons.

A few seconds later, a muffled cry rose above the thrum of the wind.

"Bang on the mark!" exclaimed Sadler. "You knocked the pistol from his hand."

"Ha, and it fell overboard!" added Sophia.

"A lucky shot," she replied, watching a small spinning shape plummet into the darkness below. "Be careful, Mr. Sadler. He may have a second one."

Sadler lifted a cautious hand to adjust a rope, but no bullet came whizzing at him. Emboldened, he stood up to tweak a few more lines.

Still no fire.

"Give me another few minutes, and I should be close enough to pluck a few of his feathers."

"That sounds like gunfire," gasped Henning, pausing at the top of a rocky rise to catch his breath. Intent on following the flight of the balloons, he and the earl had left the carriage to make their way on foot along the sea cliffs.

"Aye," growled Saybrook. "Though between your God-benighted wheezing and the crash of the surf, it's hard to be sure." Snapping open the spyglass, he drew a bead on the fast-closing orbs. "Damn, damn, damn," he muttered after a long moment. "The light is too muzzy to make out what's happening. All I can tell is that there are three people in each balloon."

"Male or female?" ventured the surgeon.

Another oath. "With my wife, outward appearances can be cast to the wind." Shoving the glass back in his pocket, he watched the two ghostly shapes float together through a slow, silent spin, as if performing an elegant aerial ballet, then head out to sea.

"Let us hope that for once, she has been sensible enough not to go where angels should fear to tread," he added under his breath.

"Lady S wouldn't hesitate to march into the deepest hole in Hell if she was hot on the heels of the Devil. And ye know it, laddie. It's one of the things ye love about her."

"At the moment," said Saybrook, "love is *not* the emotion boiling in my breast." He pointed to an outcropping up ahead. "Hurry, let's keep them in sight as long as possible."

Through a mare's tail of mist, Arianna saw Lady Urania tending to her brother's injured hand. A pale strip of cloth and a wink of silver fluttered in her fingers as she sought to cleanse the viscount's wound with brandy and bandage the mangled flesh. They seemed to be arguing, for the sound of their shrill voices rose above the thrum of the taut ropes and the keening whistle of the wind.

Deciding the twins were beyond reason, Arianna directed her shout to the French aeronaut. "This is your last warning, Le Chaze! Head back to land and set your balloon down, else my next shot will be aimed at your heart."

They were now close to the other balloon—close enough to see Le Chaze abandon his efforts in the rigging, close enough to see Canaday wrest free of his sister's grip.

"Steady yourselves," warned Sadler. "We're hitting a pocket of turbulent air."

"You dare to challenge Prometheus?" The viscount's enraged roar was edged with a note of hysteria. "Ha! No man or woman alive can match my fire." As he spoke, he whipped up a knife and wrapped the bloody handkerchief around its hilt. "Rainnie, give me a light! Together we'll triumph, as always."

"Good God, he's pouring the liquid from his flask onto the cloth," exclaimed Sophia. "I think he means to make a torch and spear our balloon."

A spark flared as his sister struck a flint to steel.

Le Chaze screamed a warning. But at the same instant a strong gust rocked the French gondola, pitching Canaday backward. The lit torch fell against the wicker, and with its fire fanned by swirling wind, flames rose up and quickly set the rigging alight.

"Bloody hell!" Sadler tugged open a release valve on his own balloon, and the big Montgolfier began to lose altitude. "Hold tight, ladies!"

Ripples of molten red raced up the ropes, and it took only a handful of heartbeats for the fire to hit the French balloon's skin with a sizzling crackle. The loud hiss of escaping gas hung for an instant in the night air, and then suddenly the sound exploded into a shuddering *BOOM*.

Arianna felt shock waves buffet her body as the hydrogen-filled sphere burst into a ball of golden fire. It burned for an agonizing moment—a brilliant, terrifyingly beautiful blaze against the black velvet sky—before disintegrating in a shower of red-gold sparks, the charred scraps plunging into the sea.

Wisps of smoke drifted above the dark waves.

There was, however, no time for the horror of what she had just witnessed to sink in. The reverberations had spun them around and their balloon was now caught in a downdraft.

"We need to shed weight," called Sadler as he fought to stop them from losing altitude. "Get rid of the main ballast bags," he added, indicating the ones to go.

Arianna and Sophia hurried to unknot the sand-filled canvas sacks and drop them overboard.

"More!" ordered Sadler after gauging the distance to the water. "Heave the rest of them!"

To Arianna's eye, their descent slowed, but not by much. He seemed of the same opinion, for after a brief hesitation, he shrugged out of his coat and tossed it over the side. "You, too, ladies, I'm afraid. Sheepskin is heavy."

"It's also w-w-warm," said Sophia through chattering teeth.

"Not when wet." Sadler glanced down. "Overboard with all boots," he ordered, kicking off his own footwear. "Hats and gauntlets as well. Leather is weighty."

Shivering as the chill air lanced through her shirt, Arianna hoped they didn't have to sacrifice every stitch of clothing. It was already colder than a witch's cackle inside the windblown gondola.

"Ladies, I have to ask you to start feeding the fire again—and with gusto, if you please. Monty seems to be stabilizing . . . but it all depends on the air currents close to the sea. We may have to trim a bit more weight." He let out a gusty chuckle. "With luck, we won't have to go to the same extremes as Blanchard and Jeffries."

"Who?" asked Sophia.

"The first aeronauts to cross the Channel. Things got a trifle testy as they approached France, and they were forced to jettison all their supplies and ended up stripping down to their drawers."

Arianna smiled. Sadler was not only a skilled flyer but also a savvy leader. Employing humor to distract an untested crew from the danger at hand was a clever tactic.

"Er, not to be indelicate," he went on, "but legend has it that the fellows saved themselves from a nasty crash by emptying their bladders, which relieved them of vital ounces."

Above Sophia's muffled snort, Arianna could hear the slap of the waves and hiss of salt spray coming, closer, closer. She had hidden the fancy dueling pistols under her shirt, fearing that their loss might spark an international incident if Tsar Alexander of Russia learned that his gift had been tossed into the sea. However, if their weight was the difference between life and death . . .

The balloon bobbed, a mere hairsbreadth from disaster, and then started to rise. From the rocky promontory she heard a faint cheer rise up.

"We're leaking air from the punctures, but we should make it safely to shore," said Sadler, his hands a blur as he tuned the rigging.

They cleared the cliffs and scraped over a stand of wind-blown trees. "There's a clearing ahead," he shouted. "Hold tight. I'm going to release all the air, so the landing may be a bit bumpy."

Out of the corner of her eye, Arianna saw the vague shapes of figures running in pursuit. There were shouts—was one of them Saybrook?—then everything was a jumbled cacophony of snapping braches, skidding stones and cracking wicker. The gondola bounced over the rough ground and turned on its side as helping hands grabbed at the collapsing balloon to keep the wild tangle of ropes and cloth from dragging into the nearby hedgerow.

Wincing, Arianna rolled over and sat up in a patch of stubbled grass, her shaky gaze encountering Sophia's soot-streaked face close by.

Do I also look like an imp of Satan who has just ridden the Devil to Hell and back?

They both began to laugh.

A pair of well-polished Hessians skidded to a stop beside them. "Miss Kirtland! Lady Saybrook!"

To her amazement, Grentham's normally impeccable grooming was three sheets to the wind. His cravat tails were in knots, his coat was covered in brambles, his hair . . .

Good God, his hair is standing on end.

Equally startling was the stream of highly improper invectives that tumbled off his tongue.

"Why are you blistering our ears?" she demanded, rubbing at her bruised elbow. "Sorry we didn't bring back a pelt to put on your wall. But the hunt is over. The Fox—or rather, the Foxes—are dead."

The minister sucked in a breath to answer, but it was her husband who replied.

"Why is he blistering your ears?" repeated Saybrook, his voice so soft that it was barely audible. Starlight skittered over his face, but not even the sun at its blazing zenith could have dispelled the look of black rage in his eyes.

"Because," the earl went on, "normal speech cannot adequately express the depths of his anger at your reckless disregard for risk."

"But—" began Arianna.

"Ignoring all constraint of common sense, you tear off in pursuit of a cold-blooded killer . . ."

"But—"

"Putting not only your life in danger, but that of Miss Kirt-land. It's one thing for *you* to be so devil-may-care about your own personal safety, but she has no experience in skullduggery and depended on *your* judgment—"

"Or lack thereof," interjected Grentham.

"—to keep her out of harm's way," finished Saybrook.

"That's unfair." Sophia tried speak up, but her protest was drowned out by the earl's rising roar.

"No, it bloody well is *not* unfair. She is always so damnably afire to charge into the fray. She likes to taunt the Devil, regard-less of the consequences."

Arianna felt her throat tighten. *Roaring? Ranting?* She had never seen Saybrook this angry.

Levering slowly to her stocking-clad feet—which were as cold as ice—she brushed a hank of hair from her cheek. "For-give me for putting Miss Kirtland in danger," she said stiffly. "You are right. It was thoughtless and selfish of me to drag *her* into harm's way."

Her husband's dark lashes flicked uncertainly. "I—I did not mean to imply . . ."

She brushed past him, blinking back the sting of salt. Through the glimmer of tears, she saw Henning stumble into the clearing. "Basil, might I borrow your c-coat?" A watery sniff. "I was *reckless* enough to lose mine over the sea."

"Auch, but of course, lassie."

The heavy wool felt wonderfully warm as it enveloped her body. To her chagrin, her limbs were trembling. "I don't suppose you have a flask of your Scottish malt. F-for medicinal purposes, of course."

"There's one in the carriage," said the surgeon, putting his arm around her shoulders. "Come along, the road is not far."

At least someone seems to appreciate my efforts. Arianna tried to summon up a surge of righteous anger to bolster her spirits. But the earl's accusations had hit a vulnerable spot.

He is right—I'm impetuous and loath to obey orders.

Was this fierce determination to assert her independence a sign of strength? Or merely petulant weakness? Aching in both body and mind, she felt her shoulders slump.

"Arianna." Saybrook caught up with them, his stride hitched and awkward as he stumbled for words. "What . . . what happened to your boots?"

"Oh, Sadler and I decided to dance a wild Druid jig to the full moon," she said sarcastically. "Impulsive, I know, but good Lord, we were having such fun."

His mouth thinned. "You have misinterpreted—"

"Have I?" she challenged. "This isn't the first time you have voiced dismay over my actions. Though in all fairness to me, you cannot claim that I ever hid my so-called impulsive nature from you."

"Arianna . . ." Saybrook halted in confusion.

Henning stopped too. Clearing his throat with a cough, he slipped away, leaving her standing facing her husband.

Avoiding Saybrook's eyes, she drew a deep breath. "Had I received a more ladylike upbringing, a more formal education, perhaps the rough edges of my personality would have been polished off," she said tightly. "But I doubt it."

"For God's sake—"

"I'm sorry if you are disillusioned. However, I did warn you."

Whatever he was going to say was cut off by the scuff of steps on the footpath. The others were now filing out of the clearing, led by Sadler, Sophia, and a still-scowling Grentham. Lawrance was also among the group, and after dispatching several men to guard the balloon, he called out a greeting.

Unwilling to continue such a painful, private scene with her husband in public, Arianna stalked away.

"Sláinte." Henning handed her his silver flask. "Drink, and that's a physician's orders. Ye need a wee bit of malt to warm yer innards."

"Thank you." The fiery whisky helped burn the ice in her belly, and as a pleasant warmth began to spread through her limbs, Arianna felt the tension start to melt.

Clack, clack, clack. The reassuring rhythm of the carriage wheels rolling over the road was a welcome reminder that she was back on *terra firma*.

Ah, but if only my emotions felt more grounded.

Saybrook leaned down to tuck the blanket around her toes. Sophia and Lawrance had gone in the minister's carriage, leaving the three of them to follow along. "Miss Kirtland told me a little of what happened today. As did Grentham—who, by the by, has a great deal of explaining to do before I blacken his deadlights."

"If you don't mind, Sandro, I'm too tired to continue fighting with you." Squeezing her eyes shut, she added, "Can't it wait until morning?" A yawn, admittedly exaggerated. "Or maybe afternoon."

"We are not fighting," he said softly.

"Ha! Sounds to me like a thumping big battle," said Henning, "with all the artillery belching smoke and cannonballs."

"Would you care to walk back to London?" growled the earl.

"Nay, I'm quite comfortable here, watching the display of pyrotechnics."

Burrowing deeper into the surgeon's coat, Arianna bit back a fleeting smile. Friendship was far easier to understand than other relationships.

A jolt over the rutted road quickly exacerbated her physical bumps and scrapes. *And her mental bruises?* Decisions, dilemmas. The earl was right—she was independent and resented any reining in of her actions. Had that been a threat to friends? Perhaps so. But war wasn't easy. One had to make split-second judgments in the heat of battle.

I am not perfect—but neither is he.

He was wrong and unreasonable to chide her with her faults. *Ye gods, he has enough of them of his own.*

And yet, Arianna felt her spirits deflate. She couldn't help but see a contrast between herself and Sophia. Strangely enough, danger had made the earl's lady friend appear to blossom rather than wilt. The scholarly Miss Kirtland looked . . . different. Confident. And the adventurous edge only accentuated her physical beauty. Perhaps it had been a quirk of starlight, or her own jostled wits, but it had seemed that Lawrance, as well as her husband, had kept sneaking sidelong looks at Sophia.

So, for that matter, had Grentham, but likely for a different reason. The minister was probably trying to think of how he could use her very private personal secrets to bully her into doing some onerous task for him.

He might be surprised, mused Arianna. She had a feeling that Sophia wouldn't allow herself to be intimidated, despite her past scandal.

As to what would become of their tentative friendship remained to be seen. Like a seedling exposed to the natural elements, it was still at a vulnerable stage in its development, so it was uncertain whether it would blossom or merely wither on the vine.

Too exhausted, too confused to wrestle with the conundrums, Arianna closed her eyes, and this time her yawn was unfeigned. An instant later, she was slumped against her husband's shoulder, the carriage wheels echoing her steady breathing as the conflicts of the day drifted far, far away.

"Arianna." A gentle shake roused her from sleep. "Come, we are home."

She blinked, needing a moment to clear the muzziness from her head. Although he was close, the weak flickers of lamplight left Saybrook's dark eyes pooled in shadows. "Basil—" she began.

"Preferred to be dropped at his residence," he replied. "It has been a long and grueling day for all concerned."

His voice was also impossible to read.

"Mmmm." Arianna looked away, feeling too vulnerable, too fragile to engage in any further discussion of her actions. For now, she simply wanted to slip under her eiderdown coverlet and sink back into oblivion. "Would that I could summon a small balloon to float me up to the bedchamber," she murmured, hoping a note of wry humor would, for the moment, lighten the mood between them. "I'm not sure my legs will consent to carry me up the stairs."

"No need to ask them. I shall assume that duty."

Duty. Ah. That did not bode well for the morning.

He gathered her in his arms, but then hesitated. His breath was warm yet strangely fluttery against her cheek. "Arianna, about earlier this evening," he said tentatively. "I . . . I spoke in anger."

She nodded, unsure of how to answer.

"I spoke in anger," repeated Saybrook, "because I was so damnably, *damnably* afraid."

"I know. I put Miss Kirtland at risk—"

His lips touched her forehead, causing her to cut off.

"We'll speak of Miss Kirtland later," Saybrook said softly. "I'm talking about you—and me."

Arianna shifted slightly, intimately aware of how familiar the muscled contours of his body had become to her. "I am sorry, Sandro. I don't mean to upset you. Truly I don't. But I cannot change who I am." A sigh. "Not even for you." She reached up and placed her palm against his whisker-stubbled jaw. "Do you think that I am not afraid for your safety too?"

That drew a reluctant rumble of a laugh from deep in his throat. "*Madre de Dios*, what a pair we make. Most couples argue about money or mistresses, while we butt heads over risking our lives for King and country."

"Eccentric, I agree. But so far we have made it work." A pause. "Neither of us would be happy trying to live conventional lives, so it seems likely that we will continue to drive each other to distraction at times. However, I hope that mutual respect and . . ." She hitched in a breath, for baring her heart was still something she found difficult. ". . . and love will help us learn to live with each other's foibles."

"Love." Saybrook tightened his hold on her, his whisper stirring the air. "That is a word which is rarely uttered aloud between us. Perhaps it should be said more often."

"We are both very guarded about expressing our emotions. That does not mean the feelings don't exist. But it is hard to change."

"It takes practice to hone any skill."

She smiled into the shadows.

"I am not asking you to change, my love," he went on. "Just promise me that you will try not to take such hellish risks in the future."

"I will try," agreed Arianna. "But you will have to accept that *try* is the full extent of my promise."

Another low laugh. "I will try." The door latch clicked open. "There is far more to say on the subject, but not now. Let us finally be off to bed and blessed sleep, which I think we've both earned."

24

From Lady Arianna's Chocolate Notebooks

Smoked Tea-Infused Chocolate Pots de Crème

6½ ounces bittersweet chocolate, finely chopped
3 cups heavy whipping cream
⅔ cup whole milk
1 teaspoon Lapsang souchong or other smoked tea
½ cup plus 2 teaspoons sugar
6 large egg yolks
¼ vanilla bean, split lengthwise

1. Place the bittersweet chocolate in a large bowl.
2. Bring 2½ cups of the cream, the whole milk, and the smoked tea to a simmer in a heavy medium saucepan over medium heat. Turn off the heat. Add ¼ cup of the sugar and stir to dissolve. Steep uncovered for 5 minutes.
3. Whisk the egg yolks and ¼ cup of the sugar in a medium bowl to blend. Gradually whisk the hot cream mixture into the yolk mixture; then strain it over the chocolate. Let

stand 2 minutes. Whisk until the chocolate is melted and the custard is smooth. Cover and chill the custard overnight.

4. Position a rack in the center of the oven and preheat to 300°F. Divide the custard among eight ¾-cup ramekins or custard cups. Cover each ramekin with plastic wrap and arrange the ramekins in a large roasting pan. Carefully add enough warm water to the roasting pan to come halfway up the sides of the ramekins.

5. Bake the custards in the water bath until just set in the center, about 55 minutes. Remove the ramekins from the water. Uncover and refrigerate until cold, at least 6 hours.

6. Before serving, combine the remaining ½ cup cream and ¼ cup sugar in a medium bowl. Scrape in the seeds from the vanilla bean and whisk until peaks form. Dollop the cream atop the custards and serve.

Their well-earned sleep was, however, all too soon interrupted, and at an ungodly hour in the morning. A messenger from the minister brought a missive to summon them to a meeting at Horse Guards, and Saybrook reluctantly decided it was best to obey.

"Have a seat," said Grentham brusquely as they entered his office. "Seeing as Mr. Henning has been part of this endeavor from the beginning, I asked him to be present as well."

Looking even more disheveled than was his wont in the morning, the surgeon sat slumped in his chair, noisily slurping a cup of coffee.

"What about Miss Kirtland?" asked Arianna. "It would seem she has earned a right to be here too."

The minister steepled his hands in front of his face, the slivered shadow making his expression impossible to read. "Miss Kirtland needs a rather lengthy session to ensure that she understands the stricture of silence by which she is bound. However, given the more intimate understanding between ourselves"—he flashed a rather sour smile—"I thought it best to confine this gathering to just the four of us. There are things to discuss that do not concern her."

Saybrook stretched out his legs and emitted an impatient sigh. "Then kindly get on with it. None of us got much sleep, so I hope you have roused us for an interesting reason, rather than simply to bore us with blather about the rules of state security."

"I shall try to keep you amused, Lord Saybrook," replied Grentham. He tapped at a dossier on his desk. "I thought you might like to hear how Renard *soeur et frère* managed to work so cunningly within Whitehall."

"I have been wondering about that," murmured Arianna. "Knowing there were two of them certainly opened up a whole new range of possibilities."

"I am assuming that Lady Urania was secretly sleeping with one of the high-ranking gentlemen on the security committee," said Saybrook. "Someone with access to the most privileged information."

Grentham looked a little miffed that his thunder had been stolen. "Correct. What made it all the more clever was that Finchley was not guilty of treason, but merely of being indiscreet in bed. He had no idea he was pumped . . . in more ways than one."

Arianna lifted a brow at the minister's risqué remark. "Women are usually far more sophisticated about using their wiles than men give them credit for."

The minister narrowed his eyes. "So I am learning."

"Bloody hell, it took you long enough to figure it out," grumbled Saybrook.

"There were layers upon layers to unpeel. I had to work my way through the suspects and examine all aspects of their lives, without them knowing. When confronted, Finchley admitted to his affair with Lady Urania and was aghast that he had played the dupe."

"What about Canaday?" asked the earl.

"That was what made Renard's trail so difficult to discern. As we once discussed earlier, it seemed as if the source of information was coming from two different sources. And it was. Canaday was blackmailing a senior official in the Foreign Office whose sexual preferences would have gotten him hanged here in England, if they had become public knowledge."

Saybrook murmured a name, earning a gruff nod from Grentham.

"You knew?" asked the minister with a hard stare.

"No, it's far easier to read between the lines when one has been handed the proper spectacles."

Henning grunted and patted back a yawn. "And when we add to the mix that both brother and sister were accomplished chemists, with inside knowledge of the institution and its members, it's easy to understand how they concocted yet another way to create havoc for England."

"Indeed," said Grentham. "With a few well-chosen friends, like Lord Reginald Sommers, they constructed a diabolical web of treachery for France. 'Why' is still a question that needs to be answered."

"I think I can help you there," said Arianna. She proceeded to repeat what the twins had told her about their family background.

"Auch, my head is starting to ache," grumbled Henning. "Is there anything else pressing to go over before we are allowed to return to our slumbers? Seeing as the threat is finally over, can't these prosy details be held until a later time?"

"There is something else to clarify." Grentham turned to him. "I assume you think I lied to you about releasing your nephew."

The surgeon answered with a wordless grunt.

"First of all, the young man put himself in danger by choosing to join a group of radical revolutionaries."

"None of us are in the mood for such platitudes, Grentham,"

snapped Saybrook. "And by the by, our government ought not force its citizens to form revolutionary groups in order to give voice to their legitimate grievances. History shows us what happens."

"Don't lecture me either," retorted the minister. "You have a seat in the House of Lords. Feel free to offer your opinion on politics there."

Arianna interrupted to forestall any further hostilities. "Do go on, sir, if you have something more to add. As Mr. Henning said, we are all tired."

Grentham cleared his throat with a brusque cough. "The sealed packet you carried north contained my orders for the young man's release. When my investigations here in London heightened my suspicions concerning Stoughton, I moved to have one of my local operatives inserted into the unit of prison guards. The plan was for him to spirit Mr. Henning's nephew to safety, but Stoughton acted too quickly."

An apology, however oblique, from the minister? Arianna arched a brow in surprise.

Saybrook's reaction was less subtle. He made a rude sound and said, "You want us to believe that you have a heart? Ha! And pigs may fly."

A dark flush rose to Grentham's cheekbones, but his only retaliation was a mocking smile. "Stranger things have been spotted floating through the skies around London, Lord Saybrook. Including your wife."

Repressing a chuckle, Arianna rose. "On that note, perhaps it's time to bring this meeting to an end—before the two of you give rise to any more insults."

"Just one last thing," said Grentham. He took a small packet of papers from his desk drawer and tossed it at the earl. "I suggest you read the contents when you get home."

"Merde," swore Saybrook. "Now what?"

"Practicing your French? I'll take that as a promising sign," shot back the minister.

On second thought, Arianna wasn't sure that she was liking Grentham's newfound sense of humor.

"No." The papers dropped onto the polished pearwood with a crackly *thunk*. "Whatever it is . . ." Saybrook took her arm rather forcefully and turned for the door. "The answer is no."

Huffing a snort, Henning got to his feet and followed.

"Enough of murder and mayhem and recipes for treason. From now on, my wife and I intend to devote our time to the peaceful study of chocolate," added Saybrook.

Grentham tapped his fingertips together as the portal slammed shut. "So you say now," he murmured, eyeing the discarded packet. "But I have a feeling that along with your exotic spices and chocolate confections, you may soon be eating your words."

AUTHOR'S NOTE

I'm often asked how I come up with my stories, and the simple answer is that the history of the Regency era is so fascinating that it inspires countless ideas. It was a time of great upheaval in all aspects of life—many consider it the birth of the modern world—and scientific explorations and discoveries served as powerful catalysts for change.

Though my scientific skills are rudimentary at best, I became fascinated by how much influence science had on society as a whole. The experiments of the early chemists and balloonists were followed with avid interest throughout Europe, and charismatic leaders in the field like Humphry Davy, Vincent Lunardi, and James Sadler were the Regency equivalent of modern rock stars.

It was fun to weave these real-life personages into my story, and many of the exploits described in these pages are based on true stories. (For those of you interested in reading more about science in this era, I highly recommend *The Age of Wonder* by Richard Holmes, a beautifully written, highly entertaining overview of the subject.) Likewise, Sir George Cayley is a real person, and his 1799 sketches of flying machines earned him the moniker of "the father of modern aeronautics." He is credited with being the first to understand the forces of flight—weight, lift, drag, and thrust—and he designed the first glider to carry a man aloft.

That said, the events and the chemical concoctions that are key to the plot are pure fiction. Also, the Royal Society and Royal Institution are real (and respected) scientific organizations, but I have populated them with some unsavory characters to move the story along.

For me, writing fiction is even more fun when it has more than a grain of truth to it. It's endlessly interesting to imagine, "What if . . ." So I hope you have enjoyed a little of the real history behind *Recipe for Treason*. For more fun facts and arcane trivia about the era, please visit my Web site at www.andrea penrose.com. I love to hear from readers and can be contacted at andrea@andreapenrose.com.

Also available
from

Andrea Penrose

THE COCOA CONSPIRACY

A Lady Arianna Regency Mystery

When Lady Arianna gifts a rare volume of
botanical engravings to her husband, the Earl of
Saybrook, she finds something even more rare
hidden inside—sensitive government documents
which would mark one they hold dear as a traitor
of King and country. To unmask the villain, they
must root out a cunning conspiracy—armed only
with their wits and expertise in chocolate...

**"A mouthwatering combination of
suspense and chocolate."
—Lauren Willig**

Available wherever books are sold or at
penguin.com

facebook.com/TheCrimeSceneBooks

OM0091

Also available
from

Andrea Penrose

SWEET REVENGE

A Lady Arianna Regency Mystery

England, 1813: Lady Arianna Hadley acts the
part of a French chef in one of London's
aristocratic households to find her father's
murderer. But when the Prince Regent falls ill
after consuming Arianna's special chocolate
dessert, she finds herself at the center of a
scandal. It soon becomes clear that someone is
looking to plunge England into chaos—and
Arianna to the bottom of the Thames...

"A thrilling ride through Regency England."
—Victoria Thompson

Available wherever books are sold or at
penguin.com

facebook.com/TheCrimeSceneBooks

C.S. Harris

WHEN MAIDENS MOURN
A Sebastian St. Cyr Mystery

When Gabrielle Tennyson is murdered, aristocratic investigator Sebastian St. Cyr and his new reluctant bride, the fiercely independent Hero Jarvis, find themselves involved in an intrigue concerning the myth of King Arthur, Camelot, and a future poet laureate...

<u>Also in the series:</u>
Where Shadows Dance
What Remains of Heaven
Where Serpents Sleep
Why Mermaids Sing
When Gods Dies
What Angels Fear

Available wherever books are sold or at
penguin.com

facebook.com/TheCrimeSceneBooks

JoAnna Carl
The Chocoholic Mystery Series

EACH BOOK INCLUDES YUMMY CHOCOLATE TRIVIA!

Looking for a fresh start, divorcée Lee McKinney moves back to Michigan to work for her aunt's chocolate business—and finds that her new job offers plenty of murderous treats.

The Chocolate Cat Caper
The Chocolate Bear Burglary
The Chocolate Frog Frame-Up
The Chocolate Puppy Puzzle
The Chocolate Mouse Trap
The Chocolate Jewel Case
The Chocolate Snowman Murders
The Chocolate Cupid Killings
The Chocolate Pirate Plot
The Chocolate Castle Clue
The Chocolate Moose Motive

Available wherever books are sold or at
penguin.com

facebook.com/TheCrimeSceneBooks